EVOL[illegible] OF THE ELEMENTS

By

T.M.Faulkner

www.tmfaulkner.com

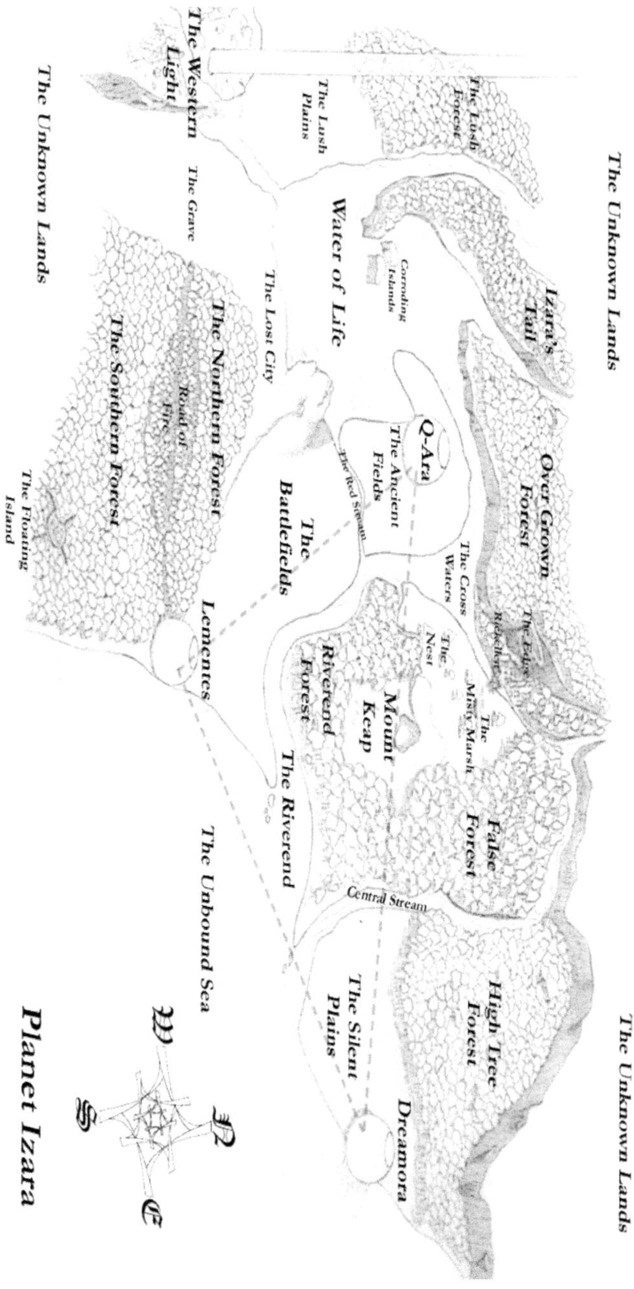
The Unknown Lands
The Lush Forest
The Lush Plains
The Western Light
The Grave
Water of Life
Corroding Islands
Izara's Tail
The Lost City
The Northern Forest
Road of Fire
The Southern Forest
Q-Ara
The Ancient Fields
The Red Stream
The Battlefields
Over Grown Forest
The Cross Waters
The Floating Island
Lementes
The Nest
The Misty Marsh
Mount Keap
Riverend Forest
The Riverend
False Forest
Central Stream
The Unbound Sea
The Silent Plains
High Tree Forest
Dreamora
The Unknown Lands
Planet Izara
N
S
E
W

Chapter 1

Determined Son

Day 1

A young man sits on the rough and dirty concrete landing bay, on top of a skyscraper. It is barely lit, but that's a good thing. It's quiet too, so he can try and have a clear mind to think; but it's difficult. The cold doesn't help. It still feels like his safe space. He visits here quite often, mostly during the night when no one is around.

His skinny arms are wrapped tightly around his knees, shaking slightly. His head is bowed. He's dressed up in dark-blue and ill-fitting old clothes with large holes showing his pale skin, his sleeves are soaking wet and stains have covered his jacket and smeared a silver logo recalling the Preyal Tournament: 9995. He slowly looks up, dark bags under his eyes showing that he hasn't slept for a very long time and his cheeks are red sore. His long dark blonde hair catches the breeze as it brushes by. At the same time, his stomach growls as he's hardly eaten anything for days.

He lifts himself up and slowly makes his way towards the edge. Tears keep falling down his face. He's given up wiping them away now. He stops and looks down seventy-one storeys.

He closes his eyes and spreads his arms out wide, feeling the wind blowing against his face. He pretends he's a flying creature soaring across the city. It doesn't matter what sort of creature either; anything will do. For a few minutes, he doesn't think about anything and he smiles. There is nothing to worry about anymore.

In his hand, is a folded piece of paper. It's old, but then it has been read so many times before. He knows every fold and crease of it now. It's the only thing that links him to that awful day, when his father disappeared. He found it in his father's office drawer, buried under a mountain of paperwork.
He opens his eyes; all the memories and all those feelings come flooding back. Even though it is exactly one year ago today, he can remember it like it was yesterday. He has been dreading this day coming, as it will hurt even more. He feels as if he's failed and every day that passes makes it worse. Tears stream down his face again. He misses him so much; he just wants to see his face or hear his voice again. His chest aches with the loss.

As he looks down, a couple of tears fall off his chin. He watches them vanish in the gentle wind; he's not scared of the height anymore as he has done this hundreds of times. He spots the sun's light rise and gleam between the two planets of Izara, his home planet, and Raziz, its twin in the binary planet system. The two rotate around each other. The sun's gleam reveals all the other grey and white skyscrapers and beautiful greenery across the city of Lementes. He hadn't realised it's morning already; he has been here all night, watching over the city.

He quickly places the piece of paper back into his jacket pocket, jumps off the landing bay and rushes into the elevator. He presses a button and wipes his face. Within seconds the blue numbers count down to twenty-one and stop. He walks out and as he turns a corner. He notices someone walking in his direction; a young dark-haired woman; and she notices him too. He lowers his head immediately, trying not to make eye contact and he quickly picks up pace.

"Hi Jaykin!" she calls from afar, waving and smiling at him.

"Hi Meara," he mumbles, uncovering his wrist and quickly swiping it against a wall. The door opens and he rushes into his apartment, closing the door as fast as he can behind him. He breathes heavily as he hasn't moved that fast for a while. He rests his head and shoulders on the door and then holds his breath so he can hear what is going on outside. "Please don't knock," he whispers, repeatedly to himself.

Meara stares at the door on the other side, puzzled. She's about to knock but stops. Instead, she just places her hand gently on it for a moment and lowers her head slightly, then walks away.
Jaykin listens and lets out a sigh of relief as he hears the footsteps fade. He turns and rests his back onto the door, sliding down it and curling up into a ball, staring into the dark rooms of his apartment.

***

The sunlight begins to creep through the gaps in the

curtains. There is suddenly a knock on the door behind him, which makes Jaykin jump out of a daydream and his heart thumps hard. He looks around quickly, trying to work out what to do. Another couple of knocks.

"Jaykin, are you in there?" a young woman's voice says, slightly muffled. He knows who it is immediately. She has a distinctive voice, calm and soothing to the ears. It's Meara again.

"Leave me alone," he whispers into his arms, so she can't hear. He lifts himself up, sighing again, trying to work out what to say. "Yeah, I'm here!" he replies, blurting it out. He shakes his head, regretting what he just said. "What are you doing?" he whispers to himself and opens the door.

"Hello again," she says, with a sweet smile on her face.

"Hi," he says clearing his throat and looking around his apartment.

"How are you?"

"I'm okay I guess." He smiles awkwardly. He knows that it isn't going to work on Meara but he says it anyway.

"Would it be all right if I come in?" she asks.

"Sure," he answers hesitantly.

"It's really dark in here."

"It's probably better that way."

"Load," she says out loud and something clicks in the centre of the room; a little digital device still responds to her voice. "Window open." The glass goes from darkened to transparent, slowly revealing the great view of the city and what was hidden in the darkness of the apartment. "Wow," she says, taking in the mess;

food packaging all over the place and heaps of clothes across the floor and strewn across the sofa and chairs. She looks over at Jaykin, who covers his face with his arms because of the light, as if he hasn't seen the sunlight for months. "How are you, really?" she asks.

"I'm okay," he replies, mindlessly.

"Oh, good," she says, not believing a word. "I'm sorry I haven't been around for a while. We've had a load of new figurines in recently and the shop has been busy in the last month or so. You know how it is."

"Understandable, it's the busiest time of the year." He avoids her eye.

"Well, it wasn't too bad this morning, so I asked Dad if I could take the day off."

"Oh cool."

"Yeah, you know, I needed to sort some things out, catch up with a good friend of mine and all that. See if he needs some help." Jaykin doesn't get the hint. "It's been a while since I've been in here."

"Well, it has been six months!" Jaykin fires back.

"I had my reasons," she strikes back. "I just ran out of patience, that's all. Plus, my dad needed help." Jaykin groans and shakes his head. "Talking about my dad, any news from yours?"

"No," Jaykin replies quickly, "still nothing."

"Oh," she says, sounding disappointed, "that's a shame. I was hoping you would have heard from him."

"No," he groans.

"Are you still searching for him?" He says

nothing and there is a pause from them both. Jaykin doesn't know how to reply. He has tried everything. He's searched the places where his father might have been, and he went to the city's Guards, but they didn't seem to be remotely interested in a missing person. He's nearly given up hope and he's certain that there is no way of finding him.

"When was the last time you showered?" Meara interrupts his thoughts, as tactfully as she can. No answer. "Come on!" she pushes him slightly towards the bathroom. "Go clean yourself up and I'll make a start in here."

"Fine!" he moans, walking towards the bathroom slowly and throwing his jacket on the sofa. She shakes her head at him, looks around and surveys the mess. She spots a pillow and some covers on the sofa; he's obviously not slept in his bed. She walks to his room. It lights up, revealing posters of creatures of multiple shapes and sizes. They fill the walls. Amongst them are the very old Preyal tournament charts, with all the boxes filled in by a child's hand; who won, who lost. The shelves are littered with the same creatures in the form of figurines, now collecting dust. The floor is covered with more old clothes and discarded food packets.

"What have you been doing Jaykin?" she whispers to herself.

Jaykin takes his time in the shower, enjoying the hot water on his cold skin. He's in there for a while, nearly forgetting that Meara is still around. When he gets out, he realizes he doesn't have any clean clothes. He opens the bathroom door to find some hanging up and detects the amazing smell of something cooking.

"I've made some food," she shouts out to him. "You need to eat something."

Jaykin walks through, to see the room has been cleaned and hot food is on the table.

"You didn't have to," he says appreciatively.

"It's fine," she says. "It's just like the old days when I used to babysit you." She scrubs the table with a cloth. "You know you can't look after yourself without me," she says cheekily.

"I'm seventeen. I am more than qualified to look after myself."

"Really?" She smirks, looking at him sideways, then walks to the kitchen, opens the nearest cupboard, and points. "Then why is this empty?" She opens another; "and this one? I couldn't even see the floor, with the amount of clothes thrown around!"

"Umm," he hesitates trying to think of something to say. "Because I'm…redecorating." He shoves food down his throat, so he doesn't have to elaborate. Her head shakes.

"Are you sleeping on the sofa too?"

"Yep," he says with his mouth full.

"Why?" she asks, sitting opposite him.

Jaykin stays quiet for a moment and then looks up at her. "Because I'm not sleeping well at the moment." He stops and places the food back on the plate. "I keep getting these terrible nightmares. It's just easier to doss on the sofa every so often."

"Oh, you still having troubles?" she asks and he nods. "Have you tried going to Dreamora?"

"No." He takes another bite of his food, nearly finishing it.

"Why not? It may help."

"In case my father returns."

Meara sighs. "Please tell me you're not still expecting him to come back?"

"No," he stares back and swallows, hard.

She shakes her head again. Jaykin hasn't changed since she had to walk away. She couldn't handle his obsession with his father, and tried her best to help him but he got worse and now he seems to be in bad shape. She needs to try again. She tries to quickly change the subject.

"Hey, the Preyal tournament is coming up soon. Do you think you'll be watching it this month?"

"Probably not."

"Why not? You used to love watching it."

"Because—"

"Don't tell me, you used to watch it with your father and it reminds you of him too much?" she says.

He nods. She's about to yell at him when a knock on the front door distracts them. They both jump slightly and exchange glances.

"Expecting anyone?" she asks.

"No," he says curiously.

Meara quickly gets out of the chair and answers the door, and, hidden by it, she greets someone. "Hey," she says in a friendly tone and there is a pause.

"Hello Meara, how are things?" a man's voice asks.

Jaykin's eyes fix on the door, wary of who is on the other side of it.

"I'm good. I haven't seen you in a while. How are you?" she asks.

Jaykin slides out of his seat and sees an elderly man at the door. "Oh, hi Thrednu," he says, surprised. "How are things?"

"Not too bad thank you Jaykin. I'm still going! I won't be going to the Western Light just yet." He chuckles while both Meara and Jaykin look at one another awkwardly. "I'm here to check your electricity if that's ok?"

"Sure, that's fine," Meara says and they move back slightly.

Thrednu turns to a wall panel, which is near the front door.

"What are you doing here Meara? Are you still looking after this one?" he asks.

"Yeah, he still can't look after himself," she replies and ruffles Jaykin's hair.

He frowns.

"Anyway, when is your father back from his trip, Jaykin?" Thrednu enquires, pressing a couple of buttons and typing the numbers onto a digital pad.

"Umm," Jaykin hesitates.

"Not for a while yet," Meara interrupts. "He's a busy guy!"

"He's been gone for a while now, hasn't he?" Thrednu questions.

"Sure has!" Meara replies while Jaykin runs his hand through his nice clean hair.

"Well, next time you see him, say hi from me." He turns off the panel. "Just to warn you both, there seems to be a couple of problems with the city's electricity supply. I need to check manually if everyone has power going to their apartments. Alarms going off here, there, and everywhere but everything looks fine to me. Nothing to fix here. Meara your place is fine too."

"Thanks, Thrednu," she replies.

"It seems like you haven't used much power this month, Jaykin."

"Everything is fine, thank you, Thrednu," Jaykin replies.

"Well, take care both of you."

"Will do. You too," Meara replies.

"Oh, before I forget, I won't be around for the next couple of months, so if you need anything fixing, you'll need to get hold of the, um…" he clicks his fingers, trying to remember, "…the other guy."

"Oh really? Why is that?" Meara asks.

"It's my ninetieth birthday next month and I'll be taking some time off, to see all the family. They're coming from Raziz."

"Oh wow, that's great news!" Meara says. "I've never been there." She looks up at the planet, shielding her eyes from the sun with her hand. "Have a great time and a happy birthday." She turns to Jaykin who stares into space. "You going to say 'bye?" she asks, nudging him with her elbow.

"Oh, I've never been there either," he mumbles.

Thrednu chuckles. "You two still make me laugh. Bye."

"Bye Thrednu. And have a great birthday!" Jaykin shouts.

They close the door behind them. "Jaykin!" Meara yells.

"What?" he shrugs.

"You were being rude…You thought it was your father, didn't you?"

He nods his head slightly in shame. "Every time I hear the door go or his name is mentioned I—"

"Look, I know you miss him," She places her hand on his shoulder. "But when someone knocks on the door, you can't expect it to be him every single time and we need to stop lying to people that he's away on holiday."

"I know that. You just don't understand."

"Not this again," she sighs. "I do understand. Since your father left, you've changed."

"He hasn't left me; he's just…gone somewhere, and I'm still the same person."

"Gone somewhere? He walked out on you. That was a year ago now and without letting anyone know? When are you going to realise, he isn't coming back?"

Jaykin sighs and looks back at his room. He can remember the time they watched the Preyal Tournaments, rooting for the biggest or even the smallest creature to win. They would laugh and celebrate with each other. 'Remember Jaykin, no matter how big they are, they can always be defeated,' his father would say to him. 'Never give up!' But it wasn't just the watching, it was the fun and enjoyment of being together.

"He is coming back!" Jaykin insists.

"I hope he does because if you carry on the way you are, you'll disappear too," She steps back, realising she's getting slightly angry with him and she doesn't want to do that again. "You need to sort your life out."

"You're right," he replies quietly.

"I'm sorry. I didn't mean to get angry," she sighs, "but you need to move on. If you carry on like this, you'll go crazy." He looks at her blankly. "You didn't listen to anything I said then, did you?"

"Yeah, I heard you but I'm never giving up on him."

She tries to ease the tension and throws the scrunched-up cloth at him but he grabs it before it hits his face.

"Put your jacket on, we're going food shopping."

He unwraps the cloth.

"I don't think this will fit me," he says sarcastically. Meara can't hide her smile.

"There's the Jaykin I know. That's the first time I've seen you smile in a long time. It's nice to see. Come on, let's go."

Jaykin goes to grab the jacket that he was wearing earlier but doesn't see it on the sofa. He starts to panic and searches frantically around the room. "Where is my jacket?" he asks.

"It's hanging up on your bedroom door, where it should be," Meara replies. He sighs in relief as he runs in and shoves his hand in the pocket, finding the piece of paper that is still inside. "What's up with you all of a sudden?"

"Nothing, I just really like this jacket, that's all." He throws it on.

"Really? It looks like it needs a good wash or be thrown away."

"No," Jaykin fires back. "I can't do that." He shakes his head. Unknown to Meara, Jaykin's father got it for him on his thirteenth birthday. Meara sighs.

"If you say so." As they are leaving, Meara stops him. "Look, you still have me, mister, you should be happy!" She grins and gives him a huge hug and a kiss on the cheek. "Tell you what; you can pick up anything you want to eat for tea tonight; my treat."

He thinks for a bit. "You're staying with me till later?"

"Of course I am, silly. I have the morning off! Talking about work, have you found a job yet?"

"Nothing yet. I'm still looking. I don't think your dad really forgave me since I dropped all those boxes a few months ago."

"Oh, he's forgiven you," she says. "You just need some more upper body strength, that's all."

"You like rubbing it in my face, don't you?" he smiles.

She shrugs. "I have no idea what you mean by that. I'm trying to help." She grabs an arm and shoves him towards the elevator. "Come on, let's go into the city."

Both Jaykin and Meara live in the same building, positioned south on the outskirts of the city. They walk into the elevator and descend to the underground floor, where crowds of people are milling around. Amongst them are Q-Roids; mechanical lifeforms shaped like humans and deployed for mundane and routine tasks. Each one looks completely different from another. Their name always begins with a Q which is derived from the city, where they are made: Q-Ara; along with weapons and armour. Their masters name them uniquely and choose their features: longer arms, thicker armour, or even changing the inside lights.

The walls and ground are all clean in the underground and it's never too crowded. Everyone is expected to respect one another and obey the laws of the city, but if they don't, there will be a terrible price to pay: exile. It is said that once anyone leaves the city, they will never be seen or heard from again.

They approach the city centre, where the largest and tallest of the buildings are located. Stores on the first several floors spread far and wide with a variety of items being sold. If you want it, someone will have it here.

"When was the last time you were here?" Meara asks.

He is about to reply when suddenly, a strange and horrible loud noise blasts out and echoes across the city. Everyone stops in their tracks and looks up and around in panic. People start to run in all different directions, staggering, hitting into each other, not knowing which way to go. The siren is only for one thing: a creature has managed to get into the city.

Chapter 2

Local Hero

A loud crackle echoes above their heads. Both Meara and Jaykin stop too, and search the sky intently. A large barka soars across the skies of Lementes and heads straight to the centre, twisting and turning around the tall buildings. This is just one of the thousands of deadly creatures on planet Izara. They know immediately what this means. This is when the shield of the city loses a small amount of power. The shield can be open to the world and anything can come in.

"This was a huge mistake; we need to leave!" Meara shouts, trying to keep calm.

"Why? We only just got here," Jaykin replies, trying to find the creature. "I want to see it!"

"You what?" she shouts.

"I haven't seen a creature up close before." Meara is speechless. "Really? Are you serious? Why would you want to?"

"I do; come on!" he says excitedly as he runs off into the crowd.

"Jaykin!" Meara shouts, panic in her voice but he doesn't reply, and she runs after him.

They both try to push their way through the screaming crowd which is surging in the opposite direction. Meara tries her best to catch up, wanting to get his attention but losing view of him and being shoved back, out of the way, by the crowd of people. The sound of a great roar from the barka echoes through the air and then it appears overhead. The crowd quickly disperses, leaving Jaykin standing alone and still. Meara finally manages to catch up with him and grabs his arm.

"Jaykin, what are you doing? We need to get out of here, now!" but he shrugs her off, watching it swerve around and come back towards them, letting out another rumbling roar. It glides down, trying to land on the hard concrete. It collides with posts and advertising screens, sending pieces of metal and shrapnel all over the place. Meara grabs onto Jaykin and they dive behind a small concrete wall and try to take cover. The creature gets its bearings and shakes its head, then observes its surroundings. Jaykin pops his head over the wall to have a quick look at it; standing twelve feet tall, and around twenty feet long to the end of its lengthy tail, with an oily umber mane. The rest is covered in tawny coloured fur. It has huge wings for a small but muscular body.

"A mature male barka!" Jaykin says. "And a strong one too!"

"Have you completely lost your mind?" Meara asks him, her face reddening.

"No," he replies, "just because you're not interested in creatures!"

"I am interested!" She glares at him. "Just not enough to be mauled by a huge barka. I actually like being alive!" Then they both hear a baby crying, followed by a woman screaming out from the creature's direction. They peer over the wall to see what is going on. It has somehow cornered the woman. In her arms, she holds a baby tightly. She screams, crying for help, trying to hold her baby away from the barka.

"No!" Jaykin gasps and lifts himself from behind the wall, picks up the nearest stone and throws it as hard as he can at the barka, hitting it directly between its eyes. "Leave them alone!" he shouts.

"Jaykin what are you doing?" Meara asks as he spreads his arms out wide and waves them frantically to distract it, moving slowly away from Meara. Startled, the barka shakes its head and lets off a loud roar. Everyone around covers their ears, trying to block the unbearable noise. It twists its head slightly in the direction of Jaykin, locking its eyes on him.

"Oh no," he gulps. The woman realises this is the best time to run away.

Meara looks up from behind the wall.

"Get out of there now!" she shouts. The barka slowly walks up to him, then stares into his eyes. Jaykin carefully walks backwards, trying not to startle it or make it even angrier. He waits, preparing to dodge anything that this thing fires at him. It releases another huge roar of anger and goes for the attack.

Suddenly, a loud continuous humming blasts out directly above them. Jaykin hardly notices as he is too focused on the barka's movements. They both get blinded by a bright light. Jaykin covers his eyes with an arm while it flickers over the barka and around its head, making it struggle to see. It stumbles slightly and lets out a roar.

The barka looks around, all over the place, disorientated; then stops. It shakes its head and tries to find the source of the light. Jaykin isn't sure whether to stay or run. It stretches it's wings out as wide as it can and thrusts them down quickly, throwing Jaykin metres away, rolling him past Meara, who is still hiding behind the wall. The barka takes off towards the light. Jaykin quickly lifts himself up and tries to brush the dust off himself, sighing with relief that he's still alive. He looks up and scrunches his eyes and keeps track of where the creature is heading.

"Are you okay?" Meara asks, giving him a hug. "What were you thinking? You could have been killed!"

"Saving that woman and baby's life. No one else would have helped," he replies and stares up at the sky. He spots the barka. It is close but something else is too; something hovering above them. A collector: a pine-coloured flying machine with two large black rotor blades on each side of it, moving with ease. It is used by the City Guards. It looks as if the rear door is fully open but it is hard to see. Someone is standing at the opening. Jaykin's eyes widen and a smile goes across his face.

"What is that light and where is that noise coming from?" Meara asks.

"It's a collector," Jaykin replies, "I think it's him too," he whispers.

"Who?" she asks, trying to focus on where he's looking.

"The only person that can help me," Jaykin replies. "Come on!" he says and runs off.

"Oh no, please tell me it's not him," Meara says

to herself, and goes after him once again.

***

High in the sky, balancing at the doorway of the collector, a dark-haired man with a long grey-coloured jacket holds a sword, and is using it to deflect the sunlight into the barka's eyes. He places his hand to his ear.

"Slow down so it can catch up," he says, deeply and firmly. "When I give the word, you know what to do."

The barka gradually gets closer, flapping its huge wings, breathing heavily as if needing to work harder to reach the collector. The man stops deflecting the light, briefly points the sword toward the creature, then folds it up. He connects it to the magnet inside the back of his jacket.

"Now!" he shouts and quickly grabs hold of a handle, which is hanging above him. The collector goes into a downward trajectory, heading to a narrow pathway. The barka roars then inhales deeply. The man swings back, preparing himself. It lets out a huge fiery breath, twice its own length, giving out some immense heat. It almost reaches the man until he thrusts his arm straight at the ball of fire. Air blasts out and easily extinguishes it. Simultaneously, the man lets go and jumps off the collector and grabs onto the barka, somehow managing to slide onto its oily mane. He unfolds his sword and strikes across the creature's right wing. It groans in pain, trying to fly away, but with no luck. Wind gusts around them as they both plummet to the ground, with the man holding tightly. Within seconds, they smash onto concrete, the barka lets out a loud cry, and all goes quiet; only the sound of cracking from the concrete underneath it can be heard. Dust is everywhere.

The man emerges, jumping off the barka's back, and looks around. He attempts to dust himself off, but the oil from the fur makes it sticky. He places his hand to his ear again.
"Barka down. Land nearby and find out if the city's shielding is back to normal. I'll wait for back-up to arrive." He takes out a tracking device from his jacket, and attaches it to the mane. The sound of several collectors is heard and he watches them descend, landing nearby.
"I'm sorry for attacking you," he says to the barka, which is still unconscious. "But it was the only way to save you and the civilians. Don't worry though, I'll make sure they take you to the right place."

Numerous City Guards in slate coloured padded uniform surround the creature with their hand-held weapons pointed at it. These weapons: Q-Azars, can shoot bolts of energy in a single shot and can cause a lot of pain to a human, a little less to barkas.

The Commander of the Guards, the golden rim of his helmet glinting impressively, approaches the man with an air of confidence and power. "We had that under control—" he says and aims his Q-Azar at the barka's head.

"Really?" the man asks.

The Commander is about to fire upon it but the man grabs onto the Q-Azar, pointing it up to the sky, and pulls it off him.
"What are you doing?" the Commander gasps, angrily. All the Guards look towards them both, braced for action.

"It's all dealt with now. There is no need to end it," he says, about to drop the Q-Azar onto the ground, but the Commander grabs the weapon back.

"Do you want me to place you under arrest?" he says, forcefully.

"You could try but I just saved the city, again!"

"Don't tempt me!" the Commander says, raising his voice and pointing menacingly at the man. "My job is to keep this city safe, and I'm not letting a thug like you get in my way!"

"My job is to save lives, both human and creatures, including this barka. Not to kill it. You should know that."

"If it wasn't for you, this thing would have been long dead and it wouldn't have harmed anyone!"

"Tell your Guards to stand down, Commander," the man says determinedly.

"I will do no such thing," he replies, leaning in closer. "You lost your rank months ago. You have no authority here anymore."

The man grabs onto the Commander's helmet and pulls him aggressively closer. All the Guards raise their Q-Azars up at him, who, ignoring them, quietly warns their leader.
"I suggest you do as I say. If not, you know where

you'll end up. The same place as that will be going. Do you understand?"

The Commander says nothing. The man lets go, pushing him backwards.

"Do what you have to do." Leaving no time for the Commander to respond, the man walks away, pressing something in his ear again. "Is the defence back up and running?" he asks.

"Yes," a strange robotic voice responds.

"Good, as I don't have time for this. I'm on my way to you now."

Approaching the Commander, a young Guard says, tentatively, "Sir—"

"What is it?" he shouts, as he watches the man walk away.

"What should we do with the barka?"

He pauses to think and sighs. "Do as he says."

"But—" the Guard stutters.

"Release it back into the wild," he shouts, and walks off in the other direction. All the Guards gawp at him and they all have the same incredulous expression. The man, however, continues walking, at a fast pace, into the depths of the city. Slowly and cautiously a large crowd gathers around the barka and the Guards.

***

Jaykin arrives just as the man leaves. A Guard stops him from getting any closer.

"Hey, kid, you can't go this way," he announces.

Jaykin ignores him and spots the man walking away.

"He's there," he whispers to himself.

"Hey kid, did you even listen to me?" the Guard demands, raising his voice.

"Sure," Jaykin replies, not really listening at all.

"Jaykin!" It is Meara's voice.

"Meara, I'm over here!" Jaykin calls as he makes his way through the crowd. Everyone tries to catch a glimpse of the creature. More people start to gather around. Jaykin just manages to see the man, and he is certain. "Kanaren," he whispers to himself excitedly. He follows and tries to keep up but the crowd is so dense he bumps into everyone. Kanaren eventually disappears from view. "Kanaren!" Jaykin shouts, and stops, searching for him. A hand grabs onto his shoulder. He turns to see Meara. "I thought you were him!" he exclaims, disappointed.

"Jaykin, what are you doing?" Meara says frustratedly.

"I need to talk to him, but he's disappeared." He looks around again but there are too many people.

"Why do you need to talk to him?"

"I was hoping he can help me find my father." She shakes her head at him. "I don't think he's going to help you." She is exasperated. She knows he is upset and missing his father badly and wants to try his best to find him. But after a year it seems pointless and she wants him to move on. "You have me; you don't need that man's help."

Jaykin sighs in disappointment and frustration, and shakes his head, "I really thought he would help."

"Come on, let's get out of here," she says, placing her arm around him.

"Yeah, okay."

They walk around the market which is now back to normal, but they can feel the tension in the air. Everyone is talking about the barka. This is the eighth time this month that a creature has managed to get past the city's defences. The defence itself is a segmental dome, that covers the huge city. It is forty-two miles in diameter and is over two thousand metres high. The buildings, which are extremely tall skyscrapers, are connected to the dome. It has a circular opening at its highest point, allowing skyships to enter or leave. The dome itself is made from millions of wind turbines that power the entire city. Beyond the turbines, layers of electrified barriers are installed to deter creatures. Some get a nasty shock.

After visiting the market, buying food to last a week, and having a Q-Roid accidentally hitting into Jaykin, they head back to his apartment. While they put away their purchases, absent-mindedly on Jaykin's part, Meara pleads with him.

"Please don't try and find that man again, he's dangerous!"

"Meara!" He looks at her straight in the eyes. "He could be the only person from Izara and Raziz that can help me find him"

"Have you seen what he does?" she asks, "He fights creatures! It's not someone you want to get involved with!"

"He's more than that; he's a good person."

"How do you know that? You don't know him;

you haven't even talked to him before."

"He's someone that helps other people Meara; that's who I need."

"Well, fine," she stops and tries to keep her cool. "Please, just think about it." But Jaykin doesn't reply. She shakes her head again and grabs her bag. "You won't need me then," she storms out and slams the door behind her.

"Meara!" Jaykin shouts and throws an elpine fruit into his room in exasperation. He stares after it then runs out of the front door.

"Wait!" he shouts to her. She stops and turns around, tears in her eyes. "I am really, really sorry Meara," he says, walking up to her. "I won't look for him, I promise."

Meara smiles back and gives him a hug.

"You're a pain you know!"

"I know."

"I need to go," she says, wiping the tears away. "I'll pop round later?"

"Sure," Jaykin smiles, "that would be great. We can work out who'll win the Preyal Tournament this month."

She smiles back. "I'll see you later."

Back in the apartment, he closes the door behind him and breathes a sigh of relief. Then he leans against the door and hits the back of his head onto it. He looks around the now tidy room, trying to work out what to do for the rest of the day. He walks up to the picture of him and his father on the small table, admiring it for a bit, then shakes his head, frowning.

"What did you know?" he asks the picture. He

places his hand in his pocket and pulls out the small piece of paper, unfolding it. It reads:

What you know places you in mortal danger. You must leave immediately. Look towards the Western Light, you will know where to go. E.K.

He places the letter back into his pocket and lays back on the sofa, having a good think about what it means, for perhaps the millionth time now, but it just doesn't make any sense to him. He has no idea what his father knows and why he is in danger. That's the part that scares Jaykin the most. Why leave and where to? The Western Light? No one ever goes there except for the elderly. Everything about this letter is strange, including the name E.K. He knows no one with those initials.

He shakes his head as his eyes suddenly feel heavy. He tries his best to keep them open but eventually gives up. Finally, he feels like he can sleep. As soon as his eyes blink several times and close for a couple of seconds, he hears a clunk and a crash. It's the front door being forced open. Jaykin jumps slightly; tries to stand, but nothing is moving. His body is numb. He tries to open his eyes but he can't, they're too heavy. He just manages to see a blur, a shadow standing still in the sunlight. For a split second, he thinks it's his father and he tries desperately, to stay awake; but he can't. Overwhelmed with fatigue, he falls into a deep sleep.

Chapter 3

Unexpected

A loud explosion goes off, echoing through the air, scaring Jaykin and taking his breath away. He opens his eyes but can't see a thing. He repeatedly blinks to make sure it isn't his sight going. No, luckily it isn't, but it's pitch black and he can feel something covering his face. A moment of silence. He tries to take whatever it is away but he can't move. His breathing gets heavy and eventually he realises he is covered in some sort of hard substance. Another explosion goes off and it is now constant all around him, making popping noises in his ears. The air is hot and he can feel the deep panting of his breath hitting back on his face and his chest feeling tighter. Something moves down his face, an insect? No, something else. Water? Sweat? Tears? Another explosion goes off near him but he doesn't feel anything. It's getting closer. He starts to wriggle his arms, hands, and fingers but they're stuck. His heart begins to thump harder and extremely fast. He struggles to breathe now, as if someone is sucking the oxygen away from him and leaving just the heat. Another explosion, but closer this time. He feels the earth scatter all over him. He lifts his head; the earth falls away from his face, revealing an even more shocking view: a city on fire.

***

"Wake up!" Jaykin is being nudged by someone. "Wake up!" Their voice sounds strange, affected and straight-toned.

"Get out of my apartment!" Jaykin shouts slurring his words and waving his arms about. He tries to look around but it's pitch black. He places his hands on his face to feel if anything is blocking his view but there is nothing. He tries to focus. "Someone, please help me!" he shouts, starting to panic.

"You are safe," the voice says. "You are not where you think you are."

He slides his hands on what seems to be a smooth floor. Not his apartment. He gasps.

"Where am I?" he asks, trying to keep his cool and glimpse some clue.

"No need to worry. You are in a secure location," the strange voice says.

"What do you want with me?" Jaykin asks, as he rubs his eyes, still trying to wake up, looking for a face to put with the voice but the darkness persists. He hesitates. "Who am I talking to?" Slowly, he stands up. A noise of footsteps walking around him. "What is your name?"

"I won't tell you. You haven't answered any of my questions properly." The footsteps walk away from him.

"Wait!" Jaykin shouts. A door opens and a dim light surrounds a figure that stands in the doorway. It's a Q-Roid.

"Please wait here until the Master arrives," it says.

"Your Master? Who is that?" Jaykin asks, while

the light slowly increases, "Wait!" he shouts, running towards the door, but it closes tight on him. "Q-Roids!" he moans. "Why am I here?" he shouts, but gets no answer. He hits the door in frustration and a slight tingle goes down his arm and through his body, making the hair on his neck stand on end.

Lights slowly turn on to a warm soothing colour. His eyes still adjusting, he looks around and tries to work out what the room is used for. The walls, floor and ceiling are all white, with a slight plastic sheen; no furniture nor windows; just one door which blends into the wall. It's about the same size as his apartment but without the rooms. He listens out for anything on the other side of the door. Nothing. Then, suddenly, he hears tapping noises, slightly muffled, sounding like footsteps. Not sure who to expect, he stands back in the middle of the room. The door opens and Jaykin gasps in excitement but only briefly. For a moment he thinks he sees his father walk through, but someone with a similar outline and height stands there instead. The legend; the hero; the only person that can possibly help him find his father: Kanaren.

"Hello," Kanaren says, his face expressionless as he slides his hand across a wall and a chair unfolds from it. Near Jaykin, the floor starts to open, revealing a white round sofa rising into the middle of the room.

"H…Hi," Jaykin hesitates, trying to get his words out. Kanaren slowly walks up to him with his arms behind his back. Looking him up and down, he offers his hand. Jaykin has never seen Kanaren up close before. He is tall, about six foot two by the looks of things, and about a similar age to Jaykin's father; around about fifty. His hair is short, clean, and dark with grey strands growing through. His shaved beard is dark, his eyes are green; he has a few lines on his face and is quite tanned. Jaykin had expected him to have scars on his face but he has none. He is still dressed as before but without his long jacket. His clothing is all dark colours, long-sleeved shirt, and baggy trousers, with a lot of pockets. A couple of holsters hang around his belt for Q-Azars; they're empty now. Jaykin holds up his hand too and they shake.

"Take a seat."

"Thank you." Jaykin is still in shock. He sits comfortably but still stares cautiously at Kanaren.

"So, you're the one that called out my name, and I don't even know yours." He has a confident and authoritative tone in his voice.

"Umm," Jaykin hesitates. He is lost for words now, unprepared for this meeting. "J-Jaykin," he replies.

"Are you sure? You don't sound so certain about that."

"I'm sure!" Jaykin quickly replies, nodding swiftly.

"Jaykin, huh? I don't recognize the name." He places his finger to his ear. "Can you check the name, Jaykin?"

"Are you talking to your Q-Roid?" he asks curiously.

Kanaren gives him a firm look, "I'll be asking the questions here." He sits down and relaxes. "How do you know my name?"

"I've seen you save the city before. I needed to know who you were. For months I searched for you and I spoke to a lot of the Guards and then eventually got a name," Jaykin explains.

"You're persistent aren't you; I give you that but they shouldn't have given you my name."

"I'm sorry but you're a very difficult person to get hold of."

"What did you want?" he asks, leaning forward slightly.

Jaykin had never met anyone so blunt before. Kanaren's facial expression is so plain, as if he doesn't have any emotion, and Jaykin feels intimidated by him.

Jaykin feels his heart skip a beat. He can feel his hands go numb and slightly clammy. Now that he has this opportunity, words seem to fail him. It's been such a long time now since he told Meara. She's the only person that listened to him and believed him too, but she doesn't know about the letter. He isn't sure if this is a good idea or not, but this is his last chance.

"Well, I thought you could help me with something." He places his hand in the pocket and takes out the folded piece of paper.

Intrigued, Kanaren walks over and takes it and reads. He instantly lowers his head and shakes it, covering his eyes and sighing deeply. He looks straight at Jaykin.

"Sorry, but this isn't my line of work anymore. Missing people are the Guards' business." He gives the paper back to Jaykin and slowly walks towards the

door. "Do me a favour, forget whoever you're looking for and forget me."
Jaykin jumps out of his seat.

"But I've spoken to the Guards loads of times, and they're not interested. They haven't even started a search!"

"I have more important missions." He swipes his hand across the wall again and the seat disappears. "It was nice to meet you."
Jaykin falls to his knees in despair and frustration. He clenches his fists.

"I really thought you would help me!" He struggles to contain his anger and hits the floor with his fist.
Kanaren gets to the door and turns.

"I'll get the Q-Roid to take you home."
Jaykin's eyes squeeze shut to contain his tears. "I cannot believe you are turning me down," he says, desperation in his voice. Kanaren is about to leave but pauses at Jaykin's words.

"You are my hero; potentially my saviour; my only hope. I have nowhere to go after this. No one is listening."

"I'm no hero," and he turns again to leave.

"Please! I'm begging you; I need your help to find my father!"
Kanaren turns again, abruptly and stares at Jaykin.

"Wait," he says, "your father?"

"Yes," Jaykin replies.

"What's your father's name?"

"Jaylin."

"Jaylin?" Kanaren whispers, saying it slowly to

himself. "I don't know that name either."

"Master Kanaren!" the Q-Roid says in Kanaren's earpiece.

"What is it?" he replies as he holds his ear again.

"Some alarming results were found concerning the name, Jaykin"
Kanaren listens intently for a few moments. "Well, that changes things. Good work. Do the same for the name, Jaylin. See if we get the same results." He takes his hand off his ear. "When exactly did your father go missing?"

"A year ago," Jaykin replies, wiping his tears away.

"The same time as…" he pauses. "Let me have a look at the letter again." Kanaren whips it away and unfolds it. He paces up and down the room, looking at Jaykin every so often, scanning every detail of the note; even the paper itself, rubbing his fingers on it. He halts, "You need to follow me. Now!" Jaykin nods and quickly jumps to his feet.

They walk through the door, which leads to a long corridor. Kanaren places his finger over his ear again. Jaykin quickly spots something just under his sleeve. He hasn't noticed it before; some sort of contraption like an arm brace wrapped around his wrist.

"Set up the room; he's coming in," he commands, looking Jaykin up and down. "No, he's no threat," Kanaren removes his earpiece and places it in one of his pockets. "Doesn't make sense," Kanaren whispers, swiping the wall to open another door to a much larger room. It is lined with trophies, old artefacts, weapons, armour, and random things in glass boxes. Jaykin gazes at them one by one. Kanaren interrogates: "Do you have any siblings? What about your mother? No mention of grandparents?"

"No, my father told me my mother died when I was born. He hadn't spoken about any other family members."

"So, you're all on your own now and that's why you're searching for him?"

"Yeah, pretty much." Jaykin nods and continues to admire everything in the room. "You have an impressive collection of stuff by the way."

"It's not 'stuff.' They all have value in them," Kanaren replies, sounding slightly cross, "from both worlds, and different periods in history."

After a few seconds in the room, Jaykin feels strange. His left hand and foot have started to sweat and pulsate slightly. It gets stronger as they near the exit. He places his hand on his chest, checking his heart is okay and still beating normally, but nothing is out of the ordinary. He looks at Kanaren to see if he has noticed anything. He hasn't. Jaykin looks over to his left, and as he does so, his face starts pulsing too. He spots a glass box all on its own with nothing else near it. Kanaren stops at the other door and swipes his hand on the wall. "This way," he commands. Jaykin looks over at the box again, trying in vain to see what is inside. They walk through the door and into the next corridor.

Jaykin looks back. The further away from the treasure

room, the better he feels; his body returning to normal. This time the door opens to a plain room. In the centre, standing at a table is the Q-Roid. As they enter, it turns off an image projected momentarily on the wall. Maybe hiding something.

"Jaykin, this is Q-Tech, my personal Q-Roid," Kanaren says.

It stands at least five feet tall. Its torso is slim but its limbs are bulky. It is transparent, enabling Jaykin to see what appears to be old and quite dirty components, moving around inside it, as well as shiny new ones; perhaps recent replacements. He waves at it but it doesn't respond. It quickly turns to a control panel and presses a couple of buttons. Jaykin has rarely seen Q-Roids, as only highly-ranking individuals have them.

"Take a seat," Kanaren says, as he walks around the other side of the table. "There's a couple of things that I'm struggling to understand. First of all, this letter," he says, throwing it onto the table. It feathers down gently. "Where did you get it from? A friend? Family? A stranger?"

"I found it a few days after my father went missing," Jaykin replies.

"Who else knows about the letter?"

"No one, you're the only person I've shown it to."

"Do you know what they are talking about in the note?"

"Umm, no." Jaykin quickly replies, "I have tried to work it out, but I can't make sense of it."

"Have you ever been to the Western Light?"

"No," Jaykin replies with a face suggesting:

"*Why would he ask a stupid question?*"

"Do you know who sent this letter?"

Jaykin shakes his head. "I haven't worked that out either." It feels like this isn't helping but he goes along with it.

"Okay, some more questions. Are you from outside the city?"

"Not as far as I know," he replies scrunching up his face and shaking his head.

"Are you from another planet other than Raziz?"

Jaykin stops to think what a strange question that is.

"No. Of course not!"

Kanaren stops and turns to Q-Tech again, "How's he done?"

"Passed every test so far, Master."

Jaykin looks at them both.

"What did I pass?" Neither replies. He persists: "Why does this feel like a one-way conversation? I've answered all your questions and you've barely answered any of mine." Again nothing. "Answer me!" Jaykin shouts and slams his hand on the table, and instantly Kanaren pulls out a Q-Azar and points it directly at him. Q-Tech does the same.

"Sit down and be quiet," Kanaren says calmly and firmly, "and I will tell you." Jaykin slowly sits back onto the chair and they both withdraw their Q-Azars. "Q-Tech was scanning your facial expressions for the truth. Our work is highly sensitive; top secret. I needed to know if I can trust you."

"Okay," Jaykin hesitates, "I'm sorry."

"It's Okay, I understand what you're going

through but I'll sort this out my way, you understand?" Jaykin nods. "No more questions for now. Q-Tech, please take him upstairs. We're taking him home."

"Are you not going to help me?"

"We'll see, but in the meantime, I need to look around at your place."

Q-Tech guides Jaykin to a wall and it slides its hand across it. Steps appear from the floor, reaching roof level, where a small door opens to the outside.

"This way please," Q-Tech says. Jaykin walks up the steps and looks over to Kanaren, who picks up the note, folds it, and places it into one of his pockets. He walks out and is hit by a cold chill in the air. He is standing on the roof of a skyscraper. The collector, its rotor blades turning slowly, is waiting. Its rear door opens and Q-Tech ushers him in. Inside, at the bottom of the walls are boxes which are used for storage, most likely for weapons, clothing, or gear. Above that are nets and long lengths of rope wrapped up, including loads of metal coils of wire. Jaykin is surprised that there is enough room for at least a hundred people huddled together or two large cages in here.

"Does Kanaren own this whole floor?" He enquires while he takes a seat on a box.

"Yes," Q-Tech replies. "He owns the whole hallway and the four apartments on this floor alone, including the roof." It makes its way to the controls at the front of the collector; a section which is separated from the rear by a wall and a door.

"That's crazy," Jaykin says, wondering how he can afford something like that. He watches as Kanaren jumps inside, jacket on. The big rear door closes and locks shut. "I've never been on one of these before."

"I would be surprised if you had. You'd better hold on." Jaykin grabs onto the nearest handle.

"What do you actually do? For a living I mean?" Jaykin asks.

"I help defend the city…and some other stuff."

"I thought that was the job of the Guards." looking at him up and down. "And you definitely don't look like a Guard."

"It is, but sometimes they need a little support and, well, let's just say I have some relevant experience. Which reminds me; impressive work on the barka, by the way. You stood up to it like it was nothing."

"You watched that?" Kanaren nods. Jaykin smiles with excitement and pride.

"How did you know it's easily distracted?"

"My father taught me everything about creatures on Izara and Raziz. I watch a lot of the Preyal tournaments too. Barkas are on there all the time."

"I know. I watch it too."

"You do?"

Kanaren nods. "You, the mother and baby could have been seriously hurt if it had gone wrong."

"I know. What else was there to do? If I wasn't there, then…" he goes quiet. "I wouldn't like to think."

"Maybe you're right," Kanaren says, pensively. "For your bravery, you'll be rewarded."

"Really?" Jaykin is surprised, not expecting any reward. "Thank you."

"Don't mention it. You deserve it for saving someone's life." He sits down opposite and stares at Jaykin.

"There aren't many people on Izara or Raziz that would do what you did."
Jaykin is silent, taking in the compliment.

"The worlds need more people like you."
Kanaren opens the letter and reads it once again. Jaykin had forgotten he still has it. "This letter; it wasn't sent to just your father."
Jaykin stares at him.

"Really? There are more? How many? Who are they?" He has so many questions.
Kanaren holds up his hand to stop him.

"Too many to count and only a handful of people know about these disappearances." He looks up at Jaykin "Now you're one of them." He gives him an uncomfortable but sympathetic look.

"I thought my father was the only one," Jaykin says. "Did you find anyone else?"

"No, but I have seen dozens of these letters. What bothers me is that everyone has disappeared at roughly the same time. Not one of them had any family. It was always a friend or work colleague reporting them missing. You're the first relative; which I find quite strange." Jaykin stays quiet, focusing on what Kanaren is telling him. "What did your father do for a living?"

"He's a scientist. He didn't really talk about his work much," he recalls.

"How long have you been living here?"

"We used to live in Dreamora when I was younger but I had problems, apparently. I slept a lot and no one could wake me. We had to move here to Lementes."

"There's a lot of that happening in Dreamora. So, it helped, moving here?"

"Yeah, a little, but recently I've been getting very vivid and horrible dreams, sometimes unbelievably realistic."

"Interesting," Kanaren considers.

"How about you? How long have you been here?"

"I don't stay in one place." A buzzing sound is heard overhead. "Good, we're here."

The engine cuts and the rear door opens. Jaykin finds the landing very smooth. He hadn't felt a thing. They walk out of the collector. Jaykin notices the familiar rooftop where he was all night. He looks over at Kanaren, smiles to himself and nods, knowing he's done the right thing. They head to the elevator and they fall silent all the way down to the apartment.

"Sorry about the mess," Jaykin says as he opens the front door.

"Q-Tech, stand guard and don't let anyone in," Kanaren says looking around.

"Understood," it confirms.

"Where's your father's room?"

"In the back, on the right," he replies and Kanaren heads in that direction.

"Jaykin? Oh!" Meara appears just outside of the door and spots Q-Tech. "What's going on?" she asks.

"Hey, Meara. She's okay, Q-Tech," It stands aside and she walks in slightly concerned. "I found some help," Jaykin says. She notices Kanaren entering Jaylin's room.

"Who's that?" she whispers, getting concerned.

"Kanaren," he whispers back.

"What's he doing here?"

"He's here to help."

"Really? He's a stranger, in your apartment."

"He's not a stranger, he's…" He pauses, "Kanaren." He grins excitedly.

"Humph." Meara crosses her arms. "You haven't been listening to anything I've been telling you, have you?"

"But I thought he could help—" Jaykin stutters.

"You go into your fantasy world Jaykin. Your father is gone. He isn't coming back; you need to get that into your head."

"He is coming back, Meara."

"Fine! Keep thinking that, but don't come back crying to me. I've had enough. I can't help you anymore." Jaykin watches her as she walks off. He sighs heavily.

"Girlfriend problems?" Kanaren asks, appearing from the room again.

"She's just a friend who's trying to help me," Jaykin replies and looks outside.

"Does she know anything about the note?"

"No, I didn't want her to find out. It'll just cause more frustration. It feels like she doesn't actually want me to find him."

"Could be," Kanaren replies. "Does she know your father?"

"Yes, but only because he asked her to look after me when he was working late nights. We've become good friends ever since." He shakes his head. "I don't know what went wrong." Kanaren spots the photos of them and picks one up to look at it closely.

"Do you have a family?" Jaykin asks.

"I did," he pauses, thoughtful for a few moments. "Many years ago."

"Really? Where are they now?"
Kanaren's mood changes.

"Let's move on." He places the photo frame on the table quite firmly and walks off to the next room. Jaykin stands there wondering if his question has caused offence. Minutes pass. "Nothing here out of the ordinary," Kanaren says. "Are you sure he didn't leave anything here?"

"Yeah, I'm sure," Jaykin nods.

"Fine." He looks around for the last time. "Grab your stuff. We're getting out of here."

"Am I not staying?" Jaykin asks.

"No, you're staying with us until I can work something out." He looks straight at Jaykin. "And for your safety."

"O…Okay," he hesitates, not expecting that reply. Why will he be in danger all of a sudden? He has been here a whole year without any problems. "Can I say bye to Meara?"

"No. It's for the best. She'll understand."
Jaykin nods slowly, uncertainly. "I'll just go get some stuff." He walks into his room and picks out a couple of things from a chest of drawers. He notices that they are neatly folded and washed. Meara has done a good job here and he starts to feel guilty about how he treated her. He places them in a bag. He overhears

Kanaren telling Q-Tech that he'll see them back at the base later and to show Jaykin to the guest room. Jaykin watches him walk past the window. Immediately, he grabs a piece of paper and a pen, writing as quickly as he can. Q-Tech walks in.

"Are you ready?" it asks.

"I am." He goes to walk out of his room but stops and turns to look around it. He has a feeling he won't be back here for a while. He feels slightly sad, but mostly excited.

"Wait a moment, Q-Tech. I just need to grab one more thing." He runs over to the picture frame and unclips the picture that Kanaren picked up earlier and places it into his pocket. He folds the piece of paper and they walk out of the apartment. As he closes the door slowly, Jaykin discreetly places the note he has written between the door and its frame. He looks towards Meara's apartment several doors away from him. "Bye Meara and thank you," he says quietly. He gently touches his door and they walk the opposite way. They enter the elevator again with an awkward silence.

"How long have you been serving Kanaren?" he asks. Jaykin has never had to make small talk with a Q-Roid before.

"Approximately forty years," Q-Tech replies.

"That's a long time," Jaykin exclaims, expecting it to be a couple. "Do you know about his family?"

"That subject is unknown."

"Oh, but you must have known about his family; parents; is he married or does he have children?"

"Master Kanaren would never talk about his

family. He keeps his work life separate."
Jaykin couldn't argue with that.

"How old is he?" he asks.

"Fifty-six."

Jaykin stares at it. "He looks really good for that age." Q-Tech doesn't respond. "Do you know what he's planning to do with me?"

"Unknown," it replies.

The number on the elevator reaches seventy-one. Jaykin smiles to himself as they walk towards the collector. Here is where he very nearly gave up. He feels like he's leaving something behind and it isn't just Meara or even the apartment; it's something deeper; the fond memories he has with his father growing up here. It feels like he is moving on, and for the better too. His emotions are mixed but powerful. They enter the collector and it takes off gently. Jaykin can't help but have a good cry.

Chapter 4

The New Hero

Day 2

Bursting out of the ground, Jaykin gasps for air and cries out. He tries to move but he can't. The air gets hotter like a blazing fire, becoming overwhelming. His lips are dry from the heat. Licking to keep them moist, he tries to reach out and grab something, anything, for comfort, but instead he grasps on soft soil. He tries to move any part of his body, but every bone feels as if it's broken into pieces.

Jaykin starts to panic. Any minute an explosion may go off on top of him. It's extremely dark here. His eyes feel like they weigh a ton and he struggles to open them. Eventually, he does so and spots a bright flash, filling the sky, then another explosion goes off nearby, making his eyes shut instantly.

He dares to open them again and all he can see is the blurry horizon. What was once a beautiful blue is now a darkish red, near the colour of blood, fused with a burning orange. A city is on fire. He tries to look away and notices the edge of whatever he is lying in. A grave? No, wait, it's a crater. He tries to move again but barely has the energy to lift a finger, let alone any part of his body. Somehow he finds some strength and moves his upper body, leaning on both his arms. A pulsating sensation rushes through him making the pain unbearable. He staggers and tries to balance, looking for a way out of there. Several explosions are going off in the city. He holds his breath to take in all the pain in his body and somehow manages to stand, but it takes a couple of attempts and, when he does get balance once again, a terrible scene is before him. People are running around screaming and all the buildings are on fire. Once a magnificent city, now just a huge mound of rubble. Then he sees them. These things; these creatures. Some fly around him miles up high, some are levitating and some begin to move the earth around them. The noise of explosions, screaming, and swords clashing together becomes overwhelming.

Suddenly everything completely stops, as if someone slowed down time itself. It is quiet; too quiet for anyone's liking. A bright light streaks across the sky and then it stops. Another blast, but this is different from any of the others. It lights up the whole battlefield. Everything that is fighting and all that are flying crash to the ground and the sea. One lands right next to Jaykin.

***

A loud crash wakens him. He opens his eyes and sees a light creeping its way into the room. He sees someone's outline, standing right next to him. It is Q-Tech placing something on the small table.

"What are you doing here?" Jaykin asks, trying to sit up.

"Good morning. Please have your breakfast. Master Kanaren needs to see you in the training room as soon as you have finished."

"Okay…thanks." Realising, with relief, that he is still at Kanaren's place, he still feels exhausted. "This is why I don't have a Q-Roid; they scare you for no reason."

While Jaykin slowly gets up from the bed and starts eating, he thinks back on the dream. It's the main reason why he can never sleep well; this nightmare will always wake him. It never varies. He doesn't know why he keeps having it. It troubles and exhausts him. After finishing his breakfast, which was a bowl of different types of fruit, he stumbles out and Q-Tech leads the way to the training room. It's the same room that he woke up in yesterday. Standing in the middle of it is Kanaren, with some weapons beside him, on a stand.

"Good, you're awake," he says. "Today we're going to do something different. Do you know how to fight?"

"I do." Jaykin hesitates and looks away.

"Oh really?" Kanaren replies, sounding quite surprised. "How?"

"My father taught me."

"Why? People don't tend to learn to fight without a reason."

"He taught me some basics. He said that to survive in this world I will need to learn to fight and defend myself, but I haven't done any training since his disappearance."

"Well then, let's see what you've got," and he

looks at Q-Tech who is standing near the door. "You'll train with the Q-Roid for the time being. It'll get you back into the fighting spirit. Q-Tech, training mode. Begin with level zero point one and gradually build up. I want to see how good he is."

"Understood Master."

"Good luck," he says, reassuring Jaykin.

"Kanaren."

"What's up?"

"Where did you go yesterday?"

"Just to sort some things out. Nothing to worry about. Good luck with your training," he says, pointing at Jaykin and leaves the training room. Jaykin faces Q-Tech and lifts his fists a little reluctantly.

"So, this is actually going to happen. I'm going to fight a Q-Roid."

"Are you ready Master Jaykin?"

He lowers his arms. "Master Jaykin? Where did that come from?" he says. "Please, just call me Jaykin."

"Understood. Level zero point one loading; title: rookie."

"Did you just call me a roo—" Before Jaykin can finish his sentence, Q-Tech is ready.

"Level loaded." Q-Tech starts to fight and swings for him. He blocks and ducks for every swing. They do this for about fifteen minutes.

"This is easy. I'm dodging every attack." Jaykin says, and they both stop.

"This is still level zero point one. Would you like to move onto level zero point two?"

"Let's make it level three at least," Jaykin says, feeling slightly more confident than earlier and lifting his fists up in readiness.

"Are you sure, Jaykin? Statistics say you will not be ready for this level quite yet."

"Don't give me the stats. Just do it, Q-Tech."

"Level three loading…ready."

"Let's do this…"

Q-Tech hits Jaykin straight into the face without warning, three times faster and stronger than before. "Ouch! That hurt." Jaykin shouts, rubbing his nose and moving back to dodge the upcoming punches. He smiles and continues fighting. He can feel his body react to anything Q-Tech throws at him. All the memories of himself and his father flood back and he's enjoying the training again.

A couple of hours pass.

***

"Pause," Jaykin says, huffing and puffing. "What level has Kanaren reached with you?" he asks. Q-Tech is about to reply but Kanaren returns to the training room. "How's it going in here?" he asks, holding a small digital device known as a Q-pad. Jaykin stands still; sweat drips off him. It's been a while since he has done anything like this. "Looks like you've trained hard." He throws Jaykin a towel and a piece of fruit. "Here, eat this. It'll get your energy back. What level did you get to?"

"Level five, I think," Jaykin smiles and gnaws on the fruit.

"Great job. I wasn't expecting you to get anywhere near that. Right, next thing to do: follow me."

They walk out of the training room, through the corridor, and Jaykin feels anxious. He knows what is coming up next: the treasure room again. He wants to get near the far left of the room so he focuses on it discreetly as they enter. He has a look at a couple of weapons.

"Are these all yours?"

"Yes," Kanaren replies, still walking towards the next room. Jaykin feels excited. He wants his body to react to whatever it is. Within seconds it does. The pulsating starts on his left side again. He quickly faces back to the training room, pretending to look around casually so as not to attract Kanaren's attention. The pulsating is now on his right side. It feels like a magnet pulling on him and his body is reacting.

"Do you mind if I check out these things over here?" he asks.

"Sure, just don't touch anything."

"Okay," Jaykin replies, acting as calm as he can. He moves around and lets the pulsating sensations direct him closer to the corner of the room. He looks at a few other objects on his way there, then stops and spots a glass box on a decorative stand. He bends down to admire it. It is about half a metre wide by another half metre high. While Kanaren checks a couple of things on his Q-pad, Jaykin steps forward to have a closer look. In the glass box lays some sort of misty white and blue crystal. It looks smooth and slightly egg-shaped. It's about four inches wide and six inches high. It could easily fit in Jaykin's hand.

"What's this?" he asks.

Kanaren looks up from his Q-pad, walks over and bends down to have a look.

"That is a very unusual crystal," he says, then focuses his eyes on Jaykin's face. "Why? Do you like it?"

"Yeah, it's beautiful," Jaykin replies, with his whole body now pulsating. "Why is it so special?"

"Because it's an extremely rare material and it's also indestructible."

"Indestructible? Cool! Where did you get it?"

"Well," Kanaren ponders. "Many years ago, when I was travelling on Raziz, I was just outside the city of Egrof and near the volcano mines. I came across something in the walls. It was this crystal." He stares at it for a couple of seconds. "I'd never seen anything like it. I've done a few tests on it and it absorbs any sort of pressure and temperature. But if you think that's impressive, there's a much larger one in Dreamora, which is about nine feet tall, I think. Have you seen it?"

"I don't think so, no, but I have heard of it," Jaykin replies.

Kanaren leans into Jaykin and whispers: "Word has it, the crystal has powers and can give you dreams." He stands back and continues: "Well, that's what the stories say anyway, but to be honest we don't really know as the emperor owns it and no one is allowed to go anywhere near it."

"Yeah, that's what my father told me," Jaykin mumbles to himself. "Isn't it in the middle of the city?"

"It is and it's protected by a dozen Guards. Anyway," he steps back, "we have other concerns to think about. Let's continue. I need to show you something important."

But the pulsating is so powerful that Jaykin can't get away. He's transfixed by the crystal; he can't keep his eyes off it. It's as if he is hypnotised. He looks at every single detail and gets closer to the glass. He finds his hand lifting towards it and has an urge to touch the glass. He taps it with the slightest touch and, suddenly, the crystal shakes slightly and moves towards him. Jaykin steps back, puzzled. He looks at Kanaren to see if he has seen what happened, but he continues to walk through the door. Jaykin slowly walks back to the glass box and does it again, and the crystal moves for the second time.

"Jaykin, you all right there?" Kanaren shouts from the other room.

"Yes, I'm fine!" Jaykin replies, startled. He quickly turns to the door. Kanaren pops his head out and sees Jaykin swinging his hands behind him.

"Sorry, just looking at the crystal again. You have an amazing collection here."

"Thanks. Come on in," Kanaren says, indicating the next room.

"Okay." Jaykin takes a couple of steps until he realises something is different. The pulsating sensation has ceased. He glances back into the glass box and notices the crystal has disappeared.

"Jaykin!" Kanaren shouts, still trying to get his attention.

"Ah!" Jaykin holds his head and collapses onto his knees and screams.

"What is it?" Kanaren asks, and rushes towards him, trying to lift him up from the floor.
He staggers up and rubs his head.

"Aargh, sorry I just had an excruciating headache." Kanaren looks at him with concern. "I've never had anything like that before."
Kanaren helps him steady. "You okay now?"

"Yeah, I'll be fine."

He takes a seat, still shocked by what happened. What if Kanaren finds out the crystal is missing? He needs to be cautious about what to say now. He focuses on something on the table. Made out of metal and with a handle on it, it looks like a blade but nothing like a sword. He has no idea what it is. Q-Tech enters the room and waits for instructions.

"What you are about to see is highly classified," Kanaren begins. "Everything you hear and see must not leave this room. You will not speak to anyone about any of this. Do you understand?"

"I do," Jaykin nods.

"Screen on." A tiny thin light pops up from the middle of the table and projects a big widescreen onto the clear wall behind Kanaren. Lines of writing fade in. "What you see here is the information on every single person who lived, was exiled or deceased. This is from all six cities and it is called the System." He points to the screen. "Name, age, parents, occupation, and sometimes recent information. What I need to show you, is this." He turns to the screen. "Search for the name, Jaykin."

"*Searching…*" a voice is heard from the light on

the table.

"What's the system for?" Jaykin asks.

"Protection—" Kanaren replies, but the voice interrupts him.

"*...Jaykin, not found.*"

"Not found?" Jaykin asks, getting to his feet. "How am I not on there?"

"That's what I want to know," Kanaren replies. "If someone is not on here, then questions need to be asked." He stops to think. "Either you're not from any of the cities, or this planet." He watches Jaykin's reaction, expecting a clue to the mystery, but he just looks confused. "Or someone is trying to protect you."

"From what?" Jaykin asks.

"I don't know. But there's something else and it's even more suspicious," he says, turning back to the screen. "Search the name Jaylin."

"*Searching...*" Within seconds it replies "*...found.*"

"He's on there?" Jaykin jumps up from his seat. "What does it say?" he asks excitedly.

"Nothing," Kanaren replies. "Except for one thing." He approaches the screen and points to three dots. "There. This means that the profile has been hacked. Just like the others who are missing."

"Why would someone do that?" Jaykin asks.

"Maybe because they don't want to be found or someone did it for them."

"The note?"

"Yes, they all knew something," Kanaren replies and he pauses, "...and I think I know what it is." Jaykin can feel the tension in the room. "Last year, a couple of days after your father and the others disappeared, I received seventeen separate video clips from an unknown source. Each clip has one letter written on it. When I gathered all the letters together, it made the words 'Project Assembling.'"

"But that can mean anything," Jaykin says. "What did the video clips contain?"

"Individually, they don't make sense, but when we combined them into one, they gave us some interesting information." He turns to the screen again. "Play Project Assembling."

The video starts with a series of blips and loses the signal every so often. Muffled popping sounds are heard, sounding like explosions in the background, and then a woman's voice emerges. She is breathing heavily as if she has been running or fighting.

"*My name is Captain Hayga from the planet Tarintia,*" She then appears on the screen, a dark-haired and blue-eyed woman. She wears bright green shining armour with darker green edging. She has noticeable cuts and bruises all over her face, as if she has been in battle. "*I am sending this out to all frequencies, and to the nearest planets.*" She looks behind her, then back at the monitor. "*We have been invaded by some sort of galactic army. This is a warning to you all. They are incredibly powerful, and we were not prepared for this. Do not make the same mistake. They have surrounded us now and they will not negotiate. All the—*" the signal loses connection and then comes back again "*—are captured, tortured, or killed. We cannot win this war.*" She turns around again, quickly, as if distracted by something and she starts to talk faster: "*They're here, I* *don't have much time, so I'll try and make this very clear. They seem to be trying to find someone and will stop at nothing. You must be prepared."* The video loses visual connections for a couple of seconds. *"Wait!"* she screams out. *"No! No!"* Then there is what seems like a long screech of communication noise and then, nothing.

There is silence in the room as Jaykin tries to take in the implications of the message. Something strikes him about the woman which puzzles him.

"She reminds me of Meara," he says.

"There's more," Kanaren says.

The connection comes back online and is clearer, but with no visuals and a scary deep voice sends out a loud deep chuckle.

"*We will have our revenge.*" Again, nothing.

Jaykin looks stunned.

"Is this what my father was hiding all this time?"

"By the looks of things, yes, and it seems they were all in danger."

"From who or what exactly?"

"I've been trying to work that out since I got these clips and it's important that we focus our attention on this message."

"I understand, but what can we do?"

"That's a good question. Which leaves me with one more thing to do." Kanaren picks up the strange object from the table, yanks it slightly and it unfolds, revealing a sword. He walks around the table. "Jaykin," he says, pointing in front of him, "please kneel." Jaykin does as he is asked.

"I normally go for someone—"

"Stronger?" Q-Tech interrupts.

"Wiser, I was going to say," Kanaren says, and shakes his head. "On behalf of the leaders of all six cities, I would like to thank you for your bravery yesterday for saving civilians from danger. It is extremely rare to see such courage. So, for that, we thank you, and now you will be rewarded." Kanaren places the sword on Jaykin's left shoulder, then the right. "I hereby promote you, Jaykin, into a class one Hunter." He lifts the sword back towards him. "Arise Jaykin!" Kanaren says, and watches him as he stands. "How do you feel?" he asks.

"Umm, I feel fine. Should I feel any different?" Kanaren stops. "You should feel proud," he says tapping on Jaykin's shoulder. He folds the sword and places it on his back. It stays in place, apparently by some magnetic force. "You're probably wondering what a Hunter is?"

"You read my mind."

"A true Hunter is a protector of the city."

"Isn't that what the Guards are for?"

"Yes, but it's much more complicated than that. Hundreds of years ago, long before the cities and the Guards, leaders from all over Izara came together. They wanted to create a group to protect their followers. That's where the Hunters came about; a large and very skilled force who served the leaders, and followers for many years. But when the cities were being built, the emperors at the time wanted more control of the Hunters and created stricter laws, reducing their freedom and power. The Hunters despised the new laws and retaliated in their own way. They didn't want to be controlled anymore and that's when the Guards were created, to protect the emperors' interests."

"So, if the Guards protect us now, then what do the Hunters actually do?"

"Many Hunters follow the emperor's laws. Some do it for good and many do it only if they're getting paid. They operate on an independent and secret basis, usually at the behest of the emperors, whose trust they retain. But to this day, Hunters hate the Guards, and vice versa."

"There are thousands of Guards," Jaykin says. "And why have I never heard of the Hunters before?" Kanaren leans on the edge of the table. "Hunters are a secret society, which keeps the cities going and operates in the background. The people of the cities are oblivious. They only know of the Guards. Hunters are around, staying and leaving whenever required. Emperor's rule. They don't want to get rid of the Hunters completely, as they're still very important to every city. A secret force is necessary for public safety and security. The people do not need to know about their missions. The Guards are never allowed to mention the word: Hunter. If they do, they will be disciplined, possibly exiled." He sighs. "But it works." He stands and walks up to Jaykin. "Every Hunter must have their own weapon. Some prefer Q-Azars, some have snipers, but mine is the sword. Compared to Q-Azars, swords are great against most types of creatures. Here, Q-Tech." It throws something over to Kanaren. "This is yours."

"Thank you," Jaykin stands there, not knowing how to hold it, staggered. "I've never held a sword before." He admires it, in awe.

"I would hope not!" Kanaren replies. "Look after it."

"I will."

"You can practise in the training room any time. Q-Tech has placed your new clothes on your bed."

"Thank you, Q-Tech," he says, still admiring his sword.

"I'm going to need your help, Jaykin. But in the meantime, you need to learn to use that. Listen to everything I say and do everything I do, unless I say otherwise. I don't honour people with the class of a Hunter randomly. I select them for a reason, do you understand?" Kanaren says firmly.

"I do. I won't let you down."

"Good. I suggest you go and get ready for your first mission. Q-Tech will assist you."

"Okay," Jaykin replies, folding the sword away. "What is my first mission exactly?"

"We're going to meet with the Emperor of Lementes."

Chapter 5

First Mission

Outside Jaykin's apartment, Meara knocks on his door and shouts for him. "Jaykin, I'm sorry for what I said. Can I come in?" but gets no answer. She knocks again, then tries looking through the window but it's all dark. When she leans back, she spots something wedged into the door. She tries to pluck it out. Eventually, being very careful not to rip it, she pulls it out and unfolds it.

"To Meara, Kanaren is helping me find my father. I'm not sure when I'll be back. It may not be for a while. I'll keep you informed if I can. Jaykin x."

"Oh Jaykin," she sighs deeply and shakes her head, "what have you done?"

***

Jaykin walks out of his room wearing his new clothing; a long grey coloured jacket, it's surprisingly light and warm. Underneath, is similar material. He can't work out where to place his sword though.

"How is this? Do I look like a Hunter now?" he asks Kanaren.

"Not bad, does it fit well?"

"Yes, it fits fine. I can't remember the last time I got new clothes."

"It is made of high polena fabric so it's resistant to dirt; an effective way to avoid changing your clothes if you're away for a few days. The jacket is for emergencies only. If the shirt or trousers are ripped, you can replace the fabric with parts of your jacket."

"That's good to know."

"We need to go." They walk through the treasure room and Kanaren swipes the wall while Jaykin glimpses the glass box.

"Are we not taking the collector?" Jaykin asks.

"No, we're walking this time; I don't use it all the time you know."

"Isn't this room connected to the elevator? How do people not accidentally go to this level?"

"Easy," Kanaren replies. "Build your own secret elevator." A ding goes off; it opens and they walk in, the number one hundred and twenty shows up on the panel. "It's also faster," Kanaren says. The doors shut. It reaches the bottom and Kanaren walks out with ease, but Jaykin struggles and holds onto anything he can.

"That was horrible," he says.

"You get used to it," Kanaren replies.

***

They head along the underground walkway towards the centre of the city. It's quiet and barely lit.

"Kanaren, I feel slightly nervous about meeting the emperor," Jaykin whispers.

Kanaren looks him up and down.

"You'll be fine."

"Why are we going to meet him?" Kanaren opens his pocket and unfolds a note. "How did you get—" Jaykin asks.

"This is one from the many that went missing." Kanaren points at the letter. "These initials are important; they're from the Emperor."

"The Emperor of Lementes?"

"Yes, Emperor Kin. We need to find out if he's still missing and we need to be discreet." He looks around. "Since the disappearances, I have tried to visit every so often, to monitor the situation."

"But who's running the city?"

"A group of people called the Knights."

"Who are they? I've never heard of them."

"They live in the Palace; as personal guards to the emperor or empress. They make an oath to protect them for life. The most senior, called the High Knight, deputises for the emperor as necessary."

"So, is this High Knight currently in charge of Lementes?"

"Yes, and they don't like to see anyone while the emperor is away." Exiting the underground via a stairway by going up some steps, they get closer to the Palace; a very large, ancient, and beautiful stone building. A group of armed Guards can be seen patrolling the entrance. "I'll do the talking," Kanaren says, and walks towards the nearest Guard.

"Halt! No further," the Guard says. He then points his Q-Azar at them both. "What do you want?"

"We wish to speak to the emperor," Kanaren replies.

"The emperor is away from the Palace," the guard says, sounding tired of saying that to people. Other Guards walk over. "Now back off."

"I wish to talk to him about what happened with the creature yesterday."

Another Guard gets involved. "We do not care about any creature or mission you have. We have our orders, now go away or we will arrest you."

Kanaren holds his hands up.

"Okay, okay. I get the picture. You don't want us here. We'll go quietly." They both walk away.

"As you can tell, it can be quite difficult to enter the Palace," Kanaren says.

"Can you not break in?"

Kanaren shakes his head.

"It's highly protected. If you get caught, you're banished from the city and I can't afford that. See what I mean about the Guards hating the Hunters?"

"Yes, ruthless," Jaykin says. "I did ask them to help me find my father a few times but they didn't do anything. I don't think they believed me."

"No, it's because they knew the job would go to a Hunter eventually and they would have to work with them. They literally guard. Investigation and search are not part of their role. That's why I received these letters. At least we know that the emperor is still missing."

***

They return to Kanaren's place and enter the elevator.

"Do all the leaders of Izara and Raziz know about Project Assembling?" Jaykin asks.

"They do but they're not doing anything about it," Kanaren sighs.

"Why not?"

"Because they don't believe in it."

"Then we should show them the video."

"Already done that. It isn't enough."

"What about the missing people and these notes? Do they know about them?"

"Not sure," Kanaren replies, "but if we can link it to the invasion then it may work. I think it's time to visit the other leaders of Izara and Raziz."

The elevator stops and Jaykin stares at Kanaren.

"Are we seriously going to meet all of them?"

"Yes," Kanaren replies, "but it won't be easy. Like you just found out, we couldn't even get through to Lementes Palace, let alone Dreamora and Q-Ara. I will prepare and we'll start tomorrow."

"What shall I do?" Jaykin asks.

"Practice using your new weapon and use Q-Tech to help with your fighting skills. You're going to need them."

***

New blade in hand, Jaykin swings it at Q-Tech several times. It is using a blunt blade that Kanaren made for it to train with. Jaykin feels like the sword may be too heavy for him. After a few hours, he asks it to stop for some rest.

"Q-Tech, has Kanaren ever trained anyone else before?"

"Yes," It replies, "a very talented young man, called Aren."

"Where is he now?"

"His last known location was in the city of Q-Ara."

Then Kanaren enters the training room.

"Good work Q-Tech," he says, "is it going well?"

"Yes, thanks," Jaykin replies. Kanaren's jacket is off, showing the device on his right arm. He noticed it yesterday and is still trying to work out what it is. Kanaren observes Jaykin's curiosity.

"Are you wondering what this is?" He lifts it up to show him and twists it around so Jaykin can have a better look. "It's a weapon," he says. "One of a kind."

"What does it do?"

"Want to find out?"

"Err…sure," Jaykin hesitates.

"Try and take it off of me." He sticks his hand out and wiggles his fingers at him. Jaykin leaps towards him but a huge gust of air forces out from the weapon. He lets out a loud gasp, his body jerking backwards against the training room wall.

"Are you okay?" Kanaren asks, giving him a hand up.

"Yeah, I'm fine, I think. That is one amazing weapon."

"It can come in handy, especially with fire breathing creatures. That was low power," he says adjusting the device. "To become a great Hunter, you will need to be faster and stronger; not just physically, but mentally too. You need to remember a few things. First, a good Hunter is to protect any civilian, inside or outside of the city, using anything necessary. Second, you will have difficult decisions to make, so choose wisely, as they can have massive consequences. Lastly, you will be travelling. This includes going to all six cities and going outside of them."

Jaykin's eyes widen.

"Outside of the city?" He hesitates; "but no one goes outside of the city. There are hundreds of deadly creatures out there."

"One hundred and eighty-four thousand different types of creatures, to be precise," Q-Tech announces.

"Yeah, thank you for that," Jaykin replies.

"Hunters do," Kanaren says. Jaykin goes silent again and his stomach churns at just the thought. Everything inside the city is fine. People like to describe it as cosy. But outside, all the nightmares come true. Everyone knows that it's the scariest and deadliest place on Izara. It's where the killers and the thieves are all sent. It's like the death penalty.

"How many times have you been out of the city?" Jaykin asks.

"I've lost count."

"Did Aren go out of the city?"

Kanaren stops and realises what is being asked. It looks as if he wasn't expecting that question.

"He did. He got used to it after a year or so. How do you know about him?"

"Q-Tech was telling me about him."

"Oh, was it now?" Kanaren stares at Q-Tech. "I think I need to start wiping your memory."

"Sorry, Master Kanaren," it replies, staying very still.

"No need for that." Jaykin says. "I ask

questions I shouldn't."

"Ask as many as you like. Anything to help you learn. I recruited Aren a few years ago. He was a great Hunter," Kanaren says, nodding his head and staring into space as if remembering something. He then looks over to Jaykin. "Go clean up, eat and get some rest. We have a long day tomorrow." He leaves the room. Jaykin expected more on Aren. It must have been another touchy subject.

Day 3

Jaykin lies in his bed trying to sleep but still struggles; his whole body is aching from all the training with Q-Tech. He tries to think about what has happened in the last couple of days, but something distracts him. He can hear footsteps and they are coming from the treasure room. He wonders who it can be, as it's in the middle of the night. Why is Kanaren up this early? Or can it be Q-Tech doing its nightly chores? Whoever it is, they're pacing up and down. He decides to get up and find out. He opens the door, but instead of being greeted by Kanaren or Q-Tech, he encounters an elderly man in a long old ragged cloak, nothing that anyone would wear in the city. He has bright white long hair and stubble. He seems to be peering into a glass box. The man looks fixated on it.

"Hi," Jaykin says, trying to be very polite. The elderly man looks up at him and kindly smiles. Jaykin suddenly feels very calm and at ease with him. He has a very kind and polite smile, Jaykin thinks. The man doesn't say anything; instead, he goes back to staring at the glass box again. Jaykin suddenly realizes it's the same box the small crystal was in. His heart drops suddenly as he knows the crystal isn't in there anymore. There are no pulsations either. The man doesn't seem angry at all; he just smiles. Jaykin nervously and quietly walks up to the man and peeks inside too. To his surprise, the crystal is back. But how? His body isn't reacting. Is it the same one as before? He stands there, shocked. It looks exactly the same; did he just miss it? He turns to ask the elderly man what he thinks about it but there is no one there. The man has gone; vanished. He twists and turns trying to find him, but nothing. He investigates the glass box again and the crystal has disappeared too. Jaykin's chest thumps.

Condensation appears inside the box and some writing can be seen. '*Your journey starts now,*' it reads.
Suddenly he feels something pulling his shoulder, then the words: '*Wake up Jaykin*' appear on the glass; then another tug. He opens his eyes and Q-Tech stands there, nudging him slightly.

Jaykin immediately sits up in his bed, still shocked. Then, realisation.

"That dream felt so real," he says, panting. "What's up Q-Tech?" he asks, still dazed.

"Master Kanaren is asking for you; you are to go to Dreamora today."

"Dreamora?" He rubs his eyes to wake himself. "What do I need to take with me?"

"All you need are your Hunter's clothes. Don't worry about your sword; Master Kanaren has it."

Jaykin gets changed and they enter the treasure room. He looks around. There's no sign of Kanaren, or the elderly man. He's desperate to check out the glass box, to see if the crystal is there. He feels strange; he doesn't know if he should feel guilty or worried about it, but now they're off to another city, so he need not think about it for at least a couple of days or so.

"Where is Kanaren?" he asks.

"Master Kanaren will be at the station," Q-Tech replies. Jaykin thinks that is strange.

***

North of the city, at the station, Jaykin searches for Kanaren but struggles, given the number of people around. However, he spots a man crouched down near some signs but with his hood over his head. It's obvious he's trying not to get any attention. Jaykin somehow knows it's Kanaren, but checks with Q-Tech, just in case.

"Is that him over there?" he asks, raising his hand to point at the person and walking towards him, but Q-Tech holds onto him.

"Master Kanaren will show himself when he is ready," it replies and hands him a small device that looks like a ticket. It has DT8 on it, which is code for destination, coach name and the table number. "Here. Q-Roids are not permitted to go to the gate. This will get you through it."

The crouching man slowly gets up and walks off.

"Okay. I'll see you when I get back then?" Jaykin asks, but Q-Tech doesn't reply. Instead, it just

walks away. Jaykin watches it and shrugs his shoulders. He searches for the platform and sees several land gliders: large and very long machines that levitate over metallic tracks. They travel to each city of Izara, in a straight-line underground, and they can reach up to four hundred miles an hour.
Jaykin can see the land glider leading to the city of Dreamora, but a gate and a small machine beside it blocks his path. He watches everyone else place the small device into the machine. It beeps every time someone goes past, so he follows suit. It beeps and turns green to confirm authorization, letting him through the gate. Guards walk around with their Q-Azars ready, checking people every so often.
A woman's voice is heard over a tannoy, sounding very calm and clear.

"*Please make sure you have all your belongings with you. There are to be no weapons, creatures or Q-Roids permitted on this journey, unless you have special written permission. Thank you.*"

Jaykin walks right next to the land glider and looks around for Kanaren, but there's no sign of him. He climbs on board and searches inside. It's busy but no one recognisable stands out to him. He finds his table seat, which is attached to the coach's wall and carpeted floor. It also has a long window view. He makes himself comfortable in the blue wavy-designed seat.

The land glider's engines start, lifting up and off the station. It slowly moves forward and gradually picks up speed. The view from the window becomes slightly blurry as it accelerates. Suddenly, just before they enter the tunnel, Jaykin hears two thuds on the roof of the carriage. He looks up, then outside, but can't see anything. The other passengers have not noticed, so he shrugs, and settles for the journey.

The driver announces: "*We will be arriving in Dreamora in two hours. Please sit back, relax and make yourself comfortable.*"

Minutes pass and people walk up and down the coach. Jaykin watches for Kanaren, but nothing. When will he show himself? Then someone walks through the doors with a hood covering their whole face. They have a familiar walk. The figure scans for a place to sit and decides to go opposite Jaykin, near the window. Then it uncovers the hood. It is Q-Tech but with human clothes on.

"What are you doing?" Jaykin asks.

"Blending in," it replies, pretending to read something on a Q-pad and trying to cover its face again.

"Where is Kanaren?"

"He will be here shortly." It makes no eye contact with Jaykin.

"Oh good, I was starting to worry I was going to Dreamora on my own." Then the same cloaked man from earlier appears at the doors and sits next to Q-Tech and opposite Jaykin. It is Kanaren.

"Hi," he says. "Here." He places something wrapped in grey cloth on the table. "You wouldn't have been able to get this through the gate earlier."

Jaykin pulls it closer and peers into the cloth. It's his sword and a Q-pad.

"What's the device for?"

"It's for you. It has information about weapons, creatures, the six cities and the lands that surround them."

"Thank you, I'll look after it."

"Good, I'm sure you will." Kanaren relaxes in his seat.

Jaykin looks around to make sure no one is listening.

"Was that noise on the roof you guys?" he whispers.

"I don't know what you're talking about," Kanaren replies with a very straight face. Jaykin can tell he's being sarcastic but can't work out why. If it was him then why would he jump onto a fast-running land glider? Something's odd. Then Q-Tech holds out a couple of circular patches. Kanaren picks them out of its hand and gives one to Jaykin. He pulls back his sleeve and slaps the patch onto his arm. "You will need these. They're adrenaline enhancers, to keep you alert while going through the city." Jaykin feels confused but shrugs his shoulders and places it onto his arm. "As we're going to be on here for a while, you can check out some of the weapons or something on there," he says, pointing at Jaykin's device.

Jaykin is keen to do just that and becomes absorbed, looking intently at the screen.

***

"*Good afternoon, ladies and gentlemen. We will be arriving in Dreamora in fifteen minutes. Please have everything ready for your departure,*" the driver announces.

"When we get to Dreamora, we will need to make our way directly to the Palace," Kanaren says quietly. "And stay near me at all times. Dreamora is a different place to Lementes."

"Okay," Jaykin replies, meekly. With that, the front part of his body suddenly starts pulsating again; just as if he were near the small crystal.

Chapter 6

The City of Dreamora

Dreamora, also known as the city of dreams. Jaykin has never travelled to this place before, as his father always said it was off-limits. He never really told him why, but now he is well aware that it is very strictly policed and well-defended, especially where their crystal is concerned.

They arrive at Dreamora station, close to the centre of the city, and exit the land glider.

"Try not to attract too much attention," Kanaren warns.

"I've heard they're strict here, but they can't be that bad, can they?" Jaykin asks.

"It's a trading city, they deal in rare and valuable items. They don't take risks."

They slowly make their way through the markets of the city, where crowds of people are busy negotiating sales from stalls, calling to potential customers, and closing deals on everything from goorit wool to exotic pets. Jaykin takes in the buzzing atmosphere, the huge skyscrapers, and crowds of people and Q-Roids walking the streets. Guards walk past, Q-Azars in hand, checking random people every so often.

Kanaren stops and points at the highest and most amazing looking building in the city.

"The Palace of Dreamora. This is where the

VIPs of Dreamora live," he says, sarcastically. They head for the extra-large doors where Guards stand to attention, then Kanaren pulls Jaykin back slightly. "Before we go in, I need to warn you that the emperor can be a bit of a…" he pauses to find the right word, "nightmare. Copy exactly what I do but I'll do all the talking, understand?" Jaykin nods his head, feeling quite nervous, but not about meeting the emperor. It's the pulsating sensation around his body that worries him. It's on his back now and he turns his head to see if something is there. Nothing out of the ordinary. His head feels the sensation when he turns. It's like his body is trying to say something. "Let's go," Kanaren says, breaking his concentration.

The Guards hold their Q-Azars tightly in their hands, pointing straight at them.

"What is your business here?" one asks. Kanaren holds his hands up and so does Jaykin. Q-Tech, however, stays outside as Q-Roids are not permitted in the Palace.

"It is a matter of great importance that we see the emperor," Kanaren replies. The Guards whisper to each other.

"What is it you need to talk to the emperor about?" one asks, but before Kanaren can answer, another Guard emerges behind them and with no helmet. He's about the same age and height as Kanaren, dark-skinned and quite skinny.

"You idiots! Can't you tell they're Hunters?" he says with a deep voice. He walks up to Kanaren and shakes his hand. "Welcome to Dreamora," he says; then, his voice lowered: "I thought you were banished from this city?"

"I am," Kanaren replies, also in low tones.

"Kanaren, you need to be careful," he says, and shakes his head. "I apologise for my colleagues. They still have a lot to learn about who matters around here." Everyone lowers their Q-Azars.

"No problem," Kanaren replies, and all the Guards relent.

"I can still throw you out," the friendly Guard says, a twinkle in his eye.

"But you wouldn't do that, would you Lesh; you owe me, big time."

"Damn," Lesh says. "Only this one time Kanaren and that's it."

"Can't promise that."

Lesh lets out a sigh. "I hope it's worth it. Do you remember what happened last time?"

"I remember like it was yesterday."

"Just don't let him turn into a raging barka this time round." Lesh turns to the other Guards. "Open the doors!" he shouts. They take some time. Lesh places his hand on Kanaren's shoulder. "Be careful in there. You too kid."

They pass through the great doors, decorated with delicate, very detailed old pieces of carved wood.

"Well, that went well," Jaykin says. "How do you know him?"

"Ex Hunter," Kanaren replies. "We need to focus on the task at hand."

They continue to an extremely long, wide, and tall hallway. The noise of their footsteps echoes around them. Jaykin has never seen anything like this before. Each side of the hallway has a long row of creatures stuffed and displayed on golden plinths; all different shapes, sizes, and degrees of strangeness. "There are some really rare creatures in here," Jaykin whispers.

"Take a good look at them. You may have to fight a few of these one day," Jaykin smiles at what he thinks is a joke but looks up to Kanaren who still has a serious face. Jaykin's heart is in his mouth at the thought.

"Fight?" His eyes widen and he gulps audibly. He admires every single one of the creatures. "Why are they all here?"

"The emperor's prized possessions," Kanaren sighs. "He has money and power; he wants to show the people his worth and how important he is. He does as he wishes," Kanaren explains as quietly as possible to limit the echo.

"He sounds crazy." The echoes agree.

Ahead, Jaykin can see someone on a beautiful, intricately decorated, golden throne. It is the emperor himself. Behind him, are two eight-foot-high faceless statues, made of gold and holding scarily large swords. They look like something that might appear in his nightmares. Below the statues stand twenty Knights, all in full amour, in a shade of indigo; and they have their weapons drawn. They are extremely still, like the statues. Another figure stands close to the throne, wearing the same armour as the Knights but with gold embellishment. This must be the High Knight. On the throne itself sits the emperor, a man in his late fifties, wearing all gold clothing and rings on every finger. His throne is set upon a raised platform, allowing him to look down at everyone in the hall. They must always look up to him. He stares down the long hallway.

"Kanaren!" he shouts, and stands at the same time. "What on Izara are you doing in my Palace?" Both Kanaren and Jaykin approach slowly.

"Emperor Lon," Kanaren says and bows. "We're here on a special mission."
Jaykin, still in awe of his surroundings, reacts just in time and quickly bows, nearly falling head-first.

"Who let you in?" Lon shouts, sounding angry.

"Your Guards."

"Oh really? I bet it was that infuriating Lesh! I'm going to have to talk to him about that," he says to the High Knight. "Remind me to find out when his retirement is, and make it sooner!"

"Yes, Emperor Lon," she replies and stands back to attention.

"Why do you look familiar, boy?" Lon asks, glaring at him. But Jaykin doesn't know how to reply. Kanaren says:

"Jaykin is a Hunt—."

"Jaykin?" Lon interrupts and relaxes into his throne. "Why does it sound familiar?" he ponders. "No matter." He looks over at Kanaren again and then sits up as if he remembers something. "Ah yes," he says with a nasty smirk on his face. "I thought I told you not to return here after our little chat last time."

"That is true, but I was only doing my job—" but then Lon gets angry and interrupts.

"You!" he yells and points at Kanaren, "you

accused me of kidnapping the Emperor of Lementes!"

"Emperor Lon, I was only speculating. I did not accuse you of anything. You and the other leaders were the last people he was seen with. That's what I tried to explain to you last time." He points to Jaykin. "Jaykin's father is also missing."

"Oh really?" Lon replies looking down at Jaykin. "And do you think I did it?"

"No…" Jaykin hesitates.

"Of course not," Kanaren intervenes. "All these missing people, I believe, are connected to one thing."

"And what is that?" Lon asks, sounding as if he doesn't want to have this conversation or to even be here at all.

Kanaren takes his time to say it.

"The invasion. It's the only thing—" Lon buries his head in his hands and grinds his jaws together, sighing out loud.

"Not this. Again!" he yells, and grabs his armrest and thrusts himself out of his throne. "Do you know how many times people, including the Emperor of Lementes himself, have told me this…" His face starts to redden. "…made-up story! It infuriates me." He starts waving his arms around. "An invasion? Aliens from another world will be attacking my city? What a load of nait's manure!"

"I know it sounds crazy but—" Kanaren starts, but is interrupted again.

"Aliens?" Lon laughs and paces up and down. He shakes his head. "If this attack was going to happen, don't you think it would have started by now?"

he says sarcastically. "All lies! I for one will not be fooled by this crazy talk. I will not let Dreamora's people believe in this nonsense, not today, not tomorrow, not ever!"

"But, if we don't prepare, millions of your people will die!" Kanaren shouts.

"No!" Lon shouts louder. "I will not place my people on high alert for an invasion that will never happen. I would look like a complete idiot and I will not be told what to do by a simple, delusional fool!" Kanaren instantly holds his tongue. He tenses up, pulling back his arms so he doesn't seem to be on the attack. He sighs slightly trying not to show his true emotions. He stares down at the steps leading up to Lon, trying not to look at him.

"I wasn't sure if we would change your mind but I thought we could at least try. We will be going now, but please, think about the right decision." Quickly bowing he turns towards the exit. "Let's go Jaykin," he says, pulling him. But Jaykin doesn't budge. Something inside of him snaps and instead of retreating, he approaches Lon, walking up two of the steps. The Knights and the High Knight all step forward too, and ready their weapons.

"Emperor Lon. You don't know me. I'm just an ordinary kid from Lementes." Lon raises his hand signalling the Knights to wait. He sits back down slowly, trying to calm down and, surprisingly, listens to what Jaykin has to say. "We hear stories about this amazing city, that it's great, powerful, wonderful. People live and work hard here," Lon smirks slightly, "and you want to take that all away? These people will die because of your arrogance and pettiness. All these lives are in your hands while you sit there drooling over your awards. Selfish. I seriously hope you make the right decision when it is needed the most."

"Why you little…no one talks to me like that!" Lon yells. Jaykin notices the High Knight quickly draws her sword and is about to swing for him. He then feels a hand on his shoulder, pulling him back, and loses his balance. He falls to the bottom of the steps; he looks up and sees Kanaren standing directly in front of the High Knight with his sword drawn against hers.

"He will die for that!" the High Knight shouts.

"Not today," Kanaren replies calmly and steps back to Jaykin's side. He puts his sword away and grabs onto Jaykin's clothing, lifting him up abruptly. "I am sorry emperor; he is still learning. I will punish him myself." He bows.

"You should. And I don't want to see you or that boy in my city again." Lon shouts and the High Knight reluctantly puts her sword away and watches them leave. Kanaren quickly turns and shoves Jaykin towards the entrance. He stumbles and falls again.

"Move it!" Jaykin quickly stands and looks back at the emperor.

"You dare not bow to me, boy?" Lon shouts and then stands in anger. Jaykin moves quickly towards Kanaren and they make a speedy exit.

"I'm sorry."

"Don't be," Kanaren replies. "I couldn't have put it better myself."

"You what?" Jaykin gasps, not expecting that reply. "Well, he was starting to annoy me."

"He is not worthy of his title," Kanaren shakes his head. "The people should always come before power. Let's just hope he'll get it into his thick skull that we need this city to be ready for anything. We need to move out to the city of Q-Ara and speak to the emperor there."

"Will he be any better than this one?"

"He's much easier to talk to than Lon. We'll have to wait and see. Sorry for pushing you by the way. I had to make it look good."

"That's okay," Jaykin replies with a smile, which Kanaren does not return. He reflects, then, that Kanaren never smiles. Lon can still be heard shouting as they are leaving.

"What on Izara did you say to him this time?" Lesh asks.

"Nothing much," Kanaren replies.

"We mentioned your name," Jaykin says.

"You what?" Lesh replies.

"It's okay Lesh, you'll be fine," Kanaren reassures him.

"Have a good retirement," Jaykin says. Lesh's jaw drops as they walk away.

"I knew I shouldn't have let them in," he says to himself.

They meet up with Q-Tech, which appears to be connected to a charging station, not that far away. Several other Q-Roids are also re-charging; it doesn't take long to fully power up. Kanaren asks Q-Tech to follow them. It unplugs itself in readiness. Jaykin has something still on his mind.

"Kanaren, did you see those tall statues behind Lon?" he asks.

"You noticed them then?"

"They're not easy to miss. What are they? I've never seen anything like them before."

"We call them Defenders."

"Defenders of what?"

"Something very powerful. And I'm going to show it to you now."

Chapter 7

Empress Mora

They head straight to a beautiful garden, named the Garden of Ezoons. Hundreds of people are enjoying the surroundings, lying around on cut grass; taking in the heady scent of exotic flowers.

They find a vacant bench and relax on it, admiring the view. Q-Tech stands alongside. Jaykin is distracted. He can feel his whole body pulsating vigorously. It's as if the cause is emanating from the centre of the garden, but he cannot ignore the extraordinary sight before him. A huge ovoid object, shrouded in a thin mist, nine feet tall. It is set on an elevated wide golden plinth. It towers over everything in the garden with its beauty and magnificence. Around it is a small and easily climbable fence, but with Guards on patrol around it.

"What's that?" Jaykin asks, genuinely awed.

"Do you know the story of Empress Mora?" Kanaren asks.

"I think so. My father told me about her when I was a child. Didn't she have the power to put people to sleep?"

"That's the children's version. No, I meant the real story?"

"Then no, I don't think so."

"Thousands of years ago, long before the city of Dreamora was created, Mora and her tribe travelled the land, searching for a place to settle. It is written that after many years, and hundreds of miles, she made a discovery. The most beautiful, precious thing in the two worlds. That crystal," Kanaren pauses to take in the spectacle. "Legends say that Mora wanted the crystal, to show it off in its beauty. But when it came to moving it from where it had lain, hidden for so long, there were repercussions. If anyone approached the crystal, they simply fell asleep. Mora believed it held some great power. She did manage to work out how it could be moved, but with consequences."

"The Defenders," Jaykin says.

"Exactly. They were originally made out of stone, until Emperor Lon covered them in gold."

"Why am I not surprised?"

"Mora had used the same oils from these patches." Kanaren shows it on his arm. "When the crystal was displaced, the Defenders emerged from the ground in force and wiped out most of Mora's followers. A small number, and Mora, managed to escape, but resolved to return with an army. A great many years passed and hundreds of lives were lost before she eventually succeeded. Long after her passing the people told of her extreme courage and determination. They moved the crystal, and what remains of the Defenders, to this place, building the village around it, which they named Dreamora, in memory of their Empress. Legend has it that there are more crystals but the new citizens of Dreamora had no interest in finding them." He looks at Jaykin. "But we can only imagine what really went on. Remember the crystal fragment at my place?"

Jaykin suddenly feels his heart thump faster. "Yes," he

replies, trying to appear calm. "Do you think the crystal has powers?" He looks over at it.

"Let's get closer and you can find out for yourself," Kanaren suggests.

"Okay," Jaykin hesitates, feeling very nervous.

"Q-Tech, stand here and wait for more instructions."

"Yes, Master."

They make their way closer to the crystal. The plinth itself is covered in very old markings. Jaykin can now feel his body thumping hard and with every step he takes, it gets ten times stronger. It is becoming unbearable but he tries to stay as calm as possible.

"Can you feel that?" Kanaren asks.

Jaykin's heart skips a beat. His eyes immediately fixate on Kanaren. Can he sense the same thing? Jaykin holds his breath.

"Yes, I can. What is that?" he asks.

"It's the crystal. Powerful, isn't it?"

"Yeah, it's quite strange."

"Sure is. People have slept here for days sometimes."

Jaykin relaxes, but without having had a good sleep for months, his eyes struggle to stay open. The adrenaline patch is not working. He tries his best to fight drowsiness but, feeling utterly depleted, he gives in.

Kanaren crouches down and reads some of the old inscription.

"Here stands the powerful crystal. No human, creature, nor weapon can damage this miracle.

Whoever stands before this phenomenon will realise their greatest dreams. This has been proven for many years. In honour and worship of Mora the Empress; in memory, and in future, we will name this land: Dreamora; the city of Dreams." Kanaren stands. "Rest in peace Mora." Suddenly he notices someone running up to him. A Guard, and it's not good. The Guard points a Q-Azar at him, and Kanaren is immediately on the defensive.

"What is he doing there?" the Guard shouts. Slightly confused, Kanaren looks back towards Jaykin and finds him climbing the golden plinth. The Guard keeps shouting, "Do not climb any further!" then points the Q-Azar directly at Jaykin.

"No! Don't fire. He won't touch the crystal," Kanaren says, blocking the Guard's view of Jaykin and trying to stop him from shooting. He turns to Jaykin who is still climbing. "What are you doing?" he shouts, but he doesn't get an answer. "He's sleepwalking. Do not shoot!" he says to the Guard. "Jaykin wake up!"

***

Jaykin awakes but everything is in a blur. It feels like time has slowed right down. Darkness descends upon him.

"Hello? Kanaren? Q-Tech? Anyone?" He can see no walls, trees, buildings, nor people; just a crystal; right in front of him. The plinth has gone. He is all alone in the park. Suddenly he hears whispers. He looks around for the source. He spots someone on the other side of the crystal; a young girl crouched down next to it, in ragged clothes and with flowers around her neck and through her hair. It sounds as if she's praying. He hears a rustling sound coming from behind him and another person appears, in similar clothing, but an older woman. Eventually, the crystal is surrounded by hundreds of people, appearing from the darkness. Where Jaykin stands there seems to be a gap for someone to pray. He slowly but surely places his knee on the soft grass, his legs unsteady. He looks at the others and he bows his head. The ground starts to rumble. A light shines from within the crystal and a woman's voice is heard:

"Find them all."

Its bright light blinds him and, suddenly, it feels as if he's being pulled into the crystal itself.

***

Jaykin wakes up, dazed, and confused, realising that he is standing very close to the crystal. His right hand is almost touching it. He panics and tries to pull it back, but nothing happens. He grabs it with his other hand and pulls it again. Nothing. He looks for help.

"Jaykin!" He recognizes Kanaren's voice instantly and spots him standing next to a Guard, who points a Q-Azar at him.

"Kanaren?" he cries out in distress.

"Commander," the Guard says in his earpiece. "I need some back up here at the crystal. Two—" Kanaren overhears him, grabs the Guard's Q-Azar, and smashes it against his head, knocking him out. He keeps hold of the Q-Azar and places it onto his back.

"Jaykin, we need to go, now!" he shouts.

"I can't move!" he yells.

"What do you mean you can't move?"

"I'm literally stuck! It's like my body is being drawn towards it!"

"You what!" Kanaren roars. He stops to think. "Okay, whatever you do, don't touch the crystal!"

"I'll try my best."

Another Guard appears from around the plinth, opposite Kanaren. She spots Jaykin and points her Q-Azar at him.

"Get away from the crystal or I will shoot!" she shouts.

"Q-Tech!" Kanaren shouts, and points at the Guard. Q-Tech shoots across the garden and grabs onto her and pulls her back off her feet, punching extremely hard, and throwing her across the grass. "Defence mode," Kanaren yells, grabbing the Q-Azar from his back and throwing it to Q-Tech. "Scan for any other Guards and keep them off us!"

"Understood, Master."

In the meantime, people from all over the park start to gather and mutter amongst themselves, partly afraid, partly curious. Kanaren quickly climbs up next to Jaykin.

"We're attracting too much attention. What's going on?" He stares at him and tries to pull him back, but nothing happens.

"I can't get away from this thing," Jaykin cries, starting to panic. He even tries to pull his fingers back, but nothing works. "What's going on Kanaren?" and he looks at him with terror in his eyes.

"I don't know." He looks all around Jaykin to see if he can spot anything out of the ordinary. He grabs onto Jaykin's arms and tries pulling again but nothing budges. Then he tries pushing sideways but it's also ineffective. "It seems like the crystal is pulling you into it. Like a powerful magnet force." Still confused, he looks around again. He notices there's still a sizeable gap between Jaykin and the crystal. "I have an idea." He squeezes himself between them both trying his best not to touch the crystal himself.

"What would happen if I touched this thing?" Jaykin asks. Kanaren stops and stares into his eyes briefly. He doesn't say anything and he doesn't have to; the stare says it all. "I guess you could do without this," Jaykin says, rashly attempting to ease the tension.

"It's definitely not on my to-do list!" Kanaren replies with anger in his voice. Jaykin can feel his face heating up and his heart staying at the same fast pace. He feels like crying; he really does not want to be here. Kanaren leans in, trying to wedge the sword's handle between the crystal and Jaykin's hand. He places his own hand onto Jaykin's chest.

"What are you doing?" Jaykin asks.

"I'm going to try something. Hold onto the sword for support." He pulls up his sleeve revealing the air weapon he used on him the previous day.

"Okay," Jaykin says uncertainly.

The air swirls around them both, like a mini-tornado. Jaykin knows exactly what's going to happen and he knows that this is going to hurt, if it works. They can barely hear anything.

"Get ready!" Kanaren shouts. A huge blast of

air erupts around Jaykin but he doesn't move an inch. Dust fills the air, covering the whole garden.

"It's not working!" Jaykin shouts.

"Q-Tech! Give us a hand here!" Kanaren shouts. It quickly jumps onto the plinth, behind Jaykin. "Get Jaykin off this plinth without touching the crystal!"

"Understood Master," it says. Grabbing underneath Jaykin's arms, it pulls, but again he doesn't budge. Kanaren retracts his arm back and sighs heavily.

"It's no good." The air around them calms, returning to normal. "I've tried everything." Jaykin lets go of the sword to release Kanaren from his cramped position. He squeezes through again and walks around him.

Voices and thumps of footsteps get closer and all around them Q-Azars are powering up. Kanaren stands behind Jaykin, facing all the Guards. More than a hundred have gathered.

"Master Kanaren, you will not survive this fight," Q-Tech determines.

Kanaren doesn't reply, he knows this may be the end of them both.

"Jaykin, listen to me very carefully," he says, as he eyes the Guards. He ignores them all, turns his head slightly towards Jaykin.

"I got you into this mess, I will take the responsibility."

Jaykin feels tired but tries to focus on Kanaren's voice despite all the other shouting going on. With tears sliding down his face, he gives a final tug of his arms to make sure. This is the end. He stares into the crystal, trying to forget what is going on around him. Something odd is happening to the crystal. Near his hands, the mist is becoming clear, almost like ice melting. He can see something inside.

Chapter 8

Awakening from the Dream

With no warning, Jaykin's hand is pulled forcefully onto the crystal. He gasps in fear.

"Kanaren!" he shouts. All the Guards lift their Q-Azars towards them. He tries pulling but nothing happens. Kanaren raises his arms.

"Don't shoot!" he pleads.

"You have placed your hands on a sacred crystal of Dreamora. You have ten seconds to remove them. If you do not comply, we will shoot!" a Guard shouts, moving closer.

"Q-Tech. Defence mode. Protect Jaykin," Kanaren says, while leaping off the plinth away from all the Q-Azars pointing at him. He lands on the soft grass, rolling and facing them all.

"Don't leave me!" Jaykin shouts. But Kanaren stands still and fires his air weapon again towards the Guards, sending many of them flying across the grass; dust and soil filling the air.

The crystal pulsates; the sensation is relayed through Jaykin's hands and up his arms. It sends shivers down his spine and around his body like blood spreading all over. Some people in the crowd feel very weak vibrations in the air making them uncomfortable. It's an alien feeling, and they start to move away from the area. Jaykin suddenly screams in pain; his arm stiffens up and a burning sensation flows through his whole body as if he's absorbing the crystal itself. The pain is unbearable. He shuts his eyes, hoping it will stop. Then, without warning, the crystal cracks around his hand. He gasps and keeps trying to pull away. Then the whole crystal breaks in half, creating a very loud cracking noise, which echoes through the garden.

The crystal slowly disappears; melting like ice into Jaykin's hand. Then, as if nothing had happened, his arm drops to his side. He falls to his knees. It has stopped at last and he relaxes, glad it is all over. He examines his hand, in disbelief. He feels no pulsating nor pain anymore and breathes a sigh of relief.

He can hear all the people running and screaming around him. Feeling drained, he looks up slowly to see something move into his field of vision. Shocked, he slides back. There is no crystal anymore. Instead, in its place, stands some sort of being. Mesmerised, he gasps in fear.

On the elevated plinth, with Jaykin, stands a human woman, roughly eight feet tall, dressed in cream-coloured rags made from wool. Metal armour covers her shins, stomach, chest, and shoulders. She wears heavy jewellery on her fingers and around her neck. Hanging from her back she has two long spears and one intricately detailed shield. With closer inspection, Jaykin notices she has a familiar symbol on each piece of her armour; a bright blue thin circle with leaves tangling around it. In the centre, a drop of water, with gold filling the rest.

Dazed and confused, the woman looks around. She takes in the tall buildings around her, reaching into the sky like they never end. She feels slightly giddy; she notices hundreds of people running around in panic.

"Where…" she says, struggling to talk and not to fall, "where am I?" Sounding exhausted and barely able to speak, she anxiously moves around as if she is hyperventilating and can just about stand on this small plinth; small compared to her. Quickly losing feeling in her legs she stumbles into a heap and she shuts her eyes. "Am I in a dream?" she asks out loud, hoping someone will answer.

"No, you're not in a dream," a young man's voice says. She immediately opens her eyes and spots Jaykin sitting right in front of her. For a few seconds, she forgets where she is and focuses on him, breathing slowly. "Are you okay?" he asks, standing quickly, and he leans forward, holding on to her, trying to keep her steady.

"I think so." Still sounding scared. She seems to have calmed down slightly but then looks behind Jaykin at all the Guards. They are brushing themselves off and preparing their Q-Azars again and people are still running all over the place. She only just manages to stand; her eyes open wide. She inhales a great gasp of air and at the top of her voice, she screams out loud, raising her hand towards the Guards. Many of them fall to the ground, but this time they don't get up. She spots more running towards her and she raises her hand again in anger but Jaykin gets caught in the crossfire as she jumps off the plinth. He falls off, landing and scraping the muddy grass.

"Q-Tech, protect Jaykin," Kanaren shouts. Then the woman kicks Q-Tech out of her way and it crashes into a nearby wall, cracking it into pieces. Stone and shrapnel fly all over the place. Jaykin struggles to get up. He's badly injured. The woman swipes her hand towards him and more of the Guards, who just fall to the ground instantly. She stops and pants hard. Whatever she does makes her very tired.

"Please, stop!" Kanaren shouts. She stares at him and points her hands at him. They're the only ones left standing in the garden. "Listen to me," he says and lifts his hands up wide to try and calm her, as he doesn't want to anger her any further. "I am not a threat to you. Nor is my friend, who is lying next to you." She looks down at Jaykin, who seems to be out cold.

While she's distracted for a couple of seconds, Kanaren quickly looks over at Q-Tech and notices it lifting itself out of the crumbled wall.

"I need to leave this place," she pleads, still sounding worried.

"Then I will get you out of here," he says calmly. "If you want to stay alive, you will need to follow me."

"But these people—" She gestures towards all the bodies on the grass.

"They were going to kill you and they still can, if they find out what happened here." He picks up his sword from the grass. "Now what is it going to be?"

"I'll follow you," she decides, sounding calmer and having no other choice. She lowers her hands to her sides.

"Good. Now can you pick up my friend?"
She kneels, and goes to pick him up but a couple of Guards run around the plinth, with more starting to appear, including Lesh.

"Get down on the ground!" he shouts, pointing his Q-Azar at her and then stares at Kanaren with disappointment in his eyes. The woman holds up her hand towards them and they also fall to the ground.

"Come on!" Kanaren shouts, as he runs over to make sure Lesh is still breathing. "I'm sorry."
She bends down and quickly picks up Jaykin and they run off together, away from the Palace. Kanaren shouts:

"Q-Tech, code word redirect Guards to area one, seven, two. Meet up in area two, two, one. Confirm?" He awkwardly shakes his jacket off while sprinting and throws it to Q-Tech. It immediately wraps it around itself.

"Confirmed," it replies and it stops, looks back at the Guards to get their attention, and heads off in another direction.

***

Meanwhile, at the Palace of Dreamora, where Emperor Lon lounges on his throne, a Guard barges through the large front doors, huffing and puffing. "Emperor Lon…" he struggles to get breath and gasps for air, "the…crystal—"

"Oh, spit it out!" Lon shouts, annoyed. "What about it?"

"It has been stolen!" the Guard replies, just managing to get his words out.
Lon stands immediately.

"What! Stolen? By whom?" he yells. Everyone in the room takes a step back.

"The two that you were talking to earlier Emperor Lon," the Guard replies.

"Kanaren, and that boy?" Lon whispers to himself. Slowly he descends the steps towards the Guard. He stands right up against him.

"Y…Yes." the Guard hesitates and gulps, stepping back slightly.

"Tell all of my Guards to search every single part of the city." He pokes the Guard's chest.

"Yes, but there is a slight problem," he replies. "There are hundreds of people and Guards sleeping all over the garden of Ezoons. I can't explain it."

"Then wake them up, you idiot!" Lon shouts.

"But…" he hesitates again, "we won't have any defence for our city."
The emperor then grabs onto him.

"I do not care how many Guards you need. I want my crystal back, now!" he shouts, throwing the Guard to the floor.

"Yes, Emperor Lon," He stumbles to his feet and runs to the main doors.

"Do I have to think of everything around here?" Lon shouts and makes his way back up the stairs to his throne. "You!" he points to one of the Knights, "place them on the wanted list and send it to every city! I want them found, now!"

"Yes, Emperor Lon," the Knight replies,

bowing out.
Lon slumps down onto his throne. He turns his head slightly towards the High Knight.

"Ready my Hunters."

***

Running through the city, Kanaren and the tall woman make their way to the outskirts. People begin to fall around them.

"Where are you taking me?" the woman asks, panting.

"A safe place," Kanaren replies and notices she is stumbling a lot. "Are you struggling?"

"I feel fine," she replies, but then hits into a wall, hurting her shoulder. Kanaren stops beside her. He is acutely aware of several Guards searching for them just around the corner. The woman swipes her arm as they come into view and they fall to the ground.

"How are you doing that?"

"What do you mean?" she stares at him, puzzled.

"The Guards and the others…how are you stopping them?"

She continues to stare and shakes her head; it looks as if she doesn't understand the question or is confused by something.

"I'll explain later when we're not being chased," she replies, trying not to drop Jaykin. They reach a quiet area in a very worn-down part of the city; deserted, far east and close to the wall.

Kanaren opens a cage door to an old building. She

stops and stares at him. "Why should I trust you?" she asks suddenly.

"I don't know," Kanaren replies, coolly, still holding onto the door. "We can't keep running through the city like this. We'll hide here until it gets dark."

"I could just put you to sleep right here, right now."

He stares at her.

"I'm the one that got us into this mess and I'm the one that will need to get us out. Plus, it isn't fair on him," looking at Jaykin.

"Very well. You are right." She walks through with Jaykin still in her arms. Kanaren closes the door behind them.

Inside the building, they pass slowly through narrow corridors, where the woman struggles to fit. The sounds of their footsteps echo around the empty rooms. Several times the woman stumbles.

"Do you need to rest a moment? I can carry him," Kanaren asks.

"I'm fine," she replies, then slides against the nearest wall.

"Are you sure? You look as if you're about to faint."

"I do feel slightly light-headed." She stops. "I think I may have used too much of my powers."

"We can rest here if you like."

"That would be a good idea," she says, sounding relieved. They find a large clear room. The woman kneels down on the dry floor, laying Jaykin right next to her with his head resting on her robes. She tilts her head back and leans against the wall. Resting, she watches as Kanaren walks in and out of adjacent rooms. She then looks at Jaykin and smiles. "Is he your—" before she can finish, Kanaren interrupts.

"No," he says quickly. "He's not my son."

"Oh sorry, I thought as you're wearing the same clothes—"

"No." He peers out of the nearest window. "His father is missing and he's trying to find him."

"Oh, poor kid." Suddenly they hear the entrance door open and close. She stares at Kanaren, wide-eyed. "What is that?" she gasps, jumping slightly.

"I don't know," Kanaren replies, flipping his sword from his back. "Take Jaykin to that empty room," he says, pointing behind him.

She stands straight away and does as he asks. They hear odd-sounding footsteps coming toward them. She sticks her head out the doorway and she and Kanaren exchange glances. "It's strange," she whispers. "I can't sense anyone there."

Kanaren looks at her, pauses and folds up the sword and places it onto his back again.

"I know what it is."

"Well?" she asks.

A couple of beaming lights come around the corner and in walks a familiar Q-Roid.

"Q-Tech," Kanaren says.

The woman stares at it, moving back slightly.

"What is that thing?"

"It's okay," Kanaren replies, acknowledging her fear, "Q-Tech is a Q-Roid. It won't hurt you. It's a lifeless being but with artificial intelligence. In other words, it has energy but no soul."

"Thank you, Master," it says.

"Q-Tech, did you redirect the Guards to where I asked?"

"Yes, they think you are hiding in the history museum." It has a small bag in its hand and gives it to Kanaren who hands it to the tall woman.

"Here, it's brought food for us."

The woman takes it from him, still staring at Q-Tech.

"Thank you," she says and slowly approaches the Q-Roid, curiosity in her expression.

"It's all right Q-Tech, she's friendly," Kanaren says, taking a bite out of something juicy.

"Hello," she says and kneels next to it.

"A pleasure to meet you," Q-Tech replies and bows a little. She moves around it and pokes its face.

"Master?" Q-Tech says.

"It's okay, I don't think she's ever met a Q-Roid before; you're fine." He walks over to the next room where Jaykin is still unconscious, checking his pulse and the rest of his body, to make sure he isn't cut or badly injured. He notices that Jaykin's body has filled out slightly as if he had been training for months. "What have you done to Jaykin?" he calls over to the woman.

"He's only asleep," she replies.

"Do your powers wake people up too?" he asks, staring at Jaykin, confused.

"Of course," she waves her hand slightly towards the next room while still staring at Q-Tech and chewing cautiously on some food from the bag. Jaykin starts twitching, then bursts into life as if woken from another bad dream. He spots Kanaren crouching above him, his expression severe. Kanaren grabs him, lifting him off the ground and shoving him up against a wall, where the woman can't see them.

"What on Izara have you done?" Kanaren asks, quietly and angrily.

"What? What have I done?" Jaykin quickly replies, bewildered.

"You touched the crystal. When I strictly told you not to, that's what you've done!" He looks out to see if the woman is listening. She isn't. She is moving around Q-Tech, still prodding it in curiosity. Kanaren looks back at Jaykin. "And how did you break the crystal with your bare hands?"

"I have no idea. It just happened."

"You better not be lying to me."

"I'm not lying, I swear. My hand was forced on the crystal and it felt like I…" he stops and raises his hands, "…absorbed it somehow." Kanaren looks intently into Jaykin's eyes, trying to detect whether he is telling the truth, but he looks terrified.

"You really have no idea, do you?"

Jaykin shakes his head vigorously. Kanaren sighs and lets him go.

The woman continues observing Q-Tech but instead of poking it, she waves her hands about as if trying to exert some power over it.

"You're such an odd thing, aren't you?" she says, and pokes it again.

"Is there something you need?" it replies.

In the next room, Kanaren is pacing up and down.

"We don't need this," he whispers harshly. "You have no idea what you've done." He stops and stares at Jaykin. "We're in a lot of trouble now."

"Trouble?" the woman calls from the other room.

"Who's that?" Jaykin mouths, wary and curious.

"That is the thing you released out of the crystal!" he whispers angrily. Jaykin gasps and covers his mouth. Kanaren grabs onto him again ensuring he has Jaykin's full attention. "Whatever you do, do not mention anything about breaking the crystal. Do I make myself clear?" Jaykin nods his head obediently. "If I don't understand, nor will she, and it'll just confuse her even more." He lets him go. "We'll talk about this another time." He tries to calm down. "I want you to meet someone."

Jaykin replays to himself what has happened. He shakes his head as if to clear his mind, then he walks out of the room to meet the woman. Dumbstruck, he just glares at her in astonishment.

"Hello," she says and waves politely. He relaxes.

"Hi, I'm Jaykin." He walks up to her to give her a handshake.

"Pleasure to meet you, Jaykin. My name is Pree."

"Nice to meet you too, Pree. This grumpy barka is Kanaren."

"Uh," Kanaren scowls at him. "Don't push it Jaykin. We'll be moving on soon, so I suggest you save your energy," he says, walking to the window and peering out of it.

"Okay," Jaykin replies, grinning slightly.

"Jaykin, you look like an intelligent young man. Could you tell me where we are exactly?" Pree whispers calmly, looking over at Kanaren with caution.

"Sure, we're on the planet Izara."

"Oh, thank goodness." She lets out a sigh of relief. "For a moment then I thought I had been captured."

"No," Jaykin smiles. "Wait! You're from Izara?"

"I am," she smiles, "but I have never seen these parts before."

"Oh, we're in the city of Dreamora."

"I've never heard of such a place. But it sounds lovely."

"It isn't," Kanaren says from the corner. "Too many people in dreamland and they don't think about anyone except for themselves and their trophies."

"I know who you're talking about," Jaykin grins.

"Pree," Kanaren walks up to her. "You've never heard of this place because this city was built around you."

"I don't understand," she says. Both Jaykin and Kanaren look at one another.

"There is no easy way of saying this," Kanaren says, calmly. "But we found you entombed in crystal." There is silence. She stares at him, disbelieving.

"Crystal?" she asks, baffled. "I don't remember anything about being in crystal. For how long?"

"I think you've been in there for a very long time," Jaykin replies, as gently as he can.

"As far as our history goes, we know it to be a good few thousand years, maybe even more," Kanaren says, "but it's difficult to say." Pree is quiet again for a few moments, as if trying to take this in.

"How on Izara did you end up in there?" Jaykin asks.

"I don't know," she replies, shaking her head.

"What is the last thing you remember?" Kanaren asks.

"It's fuzzy." She looks intently at Kanaren, then Jaykin, trying hard to recall. "I remember I just finished helping a patient of mine. She was having bad dreams. Then I heard screaming. It sounded like people were being attacked. I went outside to find out what it was and that's when I saw the explosions in the distance; very bright lights everywhere." She pauses. "That's when I woke up here and I thought I may have been caught up in the fight." She starts to weep.

"It's okay," Jaykin says, trying to reassure her.

"Pree, you mentioned explosions. What were they about?" Kanaren asks.

"The Great War." She stops and stares at both their blank faces. "You, you don't know what I'm talking about, do you?" They both shake their heads. "Oh my," she gasps, "what on Izara happened?"

"What was it?" Jaykin asks.

"The Great War is," she stops and lets out a sigh, "was, between the two lands of Izara and Raziz. You must have heard of it?"

"We have had many wars between the cities

but never between the two planets," Kanaren replies.

"It doesn't make sense," Pree says, and struggles to remember.

"Did you have cities at that time?" Jaykin asks.

"No, we had small tribes; no such thing as these cities you have or…" she looks at Q-Tech, "walking, lifeless metal things." Then she stares at Kanaren, "That explains why you don't know about my powers, but you must know about the Solutions or the Elements, right?" Both Jaykin and Kanaren shake their heads again. "No?" She stops and tries her best to hold in the tears but they still break through. "My family, my friends." She weeps as if remembering is painful. "We've fought for so long, for what? To never be remembered? I can't believe no one survived, not even one." Then she starts to panic. "I can't be…" she holds her head to try and keep it steady "…I can't be the only one left?" She is clearly distressed.

"It's all right Pree," Jaykin says, trying to calm her. "When you talk of the only one left - last of what exactly?"

She breathes in, then out, slowly, and wipes the tears away using the fabric from her clothing. "Of the Elements…I am an Element and I have the power of dreams."

"What is an Element exactly?" Jaykin asks.

"Where I come from, we begin life as humans; growing, developing and embracing every opportunity for happiness. Just as any other human, we grow old and our fragility increases. But then we are given an opportunity; a choice: to be laid to rest and be at one with the elements, or to be truly embraced by them and evolve into a new form of being. That choice depends on our response to a Life Element. Those wishing to evolve are transformed by using the Elements' power. The experience is…" she ponders, "unique to the individual and irreversible. The next stage of the evolution is called 'Solution', and is spent in determining which Element they wish to become. Once they have made their decision, they must seek permission to evolve from the original Element, who has the power to set the evolution in motion. Once having evolved, there is no going back."

"Wow," Jaykin says. "That sounds amazing."

"It is certainly intriguing," Kanaren says, pondering the implications of Pree's words.

Pree wipes the rest of her tears away, and lets out a sigh.

"We will find out what happened to the Solutions and Elements," Jaykin says, sounding determined.

"We will try, Jaykin," Kanaren interrupts, "but we cannot promise anything."

"My father told me to never give up," Jaykin says.

"You're giving Pree false hope," Kanaren replies, raising his voice slightly. "Pree, I'm sorry but it was a very long time ago, we barely know what happened to Empress Mora, let alone anything from your era. You could have been in the crystal for much longer."

"I understand, of course," she replies, "I like your determination though Jaykin. I just don't know what I'm going to do now." The noise of people talking outside distracts them and Pree gasps. "I forgot that we're being hunted."

"Who is hunting us?" Jaykin gasps.

"Guards. The emperor must know about us by now," Kanaren says.

"What have I done?" Jaykin worries and covers his head in shame.

"What's wrong?" Pree asks.

"Jaykin did something he shouldn't have," Kanaren replies, hastily.

"Go easy on him, Kanaren, I'm sure he didn't mean to do it, whatever it was." She gives him a little smile but they both stay silent.

"We need a plan," Kanaren says. "We can't stay here. They will find us here eventually. We need to leave the city."

"But to go where?" Jaykin asks. "Wherever we go we're going to be hunted."

"Certainly not to any other city," Kanaren replies.

"Wait, what?"

"We need to stay away from the cities until we can figure out what to do with Pree."

"So, what do you suggest?" Pree asks.

"We leave Dreamora and find cover out in the forests."

"Wait, no! We can't do that," Jaykin says.

"Wherever we go, they will be looking for us. We have no other choice," Kanaren says.

"What's wrong with leaving the city?" Pree asks, trying to get an answer from either one.

"But only the elderly or the guilty leave."

"Hunters leave too. I did warn you about this Jaykin," Kanaren says.

"Is there something to fear outside the city?" Pree asks.

"Outside is full of powerful creatures. It's a death trap. No one ever just walks out of the city!" Jaykin argues.

"Really?" Pree replies, puzzled. "That doesn't sound right. We had no problem with creatures."

"Times have changed," Kanaren replies. "Creatures have been dominating us for centuries, that's why we built the wall around us – as a defence against external threats."

"But Kanaren, we won't survive," Jaykin says, getting slightly worked up.

"First of all, you're the one that got us into this mess. Second, we don't have a choice. Can you imagine what they'll do to Pree if they discover her? They'll hang her up on a plinth, like all the other trophies Lon has."

"I don't want to be someone's trophy," Pree says, almost timidly.

"Then it's settled. We go and that's the end of it," Kanaren says.

"Then how exactly are we going to get out of here?" Jaykin asks.

"First of all, we need to get a collector," Kanaren replies.

"What is a collector?" Pree cannot resist asking.

"It's a flying machine that carries people or cargo from one place to another and it's our quickest way out of here too," Kanaren replies. "Q-Tech, is it possible to get to Dreamora's base from here?"

"Yes, but high chance of Guards surrounding the building," it replies.

"Damn," Kanaren replies. "Then we'll need to steal one."

"We what?" Jaykin gasps.

"Yes, I'm saying we need to break into the Guards' main base and take a collector."

"And how on Izara are we going to do that?" Jaykin asks.

"We'll go after dark."

"It will be soon Master," says Q-Tech.

"Pree, we will need your powers for this part of the task. We're going underground," Kanaren says.

"Whatever you need," she replies.

"Good, as we need to disable anyone we meet." He turns to the Q-Roid. "Q-Tech, locate the Guards' main base and lead us there. We go straight there and then out of the city. Jaykin, you will stay behind Pree. We must protect her at all costs. She'll be doing most of the work."

"Right," says Jaykin, feeling both nervous and excited.

A few minutes pass and Q-Tech leads the way, along with Pree. Kanaren holds Jaykin back.

"Before we go, Jaykin, if anything happens to me outside of the city, I want you to take Q-Tech and Pree and go straight to Q-Ara. Search out the emperor there.

"I will," Jaykin promises.

"And remember what I told you earlier: keep your crystal-absorbing to yourself."

Chapter 9

The New Mission

Emperor Lon waits impatiently. He sits on his throne, gulping down a strong drink. He stands suddenly and stares at his Knights.

"Where are those Hunters?" he shouts and throws his glass at the floor, near their feet. He hears the doors shut, with a loud thud. A group of five appears, marching towards him. "Finally!" he yells, "where on Izara have you been?"

"Emperor Lon," one of them replies, "we were preparing the creatures for the next—"

"Don't!" Lon shouts, holding his hand up, stopping the Hunter mid-sentence. "I do not care about that anymore. This is much more important." He waves his hand for another drink and tries to calm down. "I am setting you another task. Bring back to me that…" he closes his eyes, to think of the right words, "…impulsive Kanaren and his thieving little friend." One Knight hands him another drink. He snatches it and gulps it down. He takes a seat, wiping his mouth. "Do anything you want to them. I just want my crystal back!" He slams his fist on the armchair, cracking the glass into pieces.

"We will bring back your crystal, Emperor Lon," one of the Hunters says, bowing solemnly.

***

Way below the city lie several miles of underground tunnels, now unused. Q-Tech leads the others, pointing its light, showing the way, and using the old brick wall to help with balance.

"Are we nearly there yet, Q-Tech?" Kanaren asks.

"Nearly, Master Kanaren," it replies. "Will be right underneath the base soon."

They walk a little further, then Q-Tech stops and looks up at a ladder, leading up to the Guards base. "Arrived at destination."

"Good work," Kanaren says and taps it on its shoulder. "Q-Tech, you will go up first, I want you to find the nearest collector and start it up." He faces the other two. "I'll follow; then Pree. Can you use your powers when anyone comes near us?"

"I can do that," Pree replies, nodding confidently.

"Good. Jaykin, you and I will be looking out for Guards and warning Pree. I don't know how many will be up there or where the nearest collector will be, but we have to be alert and focused on getting out of the city."

"Understood," Jaykin replies, nervously.

"We get in and we go as fast as humanly and…" Kanaren pauses, "…Elementally possible?"

Pree smiles. Q-Tech stands and waits for him to say something about Q-Roids too.

Jaykin fills the void: "And at maximum Q-Roid speed."

Then they all move towards the ladder.

Q-Tech makes its way up first, much faster than the others, and reaches the top before they are halfway. It reaches a drain cover and places its robotic hands on it firmly, feeling for vibrations, but detects nothing. It lifts the cover ever so slightly to scan for signs of life; a full three hundred and sixty degrees; then lowers the cover.

"Two Guards with Q-Azars, eight metres southwest and three with same Q-Azar quality southeast." It pauses with its hand still planted on the drain. "Three to four metres away."

"Good work, Q-Tech. Right, everyone, remember the plan. Go as fast as you can." Kanaren says. He looks back up at Q-Tech who is still scanning. "Okay let's go." It lifts the drain cover and peers towards the Guards. Seeing their backs are turned, it climbs out and sprints to the nearest collector. None of the Guards spot it. Looking around for the opening, Q-Tech then presses the button near the back.

The rest of the group quickly crawls out of the drain hole. Pree, given her size, only just fits through.

"Hey, what is that?" someone says from amongst the Guards.

"Oh no," Jaykin whispers.

"Get into the collector, now!" Kanaren says. Pree sticks out her hand to the Guards before they can fire their weapons. They all drop, one by one, falling asleep, while both Jaykin and Kanaren run onto the back of the collector. Its engines fire up and it hovers off the ground slightly. Pree panics and runs towards them and jumps up with the help of the others.

"Okay Q-Tech, let's get out of here!" Kanaren shouts out to the front.

"Yes Master," it replies. They all grab onto

random parts of the craft while it lifts higher. As it ascends, Kanaren makes his way to Q-Tech, at the front.

"Head to the exit to the west of the city," he says. Q-Tech pulls back on the lever and the collector stealthily exits the base. Kanaren turns to the others.

"We need a plan to open the shield gate or else we're not getting out of here." He pauses to think about it. Pree and Jaykin look blankly at each other. "Right," he says, "I'll take over flying. Q-Tech, load level ten attack-mode on the Guards that defend the shield, set to stun, do not kill. I repeat, do not kill. Take down the shield while we pass through, then raise it back up, understand?"

"Understood, Master Kanaren."

"We'll meet you on the other side of the wall. We'll pick you up. Good luck."

He hovers near the city wall, close to a very large door. Collectors may pass through, but they all need authorisation. Kanaren opens the rear door of the collector and Q-Tech steps forward, grabs onto the bottom of the collector and hangs. It scans the ground.

"*Collector seven, three, one, five. You do not have permission to pass this point,*" a soulless voice says over the radio.

"Yes, I won't be listening to you, thanks," Kanaren says and switches it off.

Q-Tech let's go and glides through the air, landing right on top of a group of Guards, knocking them unconscious. It stands, and sensing another Guard is behind it, quickly dodges the blasts and disarms the

Guard, stunning him. It finds the controls for the shielding and turns it off. A huge panel clunks and clicks in several places, disconnecting from the main dome shielding, moving sideways like a gigantic sliding door, allowing a way through to the outside. Kanaren steers the collector through the gap and lowers it to the ground. Q-Tech turns the power back on and the shield slowly begins to reinstate, allowing it time to jump through. It glides back into the collector.

"Good work Q-Tech. You can take back control now," Kanaren says, vacating the pilot seat. Q-Tech takes its place, pressing a few buttons and switches. The collector hovers slightly. "Let's get out of here. Head west for the time being," Kanaren instructs.

"Understood," it replies.

Pree looks out of a small window panel, back towards the city full of sparkling lights of all different colours and brightness.

"It sure is beautiful," she says.

Kanaren notices Jaykin staring at his hands, quietly resting at the front of the collector.

"You, okay?" He asks.

"Yeah, I guess," Jaykin replies. "Where are we heading?"

Kanaren takes a seat next to him.

"We're going west. Between the three cities is a place called the Battlefields. Strangely enough, it's the safest place I can think of."

Jaykin shakes his head.

"No," he whispers, "we need to head northwest!"

"Why there?" Kanaren also whispers, sounding

intrigued.

"I don't know," he hesitates slightly. "I can't explain it but ever since the crystal incident, I can…" he looks over to Pree to make sure she isn't listening, "I can sense something."

"What are you talking about?"

"It's a strange feeling like…my body is reacting to something far away, like it's calling out but I can't hear or see it. It feels like it's…" he pauses "…pulling me towards something."

"Right," Kanaren says, sceptically.

"Do you think it could be a crystal?"

"Possibly," Kanaren waits to think about it. "It all sounds very strange. Are you sure?"

"I feel pretty confident about it. There could be another…" he points at Pree "…inside."

"Fine, we'll head northwest then. It's not like we have anywhere else to go for the time being." He stands and gives the order to Q-Tech. The collector quickly responds.

"Are we changing direction?" Pree asks.

"Yes," Kanaren replies. "The Guards of Dreamora will be looking for us. So, we're going in a direction they're least likely to take." He looks over to Jaykin to reassure him.

"Oh, that's a good idea," she says. She looks from one to the other. "You two are a good duo."

"Thanks, Pree," Jaykin replies.

"What were you both doing in Dreamora?" she asks.

Jaykin stays quiet. He can't think of anything to say in case he blurts something out and gets told off for it. He waits for Kanaren to answer.

"We were just finishing debating with the Emperor," Kanaren replies.

"Oh, I see," she says. "Important business I imagine. Is he a good ruler?"

"No," Jaykin interrupts before Kanaren can respond.

"Oh." She looks out of the window. "He's probably from Raziz then." She starts muttering to herself. "Lying, thieving, pathetic Barkas!" Both Kanaren and Jaykin stare back at her, in shock at her words. "Oh, I'm sorry," she says, "I'm so used to saying that. I didn't even think. Are you both Izarian?"

"Nothing to worry about Pree. Yes, we're both Izarian," Kanaren replies. "Well, as far as I know," he adds and looks at Jaykin, who nods. "To be honest it's probably difficult to distinguish who is Izarian or Razilian nowadays."

"You really don't like them, do you?" Jaykin asks.

She stays quiet for a moment.

"It would be difficult for us Elements to see Razilians in a good light, as we've been at war with them for so long."

"Why were you at war?" Jaykin asks.

She stops to think about it.

"Do you know, it's almost impossible to say. When I was human, we were told from a very young age that the lands in the sky were a forbidden place. No one ever questioned it, maybe because we were scared and it was the law. So, for many years we all had a happy and peaceful life where there was nothing to worry about." She pauses. "Until one day, the sky fell upon us. Hundreds of thousands of Razilians attacked my people and thus the Great War began. No one knows why they attacked us," she says sadly. Both Kanaren and Jaykin look at one another awkwardly.

"How long did it go on for?" Jaykin asks. She sighs out loud and shuts her eyes.

"Oh, it lasted for hundreds of years and countless people died because of it." There are tears in her eyes and great sadness on her face for a few moments. "But it seems like it has finally ended, which I'm extremely grateful for."

"It's okay Pree. I'm sure they've forgotten about the Great War as we have," Jaykin says, with a sympathetic smile on his face.

"Well, I don't think we'll be going to Raziz anytime soon," Kanaren says.

"I trust you two will make the right decisions," Pree says with a smile. Jaykin moves closer to Pree. He's intrigued by her.

"How would you get to Raziz without a skyship?" he asks.

"Elements," she replies, as if it's obvious. "Gravity and Air Elements use their powers to take others to the land in the sky. My friend, Aura, was an Air Element. She used to tell me about her adventures there. They could be horrific." She stops and looks at Jaykin. "I hope we find more Elements."

"I hope so too, Pree. I would love to meet them all." They both smile in accord.

"What is a skyship?" she asks.

"It's a machine like this, but much larger. It can

take at least a hundred people to each city, including the cities on Raziz, but I've never been on one." Pree looks at Jaykin's slightly sad face.

"Kanaren told me you're looking for your father." He nods. "Well, I'm sure wherever he is, he is safe," she says.

"I hope so. Hopefully, when we get to Q-Ara, I'll get some answers."

"Family is important."

"That's what I keep saying to myself," Jaykin replies and looks over to Kanaren.

"He reminds you of him?"

"He does. I don't know what it is. The way he stands; looking out for me. He just reminds me of what I miss."

"Your father must be very special to you."

"He is. He's the only family I have left and I miss him, a lot," he replies, lowering his head.

"I'm starting to know what you mean." Pree looks as if she is in another time.

"Do you have a family?" he asks, calmly.

"I do." She lowers her head, forgetting where she is. "Or, I did."

"I'm really sorry to hear that."

"I'll be okay. It will take time to come to terms with. You should not give up on your father. Unlike for me, there's a possibility yours can be found."

"Thank you," he says. "Not many people tell me to keep going. It's mostly to give up and move on." He stops and gives her a huge hug. She leans back slightly, not really prepared for it, then hugs him back. Stepping back, he spots the logo of the water droplet on and around her armour and jewellery.

"That symbol..." Jaykin says "...I recognise it...but it's different." Pree looks down and takes her necklace off.

"What, this? It's the symbol of where I'm from." She shows Jaykin. "A little village called Lementes. Both Jaykin and Kanaren stare at one another. "What's wrong?" she asks.

"That place is now one of the six cities. It still has the same symbol but it's a darker shade of blue and instead of a drop, it's more of a wave." Kanaren answers. Pree doesn't know whether to be excited or sad about the news.

"I would like to visit there," she says.

"We will, but not right now," Kanaren says. "We'll stay on track."

Jaykin places his hand over his mouth and yawns.

"Tired?" Pree asks.

"A bit," he replies. "I suppose I won't be getting much sleep while we're running from the Guards."

Pree laughs out loud.

"Not while I'm around," she says. "I can absorb your tiredness and make you feel wide awake."

"That sounds like a great power," Jaykin says. "Can you try it on me?"

"Sure, just relax." She places her hand on his forehead, with her thumb and small finger spread to each temple.

"This is an experience I'll never forget," Jaykin says.

Suddenly he feels a strange sensation flow through his

body like thousands of adrenalin patches slapping into him in one go. He's full of energy now and ready to take on anything.

"How are you feeling now?" Pree asks.

"Very awake. You want to have a go Kanaren?"

"Sure," he walks over to Pree and she does the same thing.

"Feel better, don't you?" Jaykin asks. Kanaren nods.

"Seemed like you needed that," Pree says. "Has it been a while since you slept?"

"You could say that," Kanaren replies. "Thank you."

"Not a problem. Your friend…" she points with her head at Q-Tech. "…does it need a boost too?"

"No, it doesn't sleep," Kanaren replies. "It's connected to the collector."

"Oh, okay," Pree says, a little confused. "If you say so."

With that Q-Tech shouts out. "Master Kanaren, there is a problem!"

Chapter 10

The Hunt is on

Day 4

Back in the city of Dreamora, on the edge of the wall, Guards are running around, jumping into collectors and taking off. In a deserted area in the base, a much larger collector, capable of holding large creatures, stays grounded.

"What do we know so far of our targets Devy?" asks Arma, a weapons expert and part of Emperor Lon's five Hunter team.

"Let's have a look," Devy, the technology expert says, from the front of the collector. She reads from a list. "Name: Kanaren; middle-aged man, last seen in Dreamora four hours ago." She starts to laugh. "Listen to this; he also saved Lementes from a barka several times this month."

"Ha!" chuckles Crata, another Hunter and creature expert. He walks up to the collector with a couple of boxes. "Barkas. Easy creatures," he smirks.

"A loner; only a Q-Roid in tow, but recently travelling with a boy who is unknown," Devy continues.

"So, nothing changed there then," Steg says. Physically, he is the strongest of the team.

"No," another says. Everyone goes silent and turns towards the last Hunter, Slayed; the leader and the brains of the team. "Kanaren is clever and he knows exactly what he's doing."

"Why did he steal the crystal then?" Arma asks.

"Nothing to show his motives there," Crata says.

"What about the boy? Do we have nothing on him?" Arma questions.

"Nothing whatsoever," Devy says.

"Hmm, could be an outsider," Crata suggests.

"Could be just tagging along? Like that other kid," Steg says.

"Wrong place at the wrong time?" Devy asks.

"No, they travelled together," Slayed says. Crata places a couple of heavy-duty weapons into the collector. "That's everything."

"Let's head out," Slayed says.

"The Guards are heading west," Devy says.

"Then we will do the same. If he's stolen the collector, then he hadn't planned for this retreat out of the city. So, with no plan, he's relying on instinct," Slayed says.

***

Due northwest of the city, Jaykin and the others fly over the vast area of High Tree Forest. The scale of the trees, seen for miles, reflects the name.

"What's the matter Q-Tech?" Kanaren asks, making his way to the front of the collector.

"Danger is heading this way." It points. Kanaren follows the direction.

"Oh, that isn't good." Jaykin joins them and looks out too.

"What is that?" he asks.

In the distance, they can make out thousands of creatures flying towards them. Pree takes a look, scrunching her eyes to get a better view.

"I can't tell what kind of creature they are," she says. Kanaren stands there in silence until he says something that sends chills down the spine.

"They're scarrags; twice as strong and as big as barkas. They hunt in hundreds, and in this case, thousands."

"Oh," Jaykin says. "What are we going to do?"

"We're going to have to stop here," Kanaren replies.

"Why? Can't we go around them?" Jaykin replies.

"We'll stand no chance against them, they're too fast," he stares at Jaykin. "We won't get past and we don't have time." He grabs onto the back of the chair. "Q-Tech, hover over those trees there and we'll get out."

"Yes, Master Kanaren."

"We're not going to fit between the trees. Grab everything you need. It's going to be a quick getaway." He reaches for his sword which is leaning against the hatch of the collector. "Pree, as soon as they get near us, target as many scarrags as you can. We'll need to grab on to them to glide down."

"Are you sure that'll work?" she asks.

Kanaren pulls the lever, sliding it across and freezing cold air gushes in. "One way to find out!" he shouts.

"Are we seriously going to do this?" Jaykin shouts.

"That or get ripped apart by scarrags."

"You do have a point there."

"Get ready to jump, Pree."

"Ready," she replies and looks down to try to see the ground, but the only light they have is from the collector itself. It is literally a leap into the dark.

"Q-Tech, keep it steady and follow when we've cleared the collector," Kanaren shouts.

"Understood, Master Kanaren."

They hover over huge trees that reach hundreds of feet in the air.

"Three…" Kanaren says. The scarrags get closer. Jaykin holds onto Pree to try and get better balance, gripping tighter. "Two…" The sounds of whistling echo through the treetops and the sound of the scarrags' screeches gets stronger and much louder. "One…" They all look up at the scarrags and prepare. "Go!" Pree swipes her hands towards the oncoming scarrags. Hundreds swarm around the collector. Some start to fall and the group all leap out at the same time, reaching as far as they can to latch on. Very loud bangs and crashes surround them while the scarrags tear into the collector, ripping it up into pieces, parts flying all over the place. Pree and Jaykin manage to grab onto a scarrag each in mid-air. But Kanaren struggles and falls into a tree. Luckily, he pulls out his sword in time and thrusts into a thick tree trunk, cutting straight through. He stops halfway down, hanging on for dear life. Jaykin's voice shouts out,

"Wake them, Pree!"

"I'm trying!" she says and tries to reach out again to the two scarrags. They slowly wake up. Pree smashes into the ground using the scarrag to cushion her fall. Jaykin manages to glide one into a high tree and jumps, rebounding off it, and rolls onto the soft leafy ground in a heap.

All is quiet for a few seconds, and it's darker down in the forest grounds. The faint noises surround them as pieces of the collector thump against the trees, branches and leaves.

The screeches of thousands of scarrags quickly fade while they pass above. Jaykin stands and searches for the others. It's very eerie.

"Kanaren where are you?" he shouts.

"I'm up here," he replies, still hanging onto his sword, which seems to be stuck in the tree, fifty metres up. He looks up to where the collector was supposed to be but there is nothing. Then something small hits the trunk, just above him. He quickly grabs onto it without letting go of the sword and admires it. He sighs regretfully. "I'm really sorry my friend," he says, then places it into a pocket inside his jacket. He spots something below him. "Jaykin! Look out!" he shouts. A Scarrag appears out of nowhere. Jaykin turns to face it. It screeches at him. This thing is huge and can barely fit between the thick trees. It has multi-coloured scales and hair from its small thin head spikes up and all the way down its back to the tip of its tail. It has large flat feet and long sharp black claws, black eyes and a dripping wet large fanged mouth.

Kanaren looks for Pree who is nowhere to be seen.

"Pree, where are you?" he yells. Hearing no reply, he places his feet against the trunk trying to pull out his sword. "Come on!" But it doesn't budge. Then he spots her. A big scarrag has fallen on top of her and isn't moving. Pree doesn't look conscious either. She must have been hit hard when she fell. "Looks like it's just up to me then." He pulls even harder but with no luck and looks down at Jaykin, who is slowly backing away from the scarrag. It inhales the mist around it, breathing heavily, licking its scaly lips like it's hungry. Jaykin starts to panic. Kanaren pulls his sword a quarter of the way. "Come on!" he shouts again in frustration. He pulls out a Q-Azar and aims it at the creature to get its attention but it doesn't respond. It's fixed on Jaykin.

Pree wakes up, slightly disorientated. She tries to move but becomes aware that a scarrag has managed to roll on top of her. She has no chance of moving the weighty creature. She looks around for the others but a tree covers her view.

Jaykin slowly draws his sword from his back and waves it around, trying to deter the scarrag but it continues walking towards him. Then, without warning, it swipes a wing at him. He skilfully fends it off with his sword but only with pure luck. But then it swings again from the other side, catching him off guard and hitting him into the nearest tree. He screams in pain and rolls onto the ground.

"No!" Kanaren shouts, watching helplessly. It's a long way down for him to jump off the tree and if he misses the creature, he can do some serious damage. The scarrag toys with Jaykin with its wings while he tries fending them off, waving his sword around and trying to scare it, but it doesn't work. He leans on the tree, trying his best to stand. It's nothing like the barkas which are easily distracted. It stares at him as if curious. It lets out small screech sounds as if getting bored playing with its food. It quickly turns its huge skinny body, striking him again with its long muscular tail. Jaykin defends again but he's too slow and it manages to hit him harder and propels him into the nearest hollow tree, crashing through the bark. Bits of bark fly out in Pree's direction, exploding all over the place. She covers her face, expecting Jaykin to appear.

"Jaykin!" she shouts out.

Kanaren looks down and anger builds in him.

"Right," he shouts, "now it's my turn." Still with the Q-Azar in his hand, he points it at the tree and fires. Bark and branches are blasted far and wide. He manages easily to pull out his sword as the tree gradually disintegrates. He quickly pockets his Q-Azar and, now thrown into mid-air, he charges up his air weapon as he falls. With only inches to spare before hitting into the ground, he points it downwards and fires. Leaves whirl all over in the blast of air, which slows his fall and allows him to land softly. Huge chunks of the tree hit the ground around him.

Kanaren is on his feet and the scarrag screeches menacingly as it catches sight of him. The creature turns but Kanaren doesn't wait and fires his air weapon at it. Pree watches as the scarrag stumbles onto the ground trying and failing to get its balance. The wind picks up suddenly like a tornado. The scarrag staggers, hitting some of the trees. It tries to run away, but keeps tripping over its own wings. Then, with a final effort and stretching of its wings, it quickly jumps onto a tree, then onto another and with room to move, it takes flight, soaring straight up into the sky.

The wind calms down dramatically and all is quiet, until Kanaren appears from behind the large tree.

"Pree, are you okay?" he asks.

"Yes, I'm fine," only just managing to push the unconscious scarrag off her. "What happened back there? I've never seen a creature so scared of a human before."

"I have a couple of things up my sleeve." They then hear a cracking noise coming from the tree next to them. It is Jaykin.

"Are you hurt?" Pree asks.

"Argh," he says, struggling to get out of it. "I'm fine. Luckily these things are hollow!" He throws his sword onto the floor and they both help him out of the hole he had made.

"Are you sure?" Pree asks, looking at the damage and picking up his sword.

"Yeah, don't worry," he says shaking his hand about and wiping bits of bark off himself.

"We need to leave," Kanaren says. "The Guards were close behind us and without our collector, they'll catch up to us quickly."

"Agreed," Pree says. "We must move on." She gives Jaykin his sword back.

"Wait," Jaykin interrupts, looking around. "Where's Q-Tech?"

Kanaren slowly pulls out something from his jacket.

"It's here; just not in one piece." He holds what appears to be an electronic component in his hand. "It's Q-Tech's memory core."

"Oh no!" Pree gasps, covering her mouth, not really knowing what she's looking at.

"Well, that answers my question then," Jaykin quietly says to himself. Kanaren sighs.

"Shame really. It was a good Q-Roid." He places it back into his jacket. "I'll get it rebuilt when we get back to a city."
Pree gently places her hands on the tree.

"Where are we exactly?"

"High Tree Forest. Why?" Kanaren asks.

"I've been here before." She smiles, sounding excited. Both Kanaren and Jaykin look at each other.

"How do you know that?" Jaykin asks.

"I helped grow this forest." She starts walking from the nearest tree, counting her steps. "The way they're positioned, they're the exact distance we planted them. We called it the New Forest."

"Pree, I know you want to find out about the past, but this isn't the right time," Kanaren interrupts and just walks away. Jaykin looks up at her.

"It's okay; it's a step closer," he says.

"It's better than that," she says. "We may be able to work out when the Great War ended just by examining the trees." They both look up and can hear scarrags hovering overhead again.

"We'd better keep going," Jaykin says. Pree holds onto the nearest tree.

"They would be proud of you," she whispers to it and smiles; then walks away.

Jaykin looks back towards the tree he fell into and can see that, deep inside, the trunk is layered in thin crystal.

Chapter 11

Nothing is What it Seems

A couple of hours pass. Kanaren leads the others northwest with Pree following and Jaykin coming up last. He has slowed down to get behind Pree for a reason. He wants to try and create crystal, as he did before, apparently by accident inside the tree. But instead of trying in front of him, he tries with his hand behind him, in case Pree accidentally looks back. Every time he thinks he has made something, he looks at Pree, then into his hand. Nothing. He keeps thinking about the tree. That crystal wasn't there already; it must have come from him, but how? How does it materialise? What were the conditions that made it work? He can't concentrate. With every step he takes, he feels the pulsating sensation in front of him, which means there must be a crystal close by.

They hear water nearby and can taste and smell it in the air. They have reached the end of the forest. The river before them is wide and slow-moving. Kanaren stops and crouches down low.

"The Central Lake," he says quietly. "We need to cross this, and we need to do it carefully." He looks across the water coursing down from the mountains beyond. A herd of skrips, harmless herbivore creatures, no more than thirty of them, are drinking from the cool fresh water a short distance away. They look back at them and slowly move on. Kanaren starts walking across the lake where the water reaches both his and Jaykin's knees, and Pree's shins. Silver nebs, big silver scaly fish, swish past their feet. Pree heaves into the water and grabs onto one which flaps frantically. She uses her powers to put it to sleep and it goes all floppy.

"Found breakfast," she says, smiling.

"Nice one Pree," Jaykin says.

"Your turn," she replies and she watches him struggle for a few minutes. She swipes her hand slightly without him noticing and a couple of the fish stop swimming and he manages to grab one. "Well done!"

"Thank you. Now what?"

"We eat them!" she replies, excitedly.

"We don't have time!" Kanaren says, as he makes it to the other side of the lake.

"But I'm hungry," Jaykin protests, holding onto his stomach. "We haven't had anything for hours."

"Fine, but we're out of here as soon as we're done."

Pree and Jaykin also reach the other side. Kanaren kneels and gathers dry sticks together and piles them up.

"Jaykin, find me longer and stronger ones like these." He opens his jacket and pulls out a small silver box, then points it at the sticks. A little red laser appears, quickly lighting a fire.

"That's an interesting item," Pree says, curious.

"Here," he says and passes it to her, swapping it for the fish. "Just be careful with it." He stabs long sticks through both the fish and places them near the fire.

***

Back at the High Tree Forest, where the collector was ripped apart by the scarrags, Guards from Dreamora make their way across the forest with the help of Q-Roids; instructed by the emperor not to come back until the fugitives are found. Over twenty collectors hover overhead, beaming spotlights onto the ground below. In one, Lesh paces nervously behind the commander of the Guards.

"I don't think we're going to find them out here," Lesh says.

"Don't give up already," the commander replies. "Leave this to us professionals."

"That's what I'm worried about," Lesh says under his breath. He's still feeling the effect of Pree's powers.

Down below the trees, one of the Guards stops and picks up something.

"Commander!" she calls, using her earpiece. "I've found parts of a collector."

"Excellent work," the commander replies. "Grab any evidence you can." He turns to Lesh with a smirk on his face. "See, I have complete confidence—"

"Sir," a Q-Roid interrupts from the front of the collector.

"What is it?"

"Scarrags are on their way to our location. What would you like to do?"

"Code name: 'Walkthrough.'"

"Understood." It presses a button and repeats

the order.
All the collectors turn to their side; with the scarrags in view. The side doors open wide.

"Let them have it!" The Q-Azars fire upon them.

***

While Jaykin and Kanaren fill their bellies, Pree uses the end of her spear to cut up pieces of fish and wrap them in big thick leaves taken from the trees nearby. Kanaren has given her some long unused wiring that was attached to Q-Tech's memory core and she uses it to tie the rolled-up parcels.

"Pree, what was Lementes like?" Jaykin asks. She looks up at him just finishing the last batch.

"Well, we were quite a large tribe." She starts to tie the parcels to the spear. "With a mixture of humans, Solutions and Elements."

"Did you have a shield?"

"He means a barrier around your tribe, to keep the creatures out," Kanaren translates.

"Oh, no. We didn't have anything like that. If we ever had issues with creatures, we Elements would take care of it."
Jaykin's body relaxes. He is feeling more comfortable to be out of the city, and knowing that Pree is good to have around.

"How does it feel to be an Element?" Jaykin asks.

"It's not so different from being a human, aside from the powers. It's an odd sensation at first but after a few hundred years, you get used to it."

"How old are you?" Jaykin asks, sounding intrigued.

"Jaykin, you don't ask people that, it's rude," Kanaren intervenes.

"No, it's ok," Pree replies with a smile. "Let's just say I'm over a thousand years old, give or take."

"Wow, how long can Elements live for?"

"Solutions and Elements can live forever, if they so wish."

Jaykin turns to Kanaren for his reaction but as he finishes his food, he stands and immediately kicks the earth to extinguish the fire.

"We should go, now," he says. "They're not that far behind us." And he walks away.

Both Pree and Jaykin look at one another.

"We should get going," Pree whispers. As they stand, they pick up their weapons and move off to catch up with Kanaren.

***

About a mile beyond the lake, they start seeing old wooden signs and covered in moss, which read: "Warning! Stay Away. Danger. Do not pass this point," but they keep pressing on, into a vast wooded landscape.

Jaykin approaches Kanaren and taps him on the arm quite roughly.

"What is it?" Kanaren asks, slightly irritated.

"I think I can sense a crystal nearby," he whispers, trying not to let Pree hear him.

"You sensing something?"

"Yes, somewhere nearby. I don't know where exactly."

"These signs are worrying me," Pree interrupts. "What are they warning us about?"

"This is called the False Forest," Kanaren responds.

"Isn't this the place where people go insane?" Jaykin asks.

"It is known to happen."

"Then why are we heading this way then?" Pree asks.

"There's a good chance the Guards won't follow us here," Kanaren replies.

"Right," she says, stopping and pondering uncertainly. "Wait. When I was in the crystal, did I somehow use my powers?"

"Well, people did fall asleep near you when you were in the crystal—"

"And the city is named after your powers," Jaykin interrupts.

"There could be a crystal nearby," she says as her face lights up.

"Maybe, but—" Kanaren says.

"We should definitely find out," Pree interrupts, excitedly.

"Yeah, let's do it," Jaykin says.

"It sounds like a Mind Element," Pree says.

"This Mind Element, is it powerful?" Kanaren asks, intrigued.

"Yes, very. So, we will need to be extremely careful. They can create unwanted visions or take over your mind completely."

"That doesn't sound good," Jaykin says, going slightly pale in the face.

"Stay focused, Jaykin," Kanaren snaps. "We must keep vigilant. Pree, what do we need to look out for?"

"Whatever you think is real, it won't be, so, do not believe it. Might be a good idea if we all say what we're seeing."

"Agreed," Kanaren says.

They walk further, looking behind trees, in bushes and under rocks. Nothing but forest. Jaykin suddenly hears a rustling in some bushes and spots someone who looks slightly familiar. It's an elderly man in an old, worn cloak.

"Hi," Jaykin says, but the man doesn't reply. "I know you, don't I?" But instead of answering, the man simply points over into the distance.

"Jaykin, who are you talking to?" Kanaren asks.

"The guy that's standing there," Jaykin replies, pointing at him.

"A man? Jaykin, there's no one there."

"Yeah, I recognize him but I'm not sure where from." He sprints in that direction.

"Jaykin, that man isn't real. I can't see him. You need to stop."

"But it looks like he's pointing at something."

"Don't go any further, Jaykin. It's not real."

"He could be telling us something though."

"No!" Kanaren says aggressively, "Listen to me - we do not follow him." But Jaykin continues running away. "Pree, can you help me here?" he asks, but she is nowhere to be seen. "Pree?" he shouts, and stops, spotting something in the sky. It's a huge spaceship, about the size of a city. "It's not real," he says to himself repeatedly.

"Kanaren? Jaykin?" Pree shouts but there seems to be no sign of them. She hears some shuffling and is extremely surprised to see a similar-sized Element standing close by and it appears to be smiling at her. The Element's skin is slightly blue, its body wrapped in dark clothing. It wears cream-coloured gloves and its trousers are baggy and tucked into its shoes. It is a muscular being with an extremely large neck. It wears the blue and gold symbol; the same as Pree's.

"Hi Pree," he says, his voice very deep.

"Mordan?" She smiles, excitedly running towards him and giving him a huge hug, so he can barely breathe, "How on Izara are you here?" she asks, emotion in her voice. He taps on her head gently.

"I'm just…here," he says sounding pleased about it.

Her smile quickly disappears and she lets go of him.

"You aren't real, are you?"

He shakes his head.

"No, but I would like to be."

"Me too. Is this your doing?" she asks.

He shrugs.

"I'm one of the thousands of Mind Elements that could be here. Please don't be disheartened if they aren't."

She pauses, not really knowing how to reply.

"I'll try," she says quietly and hugs him again and buries her head into his shoulder.
She opens her eyes and sees that Mordan has gone. She feels the loss acutely. Tears are streaming down her face. She wipes them away and stares at the empty space.

"Pree!" Kanaren shouts nearby.

"I'm over here," she replies.

"Jaykin is following someone and I can't stop him."

They reach a clearing with few trees and some evidence of habitation. They scan the view for signs of movement.

"Seems like there was a village here once," Pree says, and kneels to examine the ground. She picks up a couple of pieces of pottery. "I wonder why they left this place?"

"I'm over here!" Jaykin shouts, waving his hand behind some foliage.

"What are you doing?" Kanaren yells.
Cautiously, they approach him. He is holding back a lot of branches to reveal large stones, and beyond those, an old crumbling doorway. An entrance to a cave.
Kanaren leans on the rock.

"Good find, Jaykin." He taps him on the back.

"How on Izara did you find it?" Pree asks.

"An elderly man showed it to me," Jaykin replies.

"What man?" Kanaren asks.

"No idea! Although I think I've met him before. Might have been from a dream."

Kanaren stares at him, sceptically.

"That doesn't really help. Where is he now?"

"Hmm, I don't know," Jaykin replies, shrugging his shoulders.

"This is no ordinary cave," Pree says. "This is someone's home." She feels the edges of the cracked rock. "It's an Element's home."

"Or used to be," Kanaren says.

Pree enters first, firmly holding onto the rocks around her.

"Careful, it's very dark," she says, as they both follow her.

"I can't see a thing," Jaykin says.

Kanaren searches through his jacket and pulls out a very straight thin stick. He breaks it into three.

"This will help," he says, and gives one each to Pree and Jaykin, who don't know what to do with them. He waves it around, making it glow brightly, and they follow suit.

The cave feels eerie and quiet; the only noise they can hear is the echo of drops that trickle down the walls and land in puddles of water. They can feel a cold breeze blowing past their ears, making the hair on their necks stand on end. This isn't a nice place to be at all. They walk down some well-worn steps leading them deeper into the cave, sliding their hands across the damp wall to support themselves. The deeper they go, the dryer it gets, and much darker. Pree notices what appear to be engravings on the wall. She gently places her fingers on them. They are painted images.

"Are you both seeing these too?"

"I am," Jaykin says. "What are they?"

"Stories of your history by the looks of things," she says.

The further they walk; the more drawings appear. All manner of creatures and monsters are depicted in the cave.

"Looks like people were here for many years," Pree says, examining the walls.

The space gets wider and taller as they progress. They continue walking until they see something shining back at them in the distance. It is a crystal, the same shape as Pree's, but this one is slightly bigger. Both Jaykin and Kanaren look at each other at the same time, surprised they have found another crystal so quickly, and that Jaykin was right. As they approach, the light falls on hundreds of valuables: colourful trinkets, jewellery, coins, and clothing; alongside the crystal; possibly tributes from worshippers over many years. Pree suddenly shouts out.

"Look out! The roof is going to fall!" She pushes both Jaykin and Kanaren away from her and covers herself with her arms as they both fall to the rocky ground.

"Why did you do that?" Jaykin asks, attempting to get up but seeing the floor cracking underneath him. "The floor is splitting open!" he shouts and hits into Pree. She screams as she thinks Jaykin is the roof crumbling around her. Kanaren stands, brushing himself off.

"You're both hallucinating. Snap out of it!" he shouts; then stops. "Wait. Something doesn't feel right." With that, the wall next to him starts to crack, and he walks back slowly, pulling out his sword. The wall crumbles away and something huge emerges. Kanaren gasps.

"Are you both seeing this?" he asks.

"Yes," Pree replies, "what is that thing?"

"A Defender!" Jaykin shouts, hiding behind her. "That's the thing that took down armies."

Pree waves her hand at it but nothing happens. She tries it again.

"It's not working," she says, getting frustrated. She repeatedly tries her powers on it to no avail. "We may have a problem." They slowly walk backwards, closer to the crystal.

Pree takes her spear off her back and points it towards the Defender.

"It's time, Jaykin," Kanaren says. "While Pree is distracted." He grabs onto him and throws him nearer the crystal. Jaykin goes to place his hands on it but it unexpectedly ignites.

"I can't go near it," he says, stepping back.

The Defender strikes away Pree's spear and grabs her. She attempts a scream but her voice isn't there. She falls to the ground as if the life is being sucked out of her. The Defender lets go and waves its hand at her. She is instantly asleep.

"Pree!" Kanaren shouts. "Jaykin! Absorb it now!"

"But the fire?"

"The fire isn't real!" he yells, pointing his sword to the Defender. But Jaykin just stands there. He wants to believe Kanaren but he can feel the heat. The Defender advances on them.

"Jaykin!" Kanaren shouts, "we don't have time for this!" Without any warning he grabs onto Jaykin's clothing and rams him into the crystal, practically headbutting it and nearly knocking him out. Without realising, Jaykin spreads out his hands wide onto the crystal. It instantly cracks around them. He gasps and tries to let go but he's stuck, just like before. He tries to turn his face away too, but it's fixed as if pulled by a magnet. He can't move. The crystal pulsates when Jaykin absorbs it. This time he can feel it being soaked up inside his fingers, crawling up his arms and his face. For some reason, it begins to feel better; not hurting him so much. It is just bearable. Near his left eye, the crystal is less misty, and he can see straight through it, spotting blue skin and huge arms.

The Defender slowly walks towards Kanaren, who is preparing to attack it. He secretly primes his air gun and points it. The air whistles through the whole cave as he fires. The Defender stops in its tracks. It tries to nudge a little closer but struggles to find balance and falls to one knee.

"Jaykin, can you do that any faster?" Kanaren shouts.

"I'm trying!" Jaykin shouts back, desperately. The Defender lifts its hand towards Kanaren who shakes his head, trying to stay awake.

"It's using Pree's power! I can't stay…" He falls to one knee too, "…awake." He drops to the ground. The Defender slowly stands and walks towards Jaykin. The crystal itself has nearly gone and the Element is in full view. The Defender waves its hand at

Jaykin who is overpowered by sleep and falls to the ground. The Element struggles to stand and looks directly at the Defender. It stares back.

"I can't sense a consciousness in you," the Element says with a deep voice. "No matter," He grabs a sword and slides it out of the scabbard on his back. He stands with effort and swings it with amazing skills. The Defender tries waving its hand over at the Element to induce sleep.

"That won't work on me," he says. With no chance to protect itself, the Defender is destroyed, falling, and breaking into pieces. The Element stops and lets out a sigh, sheathing his sword.

"I've never had to use my swords until now. You thoughtless thing, whatever you are." He becomes conscious of Jaykin and Kanaren, and Pree lying nearby.

"Pree?" he shouts, running towards her and lifting her up. "Are you asleep?" he whispers. He places his hand on her forehead. "Wake up," he whispers again. She opens her eyes immediately and stares at him.

"Mordan?" she asks excitedly, giving him a huge hug. Then she pulls back slightly to see his face. "Are you real this time?" Then she punches him, not too hard, on the arm.

"Ouch! Yes, I'm real!" Mordan replies.

"Oh, I'm so happy it's you," she says, giving him another hug.

"Me too, I think," Mordan replies doubtfully, not sure how to respond. He pushes her away slightly. "Pree, where are we?"

"I'll explain later," she replies, then turns to Jaykin and Kanaren. She places her hands on their foreheads. "It's okay, they're only sleeping. Time to wake." They both open their eyes at the same time. "How are you two doing?" she asks, gently.

"I'm feeling fine," Jaykin replies. He feels something in his hand and discreetly places it in a pocket as Pree helps him up.

"I'm fine," Kanaren replies, standing and taking in the remains of the Defender.

"Mordan, I would like you to meet both my human friends: Kanaren and Jaykin,"

"Nice to meet you both," Mordan says and bows. "You both look very…" he stares at them both, mostly at their clothing, "…different."

"We're going to get a lot of this aren't we?" Jaykin asks.

"Good to meet you too," Kanaren says formally, then makes his way to the Defender. "That thing was strong."

"Yes, I have a feeling it absorbed my powers," Pree says.

"I've never seen anything like it," Mordan says, crouching down to take a better look. Its body is made from very hard rock.

"Hey, we did it, guys!" Pree smiles. "There are still Elements all over the land." She holds onto Mordan's arm. "We just need to find them." Kanaren ponders, walking towards the exit.

"It could be to our advantage."

"Really?" Jaykin asks, not expecting that response.

"Sure. Think about it: the more Elements we find, the better chance we have for our missions."

"Sorry to barge in here, but what is going on?" Mordan asks.

"I'll explain on the way out," Pree replies.

***

They make their way slowly up the steps as Pree tells their story. Mordan listens intently but is distracted several times by the artwork on the walls.

"What on Izara?" he says, his voice echoing through the cave, his gaze taking in the striking images.

"We're not exactly clear on how we have ended up here yet," Pree says.

"It's a lot to take in. I'll need time to think about this," Mordan replies. They emerge from the cave and the morning sunlight hits them.

"Oh, that feels good," Jaykin says.

"What's that strange noise? It's coming from that way I think." Mordan says, pointing south.

"Collectors," Kanaren says, in a chilling voice. "Dreamora's Guards are still searching for us, and they're close."

Jaykin stays quiet and stares west, towards mountainous terrain.

"I suggest we go to higher ground," he says pointing. "Like there."

"Mount Keap?" Kanaren questions. "Good thinking. We can head there next and then review our options. Jaykin, take Pree and Mordan with you. Be vigilant."

"Sure, but what are you going to do?"

"I'm going to lead the Guards north; I'll catch up with you when I'm done."

"Is it a good idea to split up?"

"You'll be fine. You have two Elements with you, Jaykin."

"We can take them on, Kanaren," Pree says.

"No, there will be too many and I can't risk it."

"What if you're captured or something happens to you?" Jaykin asks.

"Remember what I said to you back in Dreamora. I'll be fine. I'm used to being outside of the cities; the Guards aren't."

"Okay."

"Oh, and Jaykin."

"Yeah?"

"Be careful."

"I will. You too."

"Lead the way Jaykin," Pree says.

***

Guards appear near the cave, not long after. They examine the scene carefully, finding footprints heading in different directions.

"This is not a good place to be," Lesh says, walking beside the commander.

"Yes, you keep reminding me, but as you can tell, we haven't lost a single Guard since we've been here."

"Just trust me, I've been here before. We don't know what is lurking around."

"I'm not listening to an ex-Hunter. I have my ways of doing things and I am not stopping this search."

"Commander," one of the Guards says. "We think someone went this way," he points north.

"There's more over here," another one shouts over. "Creatures too, by the size of the footprints."

"Okay, we'll split up," the commander shouts. "Lesh, you can take your team to the North and we will go south-west."

"Sure," Lesh replies with a crafty grin.

***

Running as fast as he can, Kanaren jumps and strides through the forest, hampered at times by dense overgrowth. He eventually slows down and stops, closing his eyes to control his breathing, slowly in and out. A faint noise of ruffling and sticks breaking tells him they're close. Then he hears gushing water; in front of him? He runs off again.

Behind him the Guards rummage through the forest, looking in every direction.

"I think I hear something," one says, calling to the others. They all run in the same direction, using their weapons as battering rams to clear the branches away. Then they stop dead, nearly falling off a cliff edge. Metres down, a gigantic river flows south-east.

***

Jaykin and the Elements run as far as they can, getting

closer to Mount Keap, until Jaykin stops suddenly, huffing and puffing.

"I can't go any further."

"Come on mate, you can do it," Mordan says.

"I can't."

"They're getting closer," Pree worries.

"It's okay, I have an idea," Mordan says. "Into these bushes." He points to an area where they can huddle together.

"Are you going to do what I think you're going to do?" Pree asks.

"Of course. I am the Mind Element after all," They hear voices and rustling of bushes but it suddenly stops. "It's my time to shine," Mordan whispers. He points his hand in the direction of the Guards.

"What are you going to do to them?" Jaykin whispers.

"Give me a minute."

Suddenly, they can hear Q-Azars firing, then shouting, then running. They peer over the bushes, watching the Guards running away, as fast as they can, heading back in the direction of the cave.

"What did you do?" Pree asks.

"I may have shown them a few false scarily large creatures heading in this direction," Mordan replies with a grin on his face. "We should keep going." Both Morden and Pree get up and head towards the mountain but Jaykin doesn't move. He looks for any sign of Kanaren, but sees nothing.

"You coming with us?" Pree asks him.

"I'll be there in a second," he replies.

"Okay, we'll wait for you up ahead."

Remembering the thing he placed in his pocket, he waits until they are just out of view. He takes it out and examines it carefully. It's a crystal, about the same size as the one from Kanaren's place. It's the same colour and texture as the larger crystals that surrounded the Elements.

"But how? How did I get this?" he asks himself. He recalls that the Defender used Pree's powers on him. It must have stopped the absorption process. What is even more interesting is that it isn't being absorbed now.

Chapter 12

The Big Blunder

A few hours pass. Jaykin, Pree and Mordan are still in the forest. It seems never-ending. Every so often Jaykin looks back to see if he can see Kanaren following them but with every turn, the worry gets to him.

"It's been too long. What if he's been caught?" Both the Elements stop.

"I'm sure he's fine," Pree says. "As he said, he's used to being outside of the city."

"Wait!" Mordan says, his expression alert, "I sense someone running towards us!"

"Me too," Pree says. They all look back.

"I can hear something," Jaykin says. "I know who it is." A figure appears. "Kanaren!" he shouts with relief.

"Hi," he replies, out of breath, and sits on the ground.

"How on Izara did you get away from the Guards?" Jaykin asks.

"I lead them to a cliff edge," he answers, still gasping for air. "Loved to have seen their faces."

"Good to see you, Kanaren," Pree says.

"You too," he replies, getting to his feet. "Come on, let's keep going. I hope you've briefed Mordan on our situation, Jaykin."

"Well, he used his powers on Pree and read her mind," Jaykin informs him.

"Ah, that's a helpful technique," Kanaren says.

"That's not the only thing he can do," Pree mentions. "Show them."

"Try it on me?" Jaykin says, waving his hand in the air.

"Sure," Mordan says, lowering himself down to Jaykin's eye level. He concentrates. "Go run off a cliff." Jaykin goes pale with fear but Mordan bursts into laughter. "I'm kidding," he says "but that's one thing I can do; also, this." He looks serious. Jaykin suddenly hears Mordan's voice but he isn't moving his lips. It's as if he is talking in Jaykin's head. "*Jaykin, I want to thank you for looking after Pree. You have been very helpful in this difficult and confusing time for us.*"

"No problem, Mordan," Jaykin says and smiles, not yet getting the hang of replying in his head. He tries. "*I'll try my best to help you both.*"

"Thank you, Jaykin," Mordan says, using his voice this time.

"What did you just do?" Kanaren asks.

"He spoke to me in my mind," Jaykin replies.

"That's a powerful skill you have there."

"It comes in handy," Mordan says.

"Here, Kanaren, I'll give you your energy back," Pree says and places her hand on his shoulder.

"Thank you. I feel much better," he replies, impressed. "We should be clear from Guards now; I didn't see anyone for miles. They should go back to the city."

They continue walking, less concerned about the Guards behind them. Kanaren leads, with Jaykin close by.

"Kanaren," Jaykin whispers, "I need to tell you something."

"What is it?" Kanaren asks, looking cautiously back at the Elements, who are engaged in their own conversation.

"I have a crystal in my pocket."

"What? Haven't you absorbed it?" he whispers. Jaykin shakes his head. "Where did you get it from?"

"I'm not sure. I found it in my hand after I woke up in the cave."

"Well, keep it safe then," He checks that the Elements are distracted. "What else can you do with it?"

"What do you mean?"

"Well, you can absorb crystal, so I'm guessing you can use it for something?"

"Oh, well I have tried, but nothing came of it so far."

"That reminds me, we need to be careful given Mordan's powers. We don't want to let them know about your…ability."

"If you say so," Jaykin sighs.

Simultaneously, Pree and Mordan are catching up with one another.

"It's so good to have you here," Pree says.

"Good for me too," Mordan replies. "Feels odd though."

"I know what you mean. I feel…" she pauses to find the right word, "…lonely."

"Yes, but we have each other now." He

chuckles and shakes his head. "I can't believe it; we actually survived the Great War."

"That is a great feeling," she agrees happily.

"I hope we find other—" Whack! Mordan smashes his face into something which is camouflaged. "Son of Izara!" he shouts, covering his face, and steps back. Everyone else does the same, wondering what is going on.

"What is it?" Pree asks.

He is wiping his face and checking his hands for blood.

"I don't think I'll be able to use my powers for a while." He grabs onto what seems to be thick metal tubing, covered in moss. "What is this thing?" Slowly he pulls the weeds back to take a closer look.

"Looks like nothing from our time," Pree replies, examining it from a distance.

Kanaren approaches and follows the mossy tubing until it stops, ending at what seems to be a small building.

"Well, I haven't seen one of these before, but I know what it is." He turns to the rest of the group. "It's an attank."

"That's an attank?" Jaykin replies. "Wow, I never thought I'd ever see one. My father told me about these." Mordan and Pree look confused.

"Hundreds of years ago we used these huge things in a war between the cities," Kanaren says.

"Some sort of war machine?" Pree whispers.

"Exactly," Kanaren replies, "made to do one thing: destroy. The huge weapon in the front fires a powerful blast, destroying anything and everything in its path." He stops and looks at it. "But this particular one isn't made for going through a forest like this." He looks around it. "It's likely to be carried with an older version of a collector. This one must've fallen from one."

"I've found a door," Jaykin says, climbing on top of the machine. He tries pulling it, then pushing it. A loud clunking noise echoes inside. He opens the door slowly and it creaks, shuddering at every inch. He peeps in and doesn't see anything straight away, but then spots some sort of control panel, covered in dust, soil and plants. Kanaren climbs up and he inspects the control panel, clearing off the debris.

"This thing is certainly old but I might be able to activate it and contact someone within the city from here. Jaykin, see if you can find any supplies." He searches but finds nothing.

"Jaykin, the war, with these things," Mordan places his hand on the attank, "how did it start?"

Jaykin climbs out of the attank and sits on top, crossed legged. Both Pree and Mordan are tall enough to be at eye level with him.

"As far as I'm aware the war began with a power struggle. Every city wanted to take over each other. That's what my father taught me anyway. It may not have lasted longer than your war though."

"A hundred years or so," Kanaren shouts from inside the attank, "Jaykin's right about the power part. It would probably be different if the Elements had been around at the time."

"That's true," Jaykin says. "Mordan, were you in the Great War too?"

"I was, unfortunately."

"What did you do before the war?"

"Before?" He pauses for a moment. "I was a finder, a healer, and an entertainer, so I was a very busy Element." He chuckles to himself. "Oh, those were the good times. Everything seemed to be perfect. That was a very long time ago though. I can barely recall those memories. Then the Great War began. I remember that perfectly, like it was yesterday." He lets out a sigh. "That day still haunts me," he says as Pree comforts him.

"Me too," Pree says.

"Can you tell me about it?" Jaykin asks.

"Imagine a sky full of powerful Elements set on destruction; hundreds of thousands of them; like all your nightmares coming true. At first, I'd thought another Mind Element was playing a poor prank with me but it turned out I was wrong. I couldn't believe it at first. I never understood why they were attacking. I mean Elements attacking their own kind? They destroyed homes and nearly took over my village, but luckily, my friends and I fought back as hard as we could, pushing them into retreat."

"For years and years, we fought back," Mordan says. Jaykin can feel the struggle in Mordan's voice. "I changed a few minds to our side, of course, but sometimes I almost gave up. It felt like it would never end."

"But it has," Pree smiles, "It's finally ended."

"Yes, but at what cost?" he sighs. "I don't see any Elements except for us. Did we win or did they?" he looks at the other planet.

"Why would it matter if either of you won?" Kanaren says as he lifts himself out of the attank. "At the end of the day, you know that both the worlds are living in peace. Sure, it took a long time and many wars to work things out but it's peaceful and settled now."

"Really?" Mordan says, "and how do you know they won't do it again?"

"I don't," Kanaren replies, "I can only hope that the leaders of the worlds will make sensible decisions."

"Terrifying isn't it," Mordan says. They all look up at the planet Raziz; silent for a moment.

"How did you get on?" Jaykin asks Kanaren, trying to change the subject.

"I can't do anything with it. We'll keep looking."

They move on.

"Mordan, what was the last thing you remember before you were here?" Pree asks.

"I was scouting. There were rumours of a group of Razilians close by. I didn't find them, so we rested.... and I woke up here."

"When was the last time you guys saw each other?" Jaykin asks.

"A long time ago," Pree replies, she looks over at Mordan to try and remember. "When was it?"

"Too long," he says.

***

They start to go higher and the trees become less dense, so they can see the dark planet of Raziz. Mordan keeps staring up at it.

"Pree," he says, prodding her on her shoulder.

"What is it?"

"I've found Elements! Hundreds of them by the looks of it."

"Are you seeing things again?"

"No, I'm not this time, I promise. Look." She raises her head and follows his gaze. Three intensely bright lights can be seen on the surface of Raziz. Pree rubs her eyes just to make sure but Mordan is certain. "Light Elements! The enemy still has them," he says. Pree's jaw drops slightly.

"I'm sorry," Kanaren says. "They're not what you think they are."

"Explain then," Mordan says.

"They're cities. Huge communities with a great many buildings - homes and workplaces for thousands of people all collected together, some might say, imprisoned, within the city walls. From here they look so insignificant."

"Cities?" Mordan says, trying to take in the explanation.

"Yes," Pree says. "I've been in one. It's amazing, and…*many* times the size of the villages we knew." She continues describing the city of Dreamora. Kanaren turns to Jaykin.

"I have a feeling we will need to teach these Elements a lot about their new world. So much will have changed for them."

Day 5

Instead of resting, the group continues walking to Mount Keap, the highest peak between all the three cities. Fortunately, Pree uses her powers on Kanaren and Jaykin, to keep them awake and energised.

"Pree, your powers," Jaykin asks suddenly, "can you remove nightmares?"

"I can. Only when you're actually having them though, why?"

"Oh, I keep getting bad ones, that's all."

"What are they about, if you don't mind me asking?"

"Mostly about an attack of some kind."

"Hmm," Pree thinks for a bit. "That could mean anything."

"I thought I'd ask as you may know why I keep getting them."

"I tell you what. I will read your dreams next time we rest. How about that?"

"Err…sure," Jaykin says, not quite sure if that's actually a good idea.

"Do you dream about your father?"

Jaykin thinks for a bit.

"No, not really."

"Yawn," Mordan says, placing his hand over his mouth.

"Mordan! That was really rude! Apologise to Jaykin!"

"What? I'm tired," he says.

Pree shakes her head at him. Her voice softens.

"All you had to do was ask." She energises him with a wave of her hand.

"You guys were busy chatting," Mordan says, grinning.

As they move on, Pree asks a question that has been

on her mind for a while.

"Do you have a mother, Jaykin?"

"My mother…yes, well…my father told me she passed away when she gave birth to me."

"Oh, I'm sorry to hear that," she says gently, placing her hand on her chest in a ball. "May she find guidance in the next life." She then extends her arm, palm upwards, as if throwing something into the air.

"Yes, I'm sorry too," Mordan says and makes the same gesture as Pree. "Did your father talk much about her?"

Jaykin smiles and nods his head.

"Yes, a lot," His smile turns into a grin. "My father always spoke about my mother like she was an Empress. He said that she would treat everyone like a guardian angel; looking after them; caring for them. She sounded so beautiful; kind, generous; but also strong-willed."

"So, what other family do you have?" Mordan asks.

"My father and that's it." He ponders for a bit. "I suppose I treat Meara as part of my family too."

"Oh, who's Meara?" Pree asks.

"She's a good friend. She looked after me whenever my father went away for his job, and also when he went missing; even though I didn't ask for help." Pree and Mordan exchange glances.

"Oh really? Is she a similar age to you, then?" Pree asks.

"A few years older than me. Why do you ask?"

"Oh, just curious," Pree smiles.

"Nice one, little man," Mordan says, nudging

Jaykin.

"What?" Jaykin asks.

"Ignore him," Pree says. "Sounds like you have a lovely relationship with her."

"I guess." He looks at both the Elements. "Do you have any family?" They both nod their heads.

"Both my parents became Air Elements," Pree says "They went to the other land together and I've never heard from them again." She lowers her head. "And I have a sister who became a Mind Element and that's how I met Mordan."

"Since then, she's wished she hadn't," Mordan grins and she shoves him playfully. "My parents split when I was a young human; my father became a Fire Element and my mother became a Water Element." He pauses. "Even as Elements they were complete opposites," He shakes his head.

"What about you Kanaren?" Pree asks, but he doesn't respond. "Is he alright?" she whispers to Jaykin.

"Yeah, he's fine; just has a lot on his mind at the moment. You know, with the invasion and all."

"Invasion?" Mordan and Pree ask in unison, shocked by the disclosure. Kanaren stops and stares at Jaykin.

"Oh no!" Jaykin says, holding his hand to his mouth.

***

In the nearest solar system, a spaceship is seen motionless over the planet Edash. Below, on the planet's surface, explosions are going off that can be heard and seen from space. Inside the spaceship, humans are at the control panels. At the rear of the control room, two enormous doors open and two figures appear from outside; one a twelve-foot-high Element- shaped figure, its entire body covered in glinting metallic armour, engraved with intricately detailed golden flames. Alongside this impressive figure is a human, smaller in stature, but in appearance an exact copy of the Element. They walk proudly through the ship. A voice from the human:

"How are you feeling?"

"Great," the Element replies. "These people were weak." He stretches his arms and neck to make them click. He finds his throne and sits down, making himself comfortable. "The people of Tarintia put up a better fight," he continues. Another throne is available for the human but he doesn't sit. Instead, he walks in front of the Element, pondering.

"You know I hate it when you're contemplating," the Element says. "Go and do it somewhere else."

"I'm just thinking, we should leave now while we have the upper hand."

The Element considers for a moment, then nods and snaps his fingers.

"Commander, where is the nearest habitable planet?"

A woman, mid-forties, approaches in dark, plain clothing, with five small stars on her right shoulder.

"My Lords. The nearest habitable planet…" She stops. "…my apologies, planets, sir; it's a binary planet system. Izara and Raziz," Both the Element and the human look at the commander, then at each other.

"Intriguing," the Element says, stroking his chin thoughtfully. "We will head there next. But not immediately. We need a plan. We'll leave in two days commander, no later."

"Understood, my Lords."

The human grins.

Chapter 13

The Highest Peak

"Why did you keep this from us?" Pree asks.

"It wasn't your concern," Kanaren replies.

"It would have been nice to be told about being on the brink of another war!" Mordan yells. Kanaren is about to reply but Mordan stops him. "Wait!" he says, looking around, "We're being watched. I can sense people all around us."

"I can sense them too," Pree says.

"How many?" Kanaren asks.

"Too many to do anything about," Mordan replies and stares at him. "I should have noticed them earlier but I got side-tracked," aiming his words at Jaykin and Kanaren.

They draw their weapons, except for Kanaren, who just stands still and looks up at the trees.

"Put your weapons away," he says. "The Keap tribe won't harm us unless we show them aggression."

"There are tribes out here?" Jaykin asks.

"A very large and powerful tribe," Kanaren continues firmly, standing before the Elements. Jaykin puts his sword away straight away. Both the Elements hesitate, looking around cautiously, then put away their weapons too.

A whistle is heard from within the trees and a young man, about the same age as Jaykin, walks into view, wearing thick leather wrapped around his body. He points a bow and arrow, slowly walking towards them. Kanaren bows with his right hand on his chest, stretching his fingers out wide. The young man is surprised by the gesture. He stops and stares at Kanaren, places his bow down to his side, then does the same thing. The group look at one another and each does the same. The young man looks up at them all individually, eyeing them up curiously, then back at Kanaren.

"You speak our tongue, am I correct?" the young man asks.

"We do," Kanaren replies.

The young man responds quickly.

"And two of you are…" he pauses, critically inspecting Pree and Mordan, up and down, "…different." Kanaren looks back at them too.

"My friends here will bring no harm to your people," he says, calmly.

"Hmm," the young man smirks, "we will see about that."

Mordan looks at Pree. "*I have a sick feeling in my stomach,*" he says, using his mind to communicate.

"*Don't worry Mordan,*" she smiles at him. "*Kanaren has this under control.*"

"*I hope so,*" he replies. "*We'll soon find out I suppose.*"

The young man approaches the Elements to have a better look at them, then makes two consecutive whistles. The rest of his people begin to emerge from cover, dressed in similar style to the young man.

"You can pass, but…" he points his finger out

to them, "…you will see the Elder first, and in honour, we will take your weapons from you."

"As you wish," Kanaren bows again.

"*Kanaren is this wise?*" Mordan asks using his powers again.

"*We don't really have a choice Mordan,*" Kanaren replies, "*Plus, you two stick out like a sore thumb.*"

They all walk in a line, together with the villagers.

"Why are you so far from your village?" Kanaren asks the young man.

"We were hunting skrips, then we heard you. You make too much noise; scared them away. We will need to hunt again soon."

Kanaren looks at him and the others. They all seemed very young for hunting. Allowing some space to open up between himself and the young man, Kanaren whispers cautiously to Jaykin:

"Something is very wrong. They don't hunt at this age." He transmits the same message in silence to the Elements.

***

A lot of climbing later, they are approaching the top of the mountain. They follow a footpath into a steep ravine. Smooth stone surrounds them, with the sky and planet Raziz visible above. Buildings are moulded within the stone. The group can see many villagers going about their daily chores, but, strangely, they do so at a very slow pace, which seems unnatural. Many of the villagers surround the entrance. Small children run up to the Elements and greet them by waving and then hugging fearlessly. The Elements respond with indulgent smiles. They make their way to the centre of the village where a crowd is gathering, and becoming noisy, the people evidently intrigued by the Elements' appearance. An elderly man, seated close by, suddenly holds up his hand and there is immediate silence.

"Oozoo, what do you bring to us?" the man asks, slowly standing from his chair and facing the young man.

"We found these people wandering our territory, Elder," Oozoo replies.

"Welcome, travellers of Izara." The Elder lifts his arms in greeting. "What brings you here?"

Jaykin steps forward and is about to say something when Kanaren discreetly holds him back.

"We are on a very long journey to the Unknown Lands; we did not mean to trespass into your territory." He places his hand on his chest again and spreads his fingers as wide as possible, then lowers his head.

"You know of our greeting sign?" the Elder says. "You have been here before?"

"I have learnt about your culture," Kanaren replies. "I have heard many stories of the great Keap tribe."

Pree spots Mordan with his eyes closed and contacts him silently: *"Mordan."*

"What?" he replies.

"What are you doing?"

"I'm trying to search through the Elder's mind but he seems to be deflecting my power somehow."

"Why are you trying? We need to be very careful here. We won't get out of this alive if we screw this up."

"They're hiding something here, Pree."

"Why do you think that?"

"I'm not sure. I read some of the people's minds and they seem to know something but I can't get it out of them."

"Okay, but please be careful," she replies. He closes his eyes again and concentrates on the Elder.

"What do you seek in the Unknown Lands?" the Elder asks.

"We are returning these people to their homeland." He indicates Mordan and Pree. While they have the conversation, Mordan still struggles to enter the Elder's mind.

"A*h, I can't read him."* He turns ever so slightly in Pree's direction. "*Pree."*

"What is it?"

"I need your help."

"What do you need me for?"

"Can you make the Elder drowsy?"

"Easy." She concentrates on the elder and his eyes flutter briefly. *"Now, Mordan."*

"Thanks." He again concentrates on the Elder.

"Homeland?" laughs the Elder. "I've never seen these sorts of people before." He gazes at the Elements, apparently in admiration.

"Yes—" Kanaren says, but is interrupted by Mordan.

"Elder, if I may speak?"

The Elder, is shocked that these beings speak his language.

"You shall!" He nods his head.

"My name is Mordan and my friend here is Pree. We are Elements," He steps forward, closer to the Elder, "I know there is no point in lying to you, as you seem to have great wisdom. Our instincts tell us that your people are struggling; that they're ill and they're worried."

The Elder takes this in for a few moments, looks around to his people and sighs deeply.

"You are right."

"We have an illness affecting the village," Oozoo says. "We have struggled in the last few months; now we can't work or hunt as we used to do. We cannot cure the illness."

"Enough Oozoo!" the Elder shouts.

Pree kneels to admire one of the children that stand near her, choosing a young girl, about four years old, who is holding onto Pree's clothing.

"Stay still little one," she says. She checks her ears, mouth, nose, then her eyes. "Oh," she says and looks up to Mordan, "they have the Nonpeels virus. We can help these people." He nods agreement.

"You, help?" the Elder asks, "How could you?"

"I'll show you," Pree replies. She places her hand on the little girl's temples. "Sleep," the girl slowly closes her eyes and goes floppy. Pree holds onto her while she leans into her arm. All the people gasp in astonishment, including the Elder.

"You have superhuman powers?" he asks.

She picks up the girl and rocks her gently.

"Sleep is all that your people need," Pree replies. The Elder gives a cautious nod, clearly willing to try anything.

"I plead for your help."

"But—" Oozoo says.

"No, Oozoo," the Elder stops him, "our people will not survive much longer if we continue the way we are." He shakes his hand towards them. "Let them help."

"Mordan, what is Nonpeels virus?" Jaykin asks.

"It's where the mind does not let you sleep. Eventually, it makes you exhausted and depleted; some people can even die from it. We have seen it a lot in our time. But never a whole village. This is where Pree does her magic."

The Elder slowly walks up to Pree, using a walking stick for stability.

"What will you need?"

"Time. So, we may need a place to stay for me and my friends."

"We have plenty of space. Your two human friends can stay in the hut at the end of the village. It is unoccupied. Oozoo will show you. For both the Elements, we will set up a place in the large barn located on the opposite side of the village. You may otherwise struggle with the height," he says, with friendly humour.

"Thank you Elder. I will help your people straight away," Pree says, and hands over the child to an adult. She walks with Mordan towards the barn, with many of the people following in curiosity.

"Follow me," Oozoo says, not sounding too happy about the Elder's decision.

"Come on Jaykin," Kanaren says.

"But the Elements?"

"They'll be fine; they're going to be busy. We may as well try and help out while we're here," He watches the villagers carefully as they deposit their weapons in a small hut near the centre of the village.

"Kanaren," Jaykin whispers.

"What is it?"

"I can sense a crystal nearby."

"Why did you not say anything earlier?"

"Didn't know when the best time was. I already blurted out one thing today, I didn't want to do the same with that."

"Okay, well try and pinpoint it exactly."

"I'll try."

***

Concealed high up in a tree not far from the entrance to the village, Arma, one of the Hunters from Dreamora, looks through a long-distance scope on his Q-Azar. He places a finger in his ear then talks into his intercom.

"Kanaren has been spotted in the village," he says.

Underneath the same tree, Slayed, the leader of the Hunters, takes a bite out of some meat carved from a spit over a camp fire.

"Good work, Arma," he replies, with food still in his mouth. He turns to the other Hunters keeping guard. "Prepare to engage the village." Then he turns back to eat some more. "I'll ask you again my friend, where is their crystal?"

Beside him, hanging upside down by his feet, a villager

is tied up on the same tree.

"I said before," he says hesitating, sweat dripping off his face, "I don't know what you are talking about."

"It's quite a simple question really," Slayed says and chuckles slightly, biting into the meat again, then continuing with a full mouth, "but your village people never understand me." He swallows hard and then shreds another piece of meat off as he stands up. "We'll just have to go get it the hard way then, won't we."

"What are you going to do?" the man asks, his voice hoarse as he struggles for breath.

"You'll soon find out, won't you," Slayed replies, sadistically, bending down to his eye level. He prods the man on the forehead, making him sway slightly. He looks up at Arma in the tree and nods. Arma draws his knife and stabs it into the rope. The villager falls to the ground; hard.

Chapter 14

The New Power

At the village, the group is cautiously settling in, as the Elements interact with the people, helping the recovery from the virus. Jaykin and Kanaren are assisting in the weapons store, sharpening and cleaning blades. The Elder enters.

"Kanaren, please walk with me," he says quietly.

"Shall I come too?" Jaykin asks.

"No, you stay here, you need to learn about this."

"What, sharpening weapons?" He sighs. "Fine."

The Elder and Kanaren slowly walk through the village. The people are resting, thanks to Pree.

"You're from a city, aren't you?" the Elder asks.

"I am, yes."

"We get people from your cities coming here from time to time. Not many," he chuckles. "But the ones that survive the creatures stay and we help them grow into better people."

"Many of the people are exiled if they break any of the laws in the cities."

"Yes, and we pick up the pieces. Is that why you're here? You broke the law?"

"You could say that," Kanaren replies, glancing back at Jaykin. "We wouldn't have found the Elements if we hadn't."

"Ah, yes, the Elements; they are good people." He points his walking stick at Kanaren's chest, "like you are."

"I try to be, Elder," he says firmly.

"You are," the Elder says insistently. "The problem is, you have a hard shell and you won't let anyone into your life. That's why you're alone; like the boy. He has a shell too. Break free of it and you'll both do fine, I'm sure." Kanaren doesn't reply but just looks intently into the Elder's eyes. "You've been here before, haven't you?"

"I have. It was a very long time ago though. We were travelling the worlds back then; we ran into the tribe too."

"I thought so." He smiles, then stops in a quiet area of the village. "Kanaren, I would like to show you something; something very secret to our people."

"Very well," Kanaren replies, on the alert. The Elder points the way. An intricately carved wooden door opens, revealing a walkway that is dimly lit. They enter a room. All around the walls are candles providing a dim light and opposite the entrance lies a large crystal, similar to Mordan's and Pree's. Kanaren tries to stay cool and to do his best impression of being really surprised. He walks up close to it, but not too close to be warned off, and he stares intently at it. He can sense something strange radiating from it but can't work out what it is. He feels awake this time; like he's buzzing, with increased energy; different to the effect the other two produced. He glances at the Elder, who has a smile on his face.

"You've felt this power once before, haven't you?"

Kanaren comes clean.

"I have."

"I can tell. That's why I have shown you this."

"You know these are a very rare thing to come by, right? Many people across the two worlds have been looking for them, for thousands of years."

"We know of the crystals," the Elder says. Kanaren turns to him quickly. "But we don't give the knowledge out lightly; only to certain…individuals. Otherwise, it becomes dangerous."

"You're right, but we could use that knowledge."

"You will receive it at the right time. Your friends are…" He pauses to think. "…interesting. They're not from the Unknown Lands, are they?"

"You saw past that too."

"They don't call me a wise man for no reason."

"You *are* wise. Your people are lucky to have you as a leader. You'd be great as an emperor, much better than the one in Dreamora at least."

The Elder chuckles.

"I have heard many stories of him. He is not wise, I think." He pauses. "Your friends; they seem different to anything on these worlds."

"That is true, just like these crystals." He admires it again.

"Ah," the Elder replies, acknowledging Kanaren's evasion.

"As you said," he turns back to the Elder with the same serious face, "some knowledge becomes too dangerous." Then, returning his thoughtful gaze to the crystal: "Even for the wisest of people."

Kanaren makes his way back. Oozoo and a few of the villagers are the only ones to be found, however.

"Where's Jaykin?" he asks.

"He wanted to know if we could see the cities from here, so I took him to the highest peak." He points. "He's still up there. Follow the steps up, he's not far."

Kanaren does so, and finds Jaykin on his own, sitting on a smooth stone, passing an unseen object from one hand to the other, abstractedly.

"You are getting out of your chores," Kanaren says.

Jaykin jumps slightly and looks up at him. He looks extremely tired. In his hand is the picture of him and his father.

"I thought you were a villager then. I needed to get away. To think."

"What about?"

"Everything that's happened recently, and this," he puts the photo away and pulls out something else; a crystal, placing it in Kanaren's hand.

"We haven't really talked about this, have we?" he says as he admires it. Jaykin shakes his head slightly. "How are you feeling? After absorbing all that crystal?"

"I feel fine, surprisingly."

"Good. Now tell me, how do you do it?"

"I don't know," he replies, staring into the distance. "It all started when I absorbed the one at your place."

"You did what?"

"At least I think I did. It vanished when I touched the glass."

"I had that for years!" Kanaren tries his best to hold back his anger, shaking his head in exasperation. "When were you going to tell me about that?"

"Soon, I guess." He shrugs. "I was scared. I thought you weren't going to help me," There is silence for a few moments.

"It's all right," Kanaren says, and takes a seat next to him. "You've just discovered this…power, haven't you?" Jaykin nods.

"I don't know what's wrong with me, Kanaren."

"Nothing is wrong with you; you just need to know all the answers." He looks at the crystal again. "Does anyone else know about this power of yours? Your father? Your friend?"

"Except for you, no one else knows." He pauses before asking his next question. "Can I tell people I have powers?"

"No; it's best to keep it quiet." He places his crystal into his pocket.

"Why?" Jaykin asks, sounding slightly resentful.

"No!" Kanaren stands immediately. "You have the power to absorb the rarest Element in both Izara and Raziz. As soon as people find out about you, they'll take advantage; use you or, worse, experiment on you. People don't like different."

"You have a point," Jaykin sighs. "What about Pree and Mordan? I shouldn't be hiding this from them."

"As I said before, they wouldn't understand it

and we can't trust them yet. We only just met them. Anyway, they have enough on their mind, trying to work out how they got here in the first place, until you blabbed on about the invasion."

Jaykin pulls back.

"I'm really sorry about that," he says, lowering his head.

"It's fine, but we need to be extremely careful what we say around them. We can't let them suspect anything."

"But Mordan has the power to read minds."

"Then focus on something else. If they ask any questions, I will answer."

"Okay." Jaykin doesn't sound confident.

"We need to be extremely careful."

"And I need to know what I can do with it," Jaykin places his hand into his pocket. "If we're keeping it just between us then I should tell you something else, because I badly need to tell someone." He rummages around. "Absorbing isn't the only thing I can do." He then pulls out another crystal. Kanaren stares at him, speechless. "You can keep that one. It'll replace the one I absorbed in Lementes."

"You can create crystal too?"

"Yes. But it takes a lot of concentration and energy. That's why I'm resting." He lowers his head again and plays with the crystal, then looks up toward the Western Light. "I wish I could tell my father about this."

"I'm sure he'd be impressed," Kanaren says, in a kinder tone, and holds onto Jaykin's shoulder for comfort. Jaykin turns with a smile of satisfaction on his face and nods his head. "Yeah, I think so too. You think we can go to the Western Light, since we're already outside of the city?"

They both admire the beam of light from the west. From their vantage point, it looks as if it's shining out of a cliff edge. Jaykin has never seen it from this angle before. Kanaren thinks for a few seconds.

"Are you sure? No one wants to go there."

"I know. Part of me is terrified of that place but I think we might find some answers about the missing people."

"Then I don't see why not, but we have other priorities, remember?" Jaykin nods. He had forgotten momentarily about the Elements and the invasion. Kanaren shares new information: "Which reminds me, the Elder showed me where the crystal is but it's going to be extremely difficult to get near it, especially with all the villagers around. We'll need to come up with a plan—"

Suddenly Kanaren stops talking.

"*Kanaren, where are you?*" Mordan uses his powers to make contact.

"*I'm at the peak. Everything okay?*"

"*There are people just outside of the village. They have weapons and a hostage, and they're asking for you.*"

"*On my way. Where are you and Pree?*"

"*We're still in the barns. There are lots more people to heal. Do you want me to sort this out?*"

"*No. I'll deal with them. You stay there with Pree, and whatever happens, don't help, understand?*"

"*That's fine, but if you need help, I am here.*"

"*I know, thanks.*"

"Everything okay?" Jaykin asks.

"No. We have a situation. Hunters are outside of the village."

"Right," Jaykin gasps and looks around, "what are we going to do? We can't run."

"I know," he takes the small crystal out of his pocket and stares at Jaykin, "I have an idea, but you're not going to like it."

Kanaren jumps down a couple of steps at a time and bumps into Mordan, who is hiding behind a wall, out of view of the Hunters.

"Mordan, I told you to stay at the barn."

"Let me help."

"No, these people are too dangerous. If we don't sort this out properly, it could go very badly for the village."

"See, I told you, Mordan. He doesn't want our help," Pree says, running up to them. "I tried to stop him, Kanaren."

"We'll manage. I have a plan; I just hope it works," Kanaren says.

"Are they from the city?" Pree asks. Kanaren nods and she covers her mouth. "They've found us," she whispers.

"Mordan, can you keep in constant contact with me?"

"I'll do my best." Both the Elements nod together. Kanaren is just about to move away, when he thinks of something. He turns to them. "If anything goes wrong, promise me you will take Jaykin and whatever is in that crystal and get out of here."

"Crystal?" Pree asks.

"Not now, Pree," Mordan says. "I promise; now go." They make their way back to the barn.

At the entrance to the village stand three of the five Hunters: Slayed, Devy and Steg, who holds a woman, gagged with rope, and has a knife at her throat.

"Where is Kanaren?" Slayed shouts out. "I demand to see him, NOW! I know he's here!"
The whole village is there with bows raised at the Hunters and Oozoo at the very front. The Elder walks through, slowly, with the aid of his stick.

"Let her go!" he shouts as loud as he can.

"I asked you first old man. Where is Kanaren?" Slayed shouts, lifting his Q-Azar and pointing it straight at the Elder. Kanaren makes his way through the crowd of villagers as quickly as he can, hands raised to the Elder and to the Hunters.

"I'm here, Slayed. There is no need to hurt anyone." He positions himself between the Q-Azar and the Elder. "What do you want?" he asks glancing at the girl, then fixing the Hunters with a stare.

"You know exactly what we're here for," Slayed replies. "Emperor Lon demands that the crystal is returned to him, and if we don't get it back, you can be sure, we will hurt these people," Steg says, sneering and pointing his knife to the woman's neck again.

"Very well," Kanaren says, quickly raising his hands in defeat, "you can have the crystal back. I don't need it. There is no need for blood to be shed here. These people have done nothing wrong."

"You stole the crystal from Dreamora?" the

Elder shouts. He stares at Kanaren. "I trusted you," he says disappointedly, "and now you have put my people in danger!"

"We had no choice, Elder!" Kanaren replies. Now is the time to call, in silence, for help. *"Mordan, ask Jaykin if he's ready!"*

"Where's the boy?" Slayed asks.

"He isn't here," Kanaren replies.

Jaykin, still on the peak, is focusing on his hands.

"Come on Jaykin, you can do it," he says to himself. He tries to relax but he keeps feeling the pressure holding him back. He closes his eyes, remembering the time he spent with his father, the time when they were watching the Preyal Tournament, talking about creatures and what would be their best tactics to win. That's Jaykin's best memory of him and it makes him smile. He opens one eye to see if it is working. It is. A miniscule crystal has appeared. He opens the other eye to get a better view of it. It is growing fast, and within seconds, it reaches his own height; but is still too small for his purpose.

***

The Hunters are impatient.

"Feels like something is not right," Arma confides.

"Agreed," Steg says. "Feels like we're being led into a trap."

"Cool it you two," Slayed says "Tell us where the crystal is!" he yells at Kanaren.

"You can have it back but it's not here in the village!" Kanaren yells back.

"What are you saying?" the Elder asks.

"Not now Elder," Kanaren replies.

"He's lying," Arma says. "I know it's here."

"Tell us!" Slayed shouts, quickly taking out his Q-Azar and pointing it menacingly straight at Kanaren.

"Fine!" Kanaren says. "It's up on the peak!" and he points that way. Slayed points too, then rotates his hand. An engine starts up not so far away.

"You're a traitor to our people, Kanaren. I should not have told you about the crystal," the Elder says, his disgust obvious.

"Mordan, tell the Elder to meet you at their crystal to prove it's still there."

"Sure."

"Go and meet with Mordan," Kanaren whispers to the Elder.

"I will not leave my people in dan—," The Elder stops abruptly. Suddenly, he walks away, towards the secret room.

"You better not be plotting something, Kanaren," Slayed shouts. "Prepare for anything, you two."

"Mordan."

"I'm here."

"Please tell Jaykin to hide from the Hunters."

"Okay."

"Let the woman go!" Kanaren shouts. Slayed is about to say something when he presses a finger to his ear, listens briefly, and smiles. He nods to Steg, who then throws the woman away from him.

Oozoo goes to her aid.

"Move Kanaren," Steg says, waving his knife at him. "You know what needs to happen." Kanaren slowly walks towards them.

"Mordan, I'm going to have to leave you for the time being."

"Why?"

"They'll take me back to the city for trial."

"I'll help you—"

"No! Stick to the plan. Get the crystal, and get out of here, as far away as possible. I can't put you all at risk."

"But—"

"Don't worry about me, just look after Jaykin. He will know what to do next."

"Sure, we'll do that."

"Come on then, move it," Steg says. "No funny business either." Kanaren slowly raises his hands in front so they can place cuffs onto him.

"You know Lon will just throw me back out of the city," Kanaren says.

Slayed chuckles.

"Doubt that. I may use you as my creature for the Preyal Tournament instead," he says, while Steg secures the cuffs.

"Maybe chained up to the city wall; that'll be a good laugh," Steg grins at the thought.

"What about tying him to a turbine?" They all grunt and laugh. "So many possibilities."

"I'll last longer than all of you put together," Kanaren replies, trying to keep cool.

Steg pushes him forward, away from the village. The Elder returns just then. He has seen that the crystal is still in place in the secret room.

"Let him go!" he shouts.

Slayed shouts advice at the Elder.

"I suggest you stay out of this, old man, or we'll come back for you too." The Elder is silenced and all the villagers watch as the Hunters move away, with Kanaren as their prisoner.

In hiding, Jaykin breathes heavily, laying on the steps, watching as the other two Hunters prepare to lift the crystal.

"I can't believe they fell for it," he thinks to himself, breathing heavily and feeling dazed.

"*Are you okay Jaykin?*" Mordan asks.

"*I'm fine.*"

"*Good…But I must tell you, they have taken Kanaren.*"

"*No! We need to get him back.*" He tries to move but his body is aching all over.

"*His instructions were to get the crystal and get out of here.*"

"*I can't let them take him.*" He tries to move again. He manages to climb a couple of steps until someone grabs his foot and he suddenly falls into a deep sleep.

Chapter 15

This Knowledge is Legendary

Airborne, a few miles from the Keap, Kanaren is forced to the floor of the collector, by a vindictively grinning Steg. Kanaren manages to sit up against the metal wall and takes in his surroundings, while Steg can't resist taunting him.

"So, the famous Kanaren," he says, with mockery in his voice. "Not so famous now are you, running away with the emperor's crystal!"

"Yeah, how stupid do you have to be to do that," Creat says, sneering. "It's like number one in the rule book."

"Actually, it's eighth in the rule book," Kanaren says, coolly, and shakes his head, knowing too well it will provoke them, "and yes, I am, and always will be famous, unlike you idiots." He uses the wall to get to a standing position.

"Get back to where you belong, thief! On the floor, with your face eating the metal," Steg says, moving to grab onto Kanaren, but he dodges aside, and sticks out his foot, tripping Steg easily. He stumbles and his head smashes into the floor. Creat makes a move but Kanaren knees him in the stomach and he falls right next to Steg. They both cry out in pain, but neatly, side by side.

Arma stands up confidently from the corner, staring at Kanaren, and drawing his Q-Azar.

"Sit down and shut up and then you may still have your limbs by the time we get back," he says. Both the other two Hunters stagger up from the floor, brushing themselves off.

"Why don't we just throw him out now?" the bloody-nosed Steg says.

"Yeah," Creat agrees. Arma smirks.

"We need him alive, remember boys." He tilts his head slightly and has a creepy grin on his face. "But we can still have a shooting target." Kanaren then spots a Q-Azar tucked into Creat's jacket.

"I have another idea," Kanaren says. Suddenly, his hands come out of the cuffs and he sidekicks Steg in the stomach, winding him instantly. Kanaren grabs onto Creat, snatches the Q-Azar and points it at his head. It happens so fast, no one knows what is going on.

Arma takes aim at Kanaren but he's using Creat as a shield.

"Why did you have to be standing there?" Arma says angrily to Creat. "Get out of the way!"

"I can't!" Creat wines, "he'll shoot me!"

Kanaren slowly walks to the other side of the collector, still shielding himself with the reluctant Creat.

"Now I'll leave you to complete your fight," he says and quickly grabs onto a parachute, hooking it over his left arm. Then he aims towards the front of the collector and fires. Something explodes and he uses the distraction to bang Creat's head against the door release button. The wind rushes in and he holds on tight, still pointing the Q-Azar at the other Hunters.

"What is going on back here?" Slayed shouts,

entering from the next cabin. He spots Kanaren holding the helpless Creat.

"Say hi to Lon for me," Kanaren says, throwing Creat to the floor and leaping out.

"No!" Slayed shouts, and watches Kanaren fall.

"We need to turn around!" Arma shouts.

"We can't," Devy replies. "He's blown out our navigation system. If we turn around now, we won't find our way back. We need to fly straight."

"Damn you Kanaren!" Slayed says under his breath, punching the button on the other side of the collector with frustration. The door closes and he gives the other Hunters a withering look. "You had one job!" he says, anger in his voice. "When we get back to Dreamora, you're all fixing the collector! You got me?"

"Sorry Slayed," Creat says, as he picks himself up. "What do we do now?"

"Check if Steg is okay, and we keep going. We'll get him back, and this time, in a body bag!"

***

Jaykin wakes up in the barn. Pree has her hand on his forehead. He is about to ask about Kanaren when the Elder walks in.

"Ah, you're awake. How are you?"

"Better, thank you," he says, looking at Pree and she smiles back.

"I'm sorry about your friend," says the Elder. "Is there anything I can do to help you?"

"If we could have our weapons back, that would be a good start," Mordan says, standing behind

Pree.

"It's done," the Elder replies. "Anything else?"

"Actually," Jaykin says, "there is something."

"What is it?"

"Information. You have a crystal here, don't you?"

"We…do," the Elder is hesitant, wary.

"Are you aware of its power?" Pree asks.

"Yes," he sighs. "Please do not tell anyone about the crystal. It is very sacred to my people."

"We won't say anything, we promise," Pree says calmly.

"What power does it confer?" Mordan asks.

"It gives us knowledge…" Both the Elements look at one another with concern on their faces. The Elder looks confused. "What is it?"

"You need to know something very important, Elder," Pree says.

"Inside that crystal, is an Element," Mordan explains.

It leaves the Elder speechless for a moment, pointing at the Elements. "You, you were both in crystals too?" They nod.

"Pree was from Dreamora and Mordan was from a cave in the False Forest," Jaykin says, lifting himself up from the long grass.

"I see," the Elder says, pausing a moment to take in the information, then moving away. "I will need to reflect on this." Once he is out of view, Mordan has something to say.

"What is there to reflect on?"

"Whether to release the Element," Pree replies.

"Yes, I understand that, but surely it's an easy decision."

"No, it's not Mordan. These people have had the crystal for as long as we've been gone from these lands."

"What if he doesn't allow it?" Mordan asks.

"I don't know," Pree replies.

"We'll need to come up with a more forceful plan," Mordan says tapping his head.

"We can't do that to these people."

"Pree, there is a rare Element in that crystal. We have to do something."

"You know what Element they have?" Jaykin asks.

Both the Elements stop their bickering, reminded that Jaykin is still there.

"We do," Pree replies. "We are in reach of the rarest of all Elements."

"The Knowledge Element," Mordan says. "Unlike myself and Pree, where there are hundreds or thousands of Mind and Dream Elements, there is only a handful of them, and having one now would be extremely helpful."

"Why are these Elements so rare?" Jaykin asks.

"There were many once," Mordan says, gloomily.

"They were hunted down during the Great War, greatly diminishing their numbers," Pree says. "If we can only get to it. What do you think we should do Jaykin?"

"I don't think we're in a position to just take the crystal. Sorry, Mordan. Kanaren and I have done that once before, and it was an accident. Now we're exiled. It's just not worth it. So, I think we should see what the Elder has to say."

"I like you," Pree says and smiles, then looks over at Mordan. "He has brains."

Mordan sighs and shakes his head.

"Are there any more people to heal?" He looks away. "If it wasn't for me, he would be with Kanaren right now." Then he angrily walks off.

"I'm sorry about that. Mordan is still getting used to being here. Will you be all right without Kanaren?" Pree asks.

"I think I'll be okay but this wasn't part of his plan."

"He'll be fine," she says, and gives him a hug.

***

A few hours pass and darkness falls. Jaykin and the Elements are in the barn. They continue helping the villagers while they wait for a decision from the Elder. Oozoo interrupts their work.

"Jaykin, the Elder wishes to speak with you." Without waiting for a reply, he runs away.

Jaykin follows, approaching the main hut, the Elements close behind. He peers inside. The Elder sits on his throne and Oozoo stands nearby.

"Welcome Jaykin," the Elder says in a friendly tone. "Please come in." Jaykin enters followed by the Elements. "I have given it much thought and I have decided that we should open the crystal." Both the Elements and Jaykin smile with pleasure and relief.

"That's great news Elder," Mordan says.

"I do not agree with this," Oozoo says.
The Elder stares at him.

"And why not?"

"The crystal has been in our village for thousands of years. Are we really going to do this to our people because of outsiders?" Oozoo replies.

"Yes," the Elder says. "There is a living being inside that crystal. We have been harvesting its power all this time. We will free the Element, Oozoo, if you like it or not."

"This isn't right!" Oozoo yells.

"You will be quiet!" the Elder yells back.
Oozoo's face reddens, either with embarrassment or extreme anger or both. "I apologise for my grandson; he still has a lot to learn."

"It's understandable," Mordan says, "But, back to the crystal, when were you thinking about releasing this Element?" Pree looks at him in disgust.

"I was thinking in a few days' time. We can have a ceremony," the Elder says.

"Great idea," Oozoo says, sarcastically. "The children will put up decorations." He sighs out loud and shakes his head. Mordan is about to speak when Kanaren bursts through.

"I think it would be best to do it soon Elder. Like…tomorrow, for example."
Everyone stares at him, startled. He seems weary and breathless but Jaykin's face lights up. He is happy and relieved Kanaren is back safe.

"Ah, Kanaren," the Elder says. "Welcome back."

"Thank you…but with all due respect…we plan to leave here soon, but we would like to be at the ceremony and meet the Element if you don't mind."

"Hmm." The Elder considers. "Yes, I agree. The sooner the better."

"Excellent, then with your permission, we will prepare for our long journey ahead. I believe our work is done here." In his weariness, he leans a little on Jaykin's shoulder for stability.

"Your people are all clear of the virus now," Pree informs the Elder.

"That is great news. Thank you so much for your help. Of course, you can prepare, Kanaren. You have done enough for us. Get plenty of rest for tomorrow."

"We will and thank you." Kanaren bows and turns to the others. "Let's go."

"Before you go…." Everyone stops in their tracks. "…how exactly do you release an Element from the crystal?" the Elder asks, reasonably. It feels eerily quiet and Kanaren takes his time to think of an answer. They all exchange glances.

"Jaykin," Kanaren says eventually, "please tell me you still have that crystal?" The Elder leans forward in his throne, intrigued. Both the Elements look at one another, slightly confused. Jaykin, now wide-eyed, nervously places his hand in his pocket. He rummages around and takes out the small crystal he made that day, and hands it to Kanaren. "This is the source of the power," Kanaren says, turning and holding it up towards the Elder.

"How does it work?" the Elder asks.

"Crystals give out powers; this one absorbs and creates crystal."

"Fascinating," the Elder says. "Can we have a demonstration?"

"It's already created a crystal today," Jaykin interrupts.

"I think it would be best to leave it till tomorrow," Kanaren replies, then throws it back to Jaykin, who nearly drops it. "We, don't want to spoil the moment, do we?"

"I like the sound of that," the Elder says, unable to conceal his excitement.

"Come on guys, let's go," Kanaren says.
The Elder relaxes on his throne and smiles.

"Things will need to change around here," he says to himself.

"I agree," Oozoo whispers to himself.

As they walk away, Kanaren sees that Pree and Mordan are looking confused.

"You probably have many questions," he says.

"You're going to have to explain to us about that crystal soon," Pree says.

"And that little thing about an invasion," Mordan says.

"I will, but not right now. First things first. We need to get ready to go tomorrow."

"Fine," Mordan says, "but you can't get out of this conversation." Both the Elements turn towards the barn. Jaykin and Kanaren make their way back to their hut.

"Quick thinking about the crystal back there,"

Jaykin says.

"It was the only thing I could think of; we needed an excuse for your special technique. Good work on the crystal by the way."

"Thanks, I actually didn't know if I could do it, and on time. It took a lot out of me."

"I had complete confidence in you."

"What if I didn't?"

"No need to think about that now."

"How do you know the Hunters are not going to come back?"

"I took out their navigation system, so they can do nothing until they get to the city, but we'll be long gone by then."

"How did you get away from the Hunters?"

"The problem with many Hunters is that they compare themselves to each other, always thinking they're doing better than you, but they're just bullies and that's their weakness."

Mordan and Pree make their way back to the barn.

"*Are you going to rest?*" Pree asks as they enter.

"*I will soon,*" Mordan replies. "*I thought about going to the peak and having a good look around.*"

"*That sounds nice. How are you feeling?*"

"*I feel fine, just a lot to take in, you know.*"

"*Yes, I know what you mean,*" she smiles. "*I'm going to help the villagers sleep.*" She sits on the floor of the barn cross-legged. She places her hands together and closes her eyes. "*Have a good night,*" she says.

"*You too Pree,*" he replies, and walks out.

Day 6

Very early in the morning; a collector enters the city of Dreamora; with a crystal as cargo. The Hunters are heading to the centre of the city. A few early risers gather, looking up curiously at the collector, and the Hunters slowly lower the crystal onto its original golden plinth. A loud clunking sound echoes through the streets.

***

In the Palace, a Knight approaches Emperor Lon's bedroom door. He hesitates and looks around. He takes a moment to think about it then knocks, then listens.

"What is it?" Lon shouts from within.

"Emperor Lon, there are Hunters in the Palace. Suddenly the door bursts open and Lon strides out with just a robe on, moving fast. He heads to his throne and sees the five Hunters advance towards him, standing and then bowing low. Some of the Guards from the entrance are standing with them, including Lesh.

"Do you have news? Well, spit it out! Come on!" Lon shouts, not letting the Hunters speak immediately.

"Emperor Lon, we have returned with the crystal to your city, as I promised," Slayed says and allows himself a smirk of satisfaction.

"Ah," Lon chuckles back and holds up his arms to them, "I knew I could count on you," he says calmly, "but what about that—" he clicks his fingers. Lesh's ears perk up.

"Kanaren?" Slayed fills in for him.

"Yes, him, where is he?"

"Well, although we have got back the crystal, we have unfortunately not brought back Kanaren or the boy." Lesh sighs in relief and grins slightly.

"No matter," Lon says, and waves his hand around. "I will keep the wanted posters out. They will not be allowed back in this city for the rest of their lives, nor their families for that matter. No, focus on the tournament in a few days' time. I want you all to be prepared."

***

Jaykin wakes up to a strange noise. He sits up and tries to work out what it is. He looks for Kanaren but he is nowhere to be seen. He hears drums playing and they are getting louder. He pokes his head out of the hut and, with astonishment, sees the villagers outside, singing and dancing together. He slowly makes his way out. He spots Kanaren talking to the Elder and approaches him.

"Ah, Jaykin," the Elder says. "Welcome. What do you think?" he says, indicating a huge throne, standing alongside his own. It is made of stone and is very finely carved. It has intricate detail in every millimetre and must have taken many hours to complete.

"Is that for the—"

"It is indeed; ready to be welcomed to its new

world," the Elder says excitedly.

"Morning Jaykin," Kanaren says.

"Morning Kanaren."

"I was just saying to the Elder that you're more than happy to open the crystal for the villagers." Jaykin nods at the Elder with feigned confidence, but has a worrying feeling in his stomach.

"Yes, thank you Jaykin," the Elder says. "We're ready when you are."

"Oh, okay," Jaykin hesitates. The villagers are gathering round, leaving a small walkway to the crystal, which is shining bright in the sun. Standing next to it are both the Elements, their faces a mixture of expectation and doubt.

"Greetings everyone—" the Elder announces, waving his hand for silence.

"Are you ready for this?" Kanaren whispers.

"Not really but I'll manage. I'm used to performing in front of hundreds of people," Jaykin responds sarcastically.

"You'll be fine. Just remember to place the smaller crystal onto the larger one first, then place your hands on it," he whispers. Jaykin nods his head.

"I won't forget," he replies, obediently.

"Because if you don't, we'll be in even more trouble than we are already."

"No pressure," Jaykin says to himself. He very slowly walks towards the crystal, looking at every single villager on the way, his legs feeling like jelly and his heart beating very fast. That or it's the crystal. The pulsating sensation triggers again, but now it feels comfortable for him. He gets halfway and places his hand in his pocket to get out the smaller crystal. He lifts his head, eyes wide open, his hand rummages around. It's not there! He looks back at the Elder and Kanaren.

"I don't have the crystal!" he shouts. Kanaren is about to reply when Oozoo interrupts. "Oh no, we won't be able to open the crystal now!" There is mockery in his voice.

"You have it!" Mordan shouts.

"No, I don't!" Oozoo replies, defiantly.

"I've read your mind! Don't lie!" Mordan shouts.

"*We need to be careful here,*" Pree says, using Morden's technique. "*We won't be able to defend ourselves with so many people.*"

Oozoo lifts his bow over his head and is about to take a shot at Jaykin when Mordan holds his hand out and points it at him. Oozoo realizes he can't move. His hunting friends all point their bows at the Elements.

"Release him!" one shouts. Mordan persists, and with no control over his body, Oozoo watches himself place his hand in the fold of his clothing and pull out the crystal.

"How are you doing this?" Oozoo shouts, trying his best to fight it, but Mordan is too strong. He extends his arm and drops the crystal, which thuds and rolls around on the ground.

Suddenly, two pairs of stony hands burst out of the ground, right next to the Elements' feet, and grab on tight to their ankles. Both the Elements fall to their knees.

Oozoo realises he is back in control of his body. Seeing the Elements are in trouble, he runs away.

"What the…what's going on?" shouts Kanaren.

"My powers are being drained," Mordan says, breathlessly.

"I feel weak!" Pree calls out.

They struggle to get up. The earth around them crumbles and starts to rise. Two huge shapes, looking exactly like Defenders, appear as dust and stones drop off them. They let go of the Elements and use Pree's powers against them, sending them to sleep. The villagers, fearful for their lives, begin to run away, but the Defenders use their stolen powers to halt them. People drop to the ground, falling asleep; some scream out that they are on fire, yet there is no visible sign of it. Some try and help their friends or family and many run off in fear. There is chaos everywhere. Villagers with bows loose arrows at the Defenders but with no effect.

"Elder, get your people out of here, now!" Kanaren shouts.

"I'll try!" the Elder replies, unable to hide his own fear and powerlessness. "What are those things?" But Kanaren doesn't reply. Instead, he runs towards them.

Jaykin is on the ground, trying to locate the small crystal. He spots it, but it is difficult to reach in the melee. Someone kicks it. It stops and Jaykin is about to grab it but someone else gets there first. It is Oozoo.

"I won't let you take away our crystal!" he says

determinedly. Then he draws a familiar sword. It is Jaykin's. "Nice weapon by the way."

"Give me back my stuff!" Jaykin shouts.

"No!" Oozoo says and grins. He points the sword at Jaykin.

"Jaykin!" Kanaren shouts, running towards the Defenders. "Catch!" He throws something over to him and he catches it. Immediately it extends as if electrified. It is Kanaren's own sword. Jaykin grins while he looks up at Oozoo.

"I don't want to fight you," Jaykin says, "but you don't give me a choice."

Kanaren continues running towards the great crystal and hides behind it, out of view of the Defenders, who are still attacking villagers. He makes slight adjustments with his air weapon on his wrist, twisting it and turning it, then pulls out a Q-Azar from his jacket, mentally thanking Creat for the donation.

"Which one stole Pree's power?" he asks himself, looking around to the right side of the crystal, then to the left, searching the crowd. He spots the culprit and waits for it to face the other away, then sprints straight towards it. He slides underneath its legs curling up into a ball and then stands quickly, firing his air weapon. The Defender is hurled metres into the air and lands hard on the top of the great crystal. The Defender crumbles into pieces. Kanaren faces the other Defender, and before it can use Mordan's powers, he raises the Q-Azar, aiming at its arm, and fires it repeatedly.

"Oozoo!" the Elder shouts. "Give Jaykin the crystal or I will banish you.!"

"No!" he shouts back. "These outsiders are taking over our village!"

Pree only just manages to open her eyes as the Defender has placed her into a daydream. She spins and sways, trying to stay awake. She places her hands on her head and shakes, waking herself up. She spots Mordan next to her and she does the same thing to him.

"Pree," he says. "Are you alright?"

"I'm fine. Where are the others?" she asks.

He focuses for a time, scanning the villagers' minds.

"Jaykin is fighting with Oozoo."

"What? Why?"

"He's trying to get the small crystal back."

Jaykin and Oozoo clash swords. They fight it out briefly until Oozoo drops to the ground. Both the sword and the small crystal fall out of his hands. Jaykin quickly retrieves them both, placing the two swords, folded, upon his back. He sprints to the great crystal, weaving his way through all the villagers. As he reaches it, he takes out the smaller one. He suddenly feels all eyes on him and his nerves kick in. The crowd watches him slowly place the small crystal onto the much larger one. His hand covers it and the crystal starts to crack.

Chapter 16

You'll Be Missed

The crystal quickly disappears and a strong vibration is felt by everyone as the new Element is revealed. It falls to its knees, gasping and breathing in much-needed air. Eventually, it lets out a deep sigh, and takes in the scene.

"Fascinating," he says.

He stands and stretches his body, all nine feet of it. His height is the only characteristic similar to the other Elements. On his back, he has a large sharp battle axe and a shield, both embellished with beautiful gold carvings. Just below the weapons, scrolls hang from golden ribbons. There is something odd about his skin too. It is cream-coloured, but with strange markings upon it which look like script. Jaykin, who is closest, cannot understand what the words mean. His clothing is covered in symbols and he wears a gold circular badge with a scroll in the centre. As he moves, his whole being glimmers. The Element looks down at Jaykin and smiles.

"Hello," he says, in a voice which is kindly, and strangely compelling. Jaykin is thinking he could listen to it for hours.

"Hi," Jaykin replies, curiously.

"You're wearing odd clothing," the Element says frankly but inoffensively, then realises he is being stared at by hundreds of people. The villagers have stopped in their tracks and remain totally silent. They all start to bow to the Element, who smiles kindly. "Oh, there is no need for that," he says.

"They see you as a saviour," Jaykin says.

"I'm no saviour," the Element replies. "Where am I exactly?"

"You are in the beautiful village on Mount Keap," the Elder answers, seated on his throne.

"Mount Keap?" the Element whispers, trying to work out how he had got there.

"Welcome. It is wonderful to finally meet you!" the Elder says, approaching the Element with arms wide.

"It's an honour to meet you all," he responds. He notices Pree and Mordan, politely greets them by placing his arm to his chest and smiles at them. They reciprocate.

"*I can't believe my eyes, Mordan. A Knowledge Element. This is a dream come true.*"

"*I know. This journey is becoming more interesting by the day.*"

"How did I get here?" the Element asks.

"I will tell you the story," the Elder says. He claps his hands and the crowd draws back, clearing the way to the two thrones. There is no sign of Oozoo. Pree, Mordan, Jaykin and Kanaren regroup.

"Now what?" Mordan asks.

"We wait," Kanaren replies.

"I'm not so sure if the new Element will go with us," Pree says.

"Me neither," Mordan says. "He's been here for too long."

"We'll see," Kanaren says, staring at the

thrones and their occupants. From the corner of his eye, he spots Oozoo just behind them.

***

Emperor Lon stands beside the crystal on a large stage, apparently presiding over some sort of ceremony, celebrating its safe return, to the accompaniment of a noisy crowd.

"Welcome back," Lon says, talking to the crystal. He slowly turns to the cheering crowd. "Thank you, thank you," he says, trying to calm them down. "Today is a great day. We finally get the heart of our great city back." He places his hand on it. He stops suddenly and slides his hand across it. Something is odd. Then he looks at it all over. He places both hands on it. "Wait," he turns to the Hunters. "Is this some kind of joke?" he says, grinding his teeth. The Hunters exchange glances. He is getting annoyed for some reason and they start to worry.

"What is it?" Slayed asks.

"That is not my crystal!" He turns to a Guard, waving his hands. "Get these people out of here!" he shouts. There is confusion in the guard.

"Yes, sir."

"Now, move!" Lon claps his hands. "Faster!" he shouts.

The Hunters all look at each other. *How could we get this wrong?* they are thinking.

"It's a fake!" Lon yells, pointing at the crystal.

"Emperor Lon, we will sort this, I promise you," Slayed says.

Lon presses right up against Slayed's face and stares menacingly into his eyes.

"Make it so, Hunter, or else I will ensure you pay for this for the rest of your life!" He stomps off.

"We will not return until we have it, Emperor Lon, I swear," Slayed says sternly, to Lon's back, raising his voice slightly. He then turns to his colleagues. "This is Kanaren's doing. Time to repay him."

***

Jaykin and the others wait to greet the Element before they leave. He has been engaged with the Elder for some time.

"I'll let the Elder know we're ready to leave," Kanaren says. "I'll be back soon."

"I'll go with you," Jaykin says. They find the Elder and the Element happily talking together.

"Ah, Kanaren, Jaykin, welcome." the Elder says.

"Elder, we will be on our way very soon. I just wanted to thank you for welcoming us to your village and for your hospitality," Kanaren says.

"You are all welcome here anytime," the Elder says, smiling graciously. "Where will you go?"

"We're not sure—" Kanaren replies.

"We will be heading northwest," Jaykin interrupts.

Kanaren frowns at him.

"Really?" the Elder asks.

"I was about to say, we may go to the city of Q-Ara, but we haven't discussed it yet," Kanaren replies, giving Jaykin a disapproving look.

"Maybe for the best. You do know what is in the northwest?"

"I know of the dangers there, Elder," Kanaren replies.

The Element slowly rises from his new throne.

"Forgive me for my rudeness. I did not introduce myself earlier. My name is, Irown."

"Good to meet you, Irown. We're—" Kanaren is about to introduce himself.

"Pleasure to meet you also, Kanaren and Jaykin," Irown interrupts. "You are on a journey, correct?" he asks with interest in his voice.

"We are," Kanaren replies.

"Yes, to find the Elements," Jaykin says.

"Interesting. Something tells me that this is a very important journey."

"You could say that," Kanaren says. Irown walks towards them and then turns to face the Elder.

"I think it would be in my best interest to join these adventurers." He turns to Kanaren and Jaykin. "If you don't mind?"

"It would be an honour to have you join us," Kanaren replies, but is curious to see what the Elder's reaction is.

"Oh really?" The Elder says, surprised.

"Yes," Irown replies. "I think it would do me good, and these people. My quest for knowledge is a powerful instinct." The Elder sighs.

"I was hoping you wouldn't say that."

"No, you can't go!" Oozoo shouts, appearing out of nowhere.

"I'm sorry young man but this is my decision," Irown says, firmly.

"But you are ours. My people found you here and we've looked after you."

"And I thank you for that, but I am no one's property and I must make my own decisions." The Elder lifts himself out of his throne.

"Oozoo, let Irown go. I feel sorry too, but he is right."

Both Pree and Mordan approach. "Are we ready to go?" Mordan asks.

"We are," Kanaren replies.

"Irown is coming with us," Jaykin says.

"And you must be Irown?" Mordan asks. "It's an absolute honour to meet you."

"Likewise, Mordan and Pree," Irown says. "I have heard about all the help you gave to the villagers."

While the Elements are greeting one another, Jaykin approaches the Elder.

"I have a question I hope to ask you, if you don't mind?"

"Of course, what can I help you with?"

"Well, I thought as you have knowledge of the crystals, would you happen to know how old they are?"

All the Elements and Kanaren listen for the answer.

"Well, I'm actually not sure. I think it's a few thousand years.

"Let's find out," Irown says, and turns to the Elder. "Where did my crystal lay?"

"I will show you." They all follow the Elder to the sacred room. "Here."

Hundreds of lines are visible on the wall, where the

crystal was embedded. Irown places his hand on the stone and wipes across it.

"What do you see?" Mordan asks.

"Counting," Irown replies, concentrating. They all wait a few moments until he says. "I think, in the range of nine to ten thousand years."

"How do you know that?" Jaykin asks.

"The layers of earth. Each one represents a hundred years or so."

"Now we know. Ten thousand years." Mordan says, sounding slightly choked up and staring at Pree. He walks away.

"We should go now," Pree says. Irown agrees.

"We have a lot to discuss."

They all move away, to be met by the villagers, to say their goodbyes. Oozoo stands in front, tears down his face. Irown kneels down to him.

"Young Oozoo, what's wrong?"

"You have been guiding our people for thousands of years. Please don't go."

"I know it's difficult." He pauses and smiles. "I have heard you are a great gatherer?" Oozoo, a little flushed, makes no reply, while Irown searches through his scrolls. He selects one. "Here, take this. Let it guide you for now."

Oozoo takes it and gasps, then unravels it. His face looks confused.

"But I don't understand it; it's in a different language," he says showing it to him.

"I know," Irown replies. "That's for you to work out while I'm gone. I have given this to you because you're strong and you think of your people first, not yourself. Stay that way." He stands and starts gently waving to all the villagers as he walks down to Jaykin and the others. He stops and turns. "Oh, and Oozoo!" he shouts. "Look after the village for me while I'm away!"

"I will," the boy smiles, clutching the scroll hard to his chest. Jaykin notices Kanaren walking up to Oozoo, giving him something and whispering too.

"Thank you all for waiting," Irown says to the others. "Saying goodbye can be difficult." Kanaren joins them.

"We should make a move." Suddenly, a little girl runs up to Irown.

"Please don't go, Mr El - e - ment," she says struggling to say the word. Irown stops and looks down to see the minuscule child holding his leg and a huge smile goes across his face. She must be about three or four.

"Oh, hello there little one," he says. She looks up at him with tears streaming down her face.

"I wanted to see you," she says sniffing. Irown kneels to her level with his hand covering most of her back, then looks up to see all the village out to say goodbye.

"It's all right," he says firmly and stands with the little one on his shoulder. "I am sorry to be leaving after a brief hello, but this isn't a goodbye forever. I must go on a new journey now and I promise I'll be back with you all and with many stories to tell." He places the little girl onto the ground gently and moves off.

As they head off, Jaykin cannot resist asking:

"What did you give Oozoo, Kanaren?"

"My sword."

"What, why?"

"He's good with a weapon and he needs it."

"But don't you need it more?"

"No, I can always make a new one."

***

Light-years away, on the small planet of Edash, vessels start to leave. Inside the leading spaceship, the darkness is lit only by the control panel. A door opens and someone walks through.

"My lords, all is prepared on the surface with our new base. The Elements worked through the night to finish the build. We now have control of this planet," the commander announces.

"Excellent," the Element chuckles from the darkened chair. "Good, good."

"Are we ready to set off to the binary planet system?" the human asks.

"We are ready my lord. The scouts are ready to be sent on your word," the commander says.

"Begin," The Element says.

"Of course—"

"Unless…" the Element stops to think and looks towards the human, "…you go with them? You can have these two planets."

The human smirks back.

"Prepare my ship," he says to the commander. "I will leave immediately."

"Yes, my lord."

"Oh, and I know what to do with the people from Edash," the human states.

"Set them to work?" the Element asks.

"Exactly."

"You know, I think that is a very good idea," the Element says.

In the depths of the spaceship, sounds of people moving around, crying, and groaning, chains rattling in every cell, can be heard. In one, the most remote, dark cell, someone is on their knees with their arms spread up high, in chains.

Chapter 17

Seventeen Types

They make their way down the mountainside. Jaykin walks behind Irown, and looks cautiously at the handful of scrolls under the great big battle axe.

"Irown, what are those scrolls for?" he asks.

"They're to keep notes while I travel. Some things are worth recording. All Knowledge Elements have these."

"What are they about?"

"All sorts, but no one can read them except for me, as it can be very…sensitive material."

"Does it have anything about the Defenders?"

"Defenders?"

"Yes," Mordan says. "We keep getting attacked by these great stony beings every time we find a crystal."

"It's like it's protecting the crystal," Pree says.

"Ah, I see. Yes, I think I do know something about them but let me just check." He pauses to sift through his scrolls, mumbling words as he checks them off. "Hmm, I don't seem to have anything on them. What I do know though, is that we call them Guardians. Similar meaning to the name you've given it."

"We've called it that for thousands of years," Kanaren says.

"Guardians?" Jaykin asks. "It sounds better."

"I have heard of them but have never seen one

before," Irown replies, "I would like to. They sound intriguing."

"Why have we not heard of them?" Mordan asks.

"They were myths. No one has ever seen them," Irown replies, "until now."

"So, what are they exactly and where do they come from?" Jaykin asks.

"I have no idea, but it has been said that they have always been here, from the time of creation. They guard, defend, protect; whatever you want to call it; the most important things in the land."

"Which is why we need to be vigilant," Kanaren says. "They're powerful."

"Yes," Mordan says, "very. It absorbed our powers."

"I clearly need to learn more about them," Irown says.

"Talking of learning," Mordan says, "when were you going to tell us about the invasion?" He stares at both Jaykin and Kanaren.

"Another war?" Irown gasps.

"Hold on!" Kanaren replies, "I only told Jaykin about it a few days ago. I don't even know if it will happen. We're in this position by pure accident."

"Why didn't you tell us about it?" Mordan persists.

"The threat of invasion was a secret shared by me, Jaykin and the leaders of both worlds. But now you seem to be aware of it, I may as well tell you all that I know."

He explains in detail about the videos and the letters. They are left speechless.

"So, what are your thoughts?" Kanaren asks.

"Are we prepared?" Irown asks.

Jaykin stays quiet and lets Kanaren answer.

"No," he sighs, "but persuading the leaders of the cities to co-operate, and finding the Elements could help."

"Then that's what we'll do," Mordan says.

"That's exactly what we are doing," Kanaren replies. Irown is not convinced.

"It may not even be enough."

"But it's worth a try," Jaykin says.

"You're right Jaykin. We can't give up." Irown scans the landscape thoughtfully. "This land is a very different place now." They resume the journey, walking and talking, trying to come up with plans to help prepare for the invasion.

***

Halfway down the mountain, Pree stops in her tracks, a perplexed expression on her face. She has something on her mind.

"Irown, what were you doing before you woke up here?" she asks.

"I was on a long journey. Like this one, I guess. My group and I were about to enter the Unknown Lands of Izara. We were searching for new territory, somewhere we could hide from the Great War. We found some astonishing places; many that held very powerful creatures that even the strongest of the

Elements would struggle with. We had just managed to find a colony of humans, not so different from the Keap Tribe. They barely survived there, but somehow managed it. That is the last thing I recall before I ended up here. Strangely though, I don't remember how I got here. It feels as if I was…asleep."

"Yes, it felt like that for me," Pree says.

"Me too," Mordan says.

"The Great War. What happened?" Irown asks. Both the other Elements shrug their shoulders. "The Elements? The Solutions? What happened to them all?"

"We don't know," Pree says. "I am fearful that we may be the only ones left."

"No one knows for sure," Kanaren says, extremely blunt. Everyone looks at him, questioning looks in their eyes.

"There must be something," Irown says. "We must have left something behind, some sign of our existence. No one can vanish into thin air. Especially thousands of Elements."

"There is no evidence left of the Great War; no written record, no physical evidence, nothing has been found," Kanaren sighs. "Many wars have been fought here and the latest was known as The War of the Three, where all the cities of Izara fought against one another. That was about four hundred years ago."

"So, what are you trying to say?" Mordan says. "We fought for our lives trying to save the ones we love and cherish, the land we lived, loved and grew for thousands of years, so the future generations can completely forget about us? Or throw away? What's the point of the Elements' existence if we will not be remembered?" He walks away in anger.

"Now I wish I had stayed in the past," Pree says and follows him.

"Sorry but maybe you all destroyed each other," Jaykin says.

"But every single Solution and Element disappearing with no trace?" Irown says, shaking his head. "It just doesn't make any sense."

"Except for the crystals," Jaykin says.

"You're right. The only thing that remains from the Great War is us," he sticks his hand out. "Jaykin, may I have a look at that crystal?"

Jaykin looks towards Kanaren who nods permission. He shuffles through his pocket, feeling its slight rough edges. He hesitates to give it away, in case Irown finds out the truth.

"Sure," he says, placing it into his hand gently. Irown plays with the crystal in one hand and rolls it around with one finger.

"Fascinating," All eyes are on him.

"What is?" Jaykin asks.

Irown lifts it close.

"Someone or something has done a very good job by collecting certain Elements and somehow placing us all into this unbreakable crystal." He squeezes it. "It's like…" He pauses and thinks. "They knew what was going to happen in the Great War, so they tried to save or protect us." The others look at each other wondering why they haven't thought of that.

"Also," Mordan says, re-joining the group, "an item like that cannot absorb crystal, it's impossible."

"Actually Mordan, there is a possibility it's from our time. We still do not know if it's something from the other lands." Irown says and looks up at Raziz.

"Where did you get it from, Jaykin?" Irown asks, but before he can reply, Kanaren interrupts.

"I found it on my travels on Raziz," he says. "Jaykin managed to accidentally acquire it. Now I've given him the title of 'Guardian of the Crystal." He holds out his hand for the crystal and Irown places it in his palm. Kanaren continues. "We still have much to learn on this and the Great War. Mordan, you'll be remembered again one day but it won't be from *that* war." He plays with the crystal throwing it up in the air. "Save your stories until we protect both the worlds and save our homes." He gives the crystal back to Jaykin and stares into his eyes. "Until then, protect yourselves and everyone around you. Don't doubt or linger, because we don't know what's out there or coming for us and we must be ready for anything." Jaykin feels his hair stand up all over his body.

"Good point there, Kanaren. I will keep thinking about this," Irown says. "I would very much like to observe this 'absorbing'. Next time we come across another crystal, would that be possible," Irown asks.

"Of course," Jaykin replies hesitantly.

"We should continue on our way," Kanaren says.

***

When the group stops to rest, eat, and drink, Jaykin takes the opportunity to look carefully at all the Elements, as if comparing them.

"Irown, how many types of Elements are there?" he asks.

"Let's see." Mordan starts counting on his fingers using both hands. He stops a moment, then says, "altogether it's about—"

"Seventeen types of Elements," Irown interrupts.

"Yes, that's right," Mordan agrees. "That actually does sound like quite a lot."

"Yes," Irown says. "And I've met every single type. Every Element is unique."

"What types are there?" Jaykin asks.

"Well, there are five classes: The Mystics, the Observers, the Conjurers, the Shifter and lastly the Evolutioner," Irown says.

"So, what category do you guys come under?" Jaykin asks, turning to Pree and Mordan.

"We are under the mystics," Pree smiles. Irown continues.

"There are four types of Mystic Element. Mordan and Pree are the Mind and Dream. Then there are the two others, Telekinesis, and the Gravity Elements. Mystics can reach considerable distances using their mind powers. Then there are the three Observers: Sense and Light Elements," Irown places his hands on his chest, "and like myself, the Knowledge Elements. There was only a handful left of us. We observe our surroundings and have the power to retain all knowledge."

"What about the Conjurers?" Jaykin asks.

"There are several types and they can be very powerful."

"Hey, so can we," Mordan says.

"Of course, you are, Mordan but I would say Pree is slightly stronger," Irown smiles. Mordan looks crestfallen. Pree laughs out loud. "So, for the Conjurers there are Ice, Water, Air, Fire, Lava, Earth, Metal and Nature."

"They sound amazing," Jaykin says.

"These Elements can conjure up specific types of powers and they can also manipulate their surroundings."

"What do you mean by that?" Jaykin asks.

"For example," he looks around on the pathway and spots a small stick. He picks it up. "A Nature Element would be able to do many things with this. They could re-plant it and make it grow, mould it into any weapon or even a sheet of armour." He passes it to Jaykin, who looks doubtful.

"All from one stick?" he asks and looks over to Kanaren who hasn't said a word in a while. "I'm looking forward to meeting one."

"Hopefully we'll find a conjurer soon, so you can see their power for yourself," Mordan says.

"There are two groups left. Both have one Element in each of them. In Shifter, there is the Beast Element, which can transform into any creature. And, lastly, and the most important, is the Evolutioner, the Life Element."

"Who can heal any wound, and also the only Element to evolve humans into Solutions," Pree says.

"Wow," Jaykin says. "They all sound amazing. There is a lot too."

"There is," Irown says, "and that makes seventeen all together."

"Seventeen," Jaykin whispers, awed by the possibility of meeting them all.

"Do you know what Element you want to be yet?" Mordan asks.

"Mordan!" Pree shouts. "You can't ask Jaykin that now!"

"Why not? He may have really liked the sound of one in particular," he coughs. "Mind Element," he coughs again.

"They all sound phenomenal. How did you decide?" Jaykin asks.

"It was easy for me," Mordan says. "I met a Mind Element when I was a young boy. After that, I always wanted to be one."

"Same for me, to be a Dream Element," Pree says. "I've always liked to help people if I can."

"Most people make their decisions based on their profession," Irown says. "For example, a blacksmith would probably like to become a Metal or Fire Element, or a farmer would probably pick the Nature Element. For myself, I had many professions, I just wanted to know everything, so it was an easy decision for me."

"I don't really have a profession yet," Jaykin says, thoughtfully.

"Well, you have plenty of time to think about it," Pree says, then gives Mordan a meaningful stare. Jaykin looks over at Kanaren who is still quiet.

"What would you choose Kanaren?" He doesn't reply, seeming to be distracted by other thoughts.

"Is something wrong Kanaren?" Pree asks.

"Sorry, I'm just thinking about the next part of our journey," he replies. All the time that Jaykin has spent with him, he has never seen Kanaren so pale in the face.

"The Elder warned us about it. What was he talking about?" Irown asks.

"The Nest," Kanaren replies.

"What? We can't go there!" Jaykin explains.

"Why not?" Pree asks.

"Never heard of the place," Irown says. "I'm intrigued."

"It's miles of land, inhabited by all the creatures in the world. Everyone on both the planets knows that," Jaykin says.

"He's right. It's the most dangerous place on Izara," Kanaren says. "It's not a place for any human, nor any Element."

"I don't want to go now," Jaykin says.

"Why do I have a bad feeling in my stomach all of a sudden?" Mordan says.

"We will see when we get there," Kanaren says. "It won't take us long."

***

A couple of hours pass and they can see their destination ahead.

"Holy Izara!" Irown says.

"Oh my!" Pree gasps, covering her mouth.

"That's The Nest?" Mordan asks.

"Yes," Kanaren replies bluntly. "You know what I mean now."

They look over a vast terrain with luxuriant trees surrounding long grassy meadows. A vast array of creatures, small and large, roam the land, calmly and peacefully. This is unexpected, and unusual.

"Scordos; rogsprinters; growlers, korbas and bladesters." Irown is impressed.

"And our good friends, barkas and scarrags," Kanaren says and turns to Jaykin. "We are not going to be able to get through there. We will need to go around them."

"But I think there is a crystal in the middle of that forest," Jaykin says, out of the blue.

"Really, how can you tell?" Irown asks.

"Well, every crystal that we have encountered so far has released its powers; Pree was making people fall asleep, Mordan was creating false visions in our heads and the Keap villagers were very knowledgeable thanks to you, Irown. Earlier you said there is a Beast Element, right? Could that affect the creatures here?"

"Yes, that's correct." They all gaze at the creatures roaming peacefully together. "You might be right Jaykin," Irown says. "An unbelievably powerful Element back in the day."

"I say we go straight through the creatures and release the Beast Element," Mordan says, clenching his fist at the group, thinking it's a great idea.

"We won't be able to get through there," Kanaren says. "We won't survive the first wave."

"So, what is your plan then?" Mordan replies.

"I think we should go east, then north, to the Misty Marsh, it'll be safer."

"Then that's what we'll do," Irown says.

"We will have to come back here at some point," Jaykin says.

"We will," Kanaren replies.

***

It takes them the rest of the day, slowly but surely and extremely quietly, making their way around The Nest. Luckily for them, they only engage with one creature during the long trip: a scordos. Mordan, unfortunately, accidentally steps on its flat tail and nearly startles the whole Nest. But Pree manages to quickly put it to sleep and they scarper. The last thing they need is thousands of raging creatures in pursuit.

Day 7

Back in the village of Mount Keap, very early in the morning, the people wake up to a loud engine noise.

"I know that sound," the Elder says. "Keep all the children inside," he instructs one of the villagers. Many look out of their huts and spot a collector hovering. The Elder watches it as it descends quickly. Dust flies all over the place and it damages some of the buildings as it lands. The Hunters all jump out of the side of the collector pointing their Q-Azars. Slayed paces up to the Elder, sliding his sword out from behind him and pointing it straight at his face.

"Where is the lying, conniving barrag?" Slayed asks, anger in his voice.

"I do not know what you mean," the Elder replies, calmly shrugging his shoulders.

"You know exactly who I'm on about!" Slayed shouts. "Kanaren, where is he?" But the Elder doesn't say anything. "Fine, if you won't tell me, I'm sure one of the kids will!" He tells one of the other Hunters to search in the village. Steg bursts into the nearest hut and very quickly throws a young boy outside onto the floor and points his Q-Azar at him.

"Okay kid, time to save your village," Steg says. Slayed slowly walks up to the boy.

"Where did Kanaren go?" he asks calmly. The boy looks over to the Elder who shakes his head and he stays silent. Slayed moves closer. "If you don't tell me, I will kill your leader." The boy screams and bursts into tears. "Do you really want that?" he pauses.

"No!" he cries. Slayed waits for an answer, but he says nothing.

"Fine," Slayed says. "I'm tired of waiting," he lifts his sword to strike the Elder's neck. He stands there with amazing pride and courage.

Metal clashes with metal, stopping the sword from reaching its target. Slayed, stunned, looks into the eyes of the defender. It is Oozoo, holding a familiar sword; Kanaren's. Slayed recognises it.

"Nice weapon kid. Maybe you can tell me where they are?"

"If I tell you, you'll leave us alone?" Oozoo replies, struggling to push back Slayed's sword.

"No Oozoo!" the Elder shouts.

"This is my decision, Elder."

"Fine," Slayed says, pulling his sword towards him and placing it on his back. "And if I find out you've lied to me, I will come back here and destroy everything. Do you understand me?"

Oozoo nods. "I do," he says proudly, looking at his Elder, who is sighing and shaking his head at him. "They're heading northwest."

Slayed looks sceptical.

"That's where The Nest is."

"I promise you," Oozoo stutters. "It's where they're heading. They're searching for crystals."

"More?" Slayed asks, visibly intrigued.

"Oozoo!" the Elder says angrily.

"I'm saving our village," Oozoo replies.

Crata approaches Slayed.

"I've found something outside the village."

"What is it?"

"Several tracks. I'm pretty sure it's Kanaren and the boy."

"Good work, Crata."

"There's something else though," Crata says, before pausing. "There are…well, larger footprints too."

"Creatures?" Slayed asks.

"No. I've never seen anything like these before. They're like humans, but larger."

Slayed thinks, then looks at Oozoo.

"Bring him with us," he orders.

"No!" the Elder shouts. Slayed shunts him out of the way and the Elder falls, while Steg whacks Oozoo from behind, knocking him out.

"Some advice," Slayed says to the Elder. "Don't mess with Hunters."

Chapter 18

The Empty Crystal

The group reaches the top of the hill, far away from The Nest. They can see the rest of their journey ahead; miles of marshland. They all rest. Kanaren looks over to Jaykin who is staring into space.

"You, okay?" he asks.

"Yeah, I'm fine, just feeling…odd."

"What is it?"

He knows the Elements are overhearing their conversation. "Nothing," he says quickly, and hesitates. "Just feel a bit homesick I guess." He then pulls out the crystal in his pocket and shows Kanaren again, then looks in front of him. Kanaren nods his head, understanding. Jaykin is trying to tell him there's a crystal nearby.

"Don't worry, we're all feeling homesick," Pree says.

"Where are we heading Kanaren?" Mordan asks.

"We're going to need to go through that," Kanaren points towards an area covered in mist.

"What is that place?" Jaykin asks.

"The Misty Marsh," Kanaren replies.

"Never heard of it."

"Can't be bad as The Nest," Mordan says.

"It's as dangerous," Kanaren says. "Miles of marshland, covered in thick fog. You won't be able to see right in front of you." They all look at each other.

"So, stick together. We need to be extra careful. The mist can trick your mind sometimes."
Mordan laughs.

"Mist won't play with the Mind Element!" he says confidently. With that, he trips over and falls into a deep boggy swamp, water splashes everywhere covering him head to toe.

"Spoke too soon," Pree laughs, while Irown gives him a hand out of it.

"Think before you speak, I always say," Irown smiles, helping Mordan take off some of the swampy green sludge.

"Mordan doesn't think, Irown," Pree says, just walking past and not helping him.
They slowly make their way through the Misty Marsh. Eventually, the mist gets thicker, gently floating around them. The further they progress, the less they can see.

"Stay together, guys. This mist is going to get thicker. You okay Jaykin?" Kanaren asks.

"Yeah, all good here. I can't see my hands though."

"If only we had an Air Element right about now, we could ask it to clear this mist. I can't see a thing either," Mordan says.
A little giggle comes from Pree, "I finally don't have to look at Mordan."

"Oh, thanks, Pree. Why are you making fun of me?"

"I'm sorry," she says gently. "I think it just helps my nerves."

"I'll let you off then."

"Joking aside though, we could do with the

other Elements here," Pree says.

"I just hope you know where you're going Kanaren," Irown says. "This mist is getting thicker with each step we take; it's nearly impossible to see you all now."

"Don't worry. I have a good idea where we're heading. Just keep going—" Kanaren says but he is interrupted by what seems to be faint cracking noises coming from a distance. They all stop and listen. Then, the sounds of water sloshing around nearby.

"Can anyone else hear that?" Jaykin asks.

"Shush," Kanaren says. More noises are heard. A couple of rumbles, one after another. Growling noises sound all around them.

"Mistican beasts," Irown whispers. "And more than one."

"Misticans?" Mordan says.

"What are they?" Jaykin asks.

"Dangerous beasts," Irown replies.

"I can sense them," Mordan whispers. "There are dozens."

"Prepare yourselves," Kanaren whispers. "This might get messy."

Everyone reaches for their weapons. Kanaren prepares his air weapon. He then grabs tightly onto Jaykin's arm, and whispers in his ear. "Go. Find the crystal. When you find it, get out of here."

"I will," Jaykin says. Kanaren is about to go on but Jaykin grabs onto him. "Go northwest, that's the next place." He then heads for the centre of the marshes.

As he runs away panting, he quickly glances back to see if the Elements are safe but he can see nothing, as the noise of them fighting misticans fades away. He finds it difficult to get across parts of the marshland. Suddenly, something rushes past, making him stop in his tracks. It cuts him and he grunts in pain. He looks around to try and find it, but no sign. He feels his cut, which isn't deep but is very painful. Several growls surround him. Something slashes the back of his knees and he screams, hitting the wet mossy grass. The attacks keep coming, with small cuts to his body every second. "Leave me alone!" he shouts but they keep attacking. He realises it must be the misticans.

***

"Everyone still here?" Irown shouts waving around his battle-axe.

"Yes," both Pree and Mordan shout in unison.

"Where are Kanaren and Jaykin?" Irown asks.

"They've gone," Mordan says, using his powers.

***

Disorientated and with blood all over him, Jaykin doesn't know where to look and starts to panic. As he tries to stand the misticans still keep attacking him. Then a huge blast of air gushes around him and the attacks stop immediately. He feels a hand under his armpit, lifting him up. It is Kanaren.

"Can you stand?" he asks.

"I think so," Jaykin replies, huffing in pain.

"Good. Do you know where the crystal is?"

"It was in front of me but I can't sense it anymore."

"What?"

They both walk slowly forward with more growls surrounding them. Then with one almighty attack from what seem to be at least five misticans at the same time, Kanaren is shunted away.

"Kanaren!" Jaykin shouts, then hears a splash.

"Go Jaykin!" Kanaren shouts back.

Jaykin limps backwards and looks out for misticans; his breathing gets heavier; he turns quickly to run, but smashes into a large, hard object. It is the crystal. His hand sticks onto it. It cracks and he quickly absorbs it, faster than usual. When it completely vanishes, he falls onto his knees. He looks up and tries to find the Element, but detects nothing.

"Where are you?" he shouts. "Element!"

Breathless, he can feel his eyes closing, getting heavier; the tiredness, the pain, and the stress. His breathing becomes heavy on his chest and eventually, he loses consciousness.

***

He opens his eyes slightly, feeling his back being dragged in the marshes, but his eyes close again.

***

"Jaykin, come on, wake up!" He hears

Kanaren, shaking him slightly.

"Kanaren?" Jaykin struggles to say.

"Are you okay?" he asks.

"No, I feel like I've fallen on sharp swords," he says, as he sits up and notices that Kanaren has been attacked as badly as him. They both have lots of cuts and blood all over them. "What about you?"

"I've felt better," Kanaren replies. Jaykin looks around. The mist has cleared slightly and everything is quiet.

"Where are the others?" he asks, as Kanaren tries his best to help him up.

"I don't know, I think they're in there still."

"I hope not. Those things are ruthless."

"Jaykin, the crystal? Where's the Element?"

"There was nothing there," Jaykin sighs. "It's like it was…empty."

"That doesn't make sense."

A strange noise comes from the mist.

"What is that?" Jaykin asks.

"It sounds like clapping," Kanaren replies.

They both look behind them.

"Well, well, well," a familiar voice says. "You guys have really done well, getting this far. The Nest and now the Misty Marsh? I really thought you wouldn't survive!"

A figure appears from the mist.

"Slayed," Kanaren says, with scorn in his voice.

"Looks like you've given us a fake crystal, Kanaren. Oh, and look who we have here," he says, smirking at Jaykin. "Kanaren's pet." Jaykin merely stares. "I'm taking you two back to Dreamora. So, get the crystal and come with me. Now."

Deep within the mist, Arma lays on the floor pointing in the direction of both Jaykin and Kanaren, leaning into his heat-seeking scope. He then pulls back and shakes his head. He leans in again for another look. His shoulders begin to relax, then his head hits the scope and he falls into a deep sleep. Walking up behind him, is Pree. "Sleep time little Hunter," she says.

"Again, we're not going anywhere," Kanaren says.

"Fine," Slayed says, his annoyance clear. "I've had enough of this place anyway!" He lifts his Q-Azar towards Kanaren, then stops. He prepares for a shot, but nothing happens. He looks as if he's struggling to move, even a finger. "Why…can't…I…move?" he shouts.

"That would be me," Mordan says as he comes face to face with Slayed.

"What the…?" Slayed says under his breath, trying but failing to point his Q-Azar at Mordan.

"*I don't need this weapon,*" Mordan says. Slayed drops the weapon onto the ground. "I sensed you guys wandering around for ages. Now I see you asking yourself, what is this thing talking to me and how is it doing this?" He turns to Kanaren and Jaykin, giving them a thumbs up and a wink. "Oh, and I forgot to mention," he turns back to the Hunter. "Your friends, Hunters? They've been taken care of by the way. They're scattered around here," he points airily. "So

now you're on your own, threatening us: my two friends and three powerful Elements. I wish you luck my friend."
Mordan grins sarcastically and sits with an air of satisfaction. He takes out some fruit and bites a huge chunk out of it. He turns to Kanaren and Jaykin again. "I found this on one of the Hunters," he smiles.

"What…are…you?" Slayed asks, still struggling to move.

"I'm an Element from Izara," Mordan replies. "And so are they," he points behind Slayed.

"What?" he turns. There, standing right behind him, with a Hunter in each arm, are Pree and Irown. Pree drops one of the Hunters onto the ground and then grabs Slayed's head.

"Sleep," she says and Slayed falls to the ground, hard.

"Nicely done guys," Jaykin says.

"All five will be asleep for a while," Pree says.

"Good work. I told you we're helpful, Kanaren," Mordan says with unconcealed satisfaction.

"Thanks," Pree smiles. "What shall we do with them now?"

"It's obvious, isn't it? We leave them here," Mordan says.

"No," Kanaren says. "If we leave them here helpless, we are no better than them."

"Even if they attacked the village?" Mordan replies. "I read all their minds. I know what they were going to do to you."

"Yes, even if they have done that," Kanaren replies.

"Erase their memories of us and let them go to the nearest safe place," Irown says.

"Good idea," Jaykin says. "Then we can search for the rest of the Elements in peace."

Mordan kneels down to the Hunters and starts wiping their memories.

"Oh, you're all going to have a bad headache when you wake up," he says.

"Search them as well. Take as much as you can carry; anything will help," Kanaren says.

They check the pockets of all the Hunters, for useful stuff such as bags, weapons, and food. Kanaren takes Slayed's Q-Azar, which has a scope attached. Then he spots his sword on Slayed's back.

"How did he get that?" he asks himself and removes it. "I gave this to Oozoo as a gift."

"Do you think he's around here?" Jaykin asks.

"Possibly." Kanaren stands and looks around but the mist is still lurking.

"Wait," Mordan says. "I'll read their minds to find out." Within a couple of seconds, he finds the answer. "Yes, he's here in a small metal box of some kind…but far away."

"Can either of you sense him?" Irown asks.

"I can't sense anything for miles," Mordan says.

"Me neither," Pree says.

In the corner of his eye, Jaykin gets distracted by something flashing near his feet. He looks down at the Hunters and notices it coming from Slayed's hand. He kneels down to open it and sees a small metal object, flashing red.

"What's this?" he asks, showing it to the others.

"Ah, that is a tracker from the collector, and it means their Q-Roids are heading this way. We need to go, now," Kanaren replies. "He must have pressed it when he was about to fall asleep."

"Wouldn't we be able to sense them?" Mordan asks.

"You won't be able to, as they are not conscious beings," Kanaren replies. "There's no way to wipe their memory without the right technology."

"What about Oozoo?" Irown asks. "We can't leave him here."

"We can't do anything for him…" Kanaren says and stops. "…He's on his own now." They all look at one another, concerned. "Come on, we need to keep going northwest." Hesitantly, they all move off, in that direction.

***

Five Q-Roids run up to the Hunters. They find them fast asleep. They try to wake them but nothing works.

"There are tracks here," one Q-Roid says, scanning the ground.

"Let's follow them," one says to the others, seeming to have taken charge. So, they head off in pursuit.

Chapter 19

The Abandoned City

Day 8

"How are we going to get away from these things?" Jaykin asks, nearly running out of breath and still in a lot of pain from the cuts all over his body.

"By my calculations, we're heading straight towards Rickellen," Kanaren says.

"Isn't that the abandoned city?" Jaykin asks.

"Not abandoned," Kanaren replies, sounding serious. "It's full of creatures."

"Is there anywhere in the land where the creatures aren't?" Mordan asks

"No, they've spread far and wide around the globes. Except for the six cities, where humans are in control," Kanaren says.

"Except for the abandoned one," Irown says.

"Well, we can go up against dangerous creatures or we get attacked by very intelligent and powerful Q-Roids," Kanaren says. "Your choice."

"I'm with Kanaren here. I'd rather we go up against something we can use our powers on," Pree says.

They notice the grass around them becoming longer and thicker, which both Jaykin and Kanaren struggle to run through.

"Jump on!" Irown shouts. He holds his hand

out to Kanaren and swings him over his shoulder and onto his back. Mordan does the same with Jaykin. As they can move quickly for their size, they manage to cover a good distance, until they start seeing an odd material in the long grass. Crumbling rock.

"What is that, Kanaren?" Irown asks.

"An old road. Vehicles, like the attanks, used these, hundreds of years ago."

"What happened to the city?" Pree asks.

"An overwhelming attack by creatures. That's why we have the wall and the dome around the cities now; to protect the people. If we didn't, humans would be extinct."

"Just shows you how much humans needed us," Irown says. Both Mordan and Pree nod in agreement. "I wouldn't mind seeing these cities of yours. They sound fascinating."

"They are," Jaykin says. Then they all stop suddenly. "Why have we stopped?" Jaykin asks. The Elements can be heard breathing heavily, all looking intently in front of them.

"It's the bridge to the city," Kanaren says. He grabs the Q-Azar with the scope and points it at the bridge. "And behind it is the city, covered in vegetation and wildlands." He stops looking. "Not far to go now."

"Let's keep moving then, shall we, Elements?" Irown says, determined.

***

As they reach the bridge, Jaykin and Kanaren jump off the Elements' backs to stand on the old, cracked concrete. They discover that the middle deck of the bridge has crumbled away, leaving an enormous gap, but they all climb onto one of the fascias that is still connected, and slowly make it to the other side. Kanaren is the first to pick up metallic sounds coming from afar. They are getting louder.

"It's the Q-Roids," he says. "Go to the city, find the highest building. There is a large green door that leads to a secret base. Stay there. I'll meet up with you when I'm done here."

"What are you going to do?" Jaykin asks.

"I'll take care of these Q-Roids."

"We can help," Mordan says.

"No, I have more experience with these things. Get Jaykin away from here." But they all stand and look at one another, uncertain.

"Kanaren's right, we can't go up against these things," Pree says. "Trust me, I've already tried. Come on, we need to go, now."

They watch as Kanaren makes his way back to where the concrete ends, about a quarter of the distance of the bridge. He looks down at the rushing water and engages with the Q-Roids. The others head into the city.

The Q-Roids halt their position when they realise that there is no way across. Kanaren starts shooting with his Q-Azar but they easily dodge his fire.

"This isn't good," he says to himself, frowning. "Next plan of action."

He unclicks two objects from the inside of his jacket and presses them. They begin to beep and flash, and he throws them as hard as he can onto the other side of the bridge. They bounce; then again; making a tinging sound every time they hit the ground. Just reaching the Q-Roids, they slow right down and stop. A massive explosion then echoes through the area and the bridge crumbles to pieces into the murky river. Somehow the Q-Roids manage to get away from the explosion and stand on the edge, looking down. Then, seeing Kanaren, the Q-Roids open something on their backs, the sound of boosters is heard and they lift off the ground, levitating across the huge gap. Kanaren steps back.

"Damn, they've been upgraded" He grabs onto his sword and prepares himself. "Fine. Let's get this done!"

***

Jaykin and the Elements reach the edge of the city where the skyscrapers have all either fallen or have been completely swallowed up by the forest. They hear the creatures but are yet to encounter any. It looks as if they have made the old buildings their homes. Suddenly there is the sound of an explosion from near the bridge, that echoes through the abandoned city.

"Kanaren!" Jaykin shouts in distress.

"He'll be okay, Jaykin," Irown says, pulling him back. "We need to keep going."

Pree points at what appears to be the tallest building which is still standing. "That's where we need to go," she says.

"Be careful everyone. We need to stand closer

together. There are creatures all over the place." Mordan says. They slowly make it through, avoiding the creatures by using Mordan and Pree's powers and the overgrown grass, that has reclaimed the city. They manage to get to the building. Irown peers cautiously inside. "Empty," he says. "We need to look for the green door. And be careful."

Despite a careful search around the building, they find nothing. Just endless abandoned spaces.
Jaykin then goes searching in the long grass. He spots wires and chains wrapped around an old smashed-up lamp post, but with some sort of flat light on top. It appears to be a device for collecting light energy. He follows the cables across cracked concrete and then back on the long grass. He discovers a handle in the ground and pulls it. The large door creaks open but not all the way. It is extremely heavy and is about to close shut again when Irown grabs onto it and opens it wide.

"Well done, Jaykin," he says with a smile on his face.

***

Meanwhile, high up in the sky in their collector, Steg nudges Slayed, who is still fast asleep.

"Wake up," he says. Immediately, Slayed sits up and is about to hit Steg in the face but stops, realising who it is.

"Why did you wake me?" he says staring at him angrily.

"Because we don't know why we're here," Steg

replies.

"I need an update. Where are we? And why does my head feel like it's been stood on by a sregnad?" he moans, both hands on his forehead.

"We have all woken up with the same pain," Crata says, giving Slayed some water. "This will help."

"Looks like we're near the Misty Marsh!" a voice says from the front of the collector. It is Arma.

"Misty Marsh? Why are we here? Were we infected by seech poison?" Slayed asks.

"Doubt it," Crata replies. "They're not around these parts. Plus, I didn't find tracks nearby."

"Another thing, all our weapons are gone," Arma says.

"Our Q-Roids are missing too. We've been cleaned out," Devy says.

"Does anyone have any ideas?" Slayed asks, but everyone shakes their heads except for Crata who looks in the cage. It is empty.

"I think we had someone in here," he says, stating the obvious.

"No chance of finding whoever it is. But they won't last long here anyway," Slayed holds onto his head. "Nearest city?" he asks.

"Q-Ara," Devy says.

Slayed stands with help from the others.

"We'll head there then."

***

Jaykin and the Elements rest in a barely lit large room. It has two beds, a table, and dozens of small furnishings and appliances. They are arranged neatly around the room and give rise to much curiosity amongst the Elements, who have never seen anything like it before. This room has been well equipped. Jaykin lays on one of the beds. He is still in a lot of pain from the misticans' attack. Pree tries to help him rest. Suddenly a loud crash hits overhead and everyone looks up while specks of dust fall off the ceiling, peppering their clothes.

"What on Izara was that?" Irown asks.

"I hope Kanaren is all right out there," Pree says.

As if in response, the large door opens and closes quickly. Everyone looks towards it, and Kanaren rolls down the steps. He is breathing heavily and lying flat on the floor.

"Kanaren! Are you alright?" Jaykin asks, hopping over to him.

Kanaren sighs loudly as if relieved.

"Yes; now I am, and now we're safe," he says, and passes out.

"Kanaren!" Jaykin shouts.

Pree checks him over, then places her hand on Jaykin's shoulder.

"He's okay, he's just exhausted."

With help from the other Elements, they lift him up and lay him on the other bed. Jaykin goes back to his.

"We'll stay here for a day or so," Pree says. "These two need the rest."

"That's fine," Mordan says. "I could do with a rest too." Irown agrees.

"This looks like a good place to stop. No one

will find us here."
Pree helps Jaykin, Kanaren and Irown sleep.
"*They've gone down well,*" she says to Mordan.

"*Good, well done Pree. We should get some rest too.*"
He lays down on the floor, taking a supply of blankets.

"*I'm glad I found you, Mordan.*"

"*And I'm glad it was you, instead of some other Dream Element,*" Mordan smiles.

Day 9

Jaykin just barely opens his eyes. He feels something wrapped around his body. Bandages. Pree must have stayed up all night. He can still feel the cuts the misticans inflicted on him. He just manages to hear the Elements talking quietly with Kanaren.

"How on Izara did you get away from those Q-Roids?" Pree is asking.

"I know how they work."

"What about the creatures?" Irown asks.

"And I know this place like the back of my hand. That's why I told you to come here. This is my little base," he says, still lying on the bed, with his back propped up against the wall.

"What are these things?" Mordan walks in view holding something.

"That is a kitchen appliance," Kanaren replies with amusement in his eyes. "You make hot drinks with it."
Pree spots Jaykin waking up.

"You still need to rest, Jaykin," she says and uses her powers to get him to sleep again.

***

Later that evening, Kanaren is talking to the Elements about fighting.

"—and that's how I got away from it," Mordan is saying, finishing off his story. Jaykin makes a groaning noise and Pree comes to check him over.

"How is Jaykin at fighting?" Irown asks Kanaren.

"He needs a little training still," Kanaren replies. "But he's good."

Irown smiles.

"I can help him hone his fighting skills, if you like?" Kanaren looks confused.

"What do you mean?" he asks.

"Well, whatever you have learnt, I can share that knowledge with Jaykin. It's like explaining something to someone but they learn it straight away," Irown explains.

"What will I need to do?" Kanaren asks.

Irown moves over to them both. He holds his hand out to Kanaren and holds onto Jaykin at the same time.

"I can only share knowledge, not memories. That's the difference between me and Mordan. Okay, so now just think about what knowledge you want to give him," Irown's skin suddenly shines brightly. Moments later Jaykin lets out a gasp and he holds onto Irown's hand tightly, then lets go.

"Do you want to test it out?" Mordan asks. Pree objects to this.

"No Mordan. Jaykin still needs to rest."

"Actually, Pree. I do want to find out," Kanaren says.

"Really?" Pree says. Kanaren nods and she sighs. "Okay." She places her hand on Jaykin's forehead and as soon as he wakes, Kanaren throws him his sword.

"Let's fight," Kanaren says.

"But…" Jaykin says, slightly confused.

"This should be a good laugh," Mordan says and Pree gives him a disapproving look, shaking her head.

Kanaren slowly scratches a circle on the ground with his sword, while explaining the rules to Jaykin,

"If you leave this circle you lose."

"Okay," Jaykin replies, still looking and feeling dopey.

"I need to know that you can take care of yourself," Kanaren says. Jaykin feels slightly nervous. They both stand opposite each other in the circle. Kanaren gets into position with a starting stance with his sword behind him. Jaykin, on the other hand, feels his body move like he isn't in control of it, reacting automatically to Kanaren. He takes up the exact same position.

Mordan raises his hand.

"Are you both ready?"

"Ready," Kanaren says, confidently, and Jaykin nods.

"Go!"

They both look at each other and wait for the other to make the first move. Jaykin flinches to try and make

Kanaren move, testing his defences, but he just stands there. Jaykin flinches again but Kanaren still does not react. He is calm and at ease, just waiting.

"Are you going to make a move?" Jaykin asks, lowering his sword. Kanaren attacks straight away and Jaykin defends. The swords clash and Kanaren punches him in the chest. Jaykin steps back and drops the sword, holding his chest. He then goes to punch Kanaren's face but he catches it and pushes his arm away.

"You can do better than this," Kanaren says. Jaykin picks up his sword and they both stand back, returning to their defensive stance. Jaykin goes for the next move, opting for a quick attack at Kanaren, who steps aside, then trips him up. Jaykin stumbles and quickly gets back onto his feet, and turns to Kanaren to attack for the second time but Kanaren beats him to it. "You're too slow. You need to get quicker," He pushes him out of the circle. "Congratulations, you're dead." Jaykin goes for an attack. Kanaren swipes the sword and grabs Jaykin's head and leans in. "And you don't have a second chance if you lose." Jaykin pulls his hand out of the hold and tenses his jaw, looking away from Kanaren. Pree turns to Mordan.

"*You might be needed here,*" nudging him.

"*I'm already on it, Pree,*" Discreetly, he lifts his hand up towards Jaykin, who closes his eyes. Mordan appears in his mind.

"Focus on something from the past; something with powerful emotion, maybe someone you love and miss. Make that your weapon," Mordan says.

"My father," Jaykin replies. *"I'll use him."*

"Good, now how will that make you fight better?"

"If he was here with me."

"Do not make anger your weapon Jaykin," Kanaren says. "Let it be your trigger; make it your 'on' switch, your determination, your passion. What are you passionate about? What are you determined to do regardless of cost?"

Within Jaykin's mind, someone walks up behind him.

"Father? I could do with some of your strength and wisdom right about now. I need your help." He hears a faint whisper of his father's voice in his mind.

"*Jaykin, I believe in you,*" the voice says. "*Let go, son.*"

Jaykin's eyes burst open and he lets out an almighty scream. He propels himself at Kanaren, swinging his sword, left, right, left again. Kanaren quickly defends with his sword and dodges the attacks. Jaykin flings the sword at Kanaren and he just manages to hit it away. Jaykin attacks with swings of punches, hitting Kanaren perfectly in sync with his defence, and managing to knock him out of the circle. Jaykin stands still, panting and staring at the shocked Kanaren, then realises what has happened. The Elements all clap and cheer.

"Kanaren, I'm sorry," Jaykin says, and helps him up from the floor.

"You don't need to apologise. I knew you had a hidden talent in there somewhere." He places his hand on Jaykin's shoulder and goes to sit back down on his bed, still in pain.

"Does that mean we won't need to protect him anymore?" Mordan says. Pree nudges him in the arm.

"*What did you see?*" Pree asks.

"*His father. That wasn't the only thing either. We were all standing behind him.*" Pree stares at him.

"*It sounds like his father gives him hope.*"

"*And us,*" Mordan says.

"You going to have another rest?" Pree asks.

"It wouldn't be a bad idea," Kanaren says. "We head out first thing in the morning."

Chapter 20

The Path to The Unknown

Day 10

Very early next morning, the weather has turned gloomy and wet while they have been resting at Kanaren's secret hideout. Irown has sewn up the holes on their jackets, using Kanaren's kit. They are ready to move on. Jaykin has had the opportunity to mention again to Kanaren the crystal he has sensed. Their plan is to head in that direction: north-west. Kanaren tells the Elements that this is the only way to get to the other city, which, in truth, is actually due west. They walk through woodland that has reclaimed the area; all the buildings have crumbled or fallen and it is eerily quiet.

They continue northwest and looming in the distance is a magnificent cliffside.

"That is where we're heading," Kanaren points. "We just need to climb."

They all look up at this gigantic cliff edge, dreading that prospect. As they get closer, Irown stops to admire it.

"I recognise this place. We nicknamed it 'The Edge of the Land' as it was close to the Unknown Lands."

"It still is," Kanaren says. "But we just call it The Edge."

"Oh, that is high," Mordan says, taking in the

view.

"A few thousand feet high," Kanaren mentions. Mordan looks even paler blue and takes a gulp.

"Did you choose the wrong Element?" Irown says as he walks past him and chuckles to himself. Pree smiles with him.

"Oh great," Mordan sighs. "You're both against me now."

"That tower is where we need to get to," Kanaren points to a small tower on top of the steepest rock face.

They get closer and find a pathway zigzagging up, four times as wide as one Element.

"They still have the pathway," Irown says.

"Of course," Kanaren replies.

"After thousands of years, it's still here," Irown shakes his head. "They would be very pleased about that."

"Who would be?" Jaykin asks.

"The Earth Elements. They created this pathway before the Great War."

They start to climb. Every so often Kanaren looks down, then continues walking.

"Aren't you afraid of heights?" Jaykin asks.

"No. You get used to it after a while. How are you with heights?"

"Not too bad I guess." He recalls the times he used to lay on one of the landing bays at his apartment. He was scared of the height at first, but got used to it after going there frequently.

Kanaren and Jaykin are three-quarters of the way up. The Elements are a little further back, having stopped several times because Mordan feels queasy. As they walk, Jaykin tells Kanaren that there is a crystal close by and, while there are no Elements around, he practises his powers by creating lumps of crystal then absorbing them. Kanaren watches with interest as he has not witnessed it close up before.

"I still have no idea how you are doing that."

"I don't know either."

"Does it hurt?"

"It did at first but I'm sort of used to it now."

"What does it feel like when you create or absorb it?"

"When I create crystal, I can feel my whole body flowing out of my hands, it's the opposite feeling when I absorb it." He creates a small crystal.

"Can you create anything else?"

"No, this is difficult enough."

"You should try when you have the chance. Imagine crystal armour and weapons. That could be very useful."

Jaykin hadn't thought of that. He has been too busy focusing on just creating crystal itself. He looks back at the Elements who are still a way off.

"Do you think there was a Crystal Element?"

"They didn't mention one when Irown was talking about the seventeen."

"Maybe there were but they're as scarce as Irown. Think about it, the Elements must've been saved by someone that can create crystal."

"Could have been but the only ones who could answer that question would be the Elements themselves and they don't seem to know anything. We may never find out."

Kanaren stops unexpectedly and so does Jaykin, who looks around but there is nothing there.

"What's wrong?" Jaykin asks, but gets no reply. Kanaren faces away from the cliffside and stares out into the sky. "Are you okay?" he asks again, getting slightly nervous, especially as Kanaren is one step away from falling off the edge. He looks as if he has been hypnotised. He slowly moves his head towards Jaykin but keeps his eyes fixed on the sky.

"Something," Kanaren says, struggling to get his words out. Then his eyes search for the other planet, but the clouds are in the way. Jaykin looks up too.

"Kanaren!" he says forcefully.

Kanaren finally faces Jaykin, staring at him intently as if he had forgotten he is there.

"Something isn't right," he says.

Jaykin looks at his face, which is pale and gaunt. This is the first time ever that he has seen Kanaren looking scared of something, but of what? A loud rumble from across the sky echoes through the forest below them.

"The weather," Kanaren says in a chilling voice. A slight shiver goes up Jaykin's spine and down to his fingertips and toes. This time it is not a crystal. Kanaren shakes his head and is instantly out of his trance.

"No, it's nothing. Let's keep going," he says. Jaykin stands still and stares at him, not knowing what to do or say.

"That was odd," he says to himself and looks out over the cliff edge to see if he can spot anything.

"Everything okay?" Irown asks, as he catches up with them.

"Yeah, I think so," Jaykin replies, feeling very confused. He looks up the pathway to Kanaren, who is picking up speed to the top. He runs on, to try and catch up with him.

***

Kanaren and Jaykin eventually reach the top of the rock face. Jaykin can suddenly feel his body pulsating again. He knows there is a crystal nearby. He searches for it but doesn't see anything, just tall trees, and vegetation everywhere.

"Follow me," Kanaren says, taking off his sword and then his jacket. They approach a tall metal structure, covered with vines and branches. It looks old and barely stable. He reaches for a rusty ladder, lodged against one corner, and starts climbing.

"What are we doing?" Jaykin asks, as he also takes off his sword and jacket.

"You'll find out when you get to the top," Kanaren replies. A few minutes pass and they reach the top: a small, cramped enclosed platform which only just fits Kanaren. He unclips a box located there, revealing a couple of switches and wires. He takes out an old battery from his pocket and uses the wires to connect it to the box.

"Do you always carry batteries in your pockets?" Jaykin asks, incredulous.

"This battery is a spare for Q-Tech. It won't need it anymore."

"I miss Q-Tech. Will you rebuild it do you think?"

"Of course. If we ever get back into a city."

"If?" Jaykin asks.

"There's always a possibility…" Kanaren pauses, focusing on the wiring task. Jaykin shakes his head.

"Where did you even get the batteries from?"

"Our good old friends, the Hunters' Q-Roids. They don't need them anymore. Plus, they had some great weapons on them too," He shows Jaykin some new Q-Azars around his belt. "You still have that Q-Pad I gave to you right?"

"Yeah," Jaykin rummages through his pockets and hands it over to Kanaren. "So, what are you doing?"

"I'm sending a message to someone I know in Q-Ara. Hopefully, it will get to him."

"Who?"

"A guy called Aren. He'll help us," Kanaren whispers.

"Aren? The Hunter?" Jaykin asks. Kanaren nods.

Jaykin can feel the excitement about meeting this Aren person. Q-Tech mentioned him in Lementes but other than that, he remains a mysterious figure. If Kanaren taught him, he might be a great Hunter and another good ally.

"Do you think that'll work?" he points at box.

"It should do. They used these for hundreds of years and we still use the old signals." A beep goes off from the pad. "Great. Looks like it's sent. Let's make a move." He places the connected pad inside the box and shuts the door.

"Are we not going to wait for a reply?"

"No, it could take a long time for him to get back to us. So, we may as well try and—"

"—and find the next Element?" Jaykin asks, excitedly.

"Of Course. Do you know where it is?"

"Umm, that way," he says and points towards the vast forest.

"Then that's the next place to go," Kanaren says. "Probably best if we don't tell the others where the next one is. They might get slightly suspicious about how we are finding them."

"Ok," Jaykin replies, wondering why he's being so secretive. They climb down the tower to meet up with the others.

"What were you guys doing up there?" Pree asks.

"Contacting a friend in the city," Kanaren replies. Irown is scanning the sky over the forest.

"The weather is changing for the worse." Gigantic dark clouds are covering most of the sky, making everything gloomy and progressively harder to see.

"We were lucky to get that message out then," Kanaren says, and picks up some of his stuff.

Mordan only just makes it to the top.

"Please can we stop now?" he asks.

"No more climbing," Pree replies, and smiles at the look of relief on his face.

***

Hours pass, flashes of light manage to get through the trees, a crackle of thunder rumbles through the skies of Izara. Rain and wind gush through the forests, making the group cold, tired, and extremely wet. This, in turn, makes it difficult to move, as the ground is covered with moss and water. The only thing that holds them steady is the roots of the tall trees. They slowly make their way through an area where hundreds of small plants provide ground cover, preventing them from seeing clearly where they are stepping. They hold onto anything that can keep them steady. Mordan and Pree are walking and talking to one another at the back.

"Ouch!" Pree shrieks, quickly jumping forward. The leaves all around her bob up and down as if something is moving underneath.

"What's wrong?"

"Something has just stung me!" she yells. "Right on my heel too!"

"I don't see anything," Mordan says, looking carefully. "Are you sure you're not daydreaming?"

"No!" she shouts angrily. Then, with no warning, a blur rushes past Mordan's foot and jumps onto his arm and bites him. He lets out a loud yelp, also jumping back and throwing it away from him.

"What was it?" Pree asks.

"I don't know. I didn't have time to see it!" Mordan answers back. They both stare intently into each other's eyes. "You feel that too, right?" Mordan asks.

"I do." They both look towards the east, but they can see nothing. "Something's definitely not right, guys," Pree shouts.

"This is not good," Mordan says.

"What's wrong with you two?" Irown asks.

"Everyone run! Now!" Mordan shouts.

"Why?" Jaykin asks.

"There's thousands of…something…heading our way!" Mordan points, jogging backwards slightly.

"Thousands?" Irown asks.

"Too many to count," Pree says.

They clamber across the wet slippery ground where they start to hear another strange sound, like tiny shrieking noises scurrying through the undergrowth, thousands of small rodent type creatures with sharp teeth; running very fast.

"Ibsters!" Irown shouts recognising the sounds they make. "Keep running!"

"Not good," Kanaren says. They turn and run in the opposite direction and as fast as they can.

"Careful of their flying spikes too!" Jaykin yells.

"Nasty creatures," Irown says, shaking his head.

"Mordan, use your powers!" Pree shouts, waving her hand behind her.

"I'm already on it!" he replies, making most of the ibsters run away or flee in terror. Kanaren turns and uses his air weapon. A huge gust of wind blasts through the thousands of ibsters.

"That should slow them down," he says.

"Not for long," Irown replies, "We may not get out of this alive!"

"Willing to change that thought," Kanaren replies.

They run fast and far deeper into the forest. Mordan uses his powers again to turn some of the ibsters against each other. Pree uses her powers also, putting some of the creatures to sleep.

"They're too many!" Irown shouts out. Kanaren looks up and spots something in amongst the trees.

"We need to get to higher ground," he shouts, pulling out a Q-Azar and pointing it to a tree, shooting at it repeatedly.

"What are you doing?" Jaykin shouts.

"Saving our lives!" he replies, still shooting. A loud cracking noise echoes through the forest and the tree slowly falls towards them. Kanaren notices and aims his air weapon at it and shoots. The tree falls in the other direction and wedges onto another. "Let's go!" he shouts, waving his hand. They run up the tree, balancing and helping each other up. As they get to the top, they see a large, thick ledge wrapped around the next tree. It reaches out approximately ten feet, with large trunks, sticks, vines, and mud working together to hold it up. It is obviously man-made. "We should be okay up here," Kanaren says, trying to catch his breath.

"Where is 'here' exactly?" Jaykin asks. As they

catch their breath, they notice a number of wooden cabins; some at eye level, some even higher. Most appear to have been damaged and broken apart; by weather, or perhaps by creatures.

"No signs of life here. Seems abandoned," Irown says.

"It is," Kanaren says. "People used to live in wild places like these before the cities were built." Jaykin looks cautiously down over the ledge, trying to see the ibsters.

"No sign of them at the moment." The wood creaks below him.

"Careful Jaykin," Pree says. "I don't think this is stable."

"Agree," Mordan says. As soon as he replies, he steps in the wrong place and it breaks underneath him.

"Mordan!" Pree Shouts.

As Irown is right next to him, he quickly grabs onto Mordan's arm before he falls all the way through.

"Hold on!"

"No one else move!" Kanaren shouts, holding his arms up to Pree and Jaykin.

"Don't let go!" Mordan gasps, looking up at Irown and holding his breath.

"I'll try not to. Hold on tight!"

"Mordan, are you okay?" Pree asks, anxiously.

"I'm…fine!" He looks down, still swinging from Irown's arms. "That's a long way down!" His vision blurs then he looks up. "No, don't like that height either. Get me out of here, Irown."

"I will, as soon as you stop swinging," Irown

replies.

"I'm trying," He looks down again. "Umm," he gulps. "We may have a problem."

"What problem?" Pree asks. Before he can answer, a spike from down below misses her face by mere millimetres and sticks into the bark close by. She stares at it. "I see what you mean." She looks down as well and sees thousands of ibsters scattering around. She can barely see the ground. "Now what?"

"We've got to keep moving. Ibsters can climb," Kanaren says. "Jaykin, is there a way off this thing?"

"Umm," he holds onto the tree and walks around it. "Yeah, there is, but I can't see where it ends up."

"Doesn't matter; anywhere is better than this place."

Irown manages to lift Mordan back up onto the ledge with Pree's help.

"This thing is not made for Elements," Mordan says, grabbing onto the tree as quickly as possible. Suddenly, an ibster appears at the end of the ledge.

"Go!" Mordan shouts.

They quickly go around the tree and onto a large wooden bridge, heading deeper into the vast, dark forest.

Chapter 21

The Group Grows

Day 11

It's midnight, and they continue walking on the unstable walkways which are connected around each large tree. The few ibsters that have climbed the trees are catching up fast. The others continue to attack from the forest floor. When the pathway comes to an end, they decide to quickly lower themselves to the ground, to continue the journey.

"Lucky we can run faster than those little critters," Mordan says, chuckling.

"Wait!" Jaykin shouts. They halt and turn to look at him. He points to what seems to be the entrance to the ancient village. They hear the noise of thousands of ibsters scuttling closer toward them.

"Everyone, follow Jaykin. Go now!" Kanaren shouts. No one argues.

They run through the entrance, into a huge space that appears to be deserted. Surrounding it are masses of bushes and enormous trees, as big as those in the High Tree Forest. The ground is solid stone, with long grass and tree roots emerging through some cracks. Much of the stone is covered by a mass of moss. Carved into the tree trunks are elaborate figures, depicted with armour and weapons. There appears to be only one way in and one way out of this enclosed space.

"Find cover!" Kanaren shouts, and moves behind a huge tree, nearest to the entrance. He takes out a Q-Azar and powers it up. Pree and Mordan hide beside another tree on the opposite side of the entrance and Irown conceals himself behind a large boulder, looking around to see what might help them. Jaykin makes his way to the far side to look for cover, but suddenly becomes aware of a pulsating sensation through his body. There is a crystal very close to him but he cannot see it.

"It must be close," he says quietly to himself. He scans the space intently and sees two stone statues standing beside a thick wall of vines and bushes. "It's here," he whispers to himself. He can see nothing obvious, so it must be behind the wall. He grabs onto his sword, unfolds it, and starts cutting the vines; but the stems seem impenetrable.

Suddenly, the ibsters, in their thousands, begin surrounding the entrance. But they seem confused for some reason.

"Why have they stopped?" Pree asks, and sees that Mordan is struggling to use his powers.

"Pree, there are too many," he says. He is clearly weakened by the effort and begins to shake and strain. His nose starts to bleed.

She holds up her hand and helps by using her own powers.

"There's a crystal here!" Jaykin shouts.

"We won't have long!" Irown shouts.

"Throw me your sword!" Jaykin shouts to Kanaren. Confused, Kanaren throws it as hard as he can. It only just reaches Jaykin, who picks it up swiftly and, using both swords now, stabs, twists, and turns them simultaneously into the huge cluster of vines, leaves and branches. With some persistence he creates a small gap for his arm to fit.

Meanwhile, lightning flashes constantly, the weather worsening by the second. A few dozen ibsters have managed to get through the entrance but Kanaren fires his air gun several times, propelling them into retreat.

"We're pinned down!" Irown shouts, taking out his battle-axe. "We're going to need a miracle!"

Jaykin quickly rests both the swords against the wall and peers through the hole he has made.

"The crystal!" he whispers to himself. "Now, I just need to get to it." He looks for another way through. A gateway would be helpful right about now. Acutely aware that the others are only just holding back the ibsters, he stares at the gap with determination. He sticks his arm inside the hole, even his shoulder, but cannot feel anything. He pushes harder without success. "Damn! I can't reach it," he stresses, stretching again as far as he can, but with all the dense foliage in the way, there is no way of getting to it.

A clash of thunder rips through the forest. Kanaren, who is still using his Q-Azar and his air weapon, can see Jaykin struggling.

"Jay—" he shouts, stopping abruptly as something catches his eye. A massive ball of light hovers in the sky. In that brief moment, he spots something and feels his blood go cold.

"Kanaren, why have you stopped?" Irown shouts to him, but he appears to be frozen. It takes a while for him to reply.

"I saw something," he says, mechanically, trying not to blink or even move while he scans the dark sky, waiting for another flash to appear. A loud rumble shakes everything around them.

Jaykin has not given up on cutting away more of the vines. As he hacks away, he is conscious of the noise and tension around him and the others, but tries to focus on getting to the crystal. He becomes aware of moss peeling away close by and of crackling noises getting louder around him. Sensing more danger, he scans the area, his arm still inside the gap. Something falls to the ground and he focuses his eyes to work out what it is. He can see bits of moss rolling and breaking apart nearby, which is making him nervous, as the only place he had seen that before was on the statues. The realisation kicks in and he gulps nervously. With a huge effort he stretches to reach into the gap as far and as fast as he can. But it is too far in. He curses in frustration.

"Ga, I can't reach it!"

Kanaren is still gazing fixedly at the sky.

"What have you seen?" Irown asks, then looks up himself, but sees nothing; just darkness.

"Wait for the ball of light," Kanaren says, still in his watchful state.

"Ball of light? It can't be."

"It shouldn't be here," Kanaren says solemnly. They both wait, alert to any sign, but see nothing until they hear a loud screeching above them. Kanaren primes his Q-Azar and waits. Another flash of lightning.

"There!" Kanaren shouts out, shaking his head slightly. His eyes search the sky. "No! Jaykin," he whispers.

Jaykin's fingers are now millimetres from the crystal. The statues begin to move ever so slightly. He stares into the eyes of the one to his left. As the moss falls away from the rest of the statue, he recognises something familiar and gasps in horror. The face of the Guardians. Scared out of his skin, he tries to use all his remaining strength, which isn't much, to stretch further.

"Jaykin, no!" Kanaren yells in warning. "Don't touch the crystal!" He runs towards him, but Jaykin cannot hear him above a massive crash of thunder. He pushes every single tendon in his arm to the limit, feeling as if he might tear apart. Crack after crack, the Guardians start to move and become animated. Both are now reaching for something behind them.

"Just…have to reach…a bit more," Jaykin says to himself, grinding his teeth.

"Jaykin, no!" Kanaren yells again, trying to stop him.

"I'm nearly there!" He holds in his breath and closes his eyes, waiting for the Guardians to attack him. Like a magnet and with the slightest scrape of his fingertip, the crystal is being absorbed.

Like the others, the crystal cracks in half, melting like ice and into Jaykin's fingertip, through his arm and around his body. As the crystal is shielded by the dense wall, any sound shoots straight upwards. A rumbling, as loud as thunder, echoes up and into the sky from beyond the wall. Kanaren stops in his tracks. It is too late. Jaykin screams his lungs out with pain while his arm feels as if it is being ripped apart from his shoulder and gets sucked into the wall. The crystal disappears quickly; into nothing. As it stops, he pulls his arm out and falls to the ground. He tries to lean up against the wall of vines. Then, all goes quiet for a few seconds. Everything stops; as if time itself has stood still. No storm, no rain; nothing; until an eerie loud screech shatters the silence. Even the ibsters are stunned.

"Jaykin, get out of there," Kanaren yells.

"Now!" Irown shouts. They both realise the Guardians are a danger to Jaykin but are powerless to protect him. Jaykin ignores their warnings and the Guardians. Instead, he hears something on the other side of the wall and tries to focus on that; getting up as quickly as he can and peering through the hole to investigate. He sees something move slightly as if struggling to stand up. Hearing strong panting from the other side, it then lifts what seems to be its head, as one of its eyes is level with Jaykin's. It stares directly at him.

"What Element are you?" Jaykin whispers, a shudder of excitement flowing through his body. "Whoever you are, I need your help."

Both the Guardians simultaneously grab their weapons from behind them and thrust down. Jaykin holds his head with both arms in defence, while two loud thuds and cracking sounds on each side of him echo through the grounds. Everyone looks up in his direction, holding their breath. Jaykin is seen uncovering his head, shaking slightly but safe for the moment. He looks up to see one thick tree trunk to his left and another to his right, each pierced with a huge sword. With some relief, he sees that the trees have saved him from the Guardians' attack.

Shielding behind one of them, he watches cautiously as the bushes and vines start to move, unwrapping and burying themselves into the ground, revealing an impressive sight beyond. The brand-new Element stands ten feet tall, green-skinned and with armour made of thick, hard bark. Here and there, deep green leaves emerge from the bark on small twisted branches. On its shoulder, and only just fitting, a large green-feathered bird pecks on small red pieces of fruit, which look as if they have grown there. Around the Element's waist are dozens of leaves wrapped in small sacks, but nothing more. There is no sign of any weapons. Jaykin notices the symbol on its armour. It is gold, but has a green circle with a leaf in the centre.

The Element is holding its arms towards the wall and appears to be the cause of its disintegration. It has a smile on its face.

"Greetings," he says with a deep voice. Both the Guardians react by trying to tug their swords out of the tree without success. Jaykin falls to the ground between the trunks and looks up towards the Element who helps feed the creature on his shoulder with more fruit.

"Fly, Elra," the Element says and the creature quickly takes off into the sky. "So, what do I call you two ugly things?" he asks, eyeing the struggling duo.

"Guardians," Jaykin answers for them, making his presence known. The Element bends down and sees him between the trunks.

"Thanks," he says smiling, then looking back towards the Guardians, he spreads his hands out wide and raises them quickly. Vines explode out of the ground beneath them, wrapping around their feet and legs, then around their torsos and arms, pulling them downwards and flat onto their backs. They try to pull away but are powerless. "And they're terrible at fighting," he says. Jaykin looks up at him, confused. He bends down to Jaykin, who is exhausted, his arm still painful.

"You're safe now." The Element helps him up. "Are you okay?"

"I should be fine now. Thank you." Jaykin smiles gratefully.

"We can't hold them back anymore!" It is Mordan's voice. Struggling to keep the ibsters away from the entrance, he has overused his power, and faints. Pree lasts slightly longer but soon falls beside Mordan, exhausted.

"What on Izara is going on?" the new Element asks.

"Long story," Jaykin replies. "But we need to get those ibsters away from us."

"I think I can help," the Element replies. With

that, spikes from the ibsters are hurled towards them.

"Take cover!" Kanaren shouts. The Element flings his arms up and over his head and green aura flows from his body, up through his arms and out of his hands. New trees suddenly explode out of the ground, protecting the group from the ibsters' assault. The new Element deftly catches a huge piece of bark as it cracks off one of the trees. He leaps towards Jaykin, who braces himself in alarm. The Element uses the bark skilfully, defending Jaykin from the ibsters' sparks.

"Wow!" Jaykin says, both relieved and impressed by the move.

"You should stand behind me," the Element says and Jaykin doesn't argue.

"Time to level out the playing field." The Element lifts his arms once more, releasing another blast of energy. Strong, twisting vines grow across the entrance, blocking anything coming in. "They will not bother us anymore."

Jaykin is impressed.

"That was amazing!"

The Element nods kindly. He spots a bent stick on the ground and somehow manages to pick it up without touching it. As it floats towards him, he grabs it and a cracking sound signals a surge of power through his arm. The stick grows longer and thicker, small pieces fall off it, transforming into a beautiful bow. Then, scanning the ground in search of something, he lifts his arm and hundreds of small sticks levitate and swirl around him in a large circle. He clenches his fist and another pump of power flows through his arm. The small sticks glow, morphing and growing into perfectly straight arrows. He closes his hand again and all the arrows bunch up together. He grabs one from the pile and quickly shoots at the remaining ibsters.

Pree just manages to wake up Mordan with the small reserve of energy she has left. As the threat from the ibsters ceases, all the Elements and Kanaren gradually make their way towards this new Element.

"Get behind me," he says.

"We are so glad we ran into you, Nature Element. Thank you," Irown says, placing his hand on the Element's shoulder.

"It is an honour to meet you all too," the new Element replies, loosing several more arrows for good measure. "My name is Eragraph."

Chapter 22

The Unexpected Split

Loud screeches are heard above them.

"Barrags," Kanaren says.

"They must have heard the noise here," Pree says, trying her best to keep Mordan standing.

"The sound of the crystal breaking will attract them," Kanaren says. "We need to get out of here, now."

"I wish that was possible, but I don't see an exit," Irown says.

With that, a group of the barrags lands nearby. Whilst similar in size to Scarrags, the barrags have shorter tails and smooth shining indigo scales covering their entire bodies.

"I can make an exit," Eragraph says, turning to Pree and Mordan. "Try and distract the barrags for me." They both nod and hobble towards the creatures. Eragraph uses his powers, lowering the foliage behind them, where the crystal used to lay. The Guardians beside it are still struggling to get out of the vines. They are forced back further away from the group and onto the mossy ground where more vines take hold of them.
"We can get out this way," Eragraph says.

They are just about to run through the exit when something massive crashes down behind them; destroying both the Guardians instantly, smashing them into small pieces; the ground around them exploding as if the planet is splitting in two. Everyone is tossed out of the way; dust and stones are everywhere. As it settles, the huge creature responsible lets out an almighty and unbearable screech, forcing everyone to cover their ears until the terrible noise stops. Then, a short silent pause follows until the barrags screech back. Even Eragraph's flying companion lets out a squawk as it swoops down around them.

The ibsters all disperse from the area and back into the forest.

"Everyone okay?" Kanaren shouts and everyone replies positively, and with relief. They all lift themselves up and try to work out what just landed.

"Is that what I think it is?" Irown shouts to the others.

"It is," Kanaren replies.

"The legendary creature," Irown says and everyone's eyes widen in both fear and curiosity. They know the rumours of this magnificent creature but no one has ever seen it and lived to tell the tale. "The barragona."

It lets out a huge screech again.

"Queen of the barrags," Kanaren says.

With that, every single barrag, on the ground and in the sky, lets out another loud screech, as if to acknowledge and salute their legendary and powerful queen. She stands up on all fours as if showing off her impressiveness. About forty feet high and twenty feet wide, with a wingspan of one hundred feet, she has a very long tail; slightly longer than one wing; and her spikey head is nearly the same size as Jaykin, with a lengthy beak and bulging dark eyes which can terrify anyone nearby. She is covered in small impenetrable scales that shine slightly green, blue, and indigo, like the other barrags, but on the back of her four legs, head, spine, and tail, they turn into spikes. She has great piercing claws but her wings are made of hundreds of large silky feathers.

"I think this is worse than the ibsters," Mordan says, becoming conscious of hundreds of barrags circling overhead in the growing darkness.

"May I suggest we split up?" Eragraph says. "It's a gigantic creature, so it will be slow. Whatever you do, do not move hastily." Although he is talking to the group, he keeps his eyes locked onto the barragona. They all nod in agreement, moving slowly and gradually, encircling the creature. Its breathing terrifies them as it surveys the scene. Then it spots them. It does not attack immediately though. Instead, it moves slowly towards the group, keeping an eye for any sudden movement from them. It lowers its head directly in front of Eragraph, as if observing him closely, looking him up and down and sniffing him too. Its head vibrates as if it is using sonar.

"What's it doing?" Jaykin asks.

"Searching for an opponent," Kanaren replies. Eragraph's pet lands back onto his shoulder and squawks suddenly. The barragona snarls back at it.

"It's okay Elra," Eragraph says trying to calm her by petting her head.

Having appraised Eragraph, as if in doubt, the barragona slowly moves toward Pree. She closes her eyes and freezes, staying completely still.

"*Pree, try putting it to sleep,*" Mordan says, using his powers.

"*I can't move,*" she hesitates, scared stiff.

"*I'll try then,*" he says, determined. He lifts his hand up towards the barragona, but struggles. "It's not working." The barragona rumbles again.

"No, it won't work," Irown says. "It has reflective scales all over its body. Your powers will not get through. We need to run." It slowly shifts its gaze from Pree to Mordan.

"Umm, hi," Mordan gulps, and waves at it, inanely. Then the creature makes a strange noise, breathing as if snickering. It rumbles for the third time.

"How on Izara are we going to get out of this?" Jaykin worries.

"We'll just have to do this the hard way," Kanaren says, flexing his fists. The creature moves on again slowly and Mordan relaxes.

"I could have sworn that thing just laughed at me," he says. It moves onto Irown.

"Okay, everyone. When she gets to me, I'll attack her. Run as fast as you can away from here, got it?" Kanaren orders, determined. The creature sniffs and growls at Irown, giving out a strong message of power and superiority.

"But—" Jaykin says.

"No buts," Kanaren snaps, gripping onto the hilt of his sword firmly, preparing himself, waiting for the right moment. The creature moves slowly towards Kanaren.

"No, we are a team," Mordan says and grabs

his sword.

"I don't know who you all are or where on Izara I am, but I'm here for you guys," Eragraph says, preparing and pointing the bow straight at the barragona. His creature squawks as if it agrees with him.

"Me too," Pree says, grabbing her spear.

"Count me in too," Irown says, already holding onto his battle-axe as the creature moves closer to Kanaren and rumbles menacingly.

"Damn," Kanaren whispers and looks over towards Jaykin. The creature senses Kanaren is about to attack as it lets out another ear-splitting screech.

"Protect Jaykin!" he yells and quickly draws his sword. "Come on then!" he shouts, taunting the massive creature. It growls back and stares at him. Kanaren thrusts his wind weapon straight into the barragona's face, sending it backwards, staggering slightly. It responds by opening its gigantic jaw, ready to clamp around his body. Kanaren lunges out of the way but the barragona quickly turns to attack him again. The others move clear of its thrashing tail. Kanaren rolls toward where the crystal had lain, then turns to the creature in a defensive stance.

"Kanaren!" Jaykin shouts.

"I'm okay, Jaykin," he shouts in reply, holding up his hand, in a warning not to interfere, as he has the creature's full attention. It goes for the attack again and Kanaren moves to evade it, but it kicks him, smashing him to the ground. He rolls several times until he hits into a barrag, his sword flying out of his hand and crashing down, out of reach. With no time to get up, he goes to hurl himself towards it but the barrag screeches, hitting the ground with its tail, trying to separate Kanaren from his sword and forcing him back towards its Queen. "This isn't good," Kanaren whispers to himself. He turns to the barragona and stares into its fiery eyes. He shouts at the others standing helplessly by. "What are you doing? Get out of here!" He waves his hand at them. The barragona pauses and turns its head to look at the others. Eragraph jumps into action.

"Not when I'm still breathing," he says, and swiftly lays his hand onto the ground. The earth below him starts to crack. Vines shoot out of it with immense speed, coiling around the barragona's legs. It screeches again trying to move out of the way but is too late. It watches as the vines wrap around the rest of its body.

Kanaren hopes for a chance to run away from it until the barragona easily breaks the vines and thrashes her tail, striking him to the ground once more. Seeing the threat, Eragraph loosens arrow after arrow at the barragona's face, trying to draw her attention away from Kanaren, but she turns her whole body and uses her tail to attack him. Boldly, he jumps onto her, skilfully dodging every deadly spike sticking out of her. The barragona pauses as she senses the pressure on her back; she inflates her huge lungs; head rearing, chest thrust forward. Eragraph braces himself against the nearest wing. Then, with one almighty stretch of her wings and body, she catapults him right across the battlefield. As he lands beside the helpless Elements, he screams out and gasps for air.

In shock, Pree runs towards him. Mordan and Irown follow.

"Where are all the other Elements?" Eragraph asks huskily, trying to get his voice back from being winded.

"This is all we have," Pree replies.

"How on Izara are we going to win this?" Mordan cries. Eragraph, recovering his voice, screeches out hoarsely.

"Elra…" he points to the barragona, now heading straight for Kanaren. "…distract!" Elra swoops down from a tree and squawks around the barragona's head. She turns her head this way and that as if maddened by the high-pitched noise. "That should keep it busy for a moment." Eragraph grins.

"Good work," Mordan says.

"We need to keep it away from Kanaren," Irown warns.

"But he told us to run," Pree says.

"We don't run away," Jaykin says, "we work together as a team!"

"He's right," Eragraph replies, standing up. "We all get out of here alive, including him." He nods towards Kanaren who is just getting to his feet.

"What are you doing Jaykin? Take the Elements and get out of here now. Find the other crystals," Kanaren orders, waving his hands and red-faced. As he does so, he attracts the full attention of the barragona again. "No sword," he quickly pats around his jacket, trying to find a weapon. "Second best," he says to himself. A couple of clicks later and he points his air weapon at the charging barragona. He fires. A huge gust of air smashes into the creature and dust billows everywhere.

"What is that?" Eragraph asks.

"Good shot!" Jaykin shouts.

"That's not going to stop it," Kanaren says to himself. He's right. The huge barragona bursts through the dust. He rapidly points the air weapon down at the ground, propelling him twenty feet into the air, to try and avoid her, but she easily smacks him hard with her left wing. He soars across the sky with immense speed, smashing straight through a hollow tree and denting another, landing face down.

"Kanaren!" Jaykin screams to him desperately but doesn't see any movement. "We need to do something!" he pleads to the Elements.

"Distract her," Irown says.

"On it," Mordan says. The group separates and encircles the creature again. Jaykin spots Kanaren's sword near a barrag.

"Pree, can you use your powers to put that one to sleep?" he calls, pointing at it. She raises her hand and the barrag falls to the ground. Jaykin runs, slides, and picks up the sword.

While the other Elements distract the barragona, Irown steps in and tries to help Kanaren. He grabs his arm and goes to pull him away, but the barragona thrashes him with her huge heavy tail. Irown screams in pain and lands in some bushes, some distance away.

Jaykin notices Kanaren moving slightly and throws his sword towards him. Kanaren sees it and slowly tries his best to reach it, but it is beyond arm's length away. The barragona's anger builds. She stomps around, making the ground shudder. Then she stops and fixates on Kanaren. She lifts her foot and presses it down on the lower half of his body. He screams in agony, feeling as if every bone has snapped.

"Kanaren!" Jaykin screams again.

The other Elements gather around the great creature, trying to get to Kanaren, but she screeches at them threateningly, as if protecting her prey.

Jaykin takes his chance to sneak up from behind and reach Kanaren without being noticed.

"Are you okay?" he worries.

"Get out…" Kanaren struggles to get any breath and looks in a lot of pain, "of…here…Jaykin."

"I can't leave you here—"

"Jaykin, listen!" he grabs onto his jacket, pulling him closer. "You have great power, do not waste it!" Kanaren says, staring deeply into Jaykin's eyes, barely moving and blood everywhere. "For Izara's sake, save yourself!" Suddenly, he hears a near-deafening screech above him. The barragona drags her foot, with Kanaren and the sword beneath it, away from Jaykin. The wounded Kanaren grabs onto his sword and the creature then moves to stamp on Jaykin. He dodges, inches away from being crushed. He rolls on the ground, only to see the large foot coming towards him again. She kicks him away with so much force that he is tossed against a tree. He yells in pain as he makes contact and falls to the ground, barely moving.

"Jaykin!" Pree screams, while running towards

him, but the barragona gets in the way. Pree looks up to the creature's eyes. "Why are you doing this?" she shouts, with tears coursing down her face. The barragona ignores her and continues to stomp and kick. Mordan leaps into action and grabs onto Pree, saving her from being swatted by the large limb.

"What are you doing?" he shouts at her.

"We can't win," she cries looking deeply into his eyes with tears and mud over her face.

"I'm not giving up just yet." He eyes up the barrags who are still watching the fight. "I have an idea." He lifts his arm towards the barrags. Pree senses what he is up to immediately.

"Good idea," she says with relief, tapping on his shoulder for support. She runs toward Jaykin and helps him to his feet.

"Eragraph—" Mordan shouts and is about to shout instructions to him but he already knows what he must do.

"I'm on it!" Eragraph replies, running towards the barragona full pelt with the barrags beside him. He thrusts his arm from the ground to the barragona. Vines blast out of the ground and wrap around her legs again. She starts to screech but this time it is different, as if she doesn't want to attack her own kind. She looks over to Mordan, then back to the barrags. She shakes her head and with no hesitation spreads her wings out wide and high, moving them around as if preparing for flight. She crouches down slightly, extending her wings fully, then leaps high into the sky, flapping hard. The vacuum she creates has a powerful effect on the group, pushing them back, nearly lifting them off the ground but easily disrupting Mordan's use of power.

"Where's Kanaren?" Jaykin shouts, searching for him.

"There!" Pree shouts, pointing at the barragona's tightly gripped foot. She watches as the vines still attached to the creature scrape across the ground. With no hesitation and no time to think, she jumps on as it slides through her hands. Eventually, she gets a grip and holds on tight. Mordan watches her lift into the sky and without thinking, he does the exact same thing. They are both flung around in the wake of the creature and Kanaren, gripped in its claws. Jaykin stares helplessly up at Kanaren, wounded and struggling to breathe.

"I'm sorry," he sees Kanaren say, without hearing the words. "Don't give up." With that, Kanaren lets go of his sword and Jaykin watches it fall till it pierces the ground.

"No! Kanaren!" Jaykin screams.

Eragraph leaps up, watching while Pree and Mordan struggle to hold onto the long vines that are still attached to the barragona. He looks in vain for a vine to grab himself. He instantly gets to work. He runs and jumps onto the nearest tree and large branches emerge from it in an instant. He very quickly uses his power to draw one of the dangling vines on the barragona towards him. He just manages to grab on, with Elra, his creature, not far behind. Jaykin watches all this, feeling helpless.

High in the sky and only just holding on to the vines,

Mordan looks up and sees Pree, still holding on too.

"Pree!" he shouts. "What are you doing?"

"Saving Kanaren!"

"On your own?" He feels the vine tugging below him, looks down and spots something on the end. "Eragraph?"

He looks up at them both while he tries to climb. Barrags fly around them. Behind Eragraph is Elra, flapping her wings as hard as she can to try and catch up. Eragraph can feel something wrong with the vine though. It is beginning to tear apart. He looks down at his pet.

"Elra!" he shouts and points towards the Elements. "Follow them!" With that, the vine snaps and he falls. Elra blasts past him. Eragraph feels the air rush as he falls to Izara. He tries to get into a good position, looking around for something in the trees. He quickly picks up speed. He points his hands to the ground and pulls them up fast. Vines burst out and wrap around the trees, growing higher and beyond the canopies. He grabs onto a vine that has made it to him just in time. He swings around a tree, into a backflip, onto another tree and slides down it, landing on the wet ground with a thud. He sighs and catches his breath.

"Damn," he says, shaking his head. He looks around and spots Jaykin, who is scanning the sky. Nothing there except for the faint noise of the barrags flying away into the darkness.

"I'm sorry. I tried." he sighs. But Jaykin doesn't reply.

"We can't do anything now," Eragraph says, wearily.

"I know," Jaykin sighs. There is a long pause.

"I can't do this on my own," he says, shaking his head and trying to hold back his tears.

"You're not on your own; you have me; that's a good start," Eragraph replies. "We just got away from a barragona. Not many people can say that."

"But my friends haven't," Jaykin replies.

They suddenly hear a faint rustle from some bushes beside them. Eragraph grabs onto his bow and Jaykin prepares his sword. A voice cries out and a stumbling figure appears.

"Irown!" Jaykin shouts. But something is wrong. He is holding his chest and crashes to the ground. They quickly notice the blood which is all over him and he is looking paler than usual.

"What happened?" Jaykin asks, standing over him in shock.

"I was attacked by the barragona and she got me pretty badly," he explains and removes his hand to show them. A deep gash between his chest and his shoulder, dangerously close to his heart. Jaykin gasps. He knows there is no one who can help them for miles.

"It's ok, I'll be all right," Irown says.

"I like your optimism, friend," Eragraph says while he leans behind and picks him up, and settles him against a fallen tree.

"Where are the others?" Irown asks.

"The barragona took Kanaren. I think he's in bad shape," Jaykin says, tears coursing down his face. Irown shakes his head. "Pree and Mordan tried to save him, but she took them too."

"Now it's just the three of us?" Irown asks,

softly, then grabs tightly onto his chest.

"Looks as if she really did some damage to you," Eragraph says. "I'll do my best to ease the pain." He thrusts his hand downwards into some soft soil, digging it up. With the other hand, he rummages through some of the leaf sacks and picks something out, dropping it into the hole. He places the soil back over it and covers it with his hands. Within seconds, he uncovers a beautiful sky-blue flower. He then picks the petals from it and places them onto Irown's wound one by one. The petals transform into a liquid balm. "This will help the pain for a bit," Eragraph says. He then turns to Jaykin, who is spellbound by what he is seeing. "Is there a Life Element nearby?"

Jaykin looks back blankly.

"We haven't found a Life Element yet," Irown interrupts, then turns to Jaykin. "We need to find one or else I'm not going to last long."

Jaykin, at a loss, nods vaguely at them both.

"We'll find that Element, don't you worry," Eragraph replies calmly and rips off a big chunk of bark from the tree where Irown is resting and places it over the wound. He pushes it hard and uses his powers. A green glow forms around it. "Try not to move," he says. The bark moulds around Irown's chest, shoulder, and arm, like a hard, sturdy wooden sling.

"Thank you, Eragraph, you are a good Element," Irown says, gratefully.

"It's an honour, especially to help an Element like yourself," he says, bowing slightly.

"Feels better already," Irown says, tapping on the bark, then moaning in pain again.

"Good. It won't last long though."

"I know," trying his best to stay comfortable.

"What do we do now?" Jaykin asks. "I think we should look for the others."

"I don't think that's a good idea, given Irown's situation," Eragraph says.

"Jaykin," Irown says quietly. "I can't guarantee how the others will do against the barragona on their own. We barely survived with all six of us."

"I won't give up hope," Jaykin replies. "I'm sure they'll be okay. Besides, they have Kanaren."

"Let's hope so," Irown says, staring at Kanaren's sword, which is sticking out of the earth. He then groans in pain once again.

"We had better make a move," Eragraph says. "I don't know what else might be lurking out here. Jaykin, do you know where the nearest village is?"

"As far as I know, there are no villages around here," he replies.

"None?" Eragraph gasps.

"There may be the city of Q-Ara. But that might be many miles away though and…" he looks at them both "…it might be difficult to get inside."

"A city?" Eragraph asks. "Does it have healers that can help?"

"I hope so," Jaykin replies and looks at Irown with a worried expression on his face.

"How do we get there?" Eragraph asks. Jaykin has no idea. Just then, he notices the rain has stopped and looks around, detecting something shining on the floor. He springs up and runs over to pick it up. It is Q-Tech's memory core. Kanaren must have dropped it while he was fighting the barragona. He looks up to find out where the light is coming from. "West," he whispers. "The Western Light. If we follow it, we will end up in the city of Q-Ara. I'm sure of it."

"Then that's our next destination," Eragraph says.

Jaykin retrieves Kanaren's sword. He looks up in search of any sign of life, but there is nothing. All is too quiet; the lightning can still be seen but it is miles away. He pulls out the sword, folds it and places it with his own on his back. He then places Q-Tech's memory core safely into the same pocket as the letter, the photo, and the crystal. He makes his way over to Irown.

"Are you okay to move?" he asks.

"I'll give it a go, but I may need a hand up." Jaykin and Eragraph proceed to lift him off the ground.

"We will take it slowly then. We can't lose you; you're one of the legendary Elements," Eragraph says.

"Actually," Irown stares at him, "we're both in the same class now."

"What do you mean?" Eragraph gasps.

"I will explain on our journey," Irown replies, and they head out of the forest.

Back where Q-Tech's memory core was found, underneath a pile of leaves and branches, Kanaren's air weapon lies; broken into small pieces.

Chapter 23

The Great Hunter

As they slowly head out of the depths of the forest, Irown gives knowledge to Eragraph of what has happened in the last few days, but it takes a lot of his energy and he is weakened by it. Eragraph asks many questions, to which Irown and Jaykin still have no answers. Jaykin has other things on his mind though, like Kanaren, Pree and Mordan. The same feeling from when his father left, all those emotions, flood back. His stomach churns every time he thinks about them, wondering if he could have done things differently. If the Elements were not with him, he might have given up hours ago but there is one thing still motivating him right now: getting Irown some help, even if that means going into the city with the Elements. He's tired, hungry, wet and in a lot of pain from all the battles. He isn't thinking about the crystals. They are not important now.

Jaykin stops suddenly; then so do the Elements.

"Jaykin, what is that sound?" Eragraph asks. A slight humming noise can be heard ahead of them.

"It sounds like—" Jaykin tries to remember where he has heard it before. His eyes widen with realisation. "It's a collector," he says, surprise in his voice. "We need to find cover, now."

"Why? What is that?" Eragraph asks.

"As far as I'm aware, it is a flying thing, that

carries people inside of it. Well, that is how Pree described it to me," Irown replies. "It's like the Air Element."

"Then they could help us?" Eragraph asks.

"Maybe, or they might be Hunters," Jaykin replies.

"No matter who they are, we will deal with them," Eragraph says and inspects Irown. "We need to get you out of here, now."

"But—" Jaykin says.

"He's right. I may not be able to last long. Besides, if it is the Hunters then there is a good chance that they won't know who we are."

"Okay," Jaykin hesitates. He tries to decide how he will catch the collector's attention. He thinks for a bit and rummages through his pocket. The photo and letter are not going to help, nor is Q-Tech's memory core, but the crystal…He looks at Eragraph. "I have a plan." They all huddle together.

Eragraph helps Irown to the nearest tree, which he holds on to for support.

"Stay here. I'll be back soon." Eragraph steps back towards Jaykin. "Are you ready?"

Jaykin nods.

"We'll get you help, Irown," he says. They run closer to the noise. "We need to make space for it to land."

"I'm on it," Eragraph replies, and places both his hands on the ground. Jaykin watches intently as he feels the roots of the large trees moving, crawling closer together. They stop and Eragraph stands. "Thank you, my friends," he says, addressing the trees.

"Okay, now the crystal," Jaykin says. He throws it toward Eragraph who catches it. Vines appear from the ground again and he places it onto them.

"Good luck," Eragraph says. With the humming getting closer and louder, Jaykin spots a light from the south. It is from the collector. The vines shoot up into the sky, then stop. Light shimmers into the crystal from the Western Light, as if it is some sort of beacon, and the light of the collector turns towards Jaykin.

"They've seen it," he says. "They're on their way here. Thanks, Eragraph." The vines drop and Jaykin catches the crystal and places it back into his pocket. He stands still, in the middle of all the trees and looks up to the sky. Eragraph re-joins Irown and they both watch the collector appear in view and hover, preparing to land.

"Impressive," Eragraph says.

"It is, isn't it?" Irown agrees, trying to look up.

"Why didn't we have anything like that in our time?"

"Maybe because instead of developing our knowledge, we were too focused on fighting amongst ourselves, not exploring our full potential."

"Never thought about it like that."

Eventually, the collector's lights beam onto Jaykin, then it lowers and lands, barely fitting through the forest's canopy. The engines cut out and the doors open from the side. A Q-Roid stands with a Q-Azar in its hands. It looks highly advanced compared to Q-Tech. It scans the area and spots Jaykin, and immediately comes to life.

"It's okay, I'm on your side," Jaykin shouts, trying to reassure it, but he doesn't get a reply. It slowly walks out, with extreme caution.

"He's in trouble," Eragraph says and is about to make a move when Irown grabs onto him.

"It's okay, he knows what he's doing. We stick to the plan."

"Hands where we can see them," the Q-Roid says clearly and very direct. Jaykin holds them out.

"See, nothing in my hands." Then he hears a familiar voice coming from the collector. Someone appears at the door.

"Meara!" Jaykin shouts. She is the last person he was expecting to see, especially outside the city, and he is taken aback. Of all the people on the two worlds, how can it be her? She stops at the door and stares at him, smiling.

"Jaykin?" she shouts, and jumps off the collector and runs towards him.

"How on Izara—" Jaykin asks as she crashes into him with a massive hug.

"I think we have our help," Irown smiles, sitting down on the ground.

"Looks like it," Eragraph agrees. "I think we should still wait though, just in case."

"I found you," Meara says excitedly.

"How?" Jaykin asks doubtfully.

"With Aren's help," she says, pulling back and noticing his face with all the cuts. "What on Izara happened to you?" She strokes his face slightly, but

Jaykin is too confused to answer. He looks over at the Q-Roid.

"You know Aren? And that's his Q-Roid?" he asks.

"Q-Five!" A loud, youngish voice echoes from within the collector. Both Jaykin and Meara watch him emerge and stomp to the ground. He appears to be a few years older than Jaykin; probably the same or just older than Meara. He wears some odd dark clothing, clean or brand new, but looking nothing like a Hunter. At first, Jaykin is relieved to see him until Aren holds a Q-Azar towards him. "Good work!" he shouts.

"I'm glad to have found you—"

"Did I tell you to talk?" Aren replies. He scowls at Jaykin.

"Oh, I see how we're playing this," Jaykin replies. Not exactly the nice guy he had hoped for. He thought that Aren would help him, not hunt him down.

"We'll play this in any way I want," Aren replies. He then turns to his Q-Roid. "Scan the area for the other one. We'll take this one in for questioning."

"Kanaren trusted in you," Jaykin says, but Aren just laughs back. "You won't find him." Aren ignores him and the Q-Roid continues searching. "You're just wasting your time—"

"You are wanted in all six cities," he moves closer to Jaykin. "He is here and I will take all the time I need to find him."

"Fine," he can feel his body starting to pump adrenaline.

"Now, get down on the floor and place your hands behind your head."

Jaykin takes his time doing it and Aren loses his patience and kicks him behind his knees. Jaykin falls and Aren grabs onto his arms and cuffs them behind his back.

"Aren, please don't do this!" Meara cries.

"Meara, can you remind me later to ask where you met this jerk?" Jaykin says. With that, Aren smacks him in the face, using the back of a Q-Azar.

"Aren!" Meara shouts, running up to Jaykin. "You told me you wouldn't hurt him!" Aren smirks back.

"Now?" Eragraph asks, holding his bow tighter.

"No, not yet," says Irown.

"I see he's given you the rank of Hunter, then," Aren says, shaking his head. "He's granting that to everyone now. Even to the weak."

Jaykin sees that Q-Five is getting closer to the Elements by the minute. He must come up with something and fast.

"What are you talking about Aren?" Meara asks.

"Stay out of this, Meara," Aren says, pointing his Q-Azar at Jaykin. "Where is the crystal?"

"Aren, no!" she shouts. He shoves her out the way.

"Tell me!" Aren yells.

"Fine!" Jaykin shouts back. He knows whatever he says, no one will believe him. "Just leave Meara out of this and I'll tell you everything."

"Deal," Aren replies and kneels in front of Jaykin, face to face. "Now, the crystal. The real one this time, not the fake that was in Dreamora."

"It's…" Jaykin takes his time to reply. "…in Q-Ara."

"Q-Ara?" Aren says in disbelief. "Why there?"

"Why not? Kanaren is there too."

"You're lying to me," Aren says in frustration.

"Why would I lie? You can look for him for days here, but you won't find him."

Aren stands, considering his next move.

"He left me here as a decoy with those other Hunters from Dreamora. They were on our tail for days."

Aren smiles.

"He knew I would be looking for him," he says. "That's why I got that message yesterday from him." He shakes his head. "And those Hunters are in Q-Ara, too."

"That's why they are there. To get the crystal back," Jaykin says quickly.

"Q-Five!" Aren shouts. "Let's get out of here. Start up the collector!" It stops searching and turns to the collector which starts up automatically. Aren approaches Jaykin.

"You're coming with me."

Suddenly, something whizzes past Aren's head and hits into Q-Five's back.

"What the…?" Aren says, watching incredulously as it is consumed and wrapped around by vines. The collector also powers down. He quickly turns but is smashed into the air and straight into the side of the collector, landing near the door, unconscious.

Standing there is Eragraph.

"Thanks," Jaykin says. "I'm so glad you're on my side." Eragraph prepares his bow again. "Which side is she on?" he indicates Meara. She has managed to pick up Q-Five's Q-Azar and is pointing it straight at Eragraph.

"What…what is that?" she hesitates.

"That is my friend, Meara. He has a name," Jaykin replies, quickly getting in front of her. "And I would die for him too." She very slowly lowers the Q-Azar, examining the Element in every detail.

"Okay," she says calmly but still shocked. "What is he?"

"I'll explain later. We need to get going. Can you please release me from these?" he asks, trying to point at the cuffs binding his hands.

"Sure." She heads for Aren, who is still unconscious, to retrieve a key.

"I'll go get Irown," Eragraph says, and runs off.

"There are more like him?" Meara asks, eyes wide open.

"Yes," Jaykin nods, while she unlocks him from the cuffs.

"You have some serious explaining to do."

"So do you. How is it I'm talking to you outside of Lementes? I thought you were scared of the outside."

"I am. I'm terrified. When I found your letter, all I wanted to do was find you. When Aren appeared out of nowhere and told me that he had received a message from you I had to come with him."

"Ok, I get it," Jaykin replies. They both look at the lifeless body of Aren. "We should really take him with us."

"He said that you'd stolen Dreamora's crystal. Is that true?"

"I'll explain it later. First, help me with him, would you?" They pick up Aren, one on each side. "Damn, he's heavy. I'll just get Eragraph to throw him in."

Eragraph then appears, supporting Irown.

"How do I get into this thing?" Eragraph asks.

"At the back," Jaykin points while he and Meara enter the collector by its side door.

"Open up!" Eragraph shouts. Jaykin quickly runs to the back and presses the button. The rear door opens.

Meara covers her mouth in shock as she watches Irown bleed, heavily.

"It looks really beaten up. Is it okay?" she asks.

"His name is Irown," Jaykin says. "And he'll be fine when we get to Q-Ara." He tries to make space for the Elements.

"How are you going to get them in there? You know what they're like about any sort of creature."

"I'll think of something," Jaykin rummages through some bags in the collector.

"Get some rest Irown," Eragraph whispers.

"Can you bring those things in here?" Jaykin asks Eragraph, referring to Aren and his Q-Roid.

"You sure you don't want to leave them for the barragona? After the way he treated you?" Eragraph asks.

"As much as I want that, we better take them with us."

"Okay, if we have to. What about her?" they both look at Meara. She steps back a little, feeling slightly intimidated.

"I really don't want to stay here," she says.

"No, she's fine. She's with us now," Jaykin replies and smiles slightly. He throws Eragraph something.

"What is it?"

"It's a tranquillizer for creatures, just in case it wakes up," Jaykin replies, nodding towards Aren.

"You're treating Aren like he's a creature, Jaykin," Meara says.

"I know. Like you were with Eragraph and Irown. For the record, the Elements aren't creatures. Just because you're not used to them doesn't mean you should treat them any differently." Jaykin moves to the front of the collector. Eragraph picks up Aren and the Q-Roid, one in each arm.

"You need to get some muscles, Jaykin," Eragraph says.

"Thanks. I'm defending you here," Jaykin replies, looking at all the buttons and levers before him. He lets out a sigh and holds the back of his head. "I don't know how to fly this thing."

He looks around and finds an odd-shaped connector near the steering controls which is slightly familiar. He takes out the memory core of Q-Tech and looks at the bottom of it. It is the same size and shape. He inserts it and the collector powers up again.

"Greetings Jaykin," it says through the speakers.

"Q-Tech?" Jaykin says, surprised and pleased.

"Yes, speaking," it replies.

"It's good to hear your voice. Can you fly this collector?"

"Scanning…yes," it replies.

"Jaykin's right, I'm sorry," Meara says, facing Eragraph, "I can be too quick to judge sometimes." She lowers her head, embarrassed. Eragraph can see she is upset. He lowers Aren and the Q-Roid onto the floor.

"It's fine. We all make mistakes." He picks off a little green stem from his armour and holds it out. Meara stares intently as a beautiful flower blooms a bright pink and he gives it to her. "Here, welcome to the group," he says smiling. She accepts the small gift.

"Thank you, I will look after this," she looks up at him, a little shyly. "May I ask you a question?"

"Of course."

"What are you? Jaykin says you're…Elements?"

"Right. Let's get going," Jaykin says.

***

Miles up high and deep within the unknown lands, a rumble of thunder and a flash of lightning opens a pair of eyes. Kanaren awakes, dazed. He surveys his surroundings: endless sky, the ground far below, and barrags swooping and screeching all around. The barragona still has him gripped tightly in its claws. Both his arms are free and he tries to move but the pain is unbearable. He hears voices on the back of the barragona.

"What the…?" he says. "Pree, Mordan! What are you doing here?"

"We're trying to save you," Pree says.

"You should have stayed with the others!" Kanaren replies.

"We are a team!" Mordan says.

"Listen, forget about me. Jaykin needs you to help him find the other Elements!"

"But—" Pree hesitates.

"Just do it!" Kanaren yells and pulls out a double-pointed dagger from within his jacket. He stares at the sharp blades. "I'm going on another journey," he says quietly to himself. Then he yells, "I have something with your name on it, barragona!" Using all his strength, he plunges the dagger into the beast's thin scaled leg. In pain, she releases him.

"No, Kanaren!" both the Elements shout out. He falls soundlessly into the clouds and disappears. The barragona works hard to keep flying. Suddenly, a small ball of light shoots up from those clouds, as fast as lightning, and smashes into the barragona's lower jaw, knocking her unconscious. Both Pree and Mordan only just barely hold on. The barragona's body slowly turns upside down as her belly points to the sky. She spins out of control, falling a great distance to Izara.

***

Back in the collector, Jaykin suddenly has a sinking

feeling in his stomach. He feels sick and dizzy. He holds onto the collector's control panel to keep steady, then he feels fine. He shakes his head and looks out west while Q-Tech pilots. The others are having a conversation about the evolution process.

"Jaykin, are you listening to this? Solutions and Elements, it just sounds amazing!" Meara says, excitedly.

"Yeah, I know," he moves around slightly to get in a better position, feeling pain all over his body.

"Are you okay?" she asks. She clambers into the co-pilot's seat.

"Yeah, I'm fine. Sorry, it's just been a busy few days that's all. We've been attacked quite a lot."

"Oh, well you're still alive," she says cheerfully, then notices his arms. They seem more muscular now; not as thin or skinny anymore. "You're looking good by the way. You look…" She tries to find the right word. "Healthier." Jaykin looks up at her, and notices the pink flower in her hair. He is slightly confused by what she's saying. He is feeling awful right now. She continues, "You look as if you've had some rest too…and have you grown?"
Jaykin laughs.

"Well, I do feel like I've had some rest. I slept for two days straight but I'm not sure that I've grown." She then realises that he is flying the collector.

"How on Izara are you flying this thing?" she asks.

"I'm not flying; it's Kanaren's Q-Roid," he points at the memory core.

"Jaykin?" Q-Tech asks. "Where is Master

Kanaren?"

"I don't know," Jaykin replies hesitantly. He turns towards the Elements. "Irown, why haven't they made contact yet?"

"I don't know. It might be a number of reasons."

"What is the limit of Mordan and Pree's powers?"

"It depends on the Element. Some can use their powers within a few metres, a very few can use them on a scale of hundreds of miles."

"Depends where they are," Eragraph says. "They seem like powerful Elements though."

"They are," Irown says. "And they can look after themselves."

"I hope they're okay," Jaykin sighs. He then stares thoughtfully at Aren. "Why would Kanaren try and get hold of *you*? Meara, where did you meet that thing again?" She turns her whole body away from him, not wanting to answer.

"School," she replies quietly, hesitant. "We sort of…dated for a year." She looks back at him. "Then, he arrived, that Kanaren, and took him away."

"Oh," Jaykin says, figuring it out. "The same thing happened to me."

"Exactly," she sighs. "I was worried you would do the same, and then you did."

"I'm sorry Meara. Kanaren—"

"It's okay," she interrupts, reading his thoughts. "It's done now." She looks at Aren. "That was nearly three years ago and I hadn't seen him since, until two days ago, when he arrived at my doorstep. He was worried about me. He somehow knew you were connected to me and he wanted to find you and Kanaren. He then told me he had received a message and that's when we came to find you here." An awkward silence follows. "Jaykin, why did you steal the crystal?" she asks in a firm voice.

"We..." he pauses. "...didn't steal it; it was an accident," he says, defending himself.

"An accident?" She raises her voice. "Jaykin, you're wanted in all six cities! You need to give it back. I'm sure they'll be fine—"

"No Meara, they won't!" he fires back. "We had no choice." He stops and wonders how much he should tell her. "Meara, there was an Element inside that crystal." Her eyes widen as she takes this in. "All of them are from crystals. Kanaren and I have taken on the role of looking after them. We couldn't walk away." She sighs in relief.

"I understand now," she says calmly. "But you need to realise; the people won't accept the Elements. You know my reaction when I first met them."

"The people will understand," he replies. "It'll just take time."

"Jaykin," she shakes her head. "You're going to get yourself killed, and them."

"What else am I supposed to do?" he says slightly raising his voice. "We don't have anywhere else to go. Q-Ara is the best option."

"Well, you do have a choice," she replies. "How on Izara are we going to get into Q-Ara without being noticed by the Guards?"

"Don't worry, I have a plan."

Chapter 24

The City of Q-Ara

They reach the outskirts of the city of Q-Ara and Q-Tech lands the collector. The engines cut out and the rear door opens. Eragraph picks up both Aren and Q-Five and places them on the long grass.

"Will they be okay out there?" Meara asks.

"No idea," Jaykin replies. "He should have thought about that when he attacked me."

While walking back, Eragraph rips off a piece of bark from his armour and, using his powers, reshapes it slightly, then threads dried-up roots through it.

"Before we get there, Jaykin, I want to give you this." He passes him a sort of wooden face-mask. "I overheard you two talking about not being spotted, so it's a just-in-case."

"Thank you, Eragraph." He tries it for size. "Perfect fit." He shows Meara who shakes her head.

"I really hope you know what you're doing," she says.

They take off again.

"Q-Tech, can you get us into the city?" Jaykin asks.

"Yes. Where would you like to land?"

"The nearest hospital," Jaykin says, checking back on Irown.

"This is collector zero, five, nine, eight, transmitting to Q-Ara command tower. Permission to enter the city?" Q-Tech says.

"Code confirmed collector zero, five, nine, eight. You have permission."

"Permission to land at location code eight, eight, four, four."

"Confirmed. Platform ninety-one is available, medical assistance will be on standby at the location."

"Good work Q-Tech," Jaykin says.

"That is one astonishing sight," Eragraph says, observing the city in front of him. The great city doors open and they fly through. Q-Ara, the city of ambition and new ideas; also known as the city of the future. Its biggest attraction, though, is its monthly Preyal tournaments.

The collector twists and turns through the tall skyscrapers, which seem to be cleaner than in the other cities, and much more greenery is in evidence, some of it climbing the outside of the buildings. They go higher and head towards a very tall building. It has numerous collector bays around it and they land on one.

"Thank you, Q-Tech," Jaykin says and is just about to withdraw it from the controls when he stops. "Q-Tech, I want to rebuild you. Where shall I take you to do that?"

"Doctor Rotnevin is the best person," it replies.

"I'll do that." He takes out the memory core and places it in his pocket. He also grabs a Q-Azar from a holster that hangs from the wall. "Okay, let me talk to the doctors first." Both Meara and Jaykin step out of the collector. While Jaykin pulls down his mask, he notices a couple of doctors stand outside waiting for them. "There is a casualty on the collector," Jaykin says.

"Okay," one of them replies and they run up to the back and look in. They immediately stagger back.

"What the…" they gasp. "Is this some sort of joke?" Jaykin pulls out the Q-Azar and points it at them.

"No. He needs treatment, and without an audience."

"But—" one doctor hesitates and they look at one another.

"No, it will be done. They won't hurt you; I promise."

"Okay, we'll try our best but it's not going to be easy," one says. "Can you get it into the hospital?"

"The 'It' you're referring to, understands you," Jaykin replies. Eragraph gives Irown a hand up and helps him to the entrance. Both the doctors and Meara enter first, to make sure the coast is clear.

"I will stay here," Eragraph says. "I think it would be for the best."

"Oh, okay," Jaykin says. "You can look after the collector then if you like? Hopefully, we won't be too long."

"Thank you for everything," Irown says. "You have been a good Element, Eragraph."

"It's been an honour, Irown. You'll be fine. They will look after you here. I will see you soon. Just get better." He places his arm on his chest as Irown stumbles in. "Look after him Jaykin, we will need Irown."

"I will. Try and stay out of view. The last thing we need is all the Guards descending on us."

They head deep into the hospital, taking precautions to avoid any confrontations. They manage to reach a large operating theatre. Meara turns to Jaykin while they wait outside.

"What now?" she asks.

"We wait," he says, and, placing his hand in his pocket, he takes out the small handheld Q-Azar and hands it to her. "I'm going to get us some help. I need you to stand guard until they're finished in there."

"Okay," she says, nervously, looking quite pale.

"It'll be fine," Jaykin says, looking for the nearest help Q-Puter. He runs up to it and swipes the screen.

"*Map of cities, loading…please choose the city.*"

"Q-Ara."

"*Loaded.*"

"My location?"

"*You are here.*" An icon illuminates their position on the screen.

"Find the nearest family member of Rotnevin."

"*Found, Doctor Rotnevin Jr, age forty-five, occupation, weapon inventor…*"

Jaykin scans the map closely and works out it is on the other side of the city, but not too far away. Then he turns to Meara and lifts the mask to uncover his face.

"I'll be back as soon as I can."

"Jaykin, please be careful," she says.

"I will; you too. If you see any Guards just act normal. The Q-Azar is for emergencies only."

Before she can reply, he pulls the mask over his face again and disappears around the corner.

***

Hundreds of miles away in the depths of the unknown lands, Pree is nudging a sleeping Mordan.

"*Mordan, wake up.*" In the absence of any reaction, she gives up and uses her powers.

"Argh…are we there yet? Why does it feel as if I landed on my head?" He sits up and feels around, checking for damage. "And why are you using your power?"

"*Because the barragona is just over there!*" she transmits, with a warning in her expression, and points to some fallen trees. "*We've got to be quiet.*"

"*Why are we still here then?*"

"*Because I needed to wake you up first, dummy.*" She pushes him in the shoulder.

"*Ouch, now my shoulder hurts.*"

"*Stop complaining. We have to be vigilant here!*" He lifts himself up with some help from Pree. "*We need to find Kanaren and get out of this place with our bodies in one piece. Come on.*"

They run toward the broken trees and hide behind one. They peer around it and spot the barragona, which can just about stand. She mopes around as if she, too, has just woken up. She lets out an almighty screech, either in anger or in pain. She shakes her head and stretches her wings one by one, flapping them slightly to warm them. Slowly but surely her wings pick up enough air and she ascends into the sky, probably to try and catch up with the storm and her barrags.

"Phew! We won't need to go up against her again," Mordan says with relief. Pree rushes over to where the barragona had crashed landed.

"*There's no sign of Kanaren.*"

"*Let's use our powers,*" he replies. They both close their eyes, focusing on their surroundings, moving their heads in different directions, searching for any sign of life. "*I can't sense anything, just wildlife.*"

"*Same here,*" Pree says, with worry in her expression. Then her face changes as if she has come up with an idea. She stares into Mordan's eyes. "We should combine," she says. Mordan looks at her, surprised.

"This isn't really the time and place, Pree."

"Mordan, be serious for one moment, please. Kanaren might need our help!"

"Okay," he replies, soberly. They both place their hands on one another's temples and close their eyes again. Minutes pass and they both blink and stare at each other.

"No, Mordan," she says. "You can't think that." There are tears in her eyes.

"Pree, that's the only thing I can think of. He's either a lot further than where we can sense him or the likelihood is that he's—"

"No!" she interrupts. "Don't say it."

Mordan looks up at the sky, calculating how far they had fallen. Pree is insistent.

"I can't think like that. He's still alive, I just know it. He must be out there somewhere."

"Pree, listen to yourself. Kanaren cannot have survived that fall unless he had the most extraordinary luck."

"We were lucky."

"We had a huge barragona breaking our fall, that's why."

"True," she sighs. "This is going to break Jaykin's heart."

"I know but we need to go."

"We can't, we can't stop looking."

"Remember what Kanaren said to us. We need to get back to Jaykin. We have to forget about Kanaren now."

"But—"

"No but about it Pree. We can't waste our time looking for someone who could be—"

"Okay. Okay," she says, pushing him to stop. "We can go, but we must not give up on him, okay?"

"Okay," he replies, trying to reassure her.

Mordan and Pree are suddenly startled by a loud squawk coming from somewhere in the trees. It sounds familiar but they cannot immediately place it. Whatever it is, it squawks again.

"There," Pree points towards the trees. "What is that?"

On a branch, a large green feathered bird is perched.

"It looks like Eragraph's pet," Mordan replies.

"I think you're right."

Mordan focuses on it and reads its memories, seeing the battle with the barragona.

"Yes, I thought so," he says. "Her name is Elra."

Pree holds her arm up and the bird swoops down

straight onto it.

"Hello Elra, you're bootiful," she says in a mushy cuddly voice, stroking the feathers just under her beak. Elra chirps in excitement.

"I'm wondering why she's here and not with Eragraph," Mordan says.

"It is strange. Do you think he sent her to help us?"

"Maybe," he replies, looking for a direction to take next.

"I think we should look after her in the meantime," she says.

***

Jaykin spots a couple of Guards. Cautiously, he tries to blend into the crowds. He eventually arrives at the address and enters, removing his mask. He approaches the reception point.

"Hi, could you tell me where Doctor Rotnevin's office is, please?"

"Do you have an appointment today sir?" the man behind the desk asks.

"No, but I just need him to fix a Q-Roid if he has the time." Jaykin worries that the receptionist has recognised him. He looks around warily but there is no one else to be seen. The receptionist looks at his screen and his expression shows surprise.

"It's very rare that he is in." He taps a couple of buttons. "You're in luck sir. He is available now if you would like to see him?"

"Sure," Jaykin replies.

"Okay, can I take a name?" Jaykin hesitates for a split second.

"Eragraph," he blurts out; the safest option.

"I will let him know you're on your way. Top floor on the right from the lift."

"Thank you," Jaykin moves quickly. "Top floor."

The lift doors close and it heads up in a flash. Seconds later, he is on the right floor and looking for the doctor's name on all the doors. He finds it and knocks. It opens straight away. He peers through, curiously.

"Doctor Rotnevin?" he calls out, but there is no answer. He opens the door further; it creaks slightly. The room is dark, but for a little light from the corridor. He can smell burning metal coming from somewhere within. "Lights on," he says quickly, but nothing happens and he still can't see anyone. He can make out piles of junk and he picks up a couple of unidentifiable items, wondering about the owner. Maybe Doctor Rotnevin is a hoarder, he thinks.

"Hello?" shouts a voice from another room.

"Hello, I'm looking for Doctor…" Jaykin stops and spots a head through the door. "…Rotnevin?" The man walks in.

"That's me. How can I help you? Oh sorry," he says, realizing the lights are off. "On!" he shouts and the lights slowly turn on, revealing a spacious room. He stands there wiping his hands and face with a piece of cloth, getting rid of some sort of dirt or black oil. He's wearing a long white coat smudged with handprints. About forty years of age, he has short brown hair and a slight stubble of facial hair. "Sorry, I'm playing around with the light system. I've always felt 'lights on' is too much to say, don't you think?"

"I guess," Jaykin replies. Rotnevin chuckles.

"I'm kidding lad. I need to entertain myself while I'm working," he says, falling and relaxing into the nearest chair, panting slightly. "Anyway, what can I help you with?" he asks, wiping more stuff off of his hands.

"I have a Q-Roid that needs to be reconstructed." Jaykin pulls out the part of Q-Tech and gives it to the doctor.

"Oh right. What happened to it?"

"It got attacked by a flood of scarrags."

"Cool. That's the best story I've heard in a while," Rotnevin laughs. "Normally, they get eaten and I need to replace the whole thing. I hope it put up a good fight." He then looks at it very carefully, twisting and turning the part. "Looks like a very old model. Let me just check the sort code." He waves his hand in front of him, activating the virtual assistant. "Let's see. Q-Puter check code number one, seven, two, two, one."

"*Searching…*" Rotnevin swirls in his chair while he waits and looks at Jaykin.

"How is Kanaren?" he asks.

Jaykin's heart skips. He doesn't know how to reply or to react. He certainly doesn't know how Rotnevin knows about Kanaren.

"He's okay. How did you know I'm with him?"

"The Q-Roid is his. I recognize the code as I've given him the parts every so often for upgrades." Jaykin just grins slightly, hoping Rotnevin hasn't recognized Kanaren from any wanted adverts. "I haven't seen him for a while."

"He's fine, just..." Jaykin pauses. "...busy. That's why he asked me to come around."
Rotnevin smiles and nods his head.

"Oh, fair enough. Busy saving Lementes or something no doubt. I did wonder why you had his sword too." Jaykin had completely forgotten about his sword on his back, and grabs onto it for comfort, making sure it is still attached properly.

"Oh yeah," he forces a chuckle. "I forgot about that."

"Yes. You had better not lose that. He wouldn't be happy."

"I'll try not to, thanks."

"*Found...version: one point two Q-T,*" the Q-Puter announces.

"Ah, fantastic timing Q-Ter." He looks over at Jaykin, who is feeling rather awkward. "My Q-Puter and I have nicknames for each other." Jaykin smiles and nods politely. "Looks like it needs an upgrade," Rotnevin says, and swipes with his finger ever so slightly.

"That would be great."

"Let's see what I have here." He turns his chair slightly towards the door to the next room and stands. He swipes his hand again. The walls slide back revealing a large workshop. A whole array of parts is in view.

"So which Q-Roid would he like this time?" he says, going around collecting pieces of Q-Roid parts. "I have boosters for both hands and feet; stealth armour; exploding heads." He picks something up and twists and turns it. "Whatever that is?" He throws it, hitting into something and crashing onto the ground, making lots of noise. "You name it, I've got it, and if I haven't got it, I can make it."

Jaykin hesitates and looks around the room.

"Umm, just an updated version will do. Maybe with some awesome weapons to go with it too?"

"Typical Kanaren," Rotnevin replies with a grin. "Okay, I'll see what I can do."

"Thank you," Jaykin replies, scanning the workshop.

"Did you know, Q-Tech was one of the first fighting Q-Roids to be made here? Looks as if Kanaren has a liking for it."

Surprised, Jaykin replies: "I think he likes his stuff from the past."

Rotnevin chuckles to himself again. "That is very true. He's a bit of a collector. He's shown me many of his favourite items from the past."

Jaykin plays around with the crystal in his pocket and is very tempted to ask about it but stops himself.

"What sort of stuff do you make here? I recognize some of it."

"I make all sorts: Q-Roids, armour, weapons, and some other unusual things too."

Jaykin spots something he recognizes.

"You create weapons for the Preyal tournament?" he asks, excitedly.

"Of course," Rotnevin replies, as if it were obvious. "Are you a fan?"

"I'm a huge fan."

"Well, that thing behind you…" he points. "…is a fire enhancer."

"To boost the Barka's fire breathing technique, right?" Jaykin says.

"That's correct," he replies, looking pleasantly surprised. "What about the thing next to it?"

"I would say it is…" He thinks for a few seconds. "…part of the armour that holds some sort of weapon. Maybe for a rogsprinter? It's too large for a bladester."

"Correct, well done. You know your creatures and their upgrades."

"My father was very much into the game and taught me everything to know about it," he says, admiring the rest of the stuff.

"A wise man," Rotnevin says.

"He is," Jaykin replies. He has not had much time to think about his father lately, with so much else happening. Then he remembers what Kanaren said about what to do next; to find the system in Q-Ara. "The weapons you create here; who are they for?" Jaykin asks.

"Oh, many are for the Guards and I get quite a few Hunters like yourself through here too. I'm a busy man," he says cheerfully.

"Yeah, the receptionist said." He looks at Rotnevin wondering something. "If you know about the Hunters then you must know about the system?" Jaykin states.

"Of course, I do. My family helped create it."

"Really? Would you happen to know where it

is?"

"Certainly. It's in the building across from the Palace. Heavily guarded though, so you'll need to be very careful," he warns.

"Thanks. You wouldn't happen to know where the Hunters hang out around here?"

"The majority in this city work for high paid betters, or thugs as I like to call them. They do a lot of deals for the Preyal tournaments, so they're outside of the city most of the time but before the tournament you'll find them hanging around the arena, signing in their new creatures—"

Suddenly an alarm goes off which makes Jaykin jump. It sounds like the city is being attacked but it is, in fact, the machine telling them the rebuild is finished.

"Good. It's done," Rotnevin says, clapping his hands together in satisfaction.

"That was quick," Jaykin says.

"Well, you have to be quick in this business, plus, to be honest, I make these sorts of things all the time. I normally input what I need for the next day and the machines do the rest for me. These things never stop, unless you have unexpected Hunters coming in," he smiles.

"Sorry," Jaykin says.

"It's okay. I owe Kanaren anyway, so this is me paying him back."

Q-Tech jumps down from the machine.

"Will it recognize me?" Jaykin asks. Rotnevin smiles in satisfaction.

"Hello, Jaykin," It replies.

"Welcome back Q-Tech; how are you feeling?" he asks quietly.
It pauses to process.

"New," it says and looks at its arms and body, parts of it begin to move. "Taller too."

"Q-Tech," Rotnevin says. "You have been upgraded with the latest weapons, armour and fighting technique modes. Familiarize these new functions and follow your master's command. Do you confirm?"

"Confirmed, Doctor Rotnevin, and thank you," it replies.

"And Jaykin. Take this." He hands him a small wristband. "This is to control Q-Tech with either voice or hand commands, whatever best suits you or Kanaren. He's under your control now but when you get back to Kanaren, just follow the instructions on the wrist command and it'll transfer to him." He kindly points to the door to let them out. "Oh, and remember, there is a lot of gadgetry on there; one in particular, for when you're really in trouble. It's the voice command F-Q, but try it out later." He smiles. "It'll be a nice little surprise for you." He winks. "I wish you luck in your travels, and if you need me for anything don't hesitate to give me a call." He then taps the wrist twice with two different fingers.

"I might actually take you up on that offer. I'll definitely be in touch," Jaykin says, grateful. Having someone like him on his side will be a fantastic bonus. "And thank you for everything you've done, Doctor Rotnevin."

"No problem at all and you can just call me Rotnevin." He smiles. "Look after Q-Tech and say hi to Kanaren for me."

"I will; bye." They head back to the lift. "It's good to have you back Q-Tech."

"It's an honour serving you again, Jaykin. Will Master Kanaren join soon?"

"I don't think Kanaren will be back for a while, so for the time being I'm going to be your Master, okay?"

"Of course," it says peaceably. "To be at your side at all times." Jaykin smiles. It reminds him of his father, hearing those words. It strikes him that Q-Tech is the Q-Roid version of his father and it makes him feel energised and positive.

The lift reaches the ground floor.

"We have a few new people in our group now. Hopefully, I'll get to introduce you to them," Jaykin says, while they go past the reception, waving 'thank you' to the receptionist. He doesn't respond as expected. Instead, he stands up and runs over to Jaykin.

"You can't go out," he says.

"Why not?" Jaykin asks.

"There has been a creature sighted inside the city."

"The Elements," Jaykin gasps.

Chapter 25

The Legend Falls

Jaykin and Q-Tech sprint the quickest way back to the hospital, slowing as they reach the door to try to be as casual as possible and move into the lift.

"Q-Tech, I need you to go get the collector. Do you remember where it is?"

"Yes."

"Good. As soon as they're done with Irown, I'll be in contact with you and we'll get out of here."

"Understood."

They get to level ninety-one.

"Jaykin!" Meara shouts. "He's still in there."

"Have you heard anything from the doctors?" he asks.

"Nothing," she replies, shaking her head. With that, a couple of Guards walk around the corner.

"You two!" one of them shouts. "What are you doing? We're evacuating this level."

"Sorry, we didn't hear the announcement," Meara replies.

Jaykin stays quiet and tries to look away. Both the Guards look him up and down, he forgot to cover his face.

"You look familiar kid," one Guard says.

"I get that a lot," Jaykin replies.

"I bet you do, especially with two swords on your back," the other Guard holds his Q-Azar tighter.

Then they look at one another. "I think he's the one."

"You're coming with us kid," says the first. Instantly, a bow swings left and hits into one of the Guards who is tossed into the wall, knocking him out. Then it swings to the right and the other Guard hits the wall. Standing before them is a tall wooden figure.

"Eragraph," Jaykin says.

"Hi," he says cheerfully. "Looked like you needed some help. Any news on Irown?"

"Nothing," Meara says.

"Then I think it's about time we found out what they've been doing in there.

Only just fitting, he steps closer to the doors and kicks them open, watching someone scurrying away.

The doctors look up at him, holding their hands up, shocked and scared. Eragraph sees Irown lying across several operating tables as he is too big for one. He is conscious but still dazed by the anaesthetic. "They have done nothing," Eragraph says, examining Irown.

"What?" Jaykin gasps.

"We can't do anything," says one of the doctors. "His body is much more complex than ours."

"What are we going to do now?" Eragraph asks. Through the window, Jaykin can see the Palace at a distance.

"Q-Tech," Jaykin instructs, using his new device. "Bring the collector to the Palace-side window on level ninety-one."

"Am I now on the wanted list?" Meara asks anxiously.

"No," Jaykin replies. She peers out of the operating room doors. Suddenly she is pulled through from the other side.

"Meara!" Jaykin shouts. "Eragraph, there are Guards outside!"

"Get back! I'll hold them off," Eragraph says, standing against the wall. He places his hand on it. Vines and bark start moving across both doors interlocking one another.

"But what about Meara?" Jaykin worries.

"We can't do anything now. Get Irown out of here."

The windows vibrate as the collector appears. Its rear door opens and Jaykin pulls out a Q-Azar and shoots at the windows, shattering the thick glass into pieces.

"They're escaping through the window!" someone shouts outside the room. Jaykin tries his best to get Irown up from the operating tables but, given his size, is struggling.

"Come on Irown, we need to get out of here!" Jaykin pleads.

Irown doesn't say anything, just mumbling and stumbling from the effects of the anaesthetic. Suddenly, blasts are shot from the Guards, drowning out the noise of the collector, and nearly destroying Eragraph's vine wall.

"Take cover!" he shouts. With that, several blasts get through and hit the wall on the other side of the room. The doctors hide under some tables in fear.

"Hold it steady!" Jaykin shouts to Q-Tech. Both Jaykin and Irown manage to get a foot each onto the collector. Suddenly Irown stops, jerking forward slightly and holding his breath. "Irown?" Jaykin says desperately, trying without success to pull him further into the collector. Irown doesn't reply either. Instead, he falls to his knees. "Irown!" Jaykin shouts louder, holding onto his shoulder. Irown turns his head slightly and faces Jaykin, staring into his eyes. He lets out a deep slow breath, leans left, and falls off the collector. "Irown!" Jaykin screams as he watches his friend fall away and drop several floors. He feels his hand is wet and warm. It is covered in blood.

With no warning, Jaykin is shoved hard by something, forcing him further into the collector and hitting the floor, hard. For a split second, he thinks it is Eragraph, but then the sharp pain starts, becoming unbearable, and he feels the warm blood on his clothing. He has been hit too.

"Jaykin!" Eragraph shouts, and runs towards him. He transforms his bow into a wooden shield, covering himself and Jaykin. "We need to get out of here!" he shouts. Q-Tech steers the collector away from the hospital. Eragraph scans the cabin.

"Where's Irown?" he gasps.

"He's gone!" Jaykin screams, in a huge amount of pain and grief. "He's gone, Eragraph! He got hit!" Tears pour down his face. "We've lost him!"

"No!" Eragraph whispers. He holds onto Jaykin to comfort him as he screams in pain.

***

Deep within the forest, unknown to anyone else, Pree and Mordan continue their own journey.

"Dam wizzigs!" Mordan yells, waving his arms

around as the insects fly around him. "Why on Izara did these things still have to be in the future?" Pree looks at him and shakes her head in disgust. As she looks ahead again, her eyes widen and she gasps.

"Mordan!" she shouts, as she grasps his arm tightly.

"What are you doing Pree?" She points. "What the…?"

Just ahead, the forest ends abruptly and, instead, a vast desert stretches miles before them. Shocked, Mordan steps back and pulls Pree with him.

"Is that what I think it is?" he says, staring into her eyes.

"I think so."

"Can't be."

"I thought it was a myth."

"Well by the looks of things, it isn't." He pulls a leaf off a plant nearby and throws it towards the sand. Halfway there, the leaf transforms; its greenness turning yellow, then brown. By the time it lands, it crumbles into tiny pieces.

"Thought so," Mordan says, bending down and having a closer look. "It's true then. The Deathly Plains actually exist."

"You don't think—"

"What?" He stares at Pree, then at the eerie desert. "Kanaren? No, he wouldn't."

"He wouldn't have known," she says.

Mordan stands and holds her tightly by both her arms, trying to make sense of things.

"Kanaren's clever. If he had survived, he wouldn't have come this way."

"What if—"

"We can't think like that. We must keep going." They both take a last look at the desert and turn the opposite way, heading south.

***

Heading northwest from Q-Ara, both Jaykin and Eragraph sit silently in the back of the collector for over an hour. Q-Tech has managed to escape the city by going through the dockyard exit.

Jaykin holds his wounded arm. He has the bark wrapped around it, as Irown had around his.

"How are you?" Eragraph asks, but Jaykin stays quiet. He looks exhausted. "I know how you're feeling. I've gone through it many times."

"How do you go through this?" Jaykin asks quietly.

"You keep going. You can't save everyone."

"It feels like everyone who gets close to me disappears," he stares at the floor. "First my mother, then my father, Kanaren, Pree, Mordan, Meara and now Irown. It won't be long until you're gone too."

"It's not your fault."

Jaykin sighs. "Well, it feels like it is. I should have tried harder; everyone would still be here and Irown would be still alive." Tears fall down his distraught face again.

"How do you know that?" Eragraph persists. "How hard do you need to work to keep everyone happy and by your side? It's impossible and foolish. You need to keep moving. You have a mission, don't you?" Jaykin nods. "Then focus on that. We Elements were in a Great War for thousands of years; did we stop to worry about what we did? No. We carried on fighting for the ones we loved, to save our lands."

"Yeah ok, I'm sorry."

"No need to apologise. I know that this is tough for you." He looks at him for a few seconds. "How's the arm?"

Jaykin looks at it and moves it slightly. "Still attached."

"Good," Eragraph chuckles.

"Jaykin, sorry to disturb you but the destination of your choice is close by," Q-Tech announces.

"Thanks," Jaykin replies.

Eragraph looks out of the window and spots water.

"Izara looks calm. I thought I'd never see these sorts of days again," he says contentedly.

"What did you do before the Great War?" Jaykin asks.

"When I was human, I spent most of the time farming, helping grow food, plants and trees for the benefit of our people."

"Is that why you chose the Nature Element?"

"Yes. Elra and I used to look after the forests surrounding the nearest villages, scaring off creatures that tried stealing our food." He mimes moving stealthily and they both laugh. He picks off a couple of pieces of fruit that are growing on his armour, then throws them into his mouth. He offers one to Jaykin, who accepts. He relaxes, leaning back onto the wall of the collector. "Those were the good old days."

"Elra is your pet, right?"

"That's correct. By accident too. I found her near the village when she was little. She had fallen out of a tree. No sign of her family either. They usually fledge within the first couple of weeks of being born. She obviously failed and damaged her wing. Her parents left her there to die. I took her to the nearest Life Element. She's been by my side ever since. Except for now, of course."

"I'm sure she appreciates you. I wished I had listened to Meara when my father went missing."

"You don't need to beat yourself up. She cares for you Jaykin; I can see that clearly and she always will, wherever she is." He throws another piece of fruit into his mouth and passes more to Jaykin. He smiles to himself as a thought occurs. "Now you have me and the rest of the Elements to look after you."

Jaykin manages the hint of a smile too.

"Thank you Eragraph. That's good to know."

"Well, it's true. We all need to look out for one another to keep going. Like Elra, she'll probably be with your friends by now."

"I'm sure she is." He pauses. "What was it like going up against other Elements in the Great War?"

Eragraph throws a bad berry away.

"Difficult," he says. "And I had no choice. When the Razilians attacked, we had to retaliate. I didn't enjoy going up against other Elements at all, but hey," he sighs out loud. "That's all in the past now, right?" He lapses into silent thought.

***

Back in the city of Q-Ara, in the depths of the Palace, no one sits on the throne but, beside it, a High Knight stands tall. He is wearing dark clothing, covering his whole body, including a full helmet. The Palace doors open and a Guard runs towards the throne.

"High Knight!" he shouts.

"Commander, what can I help you with?"

"Hunters are outside the doors. They wish to enter."

"What is the reason?"

"They claim they have captured a creature like nothing seen before and they wish to bargain with you."

"Intriguing," the High Knight says. "Bring them in. I want to see this thing for myself."

The Guard turns towards the entrance and waves to colleagues at the doors.

"Let them in!" he shouts. The doors open wide and five people walk in, one ahead of the others, who are holding long chains, each connected to a huge cage on wheels, its contents concealed by a cover. The High Knight walks down the steps to look at this creature closely. The lead Hunter speaks.

"My name is Slayed; we are Emperor Lon's personal Hunters."

The High Knight lifts his hand up to stop him.

"I know who you are. The question is, why are you in the city?"

"We were here preparing for the Preyal tournament, but we were near the hospital and, well, we have an offer we would like to make to Emperor Mor."

"The emperor is detained with other important business. I will handle this."

"Very well," Slayed replies. "You pay us one

billion digits," he pauses and smiles. "Each."
The High Knight doesn't reply but instead walks a step further down.

"Interesting," he says. "Let's have a look at this creature that's worth five billion digits then."
Slayed points to Steg, who pulls the cover from the cage and reveals the creature. Face down and clinging onto the cage bars with barely any strength, is Irown. He is still struggling to stay awake.

"Hmm," the High Knight says and approaches the cage for a closer look. "What abilities does it have?"

"We haven't found out what it can do—" Slayed replies.

"Doesn't look like it does much," the High Knight says and walks around the cage. "Looks as if it's nearly dead."

"It fell from a building," Arma says.

"And it is one of a kind," Creat says.

"I will not give you a single digit for this thing," the High Knight's tone is complacent.

"Fine! We will take it to Emperor Lon. He will pay what is due to us," Slayed smirks.

"Highly unlikely," the High Knight replies. "May I remind you of rule thirty-four? Any creature found within the walls of any city is already the emperor's property."
Slayed looks at the other Hunters dumbly and wonders why no one has reminded him of that rule.

"Why you—" he shouts at the High Knight.

"It is not wise to argue with me Hunter. Rules are rules."
Slayed's face boils with anger.

"I will not let you get away with this," he says, then turns and walks away. The others follow, leaving the cage and Irown to an uncertain fate.

"And Hunter!" Slayed turns to face the High Knight. "Say hello to Emperor Lon for us!" Although the High Knight wears a helmet, the others can somehow tell he is grinning.

"Let's go," Slayed says to the other Hunters, giving the High Knight a resentful stare as they move away.

"What shall I do with you?" The High Knight says, inspecting Irown curiously. Irown looks up at him and gazes at the mask. "You understand me, don't you?" Irown nods his head ever so slightly, staring fixedly at the dark helmet. "Can you talk too?"

"I can," Irown replies, sounding croaky and in pain.

"You talk in our language? Good. Emperor Mor is going to like you."

"You sound familiar," Irown says.

The High Knight unclips his helmet and uncovers his face. Irown's eyes widen.

Chapter 26

The Evolution Can Continue

"There," Jaykin says, pointing with his good arm. Q-Tech hovers around a grassy piece of land. "Can you land here?" Jaykin asks. The collector lowers on a clear patch on the outskirts of a forest.

"What are we looking for?" Eragraph asks. Jaykin stares into his eyes.

"The next Element."

Eragraph is clearly astonished. Then confusion hits him. How does Jaykin know where the Element is?

"We need to split up," Jaykin says, interrupting Eragraph's train of thought. He steps out of the collector. "Q-Tech we're looking for a crystal, the same as the one in Dreamora."

"Understood," then it steps off too and scans the landscape.

"Crystal?" Eragraph whispers, and alights from the collector, still feeling confused. He notices the grass which reaches up to his knees. "We're not going to find it at this rate." He sticks out his hand and a large circle of grass shrinks away. "That should help."

"Thanks," Jaykin says. He walks to the left then to the right; as if struggling to sense the crystal. Eragraph spots something on the ground. He bends down to wipe his hand across the grass and rubs his fingers together. It is dry blood. Whose?

"Careful Jaykin, there might be creatures lurking around here."

"I've found it!" Jaykin shouts.
Eragraph gets up and walks towards him.

"Where is it?" he asks. Jaykin points downwards. "Underground?"
Jaykin nods.

"It's down there somewhere." He smiles in satisfaction.

"How do you know there is a crystal in this place?" Jaykin stops and looks him in the eyes.

"Because of this." He pulls out the small crystal. "It draws towards other crystals. That's how we find you all," he says, using the same response as Kanaren. Now isn't the right time to tell Eragraph the truth about his powers. Still confused, Eragraph nods. He suspects Jaykin is not telling the whole truth but he goes along with it anyway.

"And I know what Element it is," Jaykin says, discarding the bark wrapped around his arm. He flexes it with no trouble at all. They both look at each other, delighted.

"A Life Element," Eragraph says.

"I hope so," Jaykin replies.

"And all the scars that were around your face have gone too."

"They have?" Jaykin asks, feeling his face. "It must be a Life Element then."

"Let's find out, shall we?" Eragraph places his hand on the ground. "Something is definitely down there; I can feel it. You may want to move out the way for this."

The earth around them starts to shake and lift higher

until it breaks apart into small pieces. The crystal emerges, meeting light for the first time in thousands of years. Covered in mud and dirt, Eragraph's vines hold it steady, ready for Jaykin.

"Good work," Jaykin says.

"Now what?" Eragraph asks.

"I do my thing," Jaykin says. He holds out the small crystal and walks up to the larger one, excitedly.

"Wait," Eragraph says. Jaykin stops in his tracks, wondering what the problem is. "Let's think about this for just a moment."

"What do we need to think about? The crystal is right here." Jaykin says, slightly confused.

"No, you don't understand." He places his hands on the crystal. "This, right now, will be the most important event to ever happen to this land." Intrigued, Jaykin listens attentively. "The Life Element isn't like any other. It has the power to evolve humans into Solutions. Without them, none of the Solutions or Elements would ever have existed."

"Is it the only Element that can do that?" Jaykin asks.

"Yes," Eragraph stares at Jaykin. "Remember this; embrace every part of this moment; as when you unlock this crystal, it will change the future, forever. Humans will be able to evolve to Solutions and then when they're ready, they can evolve into Elements. We can continue the evolution process all over again." Jaykin pauses. Just thinking about all that makes him extremely excited about the future. He feels full of emotion at this moment.

"We will need to protect this Element as if our

lives depend on it." Eragraph sounds extremely serious and solemn.

"I understand," Jaykin responds. "We will be very cautious now."

"So, shall we change the future?" Eragraph smiles.

"Let's do it," Jaykin replies smiling back, and with determination he thrusts the small crystal onto the larger one, wrapping his hand around it, so he can still touch it with his fingers and absorb it. A pulse vibrates through them, while the crystal quickly disappears.

"That was amazing," Eragraph says quietly to himself, conscious of the possibilities ahead.

Standing before them is an Element of great height, at least eight feet tall, with long white hair. Its silver cloak is adorned with shimmering beading. Light leather straps wrap around its shoulders, holding the weapons on its back: a staff with blades at the end, a small sword, and a shield, together with a small sack. This Element's symbol is a pink circle with a heart at its centre.

"Where am I?" she gasps, looking warily around.

"Welcome back to Izara," Jaykin says politely.

"Where have I been?" she asks.

"You have been sleeping for a very long time. It is a pleasure to meet you. My name is Eragraph."

"And I'm Jaykin."

"Pleasure…to meet you both. My name is Eveara," she replies, sounding confused.

"I'm sure you have many questions," Jaykin says. He stretches his arms, feeling somehow stronger after absorbing the crystal. "We'll explain everything to you in due course but—"

Suddenly Jaykin and Eragraph hear a familiar noise. A loud screech echoes around them.

"It can't be," Jaykin says.

"Is that what I think it is?" Eragraph asks. They exchange worried glances.

"What is that?" Eveara asks, cautiously.

"Barragona," Eragraph replies. "She knows we are here."

"Take cover in the collector," Jaykin says. Q-Tech points and directs both the Elements towards it. Eveara is staring at Q-Tech as if slightly scared. Jaykin stays back.

"Jaykin?" it says.

"I'm not leaving, Q-Tech," he says. "Kanaren must be nearby."

"But—"

"No. Start the collector up for the Elements. If I don't survive, then take them back to Q-Ara."

"Understood," Q-Tech obeys and runs to catch up with the Elements.

Jaykin stares in the direction of the screech. Both the Elements reach the collector. Only then, Eragraph realises that Jaykin isn't nearby.

"Jaykin?" He spots him walking away. "Jaykin!" he yells. "What are you doing?"

The barragona smashes through the trees. It stops in its tracks, panting slightly as it takes in its surroundings. It still has vines wrapped around its body and looks a little weary. Eventually, its angry eyes alight on Jaykin.

Suddenly it charges, screeching loudly at him. She is clearly not happy but Jaykin continues to stand his ground.

The back of the collector opens and Eveara is pushed in by Eragraph, who keeps his eye on Jaykin. He shouts his name again trying in vain to get his attention. The barragona gets closer.

"I've had enough of this!" Jaykin yells, and lifts both his hands up towards the barragona, letting out an almighty scream, enough to tear his lungs apart. "You will leave us alone!"

Crystal bursts out of his hands and hits straight into the barragona's eyes, blinding it instantly. It falls and scrapes its head across the grass. Crystal forms, and completely covers its head.

"What the—?" Eragraph is dumbfounded.

"What on Izara is going on?" Eveara asks, as the collector blocks her view. Eragraph is speechless. Jaykin still screams, blasting crystal at the barragona. She tries to get up using her wings to stand. Unable to shake the crystal off, she slams her head onto the nearest trees but nothing will budge it. The crystal continues to grow, extending from her head, down her long neck. She tries to fly off, but it is too late. The crystal reaches her wings before she can get any air. She gradually gives way to Jaykin's power.

"I'm sorry," Jaykin whispers to her, while the last part of her body and the long tail is covered. All is quiet. Exhausted, Jaykin falls to the ground in a heap.

"Jaykin!" Eragraph shouts, and runs towards him. He picks up Jaykin's unconscious body. "Jaykin?

Wake up!" he shouts, jolting him slightly to try and wake him, but nothing.

"Is he—" Eveara hesitates, running up to them both.

"I think he's completely drained of energy," Eragraph says. He places his hand on the short grass to make it much longer again and lays Jaykin on it. "Could you check on him?"

"I'll see what I can do," she says.

Eragraph stands and paces up and down. Then he approaches the barragona to take a closer look.

"How on Izara did you do this Jaykin?" he says to himself, then places his hand on it. "*It's the same crystal as for the Elements.*"

"Eragraph!" Eveara shouts, her hand on Jaykin's forehead. "He's still breathing. He just has a mild concussion and the poor thing is exhausted. Is there a Dream Element nearby?"

"No," Eragraph replies. "Long story. We should get out of here before anything else turns up. There's a good chance that barrags are nearby." They both look at the barragona. Eveara's expression is a question but she gets no answer from Eragraph. Instead, he picks Jaykin up again and they both run toward the collector. Eragraph places Jaykin on the floor. "Can you keep an eye on him Eveara?"

"Of course."

"You might want to hold on tight too." He makes his way to the front, where Q-Tech awaits instructions. "Can you fly around, see if you can see anyone? We may be able to spot the others."

"Understood," Q-Tech replies. The collector

starts up and takes off, circling slowly.

"Please be around here," Eragraph whispers continuously to himself.

***

They fly over trees for half an hour but see nothing.

"Keep looking. They must be around here somewhere," Eragraph says.

"Don't worry about it," Jaykin says, just waking up. He looks out of the window. "We should head off. It'll be getting dark soon." He lifts himself up, with some help from Eveara.

"Where do we go now?" Eragraph asks

"Back to Q-Ara."

"Are you sure?"

"Yes. It's too dangerous out here. We need to go back for Meara. I got her into this mess," he replies and lowers his head in disgust.

"Then that's what we'll do," Eragraph says. "They're going to expect us this time though."

"Yes, I know. We will need to think of something."

"We will," Eragraph says.

Jaykin looks at his hands which feel as if they are on fire. The last time they did this was when he made the crystal for Kanaren at Mount Keap. He stands but feels very dizzy, weak, and exhausted again. He takes the nearest seat and tries to relax. Eragraph looks over at him, and decides that this is not the right time to ask him about his powers.

"Why don't you let our new friend know what has been going on, Jaykin. I'm going to check how far we have to go," Eragraph suggests. Jaykin nods and moves closer to Eveara. He begins the story, about his father, the Elements, and his unexpected journey. In the meantime, Eragraph listens in carefully, then moves up close to Q-Tech. "How are we getting on? Have we got far to go?"

"Approximately one hour until arrival," Q-Tech replies.

"Good," Eragraph says, looking back at the others. "I have an important question to ask you…" He pauses, trying to phrase the question in his head. "…do humans have powers in this land?"

"The question does not make sense, Master Element," Q-Tech replies.

"Do humans have similar powers to Elements? Telepathy, flight, mind control?" Eragraph asks again. Q-Tech takes its time to process; maybe a bit too long.

"In all the history of humankind, there has been no sighting of Elemental powers in humans," it replies.

"Really?" Eragraph says, surprised. "How does he have these powers then?" he whispers to himself and turns to watch them chatting. He thinks for a while, barely able to believe his own conclusion. "It can't be. A new Element?"

Chapter 27

Progress

Night falls and Guards on Q-Ara's wall pace up and down. One of them hears something odd just outside of the city, like a cracking noise, something he's never heard before. He looks down the wall and a tree appears out of nowhere in front of him.

"What the…?" he says, confused.

With that, a green, wooden arm explodes out of the tree and pulls the Guard towards it, hitting his head, knocking him unconscious. Eragraph jumps out and off the tree and takes a look around. He drops the Guard onto the ground.

"Coast is clear," he whispers.

Eveara and Jaykin jump off the tree and onto the wall.

"According to Q-Tech, there should be a control panel for the shielding around here," Jaykin says.

"This thing?" Eragraph asks, pointing.

"Exactly," Jaykin replies. He runs over and examines the controls, while Eragraph stands guard. Eveara checks out the unconscious Guard and notices some bruising on his face. She places her hand on his forehead.

"There you go; you're all healed," she says, and leans him against the wall. Jaykin pulls a handle and part of the shielding slowly slides open.

"Okay Q-Tech, bring her in," he says, using his

intercom. The collector flies through and hovers nearby. Eragraph faces the tree.

"Thank you, you can go now," he says and lowers his hand. The tree hides behind the wall. They all jump back into the collector and it hovers off.

"Do you think Meara is going to be at this hospital?" Eragraph asks.

"No," Jaykin replies. "But it's a good place to start. Q-Tech, can you land on level ninety-two?"

"Yes," it replies. "Circling the hospital now."

"As they're expecting us," Jaykin says, "they'll have level ninety-one well-guarded I assume." The collector lands. "Q-Tech, protect the collector until we're back."

"Understood," it replies.

Jaykin, Eragraph and Eveara enter the hospital, making their way through the corridors until they end up where Irown and Meara were last seen.

"Wait," Eragraph whispers, holding the others back. He peers around the corner. "A couple of those Guards are still hanging around outside the room." Jaykin looks too.

"I thought there would be more of them," Jaykin says.

"Let's find out," Eragraph says. Luckily for him, the vine wall he made is still there, although now in pieces.

"Why do we always get the clean-up jobs?" one Guard is saying.

Eragraph turns the corner.

"Hallo," he says, boldly. The Guards turn and gape at him. Eragraph pulls his arm towards his body, clenching his fist, and vines explode out of the broken wall of branches and wrap around the Guards' wrists and ankles, pulling and pinning them both to the wall. The wall starts to repair itself and the Guards both drop their weapons. Jaykin covers his face with the wooden mask and runs over to one of them and knocks him out using the Guard's own weapon. The other is struggling to get out of the vines. Jaykin peers into the operating room. Now it is just a quiet and messy room, with the window destroyed.

"Nothing in here," Jaykin says. Eragraph approaches the other Guard, intending to knock him out.

"Wait!" Jaykin shouts, halting Eragraph's blow to the Guard's head. Jaykin looks the Guard in the eyes. "Where is the girl?"

"No point kid, I'm not saying anything," he replies with his chin up high, smirking. "You're all wanted fugitives and you are not getting out of here." Eragraph slowly moves up to him and bends down, nose to nose. The Guard gulps out loud.

"I suggest you talk little pink friend, unless you want to end up like your mate over there." They both look at the other Guard, who does not look his best.

"I'm still not going to tell you," he says, although the smirk is gone from his anxious face. He takes in Eragraph's huge size and his worrying grin. "Okay, okay. They took the girl to the secure holding facility west of here."

"What about the Element?" Eragraph asks.

"I have no idea what you're talking about."

"The one you shot! He fell from the building!"

Eragraph's voice rises. "One of you killed my friend and I'm going to find out who did it eventually, even if it means killing every single Guard in this city," he says chillingly. Jaykin goes to the broken window and looks downwards. Fleetingly, he is reminded of those nights when he was back at his apartment.

"I don't know anything about it. I'm not sure where the Element is," he persists.

"Better not be lying to me," Eragraph says.

"That's all I know, I swear," the Guard replies. Jaykin turns to Eragraph, then nods his head. Eragraph then knocks the Guard unconscious, letting him hang from the vines. He approaches Jaykin who is still taking in the view from the window.

"Do you know where this facility is?"

"No, but I'm sure Q-Tech will know." He makes contact. "Q-Tech, can you locate the secure holding facility. The Guard said it's in the west."

"Yes, but Hunters are not allowed there. To locate Meara's cell, you will need to go to the system. It has all the information required, including video recordings."

"Then that's where we'll go next."

"Understood."

"What's our next move?" Eragraph asks. Jaykin pauses for a moment.

"A rescue mission," he replies.

Behind them, Eveara holds both the Guards' heads at the same time, healing their bruises.

"Will I need to do this for everyone I meet?" she asks.

"I hope not," Jaykin replies, walking past her.

The Elements are about to follow him back to the collector when Eveara notices sleeping people in the wards. She has a closer look. Eragraph joins her.

"There are so many people that are sick, Eragraph," she says, sadly.

"I know. We'll help them all one day but now is not the time," he replies.

"I hope that will be possible."

"Come on, let's get going," Eragraph says in a kind and calming voice.

They enter the collector and head west, flying past building after building. As the night draws on, hundreds of lights go out. Slowly but surely, the collector lands on another building, not far from the Palace. The rear door opens once again.

"For somewhere so highly populated, it sure is quiet," Eveara remarks.

"It always is during the night time," Jaykin replies. "It's probably best if you guys stay here. Q-Tech and I will sort this out."

"We'll be here if you need us," Eragraph replies. "Be careful and good luck."

They try the door, which, not unexpectedly, is locked.

"No one's here," Q-Tech says, stating the obvious.

"That's a good thing," Jaykin replies. "No one can see us getting the information we need. Can you get into this thing?"

Q-Tech's arm holds onto the handle and pushes it with huge force. The lock breaks and the door swings open.

They walk down some steps leading to long and narrow corridors. No lights are on so it is difficult to see. Q-Tech turns on its newly built-in lights.

"This way," it says, leading, a torch personified.

"Do you remember the mission, 'Project Assembling'?"

"Of course," it replies. "It has been Master Kanaren's mission for just over a year."

"Well, I want you to focus on that. We want to look at any files linking up to my father's disappearance too, while finding Meara. Can you do that?"

"That can be done. Do you want to continue Master Kanaren's previous investigations?"

"Sure," Jaykin replies. "What was he looking for last time?"

"Master Kanaren was searching for a list of missing persons." It stops and turns to another door but this one appears to need a specific key code. Luckily Q-Tech has it. "Here it is," it says, swiping its metal hand. The door opens but Q-Tech stops and turns to Jaykin. "Just to warn you, it can be quite disorienting for first-time Hunters to enter the system."

"Why is that?"

"You will find out." They enter a gigantic oval room. "System upload," Q-Tech says. A much bigger projector than Kanaren's rises out from the floor and projects onto the whole ceiling.

"Okay, let's start by looking back where you were last time, Q-Tech."

"Upload CCTV recordings of this building from last year," Q-Tech says. With that, thousands of small videos play at the same time. "Scanning. This is everything, a week after the people went missing last year." Jaykin has a closer look.

"There are too many to focus on. Is there anything out of the ordinary we can look at?" When did Kanaren visit this place?" Two videos highlight on the wall, footage of Kanaren and Q-Tech entering the building. "Good, when was this taken?"

"Last time Master Kanaren was here, a couple of days after he had received the letters and video clips."

"So, you both came here to check the system to try and find them. That makes sense."

"Yes, Master Kanaren checked all the names and they didn't appear in the system."

"And the only people that can change the system are Hunters, right?"

"Correct. Look at these." Dozens of clips highlight on the wall.

"What are these?"

"This is where Master Kanaren finished with the investigation. These show the Hunters who were in this building the most often. Some came in many times during this week."

"What did he do with this information?" Jaykin asks.

"He interrogated all these Hunters," Q-Tech replies. Jaykin is staring at them.

"Then what happened?"

Q-Tech stops and processes. "Under Master Kanaren's orders, permission is not granted to answer."

Jaykin wasn't expecting that reply.

"Tell me, Q-Tech. Kanaren isn't here and I'm

your new master now."

It considers the logic to answer. "Understood." It twitches slightly, as if unlocking that information, "For many years and from a young age, Kanaren was a high-ranking Hunter. As soon as he started investigating Project Assembling and interrogating Hunters for crimes, they denied and attacked him. He had lost the trust of the other Hunters."

"But he was the only one doing his duty." Jaykin sighs. He watches a couple of videos. "But it must have been a Hunter. Maybe you were looking at the wrong person." He stops and thinks. "Or the wrong time."

"Not understood," Q-Tech says.

"Think about it. Why would the Hunters come in after those people vanished? Why not before?" Q-Tech stares blankly at Jaykin. "Check the video clips a week - no, a month before the disappearances."

"That will take some time," Q-Tech replies.

"Yes, but we have time," Jaykin replies. "We need to know. In the meantime, can you show me where to find Meara?"

"Search western secure holding facility CCTV footage of the last twenty-four hours," Q-Tech says. A few hundred or so videos appear. Q-Tech waves a part of the projection over to Jaykin making a small square space for him amongst all the video clips. "You should be able to find her with this."

Jaykin faces the wall and quickly scans through the information.

***

Meanwhile, Eragraph and Eveara hide in the collector.

"Do you think he'll be all right?" Eveara asks, as she admires the view of the city from the collector's window.

"He can look after himself," Eragraph replies, as he practices using his powers by carving something on his bow. "He's a lot stronger than you think."
She turns to look at him.

"I'm still not sure what happened back with the barragona."

"Me neither, but I don't think we should worry about it too much for now."

"Good idea. It's too much to take in."

"It is." Eragraph lowers his bow. "I haven't been awake for long. It feels as if I have been thrown into a dream."

"I know what you mean. It all doesn't feel real, does it?"
Eragraph shakes his head and stares at her. Something else is on his mind.

"I think I've heard your name before. Why is that?"

"Well, I used to travel a lot before the Great War, or it could be because I was the first human to evolve into a Solution."

"Wow! That is quite a title," Eragraph says, sitting back and feeling quite spellbound by her. "So, you must have known Izara?"

"I did." She smiles.

"What was she like?"

"She was like…no one I had ever met before.

She was such a generous, courageous and confident Element."

"I heard. Whatever happened to her? I was told she died in battle?"

"I was told the same. There were rumours that she had survived but I suppose we will never know."

"We might find out one day."

"That would be good."

In the quiet that follows this exchange, they suddenly hear shouting outside. They exit the collector and peer down the side of the building. Several people are entering.

***

Both Jaykin and Q-Tech are still scanning the CCTV footage.

"Found something," Q-Tech says.

"So have I. She's in cell eighty-eight. We will go there next. What have you found?"

"A Hunter coming into the building regularly in that month. Twenty-one times to be exact, more than anyone else has visited."

"Good work, Q-Tech. Do we know who this person is?"

"No, facial recognition cannot pick them out as they keep covering their face."

"How did you know it's the same person then?"

"Height, build, and they wear the same cloak every time."

Jaykin looks closer at the clips.

"Doesn't look like a Hunter. No weapons, no Q-Roids. Is there anything out of the ordinary? Something we can focus on?" Q-Tech checks the images. "I'm getting closer to finding you, father," Jaykin says to himself. Suddenly, alarms start going off. "That's all we need right now. Do you have a data stick?"

"Yes," Q-Tech replies. Something clicks on its hand and pulls out a small box shape. It connects it to the system mainframe which is located in the middle of the room.

"Then get as much information as you can. We need to get out of here, now." Jaykin says. He rushes over to the door but can't see anything yet. He looks back to Q-Tech. "How long are you going to be?"

"One minute and two seconds," it replies. Jaykin then makes his way through the dark corridor to take a look down the staircase. He sees a couple of lights moving around, checking each level. He curses and quickly makes his way back to Q-Tech.

"We don't have a minute," Jaykin whispers. He places his hand on the wall opposite the entrance to the system room. "Please work," he whispers to himself, but nothing is coming out. "Come on," he says, trying to create crystal, without success. He takes his hand off and sees the lights beaming closer. Suddenly vines appear from the wall and creep across to the system room's entrance. Jaykin looks behind him and spots Eragraph.

"Thanks," Jaykin whispers, appreciation in his voice.

"No problem. Get the metal thing; we need to

go."

"It's done, Jaykin," Q-Tech says.

"Good timing. Let's get out of here."

Q-Tech closes all the programmes and they exit fast. In that same second, the light from the other side of the vine wall shines on them. It is impossible to see who is there through the tiny gaps. They both head off back to the collector with Q-Tech following.

"At last. Are you okay?" Eveara shouts down through the corridors, hearing the alarms.

"We're fine!" Jaykin shouts back. They rush into the collector and it quickly takes off, up and away. "To the western facility, Q-Tech."

"How did you get on?" Eveara asks.

"We found out where Meara is held and we're heading there now," Jaykin replies, panting slightly. "And I'm a little closer to finding my father too." He smiles.

"Well done," Eragraph replies, patting him encouragingly on the back.

Jaykin looks at his hands pensively, wondering what happened back there. No crystal.

***

Resting on the bench of a prison cell, Meara waits, fidgeting. Guards walk past every five minutes to check on her. She sighs, desperately wishing she wasn't there. With that, the window breaks, then comes a thud. She shoots up from the bench and looks at the window. The glass has a small hole in it as if someone had thrown a stone through it, but she can't find any stones or rocks on the floor. She has a closer look and sees something on the opposite wall; an arrow sticking out.

"What on Izara…" she whispers to herself, pulling it out. At the exact same time, the wall around the window explodes, scattering rubble and dust all over the place. Alarms go off and Meara screams. When the dust clears, she notices something hovering in the sky. It's Jaykin and the others. The collector reverses, getting closer to the building. Eragraph jumps into the prison cell, landing with a loud thud.

"Hi, how are you doing?" he asks.

"I'm fine," she gasps.

"Let's get you out of here, shall we?" He extends his arm and lifts her up onto his back. The bark from his armour wraps around her. "You'll be safe there," he says. "I'm about to jump now."

"Okay," she says nervously.

Eragraph nods his head back to the others who prepare to catch them. He jumps again and Eveara helps them in.

"Let's go!" Eragraph shouts. The bark unwraps from around Meara and she slides off him. Jaykin gives her a huge hug.

"I'm really sorry Meara," he says, muffled into her shoulder.

"It's okay," she replies, "I never thought I'd get out of there."

"We need to find somewhere safe," Jaykin says.

"There is a place north of here. It will be very useful to you all," Q-Tech informs them, attracting questioning looks from them all.

"There is?" Jaykin asks.

"Yes. Arrival time is approximately one minute, seventeen seconds," it replies.

At the same time, Eragraph kneels to be nearly the same height as Meara, although still tall in her eyes.

"Do you know anything about Irown?" he asks.

"I heard a couple of the Guards talking about some sort of creature," she replies.

"That sounds about right," Jaykin interrupts. "No one knows about the Elements; they all think you're creatures."

"Meara, do you know if he is still alive?" Eragraph asks.

"I don't know anything after that Guard grabbed me in the hospital. What happened?"

"Irown was shot, I think, and fell from the window," Jaykin replies.

Meara gasps, covering her mouth in shock.

"I'm so sorry."

"If we find him, there's a chance we can heal him. Meara, can you remember anything, any information at all?" Jaykin pleads. She thinks long and hard.

"I think they said that someone has taken a creature to the emperor."

"That's not good news," Jaykin says and paces up and down.

"Why not?" Eveara asks.

"If he's anything like the emperor from Dreamora, then we have a bigger problem on our hands. We need to find Irown and get him back to health before it's too late."

Chapter 28

Let Battle Commence

They set down on the highest landing bay of a tall skyscraper, located furthest away to the north of the city. The building is close to the city wall and is connected to the dome shielding. They all walk through the entrance and take a good look around. One large room connected to several others. The place is huge. Jaykin is thinking it is almost the same size as Doctor Rotnevin's place, or even bigger.

"Where are we?" he asks.

"This is Kanaren's home," Q-Tech replies. Both Meara and Jaykin look at one another in astonishment.

"You're not serious," Meara says. "It's like four of our apartments in one." She stares at Jaykin in shock.

"Two levels and the hallway," Q-Tech replies.

"What? How many places does Kanaren have?" Jaykin asks.

"Master Kanaren has one floor for a home in each city," it replies.

"How in Izara can he afford them?" Jaykin asks.

"He works hard as a…" it looks over at Meara, "…Defender of the city."

"It's okay Q-Tech, Meara has heard the word Hunter, before," Jaykin says. "I will get around to explaining it to you."

"Many Hunters are very wealthy; selling creatures, competing in tournaments and serving the emperors and empresses," Q-Tech informs them.

"That all makes sense," Jaykin says.

"I like it," Eveara says, taking in the surroundings. "Fit for an Element like myself."

"We should rest here tonight; then, in the morning, work out how to get to Irown," Eragraph suggests.

"Good idea," Eveara agrees.

"Us girls will take the Master bedroom," Meara says.

"That's fine with me," Jaykin replies. "We'll take the spare rooms. Anything's better than that hard floor."

"Please rest well," Q-Tech says, then heads off into another room.

Day 12

Late that night, Pree and Mordan settle down to rest and to make sure they're safe. Elra settles on a nearby branch after flying for several hours and eating her own weight in her favourite fruit. They have travelled miles into an unknown forest and they take it in turns to keep an eye out. Pree decides to go first. During this time nothing much happens and so she makes a game to entertain herself; throwing stones onto a tree stump and seeing how many she can land on without knocking any of the others off. A couple of hours pass and Mordan is awake for his turn. Pree gives him the chance to beat her high score of one hundred and seventy-eight stones on the stump. He throws a stone and hits the target perfectly.

"One hundred and twenty-nine." He smiles to himself. "The age I met you." He turns to Pree to see if she had heard him but she's fast asleep. "Damn. That would have been such a romantic thing to have said if you were awake." He stares at her for a few seconds then shrugs. "Oh well. What a perfect shot from me though. Boom!" he says congratulating himself and punching the air.

Suddenly, an explosion echoes overhead. Pree sits up immediately and stares at Mordan.

"What was that? What have you done now?" she asks.

"Wasn't me, I swear," he replies, then looks up. Out of nowhere, a ball of light slowly makes its way across the sky, with a crackling noise in the background and leaving a thick black trail of smoke behind it. "What on Izara is that?" he asks.

"I have no idea." They watch it until it vanishes from view.

"Look, another one." They see a second object, but this time it isn't lighting up, nor leaving a trail of smoke behind it. This thing is much bigger and a lot faster than the previous one.

"What shall we do?" Pree worries. "People may be in danger."

"Let's find out," Mordan replies. They pack their belongings.

"Did you beat my score in the end?"

"Yes, easily."

"Liar," she grins.

"Damn you're good at that," he says with a smirk on his face. "Anyone would have thought you were the Mind Element."

They head off into the forest.

***

Eragraph is lying on what seems to be a bed fashioned from all sorts of foliage, leaves and vines. On the spare bed, Jaykin lays wide awake. After a few days of getting used to his energy being replenished with Pree's help, he cannot sleep even on a lovely, comfortable, warm bed. He looks over to Eragraph who has his eyes closed, snoring loudly. He has too much on his mind with what went on at the system and with Irown; with the Hunter, and not managing to create the crystal. He decides to give up trying to sleep and sits up, hoping not to wake Eragraph, and tiptoes in search of Q-Tech. He pauses at a nearby door and taps on it.

"Q-Tech are you in here?" he whispers.

"Yes, Jaykin, can't you sleep?" it replies.

"No, I'm too worried about everything. What are you doing?" he asks, opening the door and trying to adjust his eyes to the light in the room.

"Master Kanaren said that whenever he rests, the task of scanning for signs of danger needs to continue, inside and outside of the cities, including off-world. Also, scanning through these images of the person from the system."

"Great idea. Have you found anything?" He notices a few screens monitoring some of the rooms, including the rooftop and a room full of cages, which Jaykin thinks is odd.

"Some scans have picked up something out of the atmosphere but they are likely to be asteroids or personally owned skyships. Other than that, nothing out of the ordinary. Maybe it would help for you to look through these images?"

"That's not a bad idea actually. May as well focus on something important while I'm up." He takes the seat next to Q-Tech and stares into the screen.

***

Jaykin is sitting in the living room admiring the view from the large thick windows, which face the centre of the city. He's been trying to create crystal in his hand but it still doesn't work.

"I thought I could hear someone moping around," says a quiet voice from behind him, making him jump slightly. He turns and sees Meara standing at the master bedroom door.

"Oh, hey Meara," he says and holds onto his chest. He feels his heart beat fast, his face goes red slightly, and he wonders if she has watched him trying to create the crystal.

"Sorry, I didn't mean to scare you," she whispers.

"It's okay. Why are you up? Can't you sleep either?" he asks.

"No, probably the same as you," she replies.

"I doubt that."

"Too much on your mind?"

"You could say that."
She walks to the window and gazes out at the city. The view is beautiful with all the different twinkling lights, looking like stars. She turns to see Jaykin staring at something on an electric pad.

"What you looking at?"

"This." He shows her. "I think this person knows something about my father's disappearance. I'm just trying to work out who it is." She just leans her shoulder on the window and smiles at him.

"I hope you find him."
Jaykin looks up at her straight away, surprised. Normally she would say something like, 'give up searching' or 'move on' by now. She knows he's thinking it too.

"You've changed since I saw you back in Lementes," she says.

"Really? I don't think I have; I still don't feel quite right."

"Well, I think you have. You look…" she looks at his face then his arms. "…different, have you lost weight?"

"Don't think so."

"Are you sure?" Jaykin looks puzzled. Why is she talking about his looks suddenly?

"I'm fine Meara. Stop worrying about me."
They stare at each other for a few moments.

"Yeah, you looked like you actually had muscles for a day or so."
He sniggers. "I've missed this," he says.

"Missed what?"

"Us, having random and weird conversations."

"Let's think, what random thing shall we talk about now?" She relaxes against the window again. "I know. The whole evolution thing. What Element would you choose?" Jaykin relaxes too.

"I don't know." He looks at his hands for a second. "I haven't really thought about it. You?"

"I think I would like to be a Life Element."

"So, you can help people, right?"

"Exactly; to fit my personality."

There is a knock at the door. They both turn around to see Eragraph.

"Can I come in?" he asks politely.

"Of course, you can. Can't you sleep either?" Meara asks.

"No, I heard some laughing and thought I'd better check it out." He smiles. "I'm kidding, I prefer sleeping outside." He takes a seat on the floor, leaning against the sofa. "Sorry but I overheard your conversation. Nature Elements are very good." Meara and Jaykin exchange glances. "But seriously, to choose an Element, you must take your whole human and Solutions life to choose, as you can't change your mind. If you have questions about any Element, all you need to do is ask."

"Thanks for the heads up, Eragraph," Jaykin says.

"No problem. This is a very interesting set-up here." He looks and points out of the window. "What's going on out there?"

Both Meara and Jaykin look out too. "Everyone's in the centre of the city getting ready for later," Jaykin replies.

"Later? What's happening later?"

"Oh yeah," Meara says, straightening up. "That's today."

"The monthly Preyal tournament. It's where creatures battle it out against one another and the owner of the creature will win anything they desire," Jaykin informs him.

"Depends if the emperor can grant it, of course," Mcara says.

Eragraph chuckles.

"It sounds very similar to the Pericoid Games."

"What were they?" Jaykin asks.

"Every year before the Great War. Humans, Solutions and Elements would come from all over the land to watch the Pericoid Games. Instead of creatures, it was the Elements who competed."

Jaykin is impressed.

"That must have been amazing. I would have loved to have seen that."

"Yes, it was a spectacular sport to watch. The winner would receive specially made armour and weapons." He shakes his head and chuckles deeply. "We would train all year round for it too."

"Did you ever enter the games?" Jaykin asks.

"I did. It was one of the most entertaining times of my Element life. Except for now of course."

"That's why you're so good at fighting—" Jaykin says, then stops and gasps suddenly.

"What is it?" Meara asks.

"I think," he says, standing up, "I think I've come up with a plan." He then walks straight into Q-Tech's room and finds it still watching the security camera footage. He spots a screen rotating around a large room and it repeats over again. Inside this room, all different sized cages are stacked on top of one another.

"Q-Tech, where and what is in that room?"

"That is the creature room. Master Kanaren would keep his creatures there. They needed to be fed every day."

"Can you show us?"

They all head downstairs, which turns out to be a warehouse, full of empty cages. Q-Azars and swords are spread across the wall and historical items on the other side, similar to Kanaren's other home in Lementes. Jaykin notices something and moves towards a large cage, looking it up and down. Then he does the same to Eragraph.

"Do you think you can fit in here?" he asks.

"Possibly. Why? What do you have in mind?" Jaykin ignores the question.

"Q-Tech, how do I enter a creature into the Preyal tournament?"

"Oh, Jaykin you're not—" Meara says.

"Oh, I am, Meara," he replies. They both look up at Eragraph.

"Oh no, I don't think I like where this is going," Eragraph says.

***

First thing in the morning, thousands of spectators are gathering outside the tournament arena. Many are dressed in odd colours and shapes, obviously dressed up as creatures like a grotesque fancy dress event. Big screens, showing clips of previous tournaments, entertain everyone while entering the building. At the rear, all is quiet. Several empty collectors are lined up at the arrivals dock, where people from all over bring their creatures. Dozens of people roam around in groups, talking to one another, hanging around empty cages.

A collector hovers over and lands in one of the empty bays. Q-Tech exits the collector with a hooded figure following. Taking in the scene, which is never seen on screen, they join the throng and enter the huge hall, where there are big bright and colourful images of all the past winners on display. Many of the pictures are of the same creature, but from different angles. Q-Tech and Jaykin approach a booth where a man appears to be taking names. He is happily chatting to and laughing with a couple of people; clearly Hunters, with their distinctive jackets; trying to hide their weapons discreetly. While Jaykin waits to be seen, he takes a look around the crowd and sees hundreds of Hunters among the spectators. He then spots a couple of Guards blocking access to a no-go area. They are keeping careful watch. One of them notices Jaykin is looking over at them and immediately squeezes his Q-Azar, as if in a warning. As he waits, Jaykin overhears a conversation.

"Did you hear that the system got attacked last night?" one Hunter says to another.

"Yeah, I did. I also heard that someone

escaped from the holding facility." He looks around. "Rumour has it that it was Kanaren," he whispers.

"I swear he's lost it," another says.

"Who's next?" The man behind the counter shouts, as the Hunters disband slowly, gulping their drinks. Jaykin jumps, remembering where he is, and approaches the counter. The man looks older than all the Hunters. Scars mark his face. Perhaps he was a Hunter once.

"Hi," Jaykin says, slightly muffled under the mask. "I would like to enter my creature into the tournament please." He spots the name tag of the man on the desk: Keeper.

"Okay," Keeper replies, looking at him strangely, "I just need to get some details from you." Looking at his screen, he swipes to the next page. "Can I get your name and the type of creature?" He grins at Jaykin.

"Of course. My name is…" he turns his head slightly to a Guard who walks past at that moment, then turns back again. "Eragraph," he says, with a determined voice. "And the type of creature is called Element."

The man stops typing and turns to Jaykin with his eyebrows raised.

"Sorry, Eragraph, there is no creature called an Element on this world nor on Raziz."

"There is, and I am signing it in," Jaykin insists. Keeper rubs his eyes and sighs in exhaustion.

"Look kid, I don't have time for your jokes. I have a lot to sort out in the next few hours. There's no creature called an Element." He stands up and looks at the nearest Guard and points. "Guards, this kid is in the wrong place!" he shouts. They walk over and move to grab onto Jaykin's hood.

"I wouldn't do that if I were you," he says. With that, they pull the hood down.

"Take your mask off, kid," one of them demands.

"Probably best to keep it on," Jaykin replies. One of the Guards loses his temper and pulls Jaykin's mask off. They both stand back.

"What on Izara?" one says.
Swollen up with dead skin flaking off, and scars all over his face, Jaykin faces the Guards.

"I told you not to," he says.

"What is that?" the other Guard asks.

"It's a poison," Jaykin replies, grabbing the mask back and placing it on his face. He leans on the table. "It's what this new creature can do." Keeper stares at Jaykin, then at the Guards.

"Okay, okay. Show me this new Element of yours, then I'll make the decision. It had better not be a joke or I'll get you arrested. You understand me?" Leaving the Guards behind, they head to the collector. Q-Tech indicates the cage which has a large cover over it, concealing Eragraph waiting within.

"Here it is," Jaykin says.
The Keeper peers underneath the cover and Eragraph snarls at him, acting as if he is distressed and hitting the cage several times.

"Right," the Keeper says, standing back. "I couldn't see much but it looks like it's one of a kind. Where on Izara did you find it?"

"In the..." Jaykin stops to think. "...Unknown Lands," he replies.

"Ballsy kid! No one goes there," Keeper says, pressing something on his pad. "You're all logged in."

"Thanks," Jaykin replies.

"You'll need to take the cage inside to bay eight." He gives Jaykin a ticket with his signature on it. "Good luck, kid."

Jaykin walks up to the cage.

"We're in. Good job Eragraph," he whispers, then heads into the collector. Eveara and Meara uncover themselves from their hiding place, another covered cage. Jaykin takes his mask off and Eveara has a closer look. She places her hands just above the worst part of his face. "This won't take long," she says. "How was it?"

"Went well," Jaykin replies.

***

"Welcome back to this month's Preyal Tournament. I'm your host, Repsa, and joining me, as always, is Jepsa." Cheers from the crowd.

"Hello everyone and welcome back to the best tournament in the universe." More cheers.

"That's right, Jepsa. Today we have some amazing line-ups for you and by the looks of things, there are some new names on the table."

"I really think this is going to be one amazing tournament, Repsa."

"Yes. I have a good feeling about this one too. Now for the rules; that everyone should know by now."

"If not, where on Izara have you been?"

"The tournament kicks off with a points contest. The more hits one creature scores against another, the more points they gain. And do we all know what you can spend these points on?"

The crowd in the arena knows the answer:

"Upgrades, upgrades, upgrades!"

"That's right ladies and gentlemen. The higher hit points the more upgrades they earn in the next battle." A crescendo of cheers as the excitement builds.

"And what are those upgrades, Repsa?"

"Glad you asked, Jepsa. Upgrades are armour, weapons and some hidden little secrets."

"We all know what they are don't we?" The crowd goes wild.

"Creatures will be fighting one versus one. In the unlikely event of a dropout or an uneven number of contestants, there will be a battle with three creatures; the last one standing goes through. Don't you worry all you spectators out there; you will all be safe with an amazing protection shield in front of you." The crowd reaches a frenzy, banners waving. "If the creature is unable to fight, or loses consciousness, then they will lose the battle and will immediately be out of the tournament!" Cries of 'Ooooh' fill the arena.

"And probably out of the city too, eh Jepsa?"

"That would be extremely unfortunate, Repsa."

"When the last creature is standing in their final battle, they win the tournament."

"And winning the ultimate grand prize." More cheers and whistling from the crowd.

"Let's see who we have up first."

***

Underneath the arena, Jaykin stands next to the cage with the cover still over it. It is dark; the only lights are from the huge doors above them. They hear the bangs and crashes of the creatures fighting. The crowd screams and cheers as the creatures battle it out.

"Sounds crazy out there," Jaykin says. "How are you doing?"

"Nervous," Eragraph replies, still sitting in the cage. "It's been a long time since I've done anything like this."

"You'll be fine." Suddenly, loud cheering and clapping is heard; and the cage lifts as the arena floor opens above them. A bright light creeps into the darkness of the underground. The screams of people get louder, becoming almost unbearable. Jaykin releases the cover and it falls away. "Keep in mind why we're doing this. We need to find Irown. He's got to be around here somewhere. And remember, you're a creature, so no weapons or powers," Jaykin says as he watches the cage move into position. "Good luck!" he shouts.

Eragraph stands and stretches his neck. It clicks in several places. He waves his arms and stretches them side to side, preparing himself. While the cage moves closer to the opening, he watches as the crowds come into view. Thousands of people stare back at him, screaming and chanting. The voices of the hosts drown the arena again.

"Next up. We have…" He stops to read it properly. "The Element!"

"What on Izara is an Element, Jepsa? Never heard of it!"

Then comes the sound of another cage clunking into position and loud crashes caused by the other creature. Eragraph cannot see it, but thinks it must be huge.

"Well, there's one way to find out, Repsa!"

"That's right, Jepsa. Let's get this fight started!"

The crowd echoes the sentiment.

***

In the secure facility, a couple of Guards watch the tournament on a small screen. They spot Eragraph.

"What the…?" one Guards says out loud. "That's the thing that attacked me at the hospital."

***

Back at Kanaren's place, Q-Tech drops off Eveara and Meara to watch the tournament. It also downloads and prints a large tournament chart with all the creature types and images, so they can follow Eragraph's progress. They settle down in front of a huge screen.

"You can do it Eragraph!" Meara shouts.

"Woo, come on!" Eveara shouts too, copying Meara's reactions to the large screen she's staring at.

***

Eragraph looks around the arena to see the soft earthy

ground. Suddenly, alarms go off and the crowd goes crazy again. The hosts and the crowd start to count down the numbers.

"Five, four…" Noises emerge from the cage which opens slightly.

"Three, two…" Eragraph starts jumping up and down.

"This is so cool," he says to himself.

"One!" everyone screams. "Go!"

The cage falls apart and Eragraph immediately sprints towards the mount in the middle of the arena. Then he stops to have a good look at his opponent. It is a strong-looking rogsprinter.

"Good start," Eragraph whispers to himself. Rogsprinters are very fast-moving creatures. They can grow up to about six feet in height, twelve feet long, and any size wide. They are very slippery too, with a gooey, greasy substance covering their backs so they cannot easily be pounced on from behind. Its head is extra thick, meaning it can headbutt other creatures with such a force that it can quite easily kill anything in its path.

The rogsprinter spots Eragraph on top of the mount and lets out a loud growl, then immediately charges. Eragraph waits till it is only a couple of metres away then easily dodges it. As it runs past, he hits its back once with each hand. He looks up as the crowd is cheering again; sounds like they enjoyed that. He then looks at his hands which now have some sort of goo on them.

"That's slightly disgusting," he says, then flaps them around to get it off.

High on the arena ceiling the words 'Element' and 'rogsprinter' show up on a huge screen. The rogsprinter score shows Zero, the Element: Two.

The rogsprinter turns and charges and Eragraph dodges it again, hitting it a few more times.

"This is easy," he says. "Let's end it now."

The numbers are now seven to zero. Eragraph runs toward the edge of the arena near the wall and taunts the rogsprinter. It goes for the attack.

"That's it, keep coming." It gets to about four metres away and Eragraph turns and sprints towards the wall. The rogsprinter gets closer. Suddenly Eragraph jumps onto the wall, using it as a springboard, leaping over the top of the advancing creature. It smashes into the wall. Eragraph lands just behind it and waits for it to react, but it falls to the ground, stunned. He lets out a sigh of relief and the crowd goes crazy.

***

Jaykin celebrates under the arena floor as he watches the contest on the screen.

***

Eveara and Meara are jumping up and down at Kanaren's place.

***

The words 'Winner – Element' flash on all the screens. Eragraph absorbs the cheering from the crowd as they start to chant one word: "El-e-ment, El-e-ment, El-e-ment."

Chapter 29

The Winner is...

A few hours and a dozen battles later, high up in the special viewing room, sitting comfortably on large cosy chairs, are Emperor Mor, the leader of Q-Ara and Emperor Lon, leader of Dreamora. Behind Lon, his High Knight stands. They have been watching the tournament with delight. Emperor Mor's High Knight appears beside them.

"Ah, welcome back," Mor says with a clap. "You've missed out on some amazing fighting; probably the best I've seen for a long time."

"Sorry, Emperor Mor, Emperor Lon, I was…" he pauses trying to find the right word. "…busy."

"Busy?" Lon asks. "With what? You need to relax." He points to one of his people. "Get him a chair."

"Thank you," the High Knight replies and sits on it slowly.

"What's the matter? Something bothering you?" Mor asks.

"Yes," he hesitates again. "We've found an intelligent being in the city."

"In my city? How?" Mor asks. Before he can reply, a loud voice shouts around the arena. It is the host's voice.

"And now, for our next match up, we have—"

"No matter," Mor continues. "Is it well contained for the time being?"

"Yes, but—"

"Then I will deal with it after the tournament. I can't miss this game; it's exciting," Mor says.

"I will join you," Lon says, while he relaxes in his chair and gulps down his wine.

"As you wish," the High Knight replies. They all settle to watch the next fight but something makes the High Knight sit forward when one of the cages catches his eye.

"I know," Lon notices. "Amazing, isn't it?"

"Yes," the High Knight replies and stares at Eragraph, who is on to his next battle.

"I've never seen anything like it, and it's doing extremely well," Mor says.

"I may have to take it off of the owner's hands," Lon muses.

Both Mor and the High Knight look at one another, then at Lon.

"What do they call it again?" Lon asks.

"It's called the Element," Mor replies.

"I've never heard of it," the High Knight says.

"Me neither," says Lon. "I think we should look for more of these Elements, it would make for much more interesting tournaments. What do you think?"

Everyone stays quiet, then the High Knight stands.

"Sorry, Emperor Mor, Emperor Lon, but I need to continue my work." Mor nods permission for him to leave and he does so.

"Mor, you really need to teach him to relax if he's going to take your position one day," Lon says.

"He's fine," Mor replies. "I think he'll do a

great job as an emperor."

Lon huffs. "You're too soft," he says, then chuckles. Mor looks at him and gives him a fake smile; then at Lon's own High Knight.

"I'm sure you change your High Knight every week." Lon's face drops and he gives Mor a long hard stare.

"I had to get rid of it. It didn't do a good enough job." He tries to relax again.

"Do you mean to say that they didn't find your crystal?" Mor says, while Lon tries to ignore him and continue watching the battle.

***

Jaykin watches Eragraph winning for the second time.

"We're actually winning a Preyal Tournament," he thinks to himself with satisfaction. He remembers all the times he had with his father, wanting to go to the tournaments but never having the chance. He takes a quick look at his father's photo, then places it back in his pocket and heads down to see Eragraph. He still wears the mask to avoid being recognised. He keeps his head down, trying not to get any attention. Many of the spectators around him have very colourful and striking clothing. Then someone walks straight up to him, wearing a plain suit.

"Excuse me, are you the owner of the Element?" the man asks.

"Who's asking?" Jaykin replies.

"Ah, good. The one I need to see," he grins and pulls out a small digital device from his back pocket and searches for something on it. "I would like to offer you something."

Sceptical, Jaykin gives him a chance to talk.

"Offer what?"

"My…" the man thinks. "…manager would like to offer you this number of digits for your creature." He shows the device to Jaykin. The number one and six zeros appear on it. Jaykin looks up at the man's face, which has a piercing grin.

"Sorry, but it isn't for sale," Jaykin replies and goes to walk away but the guy persists.

"This is a fantastic offer. My manager will give you so many digits; much more than you will receive from the tournament."

Jaykin laughs.

"As I said before, it is not for sale," and again, he goes to walk away but the guy grabs his arm this time. Jaykin turns and stares intently at him, showing his irritation.

"This is a one-time deal. You'll never get this offer ever again."

"Look, I'm not going to repeat myself for the third time. Now, let go," he pulls his arm away from the guy and walks away again.

"You'll regret this!" the man shouts.

Jaykin looks behind him to see if the man is following. He isn't, but instead, he is pressing something on his pad. Jaykin starts to panic and picks up speed.

Down the windy corridors and a few steps later, he is stopped by a couple of tall, scary-looking men. They block his pathway. He turns to go the other way and two more appear, blocking the other side. He steps back and tries to work out if they're Hunters or not, but it's difficult to see the difference as they're wearing suits, just like the man with the device. These can't be Hunters; they look too clean.

"Okay, I have a feeling something's going on here," Jaykin says to himself.

All four take out Q-Azars. "Get down on the ground!" one shouts out.

"No!" Jaykin replies.

Then one whacks him in the back, forcing him onto his knees.

"We'll be taking the Element," another says and raises his Q-Azar at Jaykin's face. He hears it powering up. Jaykin braces himself, then suddenly the Q-Azar fires, but into the roof. Rubble and smoke explode in every direction. He tries to see what happened. As his eyes focus, he makes out two figures standing next to each other.

"Kanaren?" Jaykin whispers to himself.

The smoke clears and standing there is a thug, and holding his Q-Azar is the High Knight, who pulls back, hitting the guy in the face. He drops to the floor. The High Knight keeps hold of the Q-Azar, then fires it at the other men's legs, wounding them all. The High Knight reaches out for Jaykin's hand and pulls him up.

"Get yourself out of here. You don't want to be up against four Hunters."

"Thanks," Jaykin says, and takes off in the opposite direction.

The High Knight stands above the four Hunters, who

are now screaming in pain.

"No one bullies anyone in my city." He then takes apart the Q-Azar into several pieces, tossing them onto the floor. Jaykin looks back to see the High Knight walk away, and makes a decision.

***

The High Knight, pursued discreetly by Jaykin, heads to a corner of the arena, where no one is around, just empty cages of all different sizes and shapes. The High Knight seems to know where he's going. In the far corner, where it is very dark, damp, and cold, he stops.

"Where are you from?" he asks someone, unseen. Jaykin can only just hear a response.

"I have told you already, I am from Izara," the muffled voice replies.

"I don't believe you. I have never seen anything like you before," the High Knight replies.

"We have been asleep for many years and now we have returned."

Suddenly, Jaykin gets a tingling sensation down his back as he recognises the voice. Irown. He's still alive! He moves around slightly to see what shape he's in but it's too dark to see clearly.

"Why have you awoken now?" the High Knight asks. But Irown won't reply. The High Knight stands back and sighs heavily. "I don't know if I can trust you, Element, but in any case, the emperor will decide your fate." Irown stays quiet. The High Knight moves away but then stops and turns. "You may like to know that there is another Element fighting in the tournament right now. I don't know why it's there but for your sake, I hope it wins." The noise of chains rattles through the cage as the High Knight walks away.

Jaykin waits till the coast is clear and approaches the cage. It is still dark but he spots dry blood all over the floor, as well as crumbs and water in bowls. He hears the faint chinking of chains from within. He then spots something moving.

"Irown?" Jaykin whispers.

"Jaykin?" the voice replies. Irown tries to wet his mouth but he is so dehydrated, he can barely speak.

"I'm here, Irown. I thought you were…" He stops and takes his mask off. "…I'm so glad to see you. We'll get you out of here."

"Is there any point?" Irown replies, then he passes out.

"Irown?" Jaykin shouts and hits the cage. "Irown!"

***

Irown awakes, he can just see an outline of someone while his eyes adjust to the light, then Eveara comes into view.

"Hello," she says in her calming voice.

"Oh, hello," Irown replies, with his voice back. He looks warmly at her, then checks out his chest which is not hurting, nor covered in blood anymore. With a sigh of relief, he relaxes with a huge smile on his face, "Jaykin, you found one," he says happily. "You found a Life Element." He looks around. "Where am I and how did I get here?"

"Kanaren's apartment, and we picked you up using the collector," Meara replies.

"Thank you. Where is Jaykin?"

"He's still at the tournament," Eveara says, and they both explain Jaykin's plan.

***

Jaykin heads back to see Eragraph, his mask back on, to tell him the good news, but he spots four people with the same suits as the Hunters who attacked him earlier. They are guarding his cage. Eragraph sits patiently and makes eye contact. Jaykin gives him a slight but discreet thumbs up. Eragraph nods his head slightly so as not to attract the Hunters' attention. Suddenly the cage goes up again and into the arena. This is Eragraph's third fight now. If he wins this, he will be in the final battle and have a chance to win the grand prize. He stretches again.

"Let's get this over and done with," he whispers to himself.

"Good luck," Jaykin says, under his breath.

The cage stops and opens immediately. Eragraph runs straight towards the middle of the arena again; looking to see what the creature is. A bladester snarls back at him. Bladesters are very small compared to the other creatures competing. This one reaches up to Eragraph's knees, but is deadly. Its skin is made of extremely sharp scales, shaped like broken glass. They attack their prey just by rubbing up against them. This one seems to be in good form too.

"No weapons, Eragraph," he says to himself. "Need to act like a creature."

***

Jaykin goes to watch the fight in the spectators' area. He looks up to where the emperors are sitting, each flanked by their High Knights. He reflects that one of those High Knights helped him and accidentally lead him to Irown and one of them went to attack him in Dreamora. Now he needs to get back to Eragraph, but how? With all those Hunters close by? Eragraph must win. It's all up to him now. Jaykin can only watch and hope.

***

Covered in scratches and blood, Eragraph is trying to dodge every attack from the bladester. He hasn't managed to get one hit on it yet. It dashes towards him then dodges and scrapes its scales against him. The pain becomes unbearable. He must come up with a plan and quickly. The face of the bladester is uncovered and with no sharp scales. So, if he can get to that, then he should be able to win. But he needs to lure it to the wall as he did with the rogsprinter. He makes his way there and faces the bladester and taunts it. It runs towards him and, with some calculation and a lot of guessing, he swings his mighty fist straight into the bladester's face. That's it. It falls and scrapes against the ground. Still alive, but only just, it stands unsteadily. Feeling dizzy and confused, it wobbles towards the middle of the arena, towards Eragraph, and then collapses. With that one hit on the bladester, Eragraph falls to his knees and lets out a huge sigh of relief.

"I'm glad that's over," he says wearily to himself. The crowd is going crazy once again. Then a loud noise is heard. He watches as he thinks it is the arena floor opening but it remains in place. He looks around to try and work out what it is. Then a large section of the wall begins to open up. It's pitch-black inside.

"Wait, what?" Jaykin gasps. "No. Not now. He needs to rest." He looks up at the numbers. "*I don't have the time to use any of the points to upgrade. I wanted to use them for the last match.*"

Eragraph checks out his body but is in no condition to fight. He has cuts all over and can barely stand. Someone has obviously played a trick on him. He tries to listen for the creature, to work out what type it is, but he can't hear anything, just the shouts and cries of the crowd. Then, out of the blue a loud roar overpowers their noise.

"That sounds big; very big," Eragraph says, staying completely still. The light finally reveals a gigantic creature, a sregnad, covered in large, thick, heavy armour and small Q-Azars, being forced into the arena. Whoever owns this creature obviously has plenty of time and kits it out with some serious technology. Eragraph gulps.

"Oh, this isn't good," he says to himself.

***

Up in the stands, the four Hunters who stood near the cage earlier now walk into a VIP room, where a plain-suited man sits on a sofa.

"Mr Vic," a Hunter says. "The deed is done."

"I see," the man says, smugly grinning and rubbing his hands, full of expensive rings. "If I can't have that creature, no one else will."

***

Eragraph hears the noise of something powering up on the sregnad. Suddenly the Q-Azars go off and the cage explodes, parts of it scattering across the battlefield. Judging from the gasps, the crowd is stunned. Eragraph rolls out of the way. Luckily, the sregnad moves slowly towards him but the Q-Azars keep firing. Eragraph can move out of the way but he struggles with the amount of pain he's in, from the last battle.

"*I'm not going to win this if I can't use weapons,*" he thinks. The sregnad moves, standing on the bladester, crushing it, making a loud cracking noise under its massive weight.

Jaykin watches helplessly while Eragraph struggles with the sregnad.

"What have I done?" Jaykin worries and starts to panic, holding tightly onto the banister in front of him. He notices the intercom on his wrist flash and he quickly presses a button.

"Jaykin," It sounds like Meara.

"What is it?" he responds.

"Look up."

He does so and spots a collector over the arena's shielding, preventing any flying creatures trying to escape and reaching high into the sky. Suddenly, Eveara jumps out and lands on top of the shielding. Surprisingly, she isn't noticed, as everyone is fixated on the battle. She kneels and extends her arms downwards.

"This is going to take all my energy," she concedes to herself.

Sparks of light pulsate around her body and flow through her arms, floating down onto the arena, unseen from the crowd. Eragraph starts to feel better; the sharp pain all over his body ceases, and he can now stand easily. He looks up at the sregnad and he can feel the small cuts that were made from his last encounter disappear. He notices the bladester. Amazingly, it is still alive, and now it is up, awake and wandering around. Eragraph senses this is Eveara's work and that he must end this battle, now. He rips off a few pieces of bark from his armour, then snaps off a stick, which quickly grows. He uses his powers to shape it into a bow. The crowd's cheers and screams slowly die and are replaced with mumbling and wondering what is going on. Even the two emperors are baffled.

"Is it me or is the Element acting like a human?" Mor asks, moving forward for a closer look. Lon does the same.

"It seems to have human traits," Lon replies.

"Intelligent life maybe?" Mor says.

"Intriguing."

The High Knight stands extremely still, watching every

movement.

The armour on the floor transforms too. It dissolves into chippings, leaving a few dozen arrows. Eragraph swings his arm and the arrows rise and collect over his head and bunch up into his new quiver, fashioned from the bark. He shoots at each of the Q-Azars on the sregnad's armour, destroying each one.

"What is going on?" Mr Vic shouts. "That thing isn't supposed to have weapons!" He throws his wine across the VIP room.

The bladester starts attacking all four of the sregnad's huge legs. It rumbles in pain and falls, crashing onto the ground. A large, thick, and transparent wall then appears between the bladester and Eragraph. More gasps from the crowd and they suddenly go crazy, cheering and clapping. Eragraph gasps for air, feeling a surge of elation. It is all over. He smiles, knowing he has just won a tournament, with a little help from a friend.

"You did it, Eragraph!" Jaykin cheers, jumping for joy.

Chapter 30

The Reward

Waiting nervously, and with his mask on still, Jaykin stands on a stage. Eragraph, who is still in the arena grounds, walks around looking at the crowd, who are chanting the word 'El-em-ent,' continuously, punching the air and waving. Jaykin turns to see if Eragraph is okay. He smiles and gives him a thumbs up and Eragraph nods slightly. His eyes then follow a long flight of stairs towards the emperor.

Emperor Mor lifts himself out of his seat, clapping his hands and raising his arms to greet everyone. The crowd goes crazy for him, shouting and screaming. Then he looks down to Jaykin, who waits at the bottom of the steps. He starts to walk up to greet the Emperor. He has seen this many times before in all the other tournaments; the proud owner of the winning creature walking up to receive their prize. With every step he takes, a surge of emotion flows through his body and he thinks about his father, Kanaren, Meara and all the Elements.

Halfway up, Jaykin is stopped by someone and is told to hand over any weapons, which he does without question.

"Welcome," Emperor Mor says, as Jaykin reaches the top. He bows. "Rise," Mor smiles. As he does so, Jaykin spots the familiar face of Emperor Lon, who stands and claps his hands.

"You have discovered one interesting creature," Lon says, smiling and clapping Jaykin on the back. Luckily, Jaykin still wears his mask, so Lon does not recognise him.

"I have never seen anything like it," Mor says. "I was nearly blown off my seat by that performance. Where on Izara did you find this amazing creature?" With that, the crowd stops cheering, leaving an eerie noise in the stands. Mumbling starts; random people start whispering and chatting amongst themselves.

"What is it doing?"

"Wow!"

"I've never seen a creature do that before." Others start pointing.

"Why is it doing that?"

Emperor Mor, still making small talk with Jaykin then realises the arena is quiet and looks all around, wondering what is going on.

"Silence?" he asks. Then he sees it. "Oh, my," he gasps, covering his mouth. He takes one, then two steps forward, passing Jaykin for a better look. Down in the middle of the arena, Eragraph is on one knee, bowing toward both the emperors. Mor is puzzled. This has never happened before.

"Fascinating," he says, having a good stare. He then looks around the crowd and smiles. "Ah, a very well-trained creature I see." He claps, and the crowd follows suit. "You have a very intriguing creature," he says, still staring into the Arena.

"Thank you," Jaykin replies, firmly but very

quiet. The crowd begins to chant again. "El-em-ent."

"Magnificent," Mor says and clicks his fingers to his High Knight. "I wish to take this conversation inside."

"But Emperor Mor, you always have it outside—" the High Knight replies.

"This is different," Mor says, trying to keep a smile on his face. "Oh, and bring the Element in with you."

"Of course," the High Knight bows, sounding cautious.

***

The party assembles in the Palace, with the exception of Emperor Lon, who is not invited. Jaykin is escorted to a small stage and Eragraph, in his cage, is rolled in and placed opposite him. Emperor Mor sits on his throne, backed by his Knights. The High Knight stands on his right and a party of the emperor's guests is present.

"So, let's see who I am talking to under that mask," Mor says.

Jaykin hesitates and looks around the room with all the emperor's guests staring at him. He really doesn't want to take it off as it will cause chaos but this is the Emperor of Q-Ara. He cannot disrespect him. He looks over to Eragraph for some sort of answer. He is a few metres away from him, and he nods ever so slightly. So, he slowly takes off the mask. No one reacts. Jaykin sees that the High Knight has leaned towards the emperor for a few seconds, mumbling something. Then Mor lifts his hand slightly to stop him. He looks over at Jaykin.

"What is your name?" Mor asks.

"My name is Jaykin," he replies.

"I hear you are the one that travels with the Hunter, Kanaren?"

"That's correct."

"Shall I arrest him?" the High Knight asks.

"No," Mor replies immediately. "Why arrest him? What has he done?" Everyone in the room looks at Mor, wondering what he knows about Kanaren and the boy, if anything.

"Emperor Mor, he is the boy who stole the crystal from Dreamora. He is wanted in all the cities and so is Kanaren," the High Knight replies.

"Ah yes, that," Mor says, staring at Jaykin. "Well, this isn't Dreamora, is it."

"Emperor Lon is still in the city," the High Knight says.

"Then we will give this boy a chance to explain his actions to Emperor Lon himself," He waves his hand for someone to go and get him. "But in the meantime, you have won my tournament, Jaykin, fair and square. What is it you desire? I will give you pretty much anything within my power. You have got this far in my tournament. You get to ask your question now."

"My question is…" This is it. He has been imagining this moment all his life, and the question has changed many times, but it has stayed the same since his father's disappearance. Jaykin has wanted this chance for over a year now and he finally gets to ask. He places his hand in his pocket and takes out the photo, letter and memory stick bearing the Hunter's image. But then he feels the crystal and remembers the Elements and the invasion that Kanaren is sworn to stop, no matter what the consequences. Is the invasion now more important than finding his father?

"So, what is it?" Mor asks. Jaykin's chest feels as if it is about to collapse and he starts to sweat. He has had no time to think about this. He never actually thought he would ever enter a tournament, let alone win it. He makes up his mind and is about to ask the question when the doors of the Palace swing open. A lot of shouting and mumbling comes from that direction, announcing Lon, with his High Knight and Hunters close behind.

"Where is he?" Lon shouts. "Hunters, seize that piece of filth!"

"There will be no need," Mor says. "He's under my authority now."

"What?" Lon roars. "Don't risk another war between us, Mor," he says pointing at him.

"No need for any violence, Lon. I have simply resolved this situation. The boy here has something to tell you, don't you?" Mor replies and looks expectantly at Jaykin.

"I'm sorry…" Jaykin hesitates, trying to find the right words. "…for taking the crystal."

"See, I told you, he finally admits to it," Lon laughs and points.

"Do not be so arrogant," Mor says. "Please, continue Jaykin."

"Thank you," he holds his breath for a moment. "I had no choice in taking the crystal."

"No choice?" Lon shouts.

"There's always a choice." Mor says.

"Not in this case, emperor," Jaykin stops to take in a huge breath of air. "There was another Element embedded inside the crystal." There are gasps of disbelief around the room.

"You trapped an Element inside a crystal?" Mor asks, directing his question to Lon.

"Of course not!" Lon replies angrily. "He's obviously lying!"

"I'm not lying! I swear. The Element was confused and the Guards attacked us with no hesitation, so we helped her escape. There were no chances to explain ourselves at any time. Every time we tried," he turns back to Lon, "we would be attacked by Guards or Hunters. That's why we had to run. That's why we couldn't return the crystal back to Dreamora."

"Lies!" Lon shouts. "All lies!"

Mor stands. "Is this the Element you are talking about?" He points to Eragraph.

"No," Jaykin quickly responds. "This is the Nature Element. He is from somewhere else entirely."

"Then where is my Element now?" Lon asks.

"She is no one's Element," Jaykin replies. "And I don't know where she is. She's with Kanaren, somewhere, maybe in the Unknown Lands."

"Well, you had better go out there and find them then, hadn't you," Lon shouts.

"Then what?" Jaykin replies. "You hang her up in your Palace, like every other trophy you have? Or place her in crystal again? No, even if I did know where she is, I wouldn't tell you."

"Why you little—" Lon says. "It's my property and I want it back, you thieving—"

"Okay that's enough," Mor interrupts. "What do you think?" His head leans towards the High Knight.

"A bit of a predicament," the High Knight replies, looking at Eragraph.

"Agreed," Mor says.

"Ha!" Lon laughs. "An emperor asking his High Knight for advice! I know what I'll do. How about me taking your winning Element." And he walks up to the cage, chuckling.

"You can't do that," Jaykin says and everyone starts arguing amongst themselves.

"Emperors of the lands," Eragraph's deep voice silences the room. "If I may have permission to speak for all Elements; we are not creatures, nor are we anyone's pet." He looks down at Lon, whose jaw has nearly hit the floor. "And we are certainly not someone's trophy."

"This is becoming even better," Mor says. "I knew you were an intelligent being by the way you fought. So, you speak as well then Element?"

"I certainly can, Emperor Mor," he bows. "One of my many techniques."

"And a sense of humour by the looks of things." Mor smiles.

"Impossible," Lon hesitates. "It speaks as well?"

"Do you have a name, Element?" Mor asks.

"Eragraph," he replies. "And I may have a solution to your crystal problem."

"Oh really?" Mor replies. "And what is that exactly?"

"Well, I would like to tell you and I do not wish to sound rude, but I don't really want to be in this cage anymore. I have been in a crystal for far too long and to be in a cage any longer can make one…claustrophobic."

"Is that wise?" Lon replies.

"Very well, Eragraph," Mor replies, and waves his hand to the nearest Knight, who slowly and hesitantly opens the cage for him.

"Thank you," Eragraph says, and he walks out and stretches. "Your crystal problem is simple," he says to Lon. He walks around, with everyone watching every single movement. "Jaykin, what about that creature outside of the city that is covered in crystal?"

"Oh, yes," Jaykin says, having almost forgotten about it. "I can give you the directions of a barragona." Mor's eyebrows lift in surprise.

"The legendary barragona?" Lon asks. "Impossible. Can't you see the lies they're telling, just to get away, again?"

"He is not lying. I was there myself," Eragraph says.

"My Q-Roid has the coordinates. I will happily give them to you," Jaykin says.

Lon looks all over the place, trying to work out what to do. He tries not to think about the crystal that he isn't going to get back. However, the more he thinks about showing off a barragona in the middle of the city, the bigger the smile on his face becomes.

"Fine," he says, giving in. "But if we don't find

this barragona, I'll come back for you boy."

"That is agreed then," Mor says. "He will be under my protection for the time being and I will also assist with some of my best Hunters."

"Fine, but it's my crystal," Lon says.
Mor nods to agree with him and Jaykin presses a button on his wrist. "My Q-Roid will be outside waiting for you."

"If I come back and find that he's left the city you will pay, Mor," Lon says.

"You have my word, Lon," Mor replies, solemnly.

"Before you go, Emperor Lon," Jaykin says, then turns to Mor. "I know what I want to ask for my question."

"Oh? and what is that?" Mor asks.

"The invasion of our worlds…" Everyone in the room starts mumbling again.

"Oh, not this again," Lon interrupts, covering his eyes.

"Can I ask for both the leaders of Izara to come together and prepare for the invasion?"

"No!" Lon replies, immediately. Mor stares at Jaykin, leaning forward with interest at the question. Then he relaxes, hums, and scratches his chin.

"I'm sorry, but I cannot help you with this." Both Jaykin and Eragraph look at each other in shock, while Emperor Lon has a good sneer.

"Why not?" Jaykin asks, sounding slightly angry in his voice.

"Because the invasion is a lie!" Lon shouts and laughs.

"How can it be?" Jaykin asks. "I've seen the message myself."

"I'm sorry to tell you this but you have both been misinformed," Mor says. "You see, the message is, in fact, real, but it was received over a hundred years ago."

"It's a fake and I will not say it again. That is the end of it!" Lon shouts.

"It can't be," Jaykin says. He shoves his hand in his pocket to take out the letter. "The Emperor of Lementes personally sent my father, and others, this letter, warning them to take refuge." Mor waves his hand for someone to collect the letter, to read it himself. "Kanaren is aware of the people going missing. He knows that Hunters were finding them and deleting their information on the system."

Mor finishes reading the letter and ponders for a bit. He is about to say something when a blipping noise sounds on the High Knight's wrist. He presses the button to stop it and looks at it discreetly, then quickly turns to Mor and whispers something in his ear. He listens attentively and sighs.

"I have some unfortunate news to tell you all," Mor announces. All eyes are on him. "One of our skyships that was heading to Q-Ara has not arrived at its expected time. Our communications to other cities are all down too. I do not want to get ahead of myself, but we may be under attack. Emperor Lon, I highly recommend you stay here for your own protection—"

"I'm not staying here. I will go to my city," he replies and makes his way towards Mor.

"Then I wish you luck," Mor says and shakes

his hand.

"You too, old friend." As he makes his way down, he stares over at Jaykin. "This doesn't prove anything, boy." Then he whispers to his High Knight. "If they are right, then we will need to prepare our defences." They walk to the doors to find Q-Tech outside, waiting for them, walking away from a collector.

"The coordinates for the barragona are here," Q-Tech says, about to give Lon a digital device. Lon completely ignores it and walks past, so Q-Tech hands it over to Slayed.

"You know what to do," Lon says to Slayed. The Hunters all run off, while Lon walks away in another direction with his High Knight close behind him.

Mor turns to his High Knight.

"Tell all our Guards to be in code red. We will need to prepare," he says and relaxes in his throne. "Unlike Lon, I believe this may be the beginning of something. I guess your question has been answered, Jaykin, and at an interesting time. We will do our best to defend the city." He sighs. "I had no idea it would come true," he says to himself. "Eragraph, will you help us if this is truly the invasion we have been dreading?"

"I don't know what a single Element can do to help but I've defended my home once before and I'm sure I will not stop now," Eragraph says, glancing at Jaykin.

"Thank you. Your words inspire us all." He nods and pushes himself out of his throne. People start to leave the room, until Eragraph stops them with his words.

"Emperor Mor, as I also won the tournament, do I get a question too?"

Jaykin notices Mor stagger forward slightly.

"Well, this is a first," he replies, amusement in his eyes. "Yes, I will do what I can." He is given help to relax in his throne again.

"For my good friend here…" He points to Jaykin. "…would it be possible to help him find his father?"

"That is an unusual request. Most people want luxuries or large amounts of money, just for themselves, but a favour for someone else, that is truly honourable, Eragraph."

"Thank you," Jaykin whispers to Eragraph.

Mor had forgotten about the letter in his hand and reads it again. "It is all very intriguing."

"My father is all I have left of my family. I will never give up hope," Jaykin says.

"I can see that;" Mor says and smiles.

Jaykin places his hand in his pocket again and pulls out a data stick. "I have files of someone that could be responsible for it all, but I have no detailed information about them. I have used all the resources I can and this is the last resort."

"I see," Mor replies and pauses. He gives the High Knight the letter to give back to Jaykin and he swaps it with the data stick. The High Knight takes his time receiving it and stares at Jaykin. Then he hands it to Mor but he refuses to touch it. "I will help you," Mor says. "But it will take time."

"Thank you," Jaykin smiles. "That means a lot to me."

"Good, that's settled." He turns to the High Knight. "You will search for his father. And Jaykin, you will stay in the city for the night. Do you have a safe place to go?" he asks.

"We do," Jaykin replies.

"Good, good." He waves his hand over to some of the Knights behind him. "You four will go with Jaykin and the Element. Protect them at all costs." They say nothing, but bow and stand to attention for instructions. Mor turns to Eragraph. "Please tell me; the Element that was in the crystal in Dreamora, is she the same as you?"

"No, there are many types of Elements," Eragraph replies.

"Types of Elements?" Mor asks, intrigued. "I would really like to meet them."

"They are waiting outside," Jaykin replies.
Mor gasps. "Please, introduce them to me," he says, excitedly.
Jaykin presses another button on his wrist. After a couple of seconds, the doors open and the Guards watch as Eveara and Irown walk through, with Meara and Q-Tech in attendance.

"I can't wait to meet the emperor," Meara whispers, admiring her surroundings and trying to keep her excitement under control. "I've heard he's very nice." They walk straight to Eragraph, who greets them all.

"It is great to see you're well again friend," Eragraph says to Irown.

"Thank you," Irown replies, placing his hand on Eragraph's shoulder. "It's good to be in one piece again. We will celebrate soon, but first..." He walks closer to the emperor. "Emperor Mor, my name is Irown, the Knowledge Element. In our time, it was a tradition for someone of your greatness to receive gifts from the Elements outside of their own village."

"Very well," Mor replies. "What are these gifts you speak of?"

"I bring you knowledge of the Solutions and the Elements from the village of my time, Leran." He goes to touch the emperor's hand. The High Knight stands in front of him and Irown stares back. "For this to work emperor, I must hold your hand."

"Very well," Mor says and nudges the High Knight out of the way. As he receives Irown's gift, he almost lifts out of his throne. He is most impressed, even humbled for a moment. "Thank you."

Eragraph steps forward.

"The Nature Element?" Mor asks, using his new knowledge of the Elements.

"I am," he replies, holding out a fruit, with a bright blue and green colour. "From the village Tesrof of my time, I bring you the luxury fruit of the Delic plant."

"Thank you," Mor replies. He takes it from Eragraph's hand, admires it and then passes it to the High Knight.

Eveara then approaches Mor.

"I am Eveara."

"The Life Element," Mor says.

"Forgive my rudeness, but I see you are in need of healing," she says. He looks down at his right leg and holds onto it tightly.

"I do, yes," Mor replies.

"Then I will give you this." She holds her hand up to him. "May I?" He holds his hand out to her and she places both hers on his. "From the village of my time, Vayval." White energy flows through her. Suddenly, there is a thud and a prosthetic leg falls away, onto the floor. Everyone gasps as a new limb is formed in its place. Eveara gently pulls the Emperor and he slowly stands. He looks down, speechless, wiggling his toes and chuckling to himself. He looks up to everyone with a smile across his face.

"I cannot thank you enough for all your gracious gifts." He looks down at his leg. "Now for mine. I hereby announce all Elements of all kinds, from both Izara and Raziz, are now citizens of Q-Ara." There is applause as the Elements acknowledge the honour with gratitude.

"Thank you, Emperor Mor," Eragraph says, sincerely.

"I will go further. I hereby announce that Jaykin and the Elements are now Knights of Q-Ara."

Chapter 31

Elements to the Rescue

Day 13

Pree and Mordan eventually reach a clearing in the forest, where trees have disappeared, probably destroyed by fire. Something very big has crash landed here.

"What is that?" Mordan asks. A huge object covered with dirt, dust and plants lies wrecked before them.

"Looks like a bigger version of a collector," Pree replies.

"I don't see anyone around."

"Is that a good thing?" She peers through the glass and sees a bank of empty seats.

"Pree! Over here," Mordan shouts, pointing to what appears to be a series of graves; twelve to be exact.

"What is going on here?"

Elra squawks above them. Then they hear a woman's voice scream from a distance on the opposite side of the machine.

"Let's go," Mordan says. They run past the machine and hide behind a large piece of wreckage. Two armoured Guards are pushing the woman around and laughing. As soon as the woman stands, they push her down again. She cries and they continue to taunt her.

"We have to do something," Pree says.

"Wait!" Mordan pulls her back. *"We need to find out what's going on here first. There might be others involved. We must be careful."* He concentrates on one of the Guards, reading his mind. *"Okay, I know where they all are. You can do what you want now, Pree."*

"Hey!" she shouts and both the Guards look up. "Try waking up from this!" She slams her hands together and both the Guards hit into one another and fall to the ground, stunned. The Elements run up to the woman. Mordan looks warily at the Guards.

"Did you put them in a coma or something?" She turns to him.

"Let's just say they won't be waking up for a very long time."

"Ouch!" he smiles and prods one with his foot.

"Are you alright?" Pree asks the woman, who still struggles to stand.

"What are you?" she stutters, looking them both up and down uncertainly. Mordan covers his eyes and sighs.

"We're going to have to explain to every single person in this land what we are, aren't we?"

"We are Elements," Pree replies. "We are friends. There is no need to worry." She smiles. The woman is still staring. "Let's find your friends, shall we?"

"I know where they are," Mordan says, looking south. "Many of the people are being held captive."

They make their way cautiously through the trees and take cover behind some large boulders.

"My family is over there," the woman whispers and points to a cage with two small girls and a man holding them protectively in his arms. Surrounding them are many other people in cages, also tied up, lying back-to-back. Armoured Guards are patrolling and by the looks of things have made camp for the night.

"We managed to get some nice stuff from these pathetic losers," one of the Guards says, holding up some jewellery. Mordan raises his hand up to the Guards and then looks as if he is struggling.

"What's wrong?" Pree asks.

"These Guards aren't Izarian nor Razilian," Mordan says. *"I can't work out where they're from."*

"Why not? You should be able to."

"Their minds have been wiped," he replies, and they stare at one another, confused. *"They only have one order."*

"And what is that?" Pree asks.

"To take control of Izara and Raziz."

"The invasion. It's already begun."

"What are we going to do?" the woman asks.

"Well, by the looks of things, they're going to keep these people for ransom," Mordan explains

"We're going to have to do something now, Mordan," Pree says.

"We need to attack them face on. Let's get them."

Mordan shows himself to the armoured Guards.

"Hey, how's it going?" They all look at him, startled at his appearance. He raises his arms to some of them. "*You want to fight each other,*" and all the Guards start doing exactly that.

"Good work Mordan," Pree giggles. "Now it's

my turn." She also raises her hands, forcing the Guards to the ground, overcome by a sudden need to sleep. "Let's open the cages."

One by one, they release the captives, who, though surprised and puzzled by the appearance of the Elements, are keen to get away. "Head to the hill. We will be there to meet you as soon as we're done," Mordan says, pointing to higher ground. They search the quiet camp just in case they have missed anything.

"Why do you think they had their memory wiped?" Pree asks.

"To keep whoever has given them their orders a secret. I'm sure it's the work of a Mind Element."

"Do you think?"

"I'm certain. The word Eram keeps cropping up. It might be a name." He shakes his head. *"Something is very wrong here. I feel…uneasy."*

"Me too, we should go."

Mordan and Pree make their way to meet the captives.

"Greetings," Mordan shouts.

"My name is Pree and my friend here is, Mordan." Some of the people step away and even tell their children to stand behind them. "There is no need to be scared of us," she says, calmly.

"They saved me and my family," a woman calls out, the first to be freed. She and her husband stand with their two girls beside the Elements; signalling trust. But still, the people are wary. Then one man pushes his way to the front from the staring crowd. He looks to be in his forties, his suit covered in dirt and mud.

"Excuse me; sorry; excuse me." He approaches the Elements. "Can I talk to you both?" They nod and walk a few paces away from the crowd. "I just want to say thank you for saving our lives. I am very grateful."

"Our pleasure," Pree replies.

"Sorry, I should introduce myself. My name is Captain Corteller, but everyone calls me Co. I was the co-pilot of the skyship that crash-landed in the forest. I thought I should let you know what happened here."

"It's an honour to meet you, Co," Mordan replies.

"Yes, please do tell us," Pree asks.

"We were on our way to the city of Q-Ara, and about three quarters through our journey, there was an explosion near the back of our skyship. We lost control and that's when we started our descent." He lowers his head. "As we had no control, we had to crash land in this forest. The last thing I remember is waking up to those thugs pushing everyone around."

"It sounds like the invasion has started," Mordan mutters.

"Invasion?" Co asks.

"No time to explain," Pree says, shoving Mordan in the arm for his indiscreet response. "Co, are we anywhere near the city?"

"I'm not sure," he looks up and around the landscape, but then stops and looks at his wrist, where a digital device has a compass on its screen. "Well, that can't be right."

"What's wrong?" Mordan asks.

"Well, by the looks of things, the Western Light is in the wrong place, which means we are further west than I had realised." He looks at all the passengers, who are all mumbling to each other, then back to the Elements. "In answer to your original question, no, we're nowhere near the city." Then, in a whisper: "I'm no expert but I think we're on the outskirts of the Lush Plains. I noticed we had flown over a large expanse of water, which is miles wide. We will not be able to cross it, as it is very deep. So, we will have to go around it, which, unfortunately, means we will have to go south." Both Pree and Mordan look at one another.

"How long do you think it will take to get to the city?" Pree asks.

Co purses his lips, trying to think. "By my calculations, probably a few days but there are people that have been injured from the crash here, so it could take longer." Pree and Mordan, absorbing this information, realise they have a very treacherous journey ahead of them.

"How many people do we have?" Mordan asks.

"I have counted eighty-eight. There were a hundred on the ship, including the staff. Unfortunately, we lost a few people, including the captain."

"We are deeply sorry," Pree replies.

"Thank you," Co says. "Our captain died doing what he loved. I'm very lucky to be here."

Pree touches Co's shoulder in a sympathetic gesture.

"Do you think you can get the skyship back to working order?" she asks.

"No," Co shakes his head and sighs. "That could take months."

"We need to tell everyone what is happening," Pree says.

"Agreed," Mordan replies.

"Do you think that's wise?" Co asks. "I don't know about you two but these people have never been outside of the cities, including me. We're in a death trap here."

"We need to tell them the truth no matter how hard it is to accept," Mordan says. "They will need to learn how to survive."

"What do you suggest?" Co asks.

***

Minutes pass and Mordan approaches all the passengers.

"To everyone that has lost someone today, we are very sorry for your loss." Both Pree and Co walk behind him. "Unfortunately, we have bad news. As far as we're aware, we are near the Lush Plains, which means we will need to go around the water that is between us and the nearest city. We are currently a few days away, maybe more." The passengers all start to panic in their own ways, some start to scream or cry, then the shouting starts and Mordan tries to calm them.

"Why should we trust you?" a guy shouts from the back. Then most of the people start shouting and agreeing with him.

"Because we got you out of the cages," Mordan yells. "And I can easily put you back if you desire." Pree holds him back.

"We will all need to work together now, as we're a long way from the city," she says. "We will head toward the Western Light…" She points. Then the passengers start to worry and shout again. "Did I say something wrong?"

"No one wants to go there," Co replies. "That's where people go to die."

"Oh," Pree says, at a loss.

"We will not go all the way to the Western Light!" Co shouts. Then he pauses. "And we will also take those attackers." Both Pree and Mordan stare at him and the passengers start arguing again.

"I better go wake them up then," Pree sighs.

"This is why I never travelled with a load of humans," Mordan moans.

***

After a long night of celebrating their win, Jaykin sits looking out of the window of Kanaren's apartment. Taking out the photo again, he says to himself:

"A Knight of Q-Ara; you hear that father? I'm moving up in the worlds." He smiles. "I'll be an emperor in no time." He takes out the crystal from his pocket. "Please work," he says and absorbs it successfully. Then he focuses to recreate it, forming it back into crystal, but tries to make it much bigger than its original size. This fails. Puzzled, he places it back in his pocket. "Right, I need to find more." He stands and holds up his hands and spins slowly. As he returns to his starting position, he drops his arms and sighs loudly. "Come on Jaykin," he says to himself. He shakes his hands and jumps in one spot. Then lifts his arms again. This time he closes his eyes and turns even more slowly, with intense concentration. As soon as his right hand faces between west and south-west, he stops and keeps it there, then places his left hand next to it, just to make sure. He smiles, sensing another crystal.

"What are you doing?" a familiar voice asks.

"Meara!" Jaykin says. "I'm—" but he can't come up with anything.

"You are a strange one, Jaykin. Q-Tech woke me up. It seemed to be talking to someone."
Both intrigued, they walk out of the room and check on Q-Tech, who is quiet and still.

"Q-Tech?" Jaykin asks.

"Jaykin, Master Meara."

"Were you talking to someone?" Meara asks.

"Yes," it replies. "A message from Doctor Rotnevin. He wanted to tell you that there are some items for you which will be available soon, and to say good luck in your travels. He is going to be busy setting up for the invasion, so he won't see you for a while."
Then a couple of bleeps sound behind Q-Tech and it answers.

"Q-Roid Q-Tech speaking, what is the message please?"

"This is Q-Roid Q-Five. The Master wishes to speak to your Master."

"Q-Five? Where have I heard that name before?" Jaykin asks.

"Aren's Q-Roid," Meara replies.

"If that's the case, then no, I don't want to talk to him. Block them."

"Jaykin. We can't do that."

"I can. I have too much to work out." He storms out. Meara shakes her head and steps forward.

"I'll talk to him." An image pops up on the screen. "Hi Aren," she says.

"Meara?" he asks. "Are you okay?"

Meara smiles and they continue talking for some time, while Jaykin stays away. He walks into the bedroom where Eragraph and Irown are fast asleep.

"I have more important things to do," he says.

***

Using their own equipment to restrain the attackers, or as Mordan prefers to call them, invaders, he leads them, and all eighty-eight passengers, out of the forest. Pree and Co walk at the rear. She overhears a conversation between two of the passengers.

"Why should we take these Growlers with us? We should leave them here chained up on their own. They'll be slaughtered for sure."

Pree feels she must intervene.

"And why would you do that?" she asks.

"Because they attacked us," he replies.

"But you're alive and free now. And you want them dead? Do you really want that on your conscience for the rest of your life? You would be as bad as them."

"We will take them to the emperor," Co says. "He can decide what to do with them."

"I'm pretty sure that the emperor would do the same as I would," the man says, then chuckles and stares at Pree. "I'm not sure what he will do when he sees you," he says, as if enjoying the prospect of an unpleasant fate. Pree shakes her head in revulsion. "*How can anyone think like that?*" she asks herself. *"Must be Razilian."*

***

"Excuse me." A young girl, who has been admiring Mordan for a couple of miles, plucks up courage to ask him something. "What is that strange noise?" Everyone around her notices it too, like a continuous rumbling. Mordan places his hand on his stomach, to make sure it isn't that, and then hears something coming from over a nearby mound. He walks over to investigate, then smiles, turning to her.

"That, my little friend, is the sound of goorit," He points. The young girl laughs.

"Goorit? Aren't they friendly creatures?"

"That's correct. Let's stop here for a minute." Over the beautiful landscape, for many miles, stand hundreds, if not thousands, of hefty goorit. These creatures are sweet, generous and extremely friendly. They have very long, fair hair which can be woven into virtually any clothing. They come in all different shapes and sizes, from human to Element height.

"These will help us get across the land," Mordan says. Co is not so sure.

"How?" he asks.

"Easy," Pree replies. "We won't need to walk from now on."

"Yes, everyone can ride one of these instead," Mordan says, gathering as much long grass as possible. Co and the passengers watch curiously from a distance.

"What on Izara are you doing?" Co asks. Both the Elements turn to him in surprise.

"You're telling me you don't know how to herd goorit?" Mordan asks.

"No, never had to do it before," Co replies.

"Then I'll show you." Mordan approaches a very big goorit. It looks at him a little suspiciously. Then, noticing the grass, it steps forward quickly, snatching it out of his hand and chomping on it. Mordan pets its head while it eats. "And that my friend, is how you do it," he says. The goorit nudges him and makes a sound between a purr and a rumble. Mordan grabs more grass and feeds it again, then he climbs on top of it and pets it.

"We will need a lot of goorit," Pree says. "So, get as many of the people to do the same as Mordan."

"I'm on it," Co agrees.

"Hey, Pree!" Mordan shouts.

"What is it?"

"After thousands of years, they still carry these little beauties." He picks something off the fur of the goorit and shows her. "It's covered with gizzads." He calls out to the others. Gizzads are useful little insects that eat smaller ones living in the goorits' fur. When crushed they produce a variety of delicious juices." He throws one, live, into his mouth, and, a couple of crunches later, says: "Try them! They taste so good and sweet." Nobody looks convinced. "The only downside is that they're very bad for the teeth." He grins widely, exposing bits of gizzad still moving over his molars.

"I swear he attracts all the most charming of wildlife," Pree says.

Chapter 32

Seek out the Islands

The sound of collectors hovering over the city of Q-Ara wakes everyone up. Four of these carry the huge, legendary barragona; its body hanging from dozens of cables. Lon wanted it to be paraded across the city to show it off, of course.

Jaykin has been summoned by Emperor Mor. They walk side by side around the beautiful Palace gardens and pause at a large pond with hundreds of silver nebs swimming through its clear water.

"Now that Emperor Lon's Hunters have found the barragona, you are free to go. What will you do now?" Mor asks.

"I'm going to try and find more Elements," Jaykin replies. "I believe they will help with the invasion."

"I agree," Mor replies. "Talking about the invasion, we still have not heard from the skyship that was attacked. I'm going to send a few of my best Hunters to conduct a search. If you find anyone out there Jaykin, please send them home."

"I will."

The High Knight approaches them, holding something in his hand: the data stick that Jaykin gave them yesterday.

"Emperor Mor, I have analysed the images and

I don't recognize the Hunter."

"Sorry Jaykin," Mor says, handing him back the data stick. Thinking it over for a few moments, Mor has a suggestion: "There is one person that should be able to help you. His name is Egamad. He is an elderly Hunter who used to work under the last Emperor of Q-Ara. He knows every single Hunter. Be careful though, he is…" he pauses. "…troubled."

"Thank you, I will keep that in mind," Jaykin replies. "Would you happen to know where I can find him?"

"He was last seen on Raziz, many years ago," Mor replies.

"Then at some point, I will need to visit Raziz."

Mor smiles and then addresses the High Knight.

"I would like to give Jaykin his own collector." The High Knight stays quiet, looking first at Jaykin then back at Mor.

"That can be arranged," he replies, not sounding thrilled about it.

"Thank you," Jaykin says. "I actually already have a collector, but it's someone else's and he should have it back; a Hunter called Aren."

"Good," Mor says; then, turning to the High Knight, "I will let you sort that out," he says, tapping on his shoulder. "I would like you to go with them." The High Knight hesitates.

"Emperor Mor, why have you suggested—"

"To get you out of this city for a bit. It will do you some good." Jaykin can feel the awkwardness through the silence and the High Knight's body language. "You might want to get to know one another," Mor says, and walks away, making it worse for them both. After a moment, Jaykin walks off too, heading back to the Elements in another section of the grounds.

They have opened a hefty crate from Doctor Rotnevin. He has sent new armour and weapons for them all to try out. Eragraph pulls out a light metal chest plate.

"I don't really see myself wearing this," he says. "I prefer mine. More natural," He taps on his wooden chest piece with a certain satisfaction.

"I don't know," Irown says. "I sort of like it."

"You would say that," Eragraph replies. "You're the one that got attacked by the barragona."

"I like it too and it fits very well," Eveara says, wearing a whole-body armour plate. She picks up a huge Q-Azar. "I'm going to have this beauty too."

"Do you know how to use that?" Jaykin asks.

"No, but I'm sure someone will show me." She grins at him.

"We need to head off, so get ready," Jaykin says. "The sooner we get back out there the faster we'll find the rest of the Elements." They all select a few more things from the crate and are ready to leave. Meara and Q-Tech walk by.

"Meara, I'm sorry if I seemed to be off last night," Jaykin says.

"No need to apologise." She pauses and looks into his eyes. "As much as I would like to go with you, it's probably for the best if I stay here."

"Oh, okay," Jaykin replies, slightly shocked.

"It's too dangerous out there for me and I'll just get in your way. I don't want to be the damsel in distress all the time."

"No, I understand."

"You better come back to me in one piece. I don't want to find out you've gone missing too." She gives him a hug, and a kiss on the cheek.

"I'll do my best." He watches her as she walks away. "I promise."

"And if you find your father, say hi from me," she calls over her shoulder.

"Will do," Jaykin smiles and waves a little awkwardly. As she moves further away, Jaykin stands there, wondering what to do next. Behind him, both Irown and Eragraph exchange smirking glances.

"I smell love in the air," Irown says.

"I feel sick," Eragraph responds.

Eveara shoves them both. "Cut it out, boys. I think it's really cute." She looks to the sky. "Aww, young love."

"We're just good friends," Jaykin insists, as he watches Meara turn and wave again. With that, a sizable collector hovers overhead and lands nearby. "Come on guys," Jaykin says, welcoming the distraction.

The rear door clicks open and the High Knight stands in the doorway, arms crossed.

"Get in," he says firmly. The Elements and Jaykin look at each other warily.

"He's not coming with us, is he?" Irown asks.

"Emperor Mor's orders," the High Knight replies.

"Yes, unfortunately," Jaykin says, placing his

new kit on a seat. Then he spots the Q-Roid in the front. It looks familiar. He turns to the High Knight, who takes off his helmet.

"Master Aren," Q-Tech says.

"Really?" Jaykin sighs, "you of all people, a High Knight?"

"Great!" Eragraph says sarcastically.

"I'm not exactly thrilled to be here either," Aren replies and places his helmet into a box nearby and locks it shut. He greets Q-Tech. "How you doing old friend?" he asks quietly.

"Doing well, thank you, Master Aren."

"Good," Aren smiles. "So where are we heading Knight of Q-Ara?" Jaykin doesn't say anything, just continues staring at him. "I'll need a direction," Aren smirks.

"To the Corroding Islands," Jaykin says, firmly.

"You heard him, Q-Five," Aren says, and takes a seat on the box.

Jaykin sits opposite him. The collector takes off and they both stare at one another while the Elements awkwardly put down their kit.

"You're the one that told Meara to stay, weren't you?" Jaykin asks.

"Well done, you worked that out all by yourself." Aren replies.

"Why?" Irown asks.

"Because I didn't want her to get hurt, following someone who doesn't know what he's doing. The city will protect her now," he says, still looking Jaykin in the eye.

"Why do you hate me so much?" Jaykin asks.

Aren stays quiet.

"It's connected with Kanaren isn't it?" Irown asks.

"No, it's not," Aren replies.

"It is, though," Jaykin insists. "Either it's jealousy or something else."

Aren smirks.

"Neither."

Everyone can hear the bitterness in his voice and he knows it. He sighs loudly and looks away, while the others remain quiet, perhaps hoping for an explanation.

"I had a great life before Kanaren appeared out of nowhere and took me away from it."

"What happened with you two?" Irown asks in a kindly tone.

"Nothing. That's the thing. I trained hard for years even though I didn't want the life he gave me. I committed. He pushed me to my limits. Then last year happened."

"The missing people," Jaykin says.

Aren stares at him.

"What happened last year, Aren?" Irown asks.

There is silence for a moment. Aren appears to struggle with himself; how much to tell; how much to hide; who to trust. Perhaps encouraged by Irown's tactful tone, he continues:

"The notes came in daily. He left me on my own. I wanted to get involved but he wouldn't have it; he kept pushing me away and wouldn't tell me anything about it. That's why I left. I had to find my way in Izara." He looks at Jaykin. "I couldn't go back to Meara. It would have been difficult for her to understand; a Hunter for three and half years not telling her where I'd been or what I'd done. So, I moved on and managed to become a High Knight. I never heard from Kanaren again."

"I think he had an important mission," Jaykin says.

"Yeah, and where has it got him? He's not a Hunter anymore. He has no friends, no one cares about him, so why should I?"

"He's a good person," Jaykin says, evenly, but Aren is dismissive.

"You've known him for what? A few days. I've known him for years."

"But you don't know anything about him, do you? If you did, you would have helped him; helped us with the crystal and the invasion. But no, you followed everyone else's instructions, as easy and as gullible as a goorit."

Aren thrusts himself at Jaykin but Eragraph intervenes, grabbing onto Aren just in time.

"Let me go!" Aren shouts, struggling to be released. Eragraph does so, but facing him away from Jaykin. Aren scowls at them both and makes his way to the back of the collector, slumping down in the corner and curling up in a ball. "You won't have your Element friends around you forever, Jaykin," Aren says, seething with pent up resentment. "They'll leave you all on your own. Just like the pathetic Kanaren did."

Jaykin simply stares back, but inwardly recognises some truth in Aren's words.

***

A few awkward hours pass. Jaykin gets out of his seat suddenly and moves to the front of the collector.

"Over there," Jaykin points. "It's on those islands."

Aren, calmer now, stands and looks too.

"Head down Q-Five, find somewhere safe to land."

"Yes, Master Aren."

The islands are similar to the Edge; they're very high but these have white chalky cliff edges. It is impossible to get to the islands without a collector. Nothing lives there; only long grass which ripples in the strong winds.

When they land, Aren is the first off the collector and takes in the landscape.

"Nothing amazing here," he says. He turns and points his Q-Azar at Jaykin. "You're not leaving me here."

"Don't tempt me," Jaykin replies. "It's got to be around here; we just need to look carefully."

Eragraph blocks Aren's view of Jaykin and stares down at him. Aren stares back defiantly for a moment, then slowly places the Q-Azar back into the holster.

"Q-Five, take the collector around the islands, see what you can find," he says.

"Will do, Master." It takes off again and circles the island several times.

"Anything?" Aren asks on his intercom.

"There seems to be a cave in the middle of the cliff edge and a path leading to it. Face south and it's just on the edge, but care is needed. It looks very narrow."

Aren moves to the edge and sees the path but it looks unreachable and is only a few inches wide.

"There's no way of getting down there," he shouts.

"I can do it," Jaykin says. "Eragraph, do you still have that vine?"

"Of course. I always carry it, just in case." He takes it out and starts to unravel it.

"I'm going with you," Aren says.

"No, I don't think that's wise," Eragraph says.

"Why not?"

"Because I only have one roll of vine." While Aren isn't looking, Eragraph and Jaykin exchange glances, both knowing that isn't true. Jaykin wraps it around his waist, then spots Aren taking out his sword and pointing it near the vine.

"So tempted," he says.

"Keep an eye on him, Irown." Jaykin kneels and places his foot on the very narrow footpath. "Hold on tight Eragraph."

"Don't you worry, I will."

He makes his way, very slowly and very carefully down. Reaching a safe place, he takes a look around. "Okay, I'm going into the cave now," he shouts, and unknots the vine. He enters a small space lined with white rock, but as he goes deeper, it gets much darker and he can only just see in front of him. He takes every step with caution, feeling around first. It is strange. His body is pulsating and it feels exactly the same as when he senses a crystal, but in this case, it feels as if the power is above him. He starts to climb the jagged wall, getting dangerously higher. He feels his way in the dim light, shredding his skin on the rough, sharp surface. The pain is intense but he is suddenly distracted by something smooth. With the last stretch he reaches out, placing his hand on what he realises is the crystal. It's embedded in the rock. It cracks and a loud noise echoes through the cave as it is absorbed. The Element slides into the gap. Jaykin quickly realises the emerging Element is upside down. Its eyes shine strangely in the dark. It grabs onto the nearest wall and rolls onto its feet.

"What on Izara…?" she says. "What is going on?"

"You're in a cave in the middle of an island," Jaykin replies. "And we need to go, now!" He turns to go back the way he came but she doesn't move. Instead, she looks around as if she can see everything around her clearly.

"Not that way," she says. "Follow me. There's a faster way; this way. Hold onto my arm and I'll guide you out." They dash through the cave. Jaykin cannot work out how she can see as there is no light coming from that direction. "Sounds like your friends are in trouble," she says. Jaykin listens out but he can't hear anything.

"I'm Seek by the way. What is your name?"

"Jaykin. What sort of Element are you?" She looks at him slightly confused. "I am a Sense Element."

They eventually find a bigger exit and, thankfully, an

easier way to get up to the top. She stops and inhales deeply.

"I love the sea air," she says.

Jaykin can't help but stare at her. She's about the same height as Pree and Eveara, about eight feet by his calculations. She has long dark hair tied back with two gold flower hair bands. Her skin looks thicker than any humans. She has no footwear either. Her dark green clothing fits tightly around her. He notices a tail wrapped around her right leg; it looks like a part of her clothing. Down her left leg is a series of holsters bearing daggers. She could easily be camouflaged if she wanted to. Now he can see her face in the light. She doesn't have human ears. Instead, they're curved around to the back of her neck. Her eyes are very wide. He also notices that on her back she has a small bow; a quiver with many arrows and two small swords, pointing upwards. He tries to find her symbol but can see none.

Just before they reach the top of the island, they see something thrown off the edge into the deep water below. Jaykin gasps for a split second, thinking it must have been an Element but then sees Eveara and the others looking down too.

"There you are!" Aren shouts at Jaykin and Seek. He is looking terrified.

"We were up against a few of those Guardians," Irown explains.

"But we took care of them," Eragraph says.

"It seems like they're growing in numbers too," Irown says.

"What on Izara are they?" Aren asks.

"No time to explain," Jaykin replies. "We need to keep going. Everyone, this is Seek. We'll do introductions properly later but we must move on."

They are all about to board the collector when Seek stops in her tracks, ears perked up, listening.

"Wait," she says. "I'm hearing something I've never heard before. What on Izara is that?" She scans the sky, in the direction of Q-Ara. "There is something coming our way," she says, pointing in the same direction. They all look round to see a dot in the distance.

"A collector," Q-Tech says.

"Do you think that's our help?" Jaykin asks.

"No," Aren replies. "Emperor Mor insisted that no one else would be leaving the city except for those finding the skyship, and us."

"Who do you think they are then?" Irown asks, squinting at the distant speck.

"My guess is they're Hunters," Aren replies.

"This isn't good," Jaykin says. "Get ready for anything."

The collector lands metres away from them and five people step out, all with bandages around their legs. One looks as though he is high status and the rest are the Hunters who attacked Jaykin. This time though, they are carrying an array of different weapons. Aren instantly knows who it is.

"Mr Vic," he says. "What is he doing here?"

"Aren!" Mr Vic shouts. "Didn't know you were

going to be here too," he laughs. "I have to thank you for attacking my Hunters." He points at them. "I had to spend a lot of digits to get them fixed up." He stops and looks at the Elements. "My, my, my! What do we have here? Four Elements? I am liking this!" He rubs his hands.

"What do you want Vic?" Aren asks.

"It's Mr Vic to you, sonny boy, but I'm glad you asked. I'm here to collect my reward."

"What reward are you talking about?" Eragraph asks.

"Wow!" he says with a big grin. "And it talks too! You, my friend, I have come all this way to collect you."

"Me? I don't think so."

"Sorry, Mr whoever you are," Jaykin says, stepping forward. "But we are on a mission from the Emperor of Q-Ara."

"Yes, leave this area, now," Irown says.

"Don't tell me what to do. As you can see, we're nowhere near the city of Q-Ara, so there are no rules here," Vic says, sneering.

"Is he Razilian?" Seek asks, and all the Elements laugh.

"I knew you weren't going to comply," Vic sighs theatrically, lifting his hand to his collector and waving. All eyes turn that way and, immediately, both Jaykin and Aren step forward. Descending from the back of the collector is Meara.

Jaykin shouts her name. She has both her hands tied behind her back. Another four Hunters appear too; all pointing their Q-Azars at her.

"Let her go!" Jaykin yells, his face reddening.

"Ah, ah, ah," Vic says, waving his index finger at him, mockingly. It takes all Jaykin's willpower to restrain himself. "I wouldn't if I were you. If you make a move, this pretty little thing will get hurt." They all back off for a moment. "I suggest you all put your weapons down." They all look at each other, waiting for someone to interject.

"Do as he says!" Aren tells the others, his eyes fixed on Vic's face.

They all drop their weapons.

"Now we're getting somewhere," Vic says. He claps his hands then rubs them together. "Well as you know, I am a dealer. Now that I know that there are more of you, I will make you an offer." He pauses briefly to sneer. "Your Elements for your girlfriend!"

"You've got to be kidding me," Aren says. Everyone looks at Jaykin but he looks down.

"I," he hesitates.

"Do it!" Aren says, without hesitation. "We don't have a choice!"

"No, there's got to be another way," Jaykin says.

"It's okay, Jaykin," Eragraph says, stepping forward.

"No Eragraph."

"Me too," Irown says, walking forward.

"No, I can't let you do this."

"Don't worry, we'll be fine," Eveara says, and she gently pulls Seek along with her.

"We're yours now, let her go," Eragraph says to Vic.

"I'll do whatever I damn want to, and when I'm good and ready, Element," Vic replies, grinning. "Now get on board your collector."

"You can't do that!" Aren shouts.

"Watch me!" Vic replies and turns to another Hunter. "Take our collector back to apartment three. We will see you there."

"Yes sir," the Hunter replies and does as he's told. The collector takes off and heads back to Q-Ara. Vic enters Aren's collector and sits in front to take in the view. He relaxes and pours himself some wine, a smug expression on his face.

All the Elements slowly make their way onto the collector too, while four of the Hunters gather their weapons and point their own at Jaykin and Aren. Meara is then untied and she runs towards them.

"I'm sorry," she says to Jaykin. "I couldn't do anything."

"It's okay," he reassures her. They all watch the Hunters enter the collector. As it begins to lift off Jaykin yells.

"Q-Tech, climb onto that collector!"

"Q-Five, do the same!" Aren shouts. Both the Q-Roids sprint and jump onto the collector, climbing nimbly up onto the roof.

Onboard, the Elements and Hunters face each other across the cabin. Eragraph waits impatiently. He moves around, tossing and twitching every so often.

"Are you okay there?" Irown asks.

"Not really," he replies. He leans forward and

picks something off his back, it's a red juicy fruit that has come off his armour. He looks at it and smiles. "Would you like one?" he asks one of the Hunters sitting opposite him, but gets no reply. "Come on you need to eat something. What about you?" he asks the Hunter beside him, who is holding onto Eragraph's bow. Again, no answer.

Suddenly the back door opens slightly. All the Hunters look in that direction. Eragraph waves his hand slightly and his bow forms huge thorns. They fly towards the Hunters' arms and legs. Wounded and yelling in pain, they drop their weapons. The Elements attempt to restrain them. The door opens completely and the Q-Roids climb in and join the fight. The Hunters are overwhelmed and are knocked unconscious.

"What is going on back there?" Vic shouts from the front.

Eragraph's response is to rip him out of his seat and lift him up to his own eye level.

"Greetings," Eragraph says, grinning. "You underestimated us; I believe."

Vic nods and gulps.

"What are you going to do?"

Eragraph glances out of the back of the collector.

"Can you swim?" he asks.

Vic shakes his head, vigorously.

"Time to learn then," Eragraph says, and tosses him out to a watery fate.

Q-Tech jumps into the pilot's seat and takes control.

"Let's get back to Jaykin," Irown says.

They head back and land once again. While the

Elements take out all the Hunters and place them in a tangled heap on the island, Aren storms into the collector and takes over the controls. Everyone jumps in. The engines quickly start up, he pulls on the lever and the collector lifts immediately, jerking everyone around.

"Where now?" Aren asks.

Jaykin takes out the letter and looks intently at his companions.

"To the Western Light."

Chapter 33

The Western Light

Meara quietly watches over Jaykin, who is reading the letter again. '*Look towards the Western Light, you will know where to go.*' He can't tell if it is excitement or nerves flowing through his body. Sensing the tension, Meara asks:

"What are you reading?"

He shows her the letter for the first time. While she reads it, he leans his head on the wall of the collector, imagining what he will find at their destination. Meara stares at him.

"How long have you had this?"

"Since the beginning," he replies.

"Why didn't you show me this before?"

"It wouldn't have made a difference. It doesn't matter now."

"It does to me. I could have helped…"

"It's ok, Meara. I feel like I'm one step closer to my father."

Aren interrupts their exchange. "Are you sure there is an Element there?" he asks, not for the first time.

"Yes," Jaykin replies. "Stop asking."

"No one goes there unless they want to die; you know that, right?" Aren persists.

"I'm aware of that. If you really don't want to be here you can go back to Q-Ara." They both look at one another, hostility in their eyes. Eventually, Aren sighs and faces the front.

"I'm intrigued. Why do people go there to die?" Eveara asks.

"Well…" Jaykin stops to think. "I don't really know why. When they've grown old, people travel there, I guess it's like their last journey."

"It's similar for us," Eveara says. "When humans evolve into Solutions, they also seem compelled to pursue their next adventure. It is instinctive"

"So, when the Elements left these lands, the humans needed something else to go to," Irown says.

"And like I said to you before, Jaykin, Eveara will change that. She can evolve humans into Solutions now," Eragraph says.

"I'll show you one day," Eveara promises.

***

As they get closer, the light grows more intense, bursting from the land in one continuous silent explosion. Its source must be deep inside the cliff. It becomes very difficult for everyone to see out of the collector. Luckily, both the Q-Roids are in control. They try to find a clear area to land close by. As the beam is so bright, everyone else must look away.

"Q-Tech, see if you can find a way in to the source of the light somewhere," Jaykin asks.

They land on a large, dark, rocky cliff edge, and, as the rear door opens, the light beams in and the Q-Roid steps out, advancing towards it.

"I don't think I'll be any good here," Seek says. "I'll be over there, keeping a lookout." She points to a cliff edge in the opposite direction to the beam and heads out towards it. Lit by the beam behind her, she follows the course of a glinting river towards the edge, where it transforms into a beautiful waterfall.

"She's a quiet Element isn't she," Jaykin says to the other Elements, sounding quite concerned.

"She definitely heard you say that," Irown says and Jaykin gasps, embarrassed. "It's okay, Sense Elements don't really like groups of people; it can be too much for them sometimes."

"That makes *sense*," Meara says, pleased at the pun. Adding in a more serious tone: "Sometimes people just need to get away for a bit."

Jaykin realises she is talking about herself, when she left all those months ago. It makes sense to him now.

Q-Tech returns.

"There doesn't seem to be an obvious entrance to the light source at this level," it reports. Everyone stays quiet, waiting for someone to come up with an idea.

"Over here!" Seek shouts, suddenly. They all join her at the cliff edge. She is pointing to the ground below, where the light behind them exposes layer upon layer of bones, reaching as far as the eye can see. But somehow it is not a horrible sight; it is peaceful and quiet. Jaykin's stomach turns. He suddenly imagines that his father might be in there somewhere but then shakes his head as if to rid himself of that thought. No, why would he come here?

"There," Seek points. In the middle of the heap of bones is a long pathway, and a solitary figure standing completely still, facing toward the east, leaning on a sword. A Guardian.

"Is that the thing that's been killing everyone all these years?" Aren asks.

"Looks like it," Jaykin replies. "There must be an entrance down there."

Everyone boards the collector again, except for Seek, who stands guard on the cliff edge. Q-Tech, at the controls, hovers just above all the layers of bones and opens the back of the collector. The Guardian is still facing the other way.

"I'll take care of this," Eveara says, moving to the doorway. She takes her new Q-Azar and braces, ready to fire. She glances at Jaykin to check she is taking the right stance. He nods slightly and she looks through the scope and shoots. The figure falls to the ground, the body crumbling into pieces. "I'll be taking care of our future adventurers from now on," she says, leaning the Q-Azar on her shoulder.

They see that the pathway ends at a large, dark cave in the lower cliff face, adjacent to the waterfall. Q-Tech lands the collector close by and they all clamber out.

"I don't like the look of that cave," Meara says, warily.

Aren tries to reassure her but Jaykin says:

"You can stay out here if you like." She looks at the bones nearby and shivers with fear.

"I don't think so," she replies.

"I think the crystal is going to be difficult to get to," Irown says. "By the time we find it, we'll be blinded."

"I agree," Eragraph says. "We're going to need something more than simply closing our eyes."

"I can always heal anyone who may be blinded," Eveara offers.

"Give me a few minutes," Eragraph says, kneeling. He opens one of the pouches on his armour and places it into the earth, then covers it with his hand. Within a couple of seconds, a tree grows to the Element's height.

"That was amazing!" Meara exclaims, incredulous.

"Thank you," Eragraph replies, picking off a few long, thick leaves and then distributing one to each of them in turn. "Here, these are leaves from the Esned tree. They're very thick and very strong, and I'm hoping that will help with our little problem."

"How are these going to help?" Aren asks, stubbornly.

"The leaf from the Esned tree is so dense, it can absorb any light," Irown replies.

"I can take it back if you want," Eragraph says. Aren huffs and keeps it.

The group passes through the cave entrance, which seems small initially but with every step they take, it becomes taller and wider. Shafts of light are visible ahead but the source is obscured by a gigantic boulder. They all agree that to reach the crystal they must try to move the boulder aside.

"Okay, everyone. Wrap the leaf around your head and remember to keep your eyes closed, even with these on," Eragraph instructs.

The Elements brace themselves against the boulder and, straining every sinew, manage to shift it slightly. Eragraph checks the size of the gap.

"Probably have space for Jaykin to climb in, but not me," he says.

"Same here," Irown says, from the other side of the rock.

"That's settled then. Jaykin you're up," Eragraph says. "Be careful what you touch in there."

"Just go straight ahead till you find something," Irown says.

"I'll see what I can do." Jaykin says as he clambers through; but he knows exactly where it is as his pulsating sense is working better than ever now. He takes a few steps forward. He stops. He can feel the sensation all over his hands. He has found the crystal. It is just millimetres away; but something is wrong, and he can feel it in his chest. He lowers his arms to his sides.

"I can't do this," he calls to the others.

"Why not?" Irown asks. Everyone waits for an answer as Jaykin falls silent. Then,

"Where will everyone go?" he says.

"He means the people," Meara says, softly.

"People come here for a good reason," Jaykin calls. "And I'm about to take it away from them; from everyone."

He goes quiet again.

"Jaykin," Eragraph says calmly. "Do you remember what I told you when we found Eveara?"

"I think so."

"I told you that this will be the most important

event ever to have happened. Now that the Life Element walks on our land of Izara again, humans will be able to evolve. Solutions and Elements will walk amongst us once again."

"I remember," Jaykin replies.

"Embrace every part of this moment because when you unlock this crystal—" Eragraph says.

"It will change the future forever," he and Jaykin finish the prediction in unison.

Jaykin is clear on the course he must take and lifts his hands in front of him, and places them both onto the crystal. It cracks and the light from within flickers, then all is dark.

***

Pree, Mordan and Co; together with the passengers and the invaders, continue across the Lush Plains. Co notices the Western Light flicker briefly.

"What on Izara?" he whispers.

"What's wrong?" Mordan asks.

"The Western Light; it's…flickering. It's never done that before." Both Pree and Mordan share the same thought: "*Jaykin.*"

The passengers start to notice, too, and begin to talk amongst themselves, concern on the faces.

"What if it goes out?" a man asks in the middle of the crowd.

"We'll be lost forever!" says a woman who appears to be having a panic attack. People around her try to calm her.

Slowly but surely the Western Light completely disappears. All over Izara and Raziz, people notice the light fading into nothingness; and they start to panic at this puzzling and inexplicable event.

Mordan, staring in the direction of the disappearing light, turns to face the passengers.

"People, please. There is nothing to worry about. We can still find…" He leans into Pree, "*what's their city called again?*"

"*Q-Ara.*"

"Q-Ara," he shouts.

"*You know who is over there, Mordan?*" Pree asks.

"*Jaykin. I bet it's him.*" With that, Elra suddenly squawks and takes off into the sky.

"*I think that answers our question. Eragraph must be there too. Why don't you see if you can contact him? I'll try and calm the people.*" Pree says.

"*I'll give it a try.*" He concentrates on the location of the now faded Western Light. A couple of seconds later, he says:

"I can read nine…no wait, eight, faint minds over in that area. Now to find someone I recognise."

***

Jaykin stands there with the protective leaf still wrapped around his head. He hears a deep voice in front of him. "Are you all right there?" the new Element asks. "Why do you have a leaf covering your eyes?"

"Oh. Is the light gone?" Jaykin asks politely.

"I guess so," the voice replies, sounding quite confused.
Jaykin removes the leaf. He is quickly mesmerized by an orb of soft light which floats right in front of him. He has never seen anything like it before. It slowly circles above his head and around the new Element. Standing in front of him is a nine-foot-tall being. He has scaly and very shiny skin, which doesn't have a particular colour. Instead, it appears to react to the orb of light, changing colour to reflect its surroundings. He doesn't have armour but instead wears clothing that seems to be made of the same scaly skin. On his back are two swords and a shield with a shiny reflective surface. He wears the symbol of the flame, in a beautiful red shade and with a red circle.

"You look at me as if you've never seen a Light Element before," the new Element observes.

"I haven't," Jaykin replies.
The Element smiles. "Oh really? Then it would be rude of me not to introduce myself. I am Blint."

"Jaykin. Nice to meet you, finally," Jaykin responds. "Welcome to the future."

"The Future?" Blint asks and chuckles as if he just heard a joke.

"My friends can update you on what has been happening here," Jaykin says, gesturing back at the others, just visible through the gap beside the boulder. They too are removing their eye protection.

Jaykin feels a breeze above him and looks up at the large opening overhead. Here, the Western Light has beamed for thousands of years. The Elements manage to move the boulder a little more, so that they can all properly introduce themselves.

"*Jaykin?*" a familiar voice says in his head and he stops in his tracks.

"Mordan?" Jaykin gasps. All eyes are upon him.

"*Jaykin, it's Mordan!*"

"It's Mordan," he confirms.

"They must be close by," Irown says.

"*Mordan? Where are you?*" Jaykin asks.

"Are you communicating with someone?" Meara asks.

"He's talking to a Mind Element," Irown replies. "We were separated from Mordan, Pree and Kanaren a couple of days ago."

Aren's ears prick up at the name Kanaren and he listens intently.

"*We're not that far from you,*" Mordan says. "*We will meet you there.*"

"*That's fine,*" Jaykin replies. "*You'll be glad to know we've found more Elements.*"

"*That is great news, Jaykin, good work,*" Mordan replies. He turns to Pree and shares the news. Her face lights up and she hugs his arm with a huge smile on her face. "Tell him, well done from me."

Mordan laughs. "You can do that yourself." He continues talking to Jaykin.

"*Is there a chance you can ask your new Element friend to use their powers to show us the way?*"

"*Sure.*" He turns to the Light Element. "Blint, can you shine some sort of light into the sky to show our location? We have a couple of friends that are looking for us."

"Of course," Blint says and catches the orb that floats around him. "I'll do one better." He pauses. "You may want to cover your eyes for this."

They all prepare themselves. The orb grows bigger and brighter. Blint's hands start to move further apart and he lifts it above his head. It shoots up into the sky, catching Seek by surprise. It becomes brighter by the second.

"There!" Mordan shouts. He and Pree watch it as it rises and floats briefly. "That is where we need to go." One by one the crowd of passengers look up and start to move again.

"It's a sign," a woman says as if reassured.

"There's still hope," another woman cries out.

"What are we still doing here? Let's keep moving," a man calls abruptly from the crowd. Mordan smiles happily at the light.

"Okay, let's head off again. Is everyone ready to continue?" Pree shouts.

"Yes, but what are we heading for now that the Western Light is extinguished?" Co asks.

"That is certainly a mystery, but let us not make these people any more anxious than they are already," Mordan says calmly, and walks on with the passengers.

***

Blint holds out both his hands and two large orbs appear and circulate around the group. Jaykin decides to explore the cave while the others introduce themselves. He comes across many old creature bones, scattered across the ground. But he also spots some colourful, beautiful, and intricate writing on the wall, right behind Blint.

"Irown, I've found something over here," he calls.

"What is it?" Irown replies staring at the wall. "Blint, can we have more light over here please?"

"Of course." The orb moves closer and so does everyone else, intrigued.

"Much better, thank you," Irown replics, and he wipes away some of the dust from the wall, staring curiously at it for a few minutes.

"What's wrong?" Jaykin asks.

"I…I can't translate it," Irown replies.

"Why not?" Eragraph asks.

"These are very ancient markings." He turns to the others. "Long before the Great War."

Chapter 34

Bad News

As they leave the cave, Eragraph explains to Blint what has brought them all to this point. Irown is busy reading one of his scrolls. He has copied the writing from the wall so that he can try and decipher it on the journey. Jaykin walks alongside him.

"What do you think it's about?" he asks.
Irown is scanning the symbols. "It might be something extremely important or it could be nothing at all, but we can't ignore it."

"How are you going to work it out?"

"Well, the scrolls I already have are full of ancient writings. With a bit of time, I might be able to figure something out."

They board the collector and head up to Seek. Blint introduces himself to her and she announces that she has spotted two Elements and many people heading this way, from the north.

"It's okay, Seek. They're friends of ours," Irown says.

"How many people can you see?" Jaykin asks.

"There seems to be quite a crowd; too many to count. They have goorit and…" She pauses. "It looks as if many are injured."

"Eveara, they're going to need your help when they get here," Eragraph says.

"Of course," she replies. "I'm ready."

Eragraph is distracted suddenly by some familiar squawks overhead.

"Elra!" he shouts excitedly. "You made it!" She lets out a few more loud squawks, swooping down and landing on Eragraph's shoulder. He strokes her and she responds by pecking his head. "I bet you're hungry." She squawks again. "Thought so." He picks off little pieces of fruit from his armour and feeds them to her. Meara watches with interest and admiration.

"Lovely looking creature."

"Thank you. Would you like to feed her?" He holds up some fruit, so Meara can join in.

"I would love to, thank you." He kneels down and drops the fruit into her hands.

Elra eyes Meara and the food cautiously. She flaps her wings in excitement, then slowly and carefully pecks at the fruit as gently as she can, as if she doesn't want to cut Meara with her very sharp beak.

***

They wait for Mordan, Pree and the others to arrive. Jaykin sees them coming over the horizon and rushes over to meet them. They both lift him up to give him a huge hug.

"It's great to see you guys again," he says.

"You too," Mordan says.

"I see you've been busy collecting more Elements," Pree remarks.

"Yeah, it's been a rough couple of days." Jaykin turns to the people and the goorit. "You have goorit?"

He pets one. "Where did you get them from?"

"We came upon thousands of them not far from here," Mordan replies.

"That's really cool. I want to ride on one sometime." Jaykin is smiling but they see that his eyes are searching for someone else. They are dreading his next question.

"Where's Kanaren?" he asks, expectantly. Mordan looks at Pree. "*He needs to know,*" he says, and she nods.

"I know. I will tell him." She kneels to Jaykin's height. "I don't really know how to say this, but…" She stops. She concentrates on holding back the tears. "We couldn't find Kanaren."

"What do you mean? What happened?" Jaykin asks.

"Kanaren stabbed the barragona and it let go of him while we were in flight," she replies.
Jaykin takes this in, trying to find some words. "I think it means he's no longer with us," Pree says as calmly and gently as possible. The words smash through Jaykin like a barragona's screech. His knees turn to jelly and he loses his balance, crashing onto the rocky ground. He struggles to breathe and bursts into tears. Both the Elements shed tears too and try to comfort him. The other Elements draw closer, unaware of the news.

"Mordan it's good to see you, old friend," Irown says and they embrace.

"How are things?" Mordan asks, softly. Wiping his tears away.

"Good, thank you. All in one piece now.

Everything okay?" Irown asks and immediately notices something is wrong. Eragraph approaches him and shakes his hand.

"It's good to know you have made it," he says.

"Not all of us, unfortunately," Mordan sighs, and they all look down at Pree hugging the teary Jaykin. "Kanaren didn't make it."

Irown sighs and lowers his head.

"He was a great friend to us," he says.

"He was. And he'll be sorely missed." Mordan pauses a few moments. "How is everyone after that battle with the barragona?" Irown holds his arm, then Eragraph buts in.

"Well actually, this wise Element did have a bit of an accident, but we managed to get him sorted in the end."

"Long story," Irown says. "Oh, you guys haven't been properly introduced yet, have you? This is Eragraph."

"No, not yet," Mordan says and they shake hands. "Great to finally meet you properly."

"An honour, Mordan and thank you for looking after Elra for me."

"Oh, it was nothing."

"What are you talking about?" Pree says, overhearing their conversation. "She looked after herself; we didn't do anything."

Jaykin stands and moves away from everyone. Meara tries to go after him but Irown stops her.

"I think it's best if he's alone for now."

Eragraph takes the opportunity to make introductions between the Elements. They greet each other warmly and commit to offering any assistance they can. Mordan takes up Eveara's offer of help straight away, since a few of the people are injured. She sets to work.

"Pree, who are those people?" Irown asks, noticing the armoured guards.

"They're from another land."

"Razilians?" Blint asks.

"No. Somewhere much further. We think they have had their memories erased by an Element." Everyone exchanges glances. Elements from a planet other than Izara or Raziz has never been heard of.

"Are they the first of the invasion?" Irown asks.

"Looks like it. We will need to come up with a plan," Pree says.

Jaykin runs towards the cliff edge and stops. He looks down at the waterfall and reaches over his shoulder to unfold Kanaren's sword. He stares at it intently.

"You can't be gone, Kanaren. We need you," he says, still tearful. "No, I don't believe it for a minute. You're still out there. I know it."

He steps closer to the edge of the cliff, taking in the view, towards Lementes now, where he and Kanaren first met. He takes in a big breath of air to try to calm himself. He rummages through his pocket and takes out the small crystal. He stares and admires every single detail of it, playing and rolling it around his hand, pensively. He closes his eyes, trying to remember Kanaren but tears come again. "You promised to help me find my father," he says, in anger, frustration, and sorrow. "Now you're gone, and you've left me here."

He holds the crystal tightly in his hand, squeezing it as hard as he can, trying to break it. Blood trickles from his hand and drips onto the ground. He feels every bit of pain from it. Opening out his hand, he sees that the crystal is still in one piece but covered in blood. He stares at it for a few seconds. "I wish I'd never had this. I didn't ask for it and I don't want it anymore." He looks up. "Do you hear me?" he screams at the top of his voice. "I don't want this anymore!" Then as hard as he can, he throws the crystal off the cliff. "There's nothing here!" he screams again. "Nothing!" He falls to his knees, sobbing his heart out. "Where are you?"

All the Elements are taken aback as they watch the crystal fly through the air and fall in the distance. Meara shouts Jaykin's name and runs towards him.

"Don't worry, everyone; I'll find it later," Seek says calmly, as Eveara re-joins them.

"I have finished healing the few people who needed it," she tells them.

"Good," Eragraph says. "Then we should leave."

"What about Jaykin?" Pree asks.

"Would it be better if he went back to the city while we carry on searching for the Elements?" Irown asks.

"No," Eragraph replies. "He just needs time, that's all."

Aren looks back at the passengers, who are getting uncomfortable being close to what was the Western Light.

"I think it would be best if I go back to the city

with my people," Aren suggests.

"Are you sure?" Irown asks.

"Yes. By the looks of things, the invasion has already started and I want to be there to defend my city. I'm no use here anyway." He looks up at the Element. "Irown, I want to apologise for what I did back in the city." He shakes his head. "I thought I was doing the right thing."

"I accept your apology," he replies, and smiles politely. "You were defending your home and your people. I would have done the same. How will you get back?"

"Take the collector," Eragraph says.

"There will not be enough room for both the people and those—" Aren stops to think.

"We called them invaders," Mordan says.

"We should take them to the city somehow," Co intervenes; "The emperor will want to deal with these people."

Aren looks at Co. "Can you fly a collector?"

"Of course."

"That's settled then. While you take the people of Q-Ara back, Q-Five and I will take the invaders on foot."

"But that will take you days," Co replies.

"It'll be fine," Aren insists.

"Well, if you are sure." Co then approaches Mordan. "I would just like to say, on behalf of the people of Q-Ara, thank you, and Pree, for what you have done for us. Without you we wouldn't have survived. We really can't thank you enough."

"It was an honour, Co," Mordan replies.

"I have a feeling I will not see you for a while."

"You never know," Eragraph says. "The future is unclear." He looks over to Jaykin.

"Good luck Co," Pree says, hugging him. "Look after them."

"Aren," Irown says. "Take the goorit with you too; it'll get you there faster."

"Thank you. You can keep a few, you will need them."

"Very well. I wish you all the best, Aren."

"Same to you and I hope we cross paths again." They shake hands. Aren turns toward Meara and Jaykin. "Meara," he shouts. "Let's go!"

Meara hears him.

"It sounds like everyone is leaving," she says. "It's time to go. Jaykin?"

"I want you to go back with them, Meara," he replies, quietly.

"But—"

"No. I've lost my father and now Kanaren. I can't afford to lose you too."

"I understand," she says. "I'll probably be more helpful for these people anyway." She gives him a huge hug and kisses him on the cheek. "Good luck. Find the rest of the Elements and your father for me."

"I will do my best. Please, be careful."

"I always am," she grins. "You too." She runs towards the collector. She makes herself known to Co and steps onboard. She looks back at Jaykin, who still faces away from her. She turns and moves through the doorway.

Pree is happy to see Q-Tech again.

"Oh, Q-Tech, you have been repaired. How are you? Do you remember me?"

"Greetings Element Pree. Brand new, thank you," it replies and moves some parts of its body in demonstration. "Yes, memory bank was not damaged on impact."

"I'm so glad to see you again. I want you to meet Mordan, my very good friend."

"Hello there," Mordan says and waves to it.

"Greetings, Element Mordan."

He kneels down close to Q-Tech. "I see what you mean about not sensing a conscious." Then, slowly prodding it, then waving his hand, he is trying unsuccessfully to use his powers. "Very interesting," he says as he stands. "Which reminds me. Irown, do you remember the stories of the Deathly Plains?"

"I do. A land where no one can pass through and should never set eyes on. Why do you ask?"

"Because I think we found it on our journey," Mordan replies, his expression showing a horrifying recollection.

"Tell me all about it," Irown says, encouragingly.

Eragraph approaches Jaykin.

"Come on," he says. "Let's keep going." Jaykin sighs as he watches the collector vanish in the distance and through the dark clouds. Aren and the invaders start their long walk towards Q-Ara. Rain starts to fall, mirroring everyone's mood. Mordan lifts Jaykin up onto a goorit, hoping it will divert him from his sadness.

"There you go." But Jaykin's face says it all. He is deeply unhappy.

"Where do we need to go now?" Eragraph asks.

Jaykin stops to think. He wants to go home and give up. Lementes is a few days away east.

"East for the time being," he says quietly.

"Jaykin, you have a cut on your hand," Eveara notices. "May I heal it?"

"No, thank you," he replies quickly and rips the jacket that Kanaren gave him and wraps some fabric around the cut on his hand, as if he wants to keep the pain.

She smiles politely.

"Very well. Let me know when you're ready, okay?" She lifts herself onto the same goorit.

They follow the cliff edge where they find a wide and very old pathway. None of the Elements, not even Irown, has seen this kind of construction before but as Irown mentions, it is similar to the pathway at The Edge.

They slowly make their way past what must be millions of bones, stacked up over time along the way. They are very careful not to stand on any. Seek spots something sparkling on the ground, covered in dried blood. She jumps off her goorit and picks it up.

"Is that what I think it is?" Eragraph calls.

"I think so."

"Do you mind if I keep it for the time being?"

Eragraph asks. "I think he'll need it back at some point," he adds, smiling.

"Of course." Eragraph admires it, then places it into one of his leaf pouches, and continues riding.

"We'll find out what you are, Jaykin; you'll see," he whispers to himself.

Chapter 35

Unravelling Jaykin's Power

Day 14

It's gloomy as they continue their journey. It has been pouring with rain. Large black clouds still fill the sky. The sea of bones is now gone and they ride the goorit through the long grassy plains. Near the back, Seek keeps a watchful eye on things. She senses something and instantly looks behind her to see Mordan and Irown walking nearby.

"What is it, Seek?" Irown asks, scenting a problem. She looks around behind them.

"Since the Western Light, I keep sensing something. It feels as if something is following us." Irown looks behind him.

"There is nothing there," he says, gently but sceptically.

"You've spent too much time in the crystal. It plays tricks with your mind," Mordan says.

"We did just come from a place where people go to die," Irown says. "Perhaps the atmosphere has upset you."

"Maybe it's nothing," she says.

"Well, we should always be on the alert," Irown says. "It's probably some little creature foraging for food. When I travelled in the Great War, there were many odd things happening; many that we couldn't explain."

"I'm glad that the Great War is over," Blint says.

"It's certainly calmer," Seek says. "There was always smoke in the air and a constant rumble in the earth."

"Yes, agreed," Eveara replies. "It feels like the time before the Great War."

All the Elements agree on that.

"Yes, but I still keep looking to the skies, wondering if another attack will happen," Pree says.

"One day we won't feel like that," Eragraph says.

"I hope so," Irown says and then changes the subject with a question for the Light Element.

"Blint, what did you do for a living?"

"Before the war, I used to create light orbs for the villagers, so that people could walk around at night with ease and safety. I also created them for the Air Elements to travel to other villages. Through the Great War, I helped as much I could with communications and again, lighting the battlegrounds."

"So, you are from the Staride Village?"

"I am."

"Where was it?" Jaykin asks.

"It was high up in the mountains in the east. It was a beautiful place."

"It was. I travelled there a few times before the war," Irown says. "Where are you from Seek?"

"I was originally from Ieten but as soon as I became an Element, I travelled the land. In the war, I ended up helping other Elements scout out Razilians."

Pree calls out to Eragraph, who is leading the group.

"Can we rest here?"

"Sure, but not for long," he replies. They all jump down from the goorit.

"Seek, keep an eye out. If you see anything give me a shout," he says.

"Okay." She crouches down low, feeling for vibrations on the ground beneath her.

Eragraph approaches Jaykin and checks on him. He helps him off the goorit, as he appears to be struggling. He notices the blood coming through the fabric on Jaykin's hand.

"How are you doing?" he asks, kindly.

"Fine, I guess," Jaykin tries to cover his hand. He sits down and starts pulling out some of the long grass underneath him. All the goorit rumble at once, as they think the grass is for them.

They rest for a few minutes, until Seek suddenly stands, looking up at the sky towards the northeast.

"Something is coming this way," she says. Everyone else looks up too, but sees nothing.

"What is it?" Irown asks.

"I'm not sure yet."

"Dangerous?" Eragraph asks.

"Possibly; it's big enough, and very fast."

"We can take it," Blint says.

"No," Eragraph says. "We don't want to draw any more attention to ourselves. Get down and stay out of sight." He places his hands into the long grass, and it grows over and around them.

"Bunch the goorit together," Irown says.

"It's getting closer."

"What is it Seek?" Blint asks, and she tries to focus but its speed is too great for her to keep track.

"No, it can't be," she says. "You're not going to believe me." She turns to the others. "I think it's an Air Element."

"Impossible," Jaykin gasps.

"I see it too; it moves like an Air Element," Irown says.

"But all Elements are in crystals, right?" Blint says, turning to Jaykin, but he is speechless.

"Anything's possible at this point," Irown replies.

"How?" Jaykin asks.

"It might be an Element not from this land," Mordan suggests, and gazes intently towards it. "Damn," he sighs in frustration. "I can't read its mind."

"Why not?" Jaykin asks.

"It must have armour on," Irown replies. "Some metals are a barrier to reading the mind."

"It's the weakness of my power," Mordan says.

"We should try to contact it. I can beam a bright light to—" suggests Blint and conjures up a small orb of light in his hand.

"No," Irown interrupts. "If it's an Element that has not come from crystal, then we cannot trust it. We must not engage."

"It's heading west," Seek says.

"To the Western Light?" Jaykin says and stands. "But it's not there anymore."

"Maybe it's looking for us?" Eragraph says, pulling him down.

"What if it gets there and then heads towards Meara and the others? We have to go there. They could get killed." Jaykin feels frustrated and powerless.

"You are not thinking straight, Jaykin. We must continue the journey. They'll be fine," Irown insists.

"But I can't lose anyone else, I can't…" He stops talking and his eyes close. He suddenly falls to the soft long grass, apparently sleeping. Pree's hand is raised.

"Sorry, I thought it would be a good idea," she says to the others.

"He has been through a lot lately," Eragraph says. They all watch as the Air Element flies overhead and onwards, in the direction where once the Western Light shone.

***

In the city of Q-Ara, a Guard is running through the Palace. "Emperor Mor!" she shouts. The emperor is in conversation with one of his Knights.

"Any news on the Hunters searching for the passengers?" he is asking the Knight, who shakes his head. Then Mor looks at the intruding Guard. "Speak. And please have some good news."

"We have had a message from a collector, outside of the city," she replies.

"Where has it come from?"

"The Western Light, and they want permission to land in the city."

"They may know why the Western Light has disappeared. Who are they?" Mor asks.

"Passengers from the crash site—"
Mor stands from his throne straight away.

"They've survived then," he says and lets out a sigh of relief. "Send them to my personal landing bay." He walks off. "I will meet them there."

"Yes, Emperor Mor," the Guard replies obediently.

A few minutes pass and the collector lands. The people move off it slowly, with Guards assisting. Emperor Mor waits for them all to alight. Co is the last one off and draws near to the Emperor with Meara at his side.

"So glad to be back home," Co says.

"Captain?" Mor asks.

"Co-pilot Corteller, sir, at your service."

"Co-pilot? Where is your captain?" Mor asks.

"He didn't make it, unfortunately," Co replies.

"I see. I'm sorry to hear that, but we will need a briefing on the situation, and soon."

"Of course," Co replies.

"I recognize you," Mor says, looking at Meara.

"Emperor Mor, I was with Jaykin."

"Yes, I remember now."

"Aren is on his way with some of the invaders who attacked Co's skyship."

"I see," Mor says." He turns to one of the Knights. "I want every single Guard on the lookout for anyone coming from the south." They all bow.

"I could take the collector for them," Co suggests.

"No, I don't want to risk any more lives and certainly not a skyship pilot. I need you both," he says to Co and Meara. "The Western Light? I'm guessing that was Jaykin and the Elements?"

"Correct," Meara says. "The light was a Light Element."

"Then things will change around here."

***

Eragraph picks something out of one of the pouches attached to his armour. It is Jaykin's crystal.

"I need to tell them," he whispers to Elra, who is on his shoulder pecking at some fruit. She squawks at him. "I know, I know." He turns to look at the others, especially Jaykin, who is still fast asleep on the goorit.

"Are you okay?" Irown asks, passing him on another goorit. "Looks as if you're not with us."

"Just thinking." He fakes a smile.

"We shouldn't worry about the Air Element. I'm sure—"

"No, it's not that…" He stops and thinks "We should rest here, just for a couple of minutes."

"But we stopped not so long ago."

"I know. I need to discuss something with everyone. It's important." His goorit stops.

"Very well," Irown replies.

All the other goorit stop. Eragraph and Irown jump off.

"What's wrong?" Mordan asks.

"All good," Eragraph replies. "Pree, how is Jaykin doing? Is he still asleep?"

She places her hand on his head.

"Out cold. He's not going to wake up for a

while yet. Do you want me to wake him?"

"No, let him rest."

"Are you sure you're all right, Eragraph? You haven't been yourself since, well, Q-Ara," Irown says. All the Elements, plus Q-Tech, gather together.

"I just have something on my mind, that's all." He stays quiet for a moment, wondering if it's the best time to talk about Jaykin.

"Well?" Irown asks, looking at Eragraph expectantly.

"I don't know how you will all react."

"One way to find out then," Mordan says.

"I'm not sure how to tell you all this, so I'll just come out and say it. When Jaykin and I were searching for Eveara, we were attacked by the barragona again." Everyone gasps and starts muttering to each other. "Please, let me finish," Eragraph says. "While Eveara and I were escaping, Jaykin stood his ground and didn't move. He attacked the barragona, with no weapons. He's the one that covered the barragona with crystal, he's the one absorbing the crystal, not this." He holds up the crystal. Everyone exchanges looks. "Jaykin has powers."

"Impossible," Blint replies.

"Are you sure about this?" Mordan asks. "You didn't imagine it?"

"On Izara's life, I saw everything with my own eyes. He was like another person altogether. So much power."

"But humans don't have powers," Seek says. "I've never heard of such a thing."

"The legend is true then," Irown says.

Everyone stops and stares at him.

"What on Izara do you mean?" Blint asks. Irown takes his time before responding. "Long before the Great War, rumours, stories, whatever you want to call them, were told of the first Elements walking the lands and how they were in the form of children. This is when their powers would grow and instead of evolving into a Solution they would instantly transform into a new Element and with no help from any other."

"I've heard of this myth," Eragraph says. "It is said that the first of the Elements would have no memory of their human life before."

"I remember these as bedtime stories," Pree says. "I think we've all heard the myths, but if it were true, Irown, wouldn't there be Elements walking the lands in this time?"

"That is true. The Knowledge Elements have been discussing this subject for as long as we can remember," Irown replies.

"Eveara, do you know anything about this? You must have heard something," Eragraph asks.

"Unfortunately, I don't. This is the first time I have heard of a human having powers. Izara herself didn't know where she came from or if she had powers when she was a human. She had no recollection of it."

"Well, if Izara didn't know, then we stand no chance of knowing," Irown says. "Pree, you were the first to see this land, can you remember anything?"

"No. The only thing that didn't make sense was when they were talking about the smaller crystal absorbing other crystals. It never even crossed my mind that it would be Jaykin."

"And he was the only one." Mordan butts in. "It's never anyone else."

"A Crystal Element though?" Eragraph says.

"There is no such thing," Blint says.

"But there must have been," Irown states. "I have been pondering about this for days. How did we end up in crystal? There must have been more people like Jaykin at the Great War."

"What if he is from Raziz or even another land?" Blint asks.

"He is not Razilian," Mordan insists. "If he wanted to kill us, he would have done it by now."

"And he isn't from another land," Pree says.

"How do we know?" Blint asks. "I've been here for a day and I hardly know this kid."

"Mordan, you must have been in his head at some point. Have you not seen anything in his memory?" Seek asks.

"Well to tell you the truth, no. Ever since I've been here, I haven't read his or Kanaren's mind," Mordan replies. "The only time I was in his head, was when he and Kanaren sparred but I didn't see anything out of the ordinary."

"Are you sure?" Pree asks.

"Very sure. Remember he kept the invasion from us."

"What else could he be hiding from us?" Blint asks. "He may know how we got in the crystal in the first place." He turns to Jaykin. "Mordan, read his mind."

"Wait," Irown says. "Before we do that, I suggest we ask him ourselves."

"Do you think that's wise?" Pree asks. "He has been through a lot recently."

"I think it's a good idea," Blint says. "We need to find out what's going on."

"Let's have a vote," Irown suggests. "Who wants to ask him for the truth about his powers?"
Blint and Seek put their hands up straight away but the others think about it first.

"I think it's too early to ask him," Pree says. "He will tell us when he's ready. So, I won't be putting my hand up."

"Me neither," Eveara says. "I'm respecting his powers."

"I'll have to agree with Pree and Eveara. He must have a reason for not telling us," Mordan says.

"That may be true, but I'm always fascinated when I find new things. I say we ask," Irown says and he turns to Eragraph, who takes his time, including looking at Q-Tech for an answer, but it stays quiet.

"I guess it's all up to me then," he says, facing the others. "I know that he has been through a lot; but so have we. We all know about his power now and it's going to be difficult to keep it quiet." He turns to Irown. "We need answers."

"Then it's settled," Irown says. "Do what you need to do Pree."
She moves slowly and stands over Jaykin.

"I'm sorry, Jaykin," she whispers. "Time to wake up." She places her hand on his forehead and he awakes. Eragraph approaches him.

"How are you feeling?"

"I feel much better after that nap," Jaykin

replies.

"Good…Jaykin, we need to talk about something very important."

"What's up?"

"We know your secret."

"What secret?" he asks, looking warily at all the Elements in turn and feeling nervous.

"Your crystal powers," Irown replies. Jaykin takes this in.

"How do you know?" he asks, eventually, lowering his head, avoiding eye contact with anyone.

"I saw you and the barragona fight. You didn't use this crystal," Eragraph says, showing it to him. Jaykin takes it out of his hand.

"I knew you had it. I just…didn't want it anymore."

"You can sense it can't you?" Irown asks and Jaykin nods. "That's how you know where all the crystals are?" He nods again and looks as if he is about to cry. "Jaykin, humans and Solutions aren't supposed to have powers," Irown says.

"I know. That's why I got confused about the whole thing."

"Why didn't you tell us?" Pree asks, looking concerned and sad.

"I'm sorry," Jaykin sighs. "There were so many times when I really wanted to tell you all, but I promised Kanaren not to say anything, to anyone."

"Kanaren?" Mordan replies. "I knew I shouldn't have trusted him."

"That's the thing. He didn't want to tell you because we only just met you. He didn't even know anything about it until I absorbed the crystal in Dreamora. He said that none of you would understand and I would be in danger too, if anyone else found out."

"He does have a point," Blint says.

"Jaykin, where did you get these powers from?" Irown asks.

"I honestly don't know. They just sort of appeared out of nowhere."

"When was the first time you used them?" Irown asks. Jaykin tries to remember.

"I think when I was in Kanaren's place. I had absorbed a crystal that he had found on Raziz. Like this one, but I didn't realise it then."

"Could that have been the cause?" Pree asks.

"Wouldn't have thought so," Eragraph butts in. "Jaykin would have had the power before that." He turns to Mordan.

"He's been telling the truth all this time," Mordan says.

"Can you demonstrate your power?" Eragraph asks.

"I can't," he replies.

"Why not?" Irown asks.

"Last time I tried to use it; it didn't work."

"When was the last time you tried to create crystal?" Irown asks.

Jaykin thinks long and hard.

"I created this crystal when I was at Kanaren's place in Q-Ara, but that's when I'd absorbed it. I couldn't create any more than that. Also, when I was at the system, I tried to create a wall, but nothing happened."

"That was after the barragona, correct?" Eragraph asks. "Pree, Mordan, Irown, myself and lastly Eveara. That makes five. Irown how large do you think the barragona is?"

"About four to five times as big as one of us," he replies.

"That would make sense and, Jaykin, I'm guessing you created crystal elsewhere?"

"Yeah, a couple of places. I created that crystal in Mount Keap, but I think the Hunters brought it back to the Misty Marsh so that one doesn't really count." Then he remembers another time and faces Pree. "Oh, and the time I fell in that tree in the High Tree Forest."

"I remember that," Pree says. "You created crystal then? I didn't notice."

"I accidentally created the crystal in the Tree," he replies.

"That's it then; you just ran out of crystal," Eragraph states.

"Ran out?" Jaykin asks, baffled.

"Yes, that's it," Irown says. "You would be classed as a Conjurer Element. They absorb the elements around them to reuse again. For most, it's all around them and is unlimited."

"But as you absorbed all five crystals from the Elements you literally ran out of crystal after you covered the barragona," Eragraph explains.

"You should be able to create some now, after you absorbed the crystal from me and Seek," Blint says.

"I'll give it a try," Jaykin says. He feels nervous showing everyone as he has tried to keep it a secret for so long. He stands and holds his hands out and then he looks around to each of the Elements. They watch expectantly. A small crystal appears out of thin air and it slowly gets larger, nearly covering his hand. All the Elements start clapping.

"Good work, Jaykin," Eragraph says. "Now, what else you can do with it?"

Jaykin looks confused.

"This is all I can do," he replies. "And absorb it of course."

"It's okay, we will teach you how to use your powers," Eragraph says. "But it's a great start."

"What else can I learn?" Jaykin asks. All the Elements are grinning.

"Many things," Eragraph assures him.

Chapter 36

Friend or Foe?

Day 15

Aren, Q-Five and a couple of the survivors of the ship continue walking with the invaders towards the city of Q-Ara. They can see it in the distance. With still a few hours to walk, Aren does not feel so good. Something eerie is in the air, and the wind picks up.

"Something isn't right," he whispers.

"Creature!" someone yells.

"Everyone, get down!" Aren shouts. He pulls out his sword. They all fall to the ground and some begin to scream. Aren stares at it trying to work out what it is. It circles above them. "That's no creature," he says.

"It's an Element!" an invader shouts. "Have you never seen an Air Element before?" he says, mocking the others for their caution.

"Is this Jaykin's doing? Did they find another one?" Aren loosens his grip on his sword. "Q-Five, prepare for anything!"

"What are we to do?" a passenger asks.

"Stay down. I can't work out if it's friendly or not." Everyone watches it hover around them, not yet ready to believe they are safe. Aren senses that something is out of place. He is trying to understand why Jaykin has sent an Element to their aid when they are so close to the city. His eyes turn to the invaders and immediately notice that their expressions have turned to a grotesque grin. "No," he gasps. "Run to the city, now!"

"We're staying right here!" an invader shouts. The Element stops in mid-air and suddenly the wind picks up faster and harder.

"Go now!" Aren shouts to the passengers. The Element swoops closer and thumps down on the ground. Everyone, including the invaders, is shoved back with a gust of air. The Element is huge; at least twice the height of Pree. With the exception of its gigantic wings, it has light armour covering its whole body, including its head.

"Who is your leader?" he demands, with a deep resonating voice. No one says anything. "You," he points at Aren. "The one with the sword; are you the leader?"

"I am. What is your business?"

"None of yours," the Element replies.

"Then I take it you're not here to help us," Aren says, brandishing his sword.

"Help you?" the Element chuckles. "No, but you will help me free my people."

"I don't think so," Aren replies, holding his sword firmly and pointing it at the Element.

"Then prepare for the full wrath of my power," the Element shouts. He swipes a wing towards Aren and a strong gust of air whirls around, throwing him off his feet, and blasting his sword from his hand. As the Element is about to unleash more of his power, a blast from the city is heard, causing an explosion nearby, barely missing Aren and the others. The

Element staggers in shock, covering its face. Another two blasts follow the first. The Element faces the city. He aims his air powers to redirect the blasts away, but he misses one and is hit, falling to the ground, and screaming in pain.

"This is our chance. Run!" Aren shouts to the passengers. The invaders stay rooted to the spot. He takes out a Q-Azar and starts shooting at the ground near their feet and they run towards the city. He watches the Element staggering to his feet, trying to use his wings to keep stable, but the explosions keep coming. He searches for his sword but can't find it anywhere. The Element curses. He somehow gets to his feet and spreads his wings out wide. Without any warning, Aren lunges onto the Element to grab its armour, trying to stop him from getting away; but it's no use. The Element takes flight and flies off, heading west, with Aren holding on, tightly.

***

Jaykin learns from the Elements how to use his powers effectively. He is a keen learner.

"As a Conjurer Element, you can do many things with your powers," Eragraph explains. "For example, creating weapons, armour or even shields. By the end of today, I want you to have created a crystal sword for me."

"Okay, I'll do my best," Jaykin replies with slight hesitation.

Seek gives him an Esned plant, the same one as they used to open the Light Element.

"I don't know how covering his eyes is going to help," Mordan says, dismissively.

"Because he needs to sharpen all other senses to help when using his power," Seek replies.

"Did you not learn your powers as Jaykin's doing right now?" Pree asks.

"Well…," Mordan hesitates.

"Thought so," she says.

"Okay Jaykin," Seek says. "You will be wearing that cover for the rest of the day while practising."
Jaykin is speechless, and obedient. He spots an orb of light hovering right next to him.

"You may have seen Eragraph use and control his environment," Blint says. "You can also do this with crystal, without using your hands. You will need to use your mind."
Jaykin doesn't argue and submits himself to their wisdom.

***

They travel for miles, heading west until the grass disappears and leaves a stone road. It looks ancient and uneven and appears to lead into a forest, of sorts. The trees are large, with thick trunks, but instead of a lush green colour for the leaves, they are bright orange, like fire. Eragraph suggests they take this part of the journey on foot, as goorit are not used to carrying heavy Elements on stony ground. Instead, they walk beside them and encourage them to move along with supplies of long sweet grass. Eveara describes their surroundings to Jaykin, who still has the leaf wrapped around his head and a strange shape made from crystal in his hand.

"It's called the Road of Fire," Jaykin says. "I wouldn't mind looking at this." And he takes off the leaf and admires the view. "Wow," he says. "It's beautiful."

"It is, isn't it," Pree agrees.

Suddenly Seek stops in her tracks. "Wait, everyone! I see something strange, straight ahead of us, but I can't work it out. We need to get closer, but take care." They follow the path a few more steps until a figure comes into view. "It looks like an elderly man, carrying a stick. And he's walking their way." They all exchange looks.

"He's heading towards the Western Light," Jaykin says.

"But there is no light," Blint says, bluntly.

"Let us speak with him," Eragraph suggests.

They get closer to the man, who seems not to notice any of them. He is very hunched over, with a small rucksack on his back, using a stick to keep himself steady. He wears an old cloak and nothing on his feet.

"This feels slightly awkward," Mordan whispers.

"Hush," Pree says.

"Hello, is someone there?" the man asks.

"Greetings," Eragraph replies, in his deep voice.

"Oh, hello there," the man replies, slightly startled. "My, my, you have an interesting voice young man."

"Thank you," Eragraph smiles.

"I thought I heard someone." The man chuckles and coughs slightly. "My name is Dezil. Nice to meet you."

"It's a pleasure to meet you, Dezil. We are the Elements," Irown says.

"Oh," Dezil says in surprise. "So, there are more of you?" He sounds cheerful about the prospect of more company.

"Yes, there are several of us," Jaykin replies.

"Oh my, where are you folks off to on this beautiful day?" Dezil asks. Everyone exchanges glances. The conditions are cloudy and grim.

"We're on an adventure," Pree replies.

"An adventure? I am too." Th Elements feel a certain awkwardness, especially Blint.

"Where have you travelled from?" Jaykin asks.

"From Dreamora.

"That's a long way. How did you get here all by yourself?"

"Oh, the usual. I made my way to Lementes, then travelled from there two days ago…"

Two days ago

…Dezil walks up to the western gates of Lementes. A couple of Guards approach him, one younger Guard learning on the job and another much older.

"Are you okay sir?" the older Guard asks him.

"Oh yes. I wish to go to the Western Light please. Am I in the right place?"

"You are. Do you have your documents?"

"All in my bag, young man," Dezil replies, undoing and rummaging through it. He passes them to the Guards.

"Thank you…" The Guard inspects them. "Dezil, you can pass. We wish you all the best," he says in a very calm and soothing voice.

"Thank you," Dezil replies cheerfully. "My new journey starts here." The doors open, and he walks through. The Guards watch him from the doorway.

"Shall I close the door now sir?"

"No. Not yet. Give it until he gets to the forest. Sometimes they go outside the wall and then they have second thoughts." They both watch him enter the forest. "Okay, you can close it now." At that moment, the Western Light flickers in the sky and then disappears.

"What on Izara?" they say in unison.

Present Day

"I packed some food for the journey but I'm afraid I may be running out," Dezil says.
Seek approaches him. "Here, I have some food." Dezil reaches out and she passes him some fruit. She turns to the other Elements and points to her eyes, then waves in front of them, indicating that he may be blind.

"How long have you been without sight?" Eveara asks, drawing closer to him. She waves to Jaykin to follow her, which he does.

"Oh, for far too long my dear," he replies.

"Jaykin, do you have that thing you've been creating recently?" she whispers.

"Yes, why?" he asks.

"I'll show you." He takes it out of his pocket and instead of taking the crystal, Eveara pushes his hand gently towards Dezil's face, raising it to eye level. She smiles at Jaykin.

"I was eighteen when I was blinded. It has been such a long time," continues Dezil, sadly.

"That is sad," she whispers. "Let us make it better for you." He is baffled by the young-sounding voice. "Would you like to see again?" she calmly whispers and without any hesitation, Dezil nods.

"Yes, I would," he replies. "But how?"

"It's probably better if I show you." All the Elements look on as Eveara moves closer, placing her index finger, with an aura around it, near the top of Dezil's forehead, but not touching him. "Okay, Dezil, just relax for me please," she says, noticing his excitement. She touches his forehead ever so slightly. He jerks back dropping his stick and, within seconds, he sees.

"Oh my," he gasps, the light slowly bursting into his eyes. Blint approaches and creates another orb around Dezil's head but this time to filter the light and enable him to become accustomed to it, gradually. "I…I can see again." Dezil is overcome and breathing heavily. Then he goes silent. Focusing, he spots the crystal in Jaykin's hand and stares at it. He comes closer. "That is beautiful," he says slowly. Jaykin looks at Dezil then back at the crystal.

"Here, it's yours."

"Really?" Dezil replies, "are you sure?"

"Of course. It's our gift."

"My goodness." He leans back, trying to see their faces as they are all so tall, but struggles with his hunched back, and with visual perspective. He leans so far back that he loses balance. Luckily Eragraph catches him and stands him up again.

"Here," Eragraph says, creating a chair out of wood and leaves, then helping him onto it.

"You aren't from around here, are you?" Dezil asks. Before Irown can reply, Dezil continues: "Are you here to take me on my new journey?"

"Where do you think we will take you?" Eragraph asks, kneeling beside him.

"I'm not quite sure," Dezil stops and thinks. "A new adventure, I hope," he says with delight.

"I know how you feel," Jaykin says.

"You're going to the Western Light, aren't you?" Blint asks. "To leave these lands?"

"That's one way of putting it." Dezil smiles. Eveara kneels next to him, on the other side of the chair.

"Well, what do you think?" she asks the other Elements. They all smile at her and start nodding.

"I think it is his time," Eragraph says.

"I am ready to go," Dezil says, sounding slightly nervous.

Chapter 37

Evolution is the Solution

Eveara moves in front of Dezil with a twinkle in her eye and holds his hands for comfort. Dezil smiles and lights up.

"My dear," he whispers. "I'm feeling very nervous about this." He shakes slightly.

"It's all right," she whispers. "I'll look after you now." She gently taps his hands.

"You have such a beautiful smile," Dezil whispers.

"Thank you. May I ask, where is your family?"

"Oh, they do not live around here anymore. They live on planet Raziz now," he says, lowering his head. "And I cannot travel there at my age."

"Well, would you like to go see them again?"

"I would like that very much."

"I have the powers to make that come true," Eveara says gently.

Dezil cannot believe what he is hearing.

"I wouldn't hesitate my dear."

Eveara moves into position.

"With your permission, your wish is granted." She prepares herself by rubbing her hands together gently, and calmly settling him. "Normally I would do this with the family around but in this special case I'll make an exception." She smiles kindly at him. She stands and holds up her hand and looks down upon Dezil. "This will be a bit uncomfortable for a couple of

seconds," she whispers. "But will soon be over."
Dezil nods his head.

"I'm ready."

Eveara inhales deeply. In a straight-toned voice, she says:

"In the law of life and regulation, from human life to Solution, I will ask you one very important question. Will this be your final destiny or do you seek one chance of eternity?" She looks at Dezil for his answer. But he looks confused. Eragraph leans in.

"Do you want to end your life here or would you like a second chance to live, for eternity?"

Dezil gasps slightly and stops to think, playing with the crystal in his hand. Eveara is waiting for his answer. He spreads his arms up as high as he can. "I choose, Eternity!" he shouts.

"Then in order of the evolution, you, Dezil, will become a mighty Solution." Eveara kneels down, moving closer to Dezil. "May the journey to find your Element life guide you on your next adventure," she says calmly, and places both her hands onto Dezil's temples. A bright light pulsates through and around his body, glowing brighter. He tries to stay as still as possible but finds himself slowly standing with new strength. His wrinkled skin starts to fill out with muscle, making him grow taller and broader. His curved back straightens up, making him much taller and his skin becomes thicker. His eyes grow bigger and wider. His nose and ears shrink and flatten, embedding back into his skull.

"Oh, I remember this," Seek reminisces.

"So do I," Blint says. "I was so excited to see

the Life Element."

"I can barely remember mine. Feels such a long time ago for me," Mordan says.

"It was a very long time for us all, Mordan," Pree reminds him.

"What's happening?" Jaykin asks, looking puzzled.

"He's evolving into a Solution," Eragraph replies. "This is the future now."

Dezil stands, amazed at what has happened, looking at his hands, then his new body. "Oh, my goodness," he says, with a similar voice but much clearer and deeper now.

"How does it feel to be the first human to turn into a Solution for over ten millennia?" Mordan asks.

"I feel amazing. And I sound like a young man again," he replies, holding his throat. He then moves his arms and hands, stretching his back, looking at every single bit of detail of his new body. He looks down at Jaykin, who seems shocked, and Eveara, who is still kneeling. "Am I taller?" Dezil asks.

"You are." Eveara smiles.

He runs on the spot then jumps. "I can move faster too." He chuckles with delight.

"Your agility, strength and speed will have improved significantly," Irown says.

Dezil stops suddenly.

"Thank you so much, but…what do I do now?" he asks in a worried voice, looking at each Element in turn.

"Whatever you like," Irown replies.

"You have an eternity to find out what you

want to be," Pree says.

"What I want to be?" Dezil asks.

"Yes," Eragraph replies, standing up to face him. "To find out what Element you want to become. You have a choice of seventeen." He looks over at Jaykin. "Possibly eighteen Elements." He uses his powers to transform the chair into some armour. "Here, this is for you."

"Oh." Dezil looks in awe at his new armour and body again. "Thank you, thank you so much."

Irown takes some time to explain all the different types of Elements to Dezil, while the others prepare, rest, drink and eat before the next part of the journey. Jaykin listens in closely as he finds it all exciting and fascinating.

"So, have you decided which Element you're going to become?" Mordan asks.

"Stop asking that," Pree says to him. "It's too soon."

"I really don't know, I think I will wait," Dezil replies, looking thoughtfully at the crystal, which is still in his hand.

"Can I suggest something?" Eveara says. "As you want to start a new journey, why don't you join us?"

"That is a great idea," Jaykin says.

"Well, I suppose…" Dezil replies, still trying to work out what is going on.

"Well, this is your second chance of life now," Eveara says.

"True. Plus, you will gain a vast amount of

knowledge with us around," Irown smiles.

"Then I suppose I don't have a choice," he says, and laughs with the group. "I will happily join you all."

"Welcome to the team," Eragraph says, patting him on the back. "You are part of the Crystal Hunting Team now."

"Thank you," he replies, uncertainly. "Crystal hunting?"

"We are searching for large crystals," Jaykin replies. "Like the one that was in Dreamora."

"But that one was stolen," Dezil says. "Oh." He looks at Jaykin. "And you're the…" Then he looks at all the Elements. "You are all from crystal…" He lifts the crystal and they all nod. "Goodness, I have a lot to catch up on."

***

In the city of Q-Ara, deep inside the Palace, the Knights keep their Q-Azars aimed at the invaders, who kneel with their hands behind their heads. They have been stripped of their armour too. They look like humans, which surprises the emperor.

"Emperor Mor, they aren't talking. They will not let anything slip," one of the Knights says.

"Bring them forward to me," Mor says.

"The Emperor of Q-Ara is demanding answers." The Knight grabs onto one of the invaders and shoves him closer to the emperor.

"What is your name?" Mor asks. The invader keeps his eyes to the floor. "Where are you from?" The invader stays quiet. "Why are you here?" Mor then grabs the invader's neck. "Why did you attack us?" he yells in his face.

The guy grins. "Are you the leader?" he asks in a creepy voice.

"I am," Mor says proudly. The man sneers.

"Your city will fall." He leans back slightly and then smashes his head into Mor's face. Mor steps back, letting go of the invader and holds onto his nose, which bleeds profusely. The Knights power up their Q-Azars.

"Back away from the emperor, now!" they shout.

"Wait!" Mor bellows. "I can handle this." He approaches the invader, who just laughs.

"We will win this war," the man says. Mor struggles to keep his cool and punches him unconscious.

"We will see about that. Take them to the creatures' cages, then they will talk." The Knights take the invaders, one by one.

"Emperor Mor!" another Knight calls out from the doorway.

"What is it?"

"The Palace is under attack!"

Mor stares at the Knight. "By whom?" he shouts.

"Unknown. But they have already killed dozens of our Guards."

"Barricade the doors. Knights to the defence! Do not let anyone in or out of this Palace!" Mor shouts.

***

Night has fallen and Blint has created bright orbs to light everyone's way. They get halfway along the Road of Fire Forest when they notice a small path leading south and they take it, only just fitting.

"Dezil, how does it feel to be a Solution?" Jaykin asks. Dezil is riding with Q-Tech on the same goorit.

"Not much different to a human, really," he replies honestly, admiring his new body again. "I feel young but then again I felt young when I was an old man."

"We share that feeling," Irown says. "Most of us are over a thousand years old."

"I can't imagine being that old," Jaykin says.

"Age has its positives," Blint says.

"Eveara, what happens when someone doesn't want to be a Solution?" Jaykin asks. "Or an Element?"

"Good questions. It's rare for someone to decline, but if I ask and they don't wish to evolve, then the life essence is taken from them, with their permission of course. It is a painless and peaceful process. I absorb it like you do with crystal and use it to help others evolve. Same with Solutions. Many cannot take the stress of deciding what Element they would like to become for eternity. It can be an extremely difficult decision to make and many believe that they shouldn't continue living for so long after all. They find the idea overwhelming, and that goes for both levels of evolution."

"If I choose an Element," Dezil says, "then what? How will the Element decide to evolve me?"

"When you are certain, we will know," Irown says. "Elements that have completed the process have described it as, 'Solutions will have a glow'. That is when we know when you are ready."

"I think our new recruit needs a weapon," Eragraph says. "What do you think?" he calls to the others who all agree. He looks at his shield and gives it to Dezil. "Here take this."

"Thank you, but don't you need it?"

"No, it's okay. I can make another one. Besides, I'm sure there's someone else who can create something for you." He looks pointedly at Jaykin with a strong suggestion in his eyes.

"Me?" Jaykin asks.

"Yes," Eragraph replies. "You will get it eventually."

"I knew someone was going to say that," Jaykin sighs. "I'll give it a try, but you might be waiting for a while."

"That is your mission, for now, Jaykin," Irown reminds him.

Dezil looks puzzled and slightly shocked.

"Can you make things from nothing?" he asks. Jaykin is hesitant to say anything.

"Not really. I have the power of crystal."

"See, that wasn't so difficult to say, was it?" Mordan says.

"They've only just realised I have this power," Jaykin clarifies, for Dezil's benefit.

"Oh, I see. Can you show me?"

Jaykin lifts his hand out towards him and a crystal

forms in his palm.

"That's all I can do at the moment. I can't make anything in particular; all I can do are these." He lifts up the small crystal.

"Not yet," Eragraph says. "But you'll be able to make so much more with practice."

Dezil is speechless and stares at him.

"I didn't know we can do that," he says.

"No, I'm the only human that can do it," Jaykin replies.

"Actually," Dezil says, quietly and very bluntly. "I think I have heard that noise of a crystal being made before."

Jaykin and the others stop their goorit in their tracks.

Chapter 38

The Others

Shooting across the sky, the Air Element descends closer to the ground, appearing to lose energy or perhaps to be in pain. He drops Aren. Its wings smash into the trees, cutting them in half. Both the Element and Aren hit the ground rolling and tumbling on the forest floor. Aren hits his head hard. Leaves fly everywhere. He shouts in pain as he ends up hitting into a tree. Then everything is quiet; the only sound nearby of branches breaking and small creatures scuttling away from them. The Element is dazed and moves slightly, trying to lift itself up from the muddy ground, looking for Aren, then at its wings, which are badly damaged from the Q-Ara blasts. Aren tries to stand too, but keeps staggering, battered, and bruised. He feels something warm on his head and carefully places his hand on his scalp. He checks his palm. It's covered in blood. With that, he falls to the ground and loses consciousness.

***

Everyone jumps off their goorit.

"Really?" Jaykin asks, feeling very confused. "That's impossible."

"Yes, I'm certain," Dezil replies. "It has a very distinctive sound when it's being made. It's like when you walk on snow; it has that scrunch sound to it but with the crystal, it also has a slight ringing."

"When did you hear that?" Jaykin asks. Dezil stops to think.

"It must have been about thirty years ago. I was in the garden of Ezoons, in Dreamora, sitting on a bench, enjoying the lovely weather. My late wife used to leave me there while she went shopping. Suddenly, I heard the alarms for a creature in the city. It was the year when dozens of barkas managed to get in and were causing havoc. I heard people running and screaming nearby. I didn't know where to go. I was in the wrong place and I was struck down by people who were running my way. I was on the ground for a long time. I was very scared. I couldn't do anything. Then from nowhere, I felt someone grab onto me and lift me up. He sounded young like you." He looks at Jaykin. "He was probably about your age. The young man asked who I was and I told him. Then suddenly I heard it; the same noise. I never forgot that sound. He then said to me that I should be safe in there. Of course, I didn't know what he was talking about at the time and I didn't know where I was. It felt like I was in a small building, with no sounds or even wind. I touched what seemed to be the walls and it was nothing I had ever felt before. After a few minutes, I heard the same thing. I asked for his name and he told me, but for the life of me, I can't remember what it was. The walls had gone then and I never heard from him again after that." Jaykin's heart is in his throat and he feels as if he is about to be sick. His thoughts are running wild, between hope and disbelief.

"You got his name?" Jaykin asks, his voice sounding croaky, unsure if he wants the answer.

"Yes, he told me what it was." He thinks for a bit but he struggles to remember. "I think it was…J-Jay something."

"Jaylin?" Jaykin interrupts.

"That's the one. Do you know him?" Dezil asks.

"Isn't that your father's name?" Pree asks. Jaykin staggers back against the goorit.

"Yes," he replies. He is astonished. He hasn't considered that his father might have the same powers as him. He has never mentioned it nor shown it to him before. Jaykin can feel everyone staring at him and his breathing gets faster. He walks away to think. Eragraph follows.

"Are you alright?" he asks.

"No. All these years and he didn't tell me anything about his powers, and he passed them onto me." His voice is angry. "Why would he do that, Eragraph?"

"Perhaps he didn't say anything because he wasn't sure how you would take it and to save you from harm."

"That's exactly what Kanaren said." He is becoming annoyed. "He said that I shouldn't tell anyone about my power because no one will understand it, especially the Elements!…" He takes in a deep breath. "…But I'm glad I did."

"Maybe it's something you should ask about when you find him," Eragraph replies. "Come on."

Jaykin follows him back to the group who are getting ready for the next stage of their journey. He approaches Dezil.

"Did you ever go searching for Jaylin?" Jaykin asks.

"No. I thanked him of course. There was no need to try and find him after that. I thought it was someone just helping me out, but now I understand. He had the same power as you." Dezil makes it sound as if he met someone random, for a brief moment, and that's it. "Did you not know?"

"No," Jaykin replies and they stay quiet. He can feel all his emotions run through him again. Now he knows where his power has come from. Then he thinks about the other people that are missing and wonders whether this means they have the same powers too.

"It's another mystery to add to our list of questions," Irown says.

Jaykin nods and looks up at all the Elements. Irown is right, he thinks, making him more determined to find his father.

Pree does her usual service of absorbing everyone's tiredness, and they all continue their journey with renewed energy.

***

Far west, Aren awakes. He looks around and sees that the Air Element is still face down in the earth. Aren still feels dizzy but manages to sit up.

"Where am I?" he says and tries to recognise the place. He manages to stand and hold onto the tree for stability. He hears a rustling in the forest behind him. He turns, then there is another. "If you're trying to scare me it's not going to work," he shouts confidently, holding onto his sword.

"That won't be difficult, Aren," whispers a familiar voice.

He freezes as he recognizes the figure walking towards him.

"Kanaren?" he whispers. "You're alive? But how? We were told you died?"

"Anything is possible," Kanaren replies, grinning.

"Wait." Aren notices something odd. "You're not Kanaren," he says, getting closer, until something whacks him on the back of the neck, and knocks him out.

Suddenly Kanaren's body fades away, vanishing into thin air. Two Elements appear, standing opposite each other. One looks like Mordan but a female version, and the other is a Life Element. They both wear similar armour to the Air Element.

"Yes, anything is possible, especially with powers like mine," the Mind Element says, and kneels to check on Aren, who is still unconscious, and injured, but not seriously. She looks up to the Life Element.

"Good hit," she smiles. "Now go and heal Ingrib; we're going to need him. I will…*question* this one and add him to the others." She looks down at Aren.

"Don't do too much damage to him Eram. He could be useful to us," the Life Element says.

"I can't guarantee that, Lufain," Eram smirks.

Day 16

It is still dark over Izara, making things difficult for everyone to see, except for Seek. Blint has created some orbs of light. Seek notices something not too far from them but can't work out exactly what it is.

"This path ends soon," she says.

They soon stop and line up beside what seems to be a very deep crater.

"Is that one of those skyships?" Mordan asks.

They can make out a large metal object, but it is small compared to a normal skyship.

"Yes, I think it is," Pree replies.

"It looks very similar to the one we saw in the Unknown Lands," Mordan says.

"This isn't from any of the cities," Q-Tech says and everyone looks at it. "Nor from these planets."

"It's not?" Jaykin questions. "Might be a good idea to head down there and see if you can open it."

It slides down the side of the crater, reaches the ship, and scans it to see if there is an entrance. Like the collector, it opens from the rear but Q-Tech struggles to access it.

"It looks as if we're going to stay here longer than we want," Eragraph says. "Let us settle here for a while. Jaykin, you can do some more training."

They find a spot and rest. Curiosity gets the better of Blint, Eragraph, Mordan and Dezil, and they head down in the crater to see if they can help Q-Tech.

"We are nearly there," Jaykin says to no one in

particular. He has just finished creating what is supposed to be a star-shaped crystal but has ended up being a blob instead.

"Where are we going exactly?" Eveara asks.

"We're going to the Floating Island by the looks of things," Jaykin replies.

"Oh," Pree says, as if she is not pleased.

"What's wrong?" Seek asks.

"It's Mordan," she replies. "He doesn't like going anywhere near floating islands. He has a phobia for that sort of thing. He'll probably tell you about it at some point."

With that, Mordan himself hops over the edge.

"We still haven't managed to get it open," he announces. "Your Q-Roid thing is still trying its magic on it." Jaykin goes to take a look.

"Mordan, we're heading to the Floating Island," Eveara says.

"Wait, what?" he stutters, looking straight at Pree as she faces the other way. "You knew about this didn't you?"

"I only just found out," she says as defensively and as calmly as possible. "I'm sorry."

"I'm staying here then," he mumbles.

"Mordan, we need to go there to find the next Element," Pree continues. The others come up from the ship.

"Yes, but…" Mordan sighs.

"What's the problem?" Eragraph asks.

"You can tell them, as you're so uptight about it," Pree replies.

"I can't," Mordan says. "You'll have to go

without me."

"Come on Mordan, we need you," Jaykin says. Pree is losing her patience with him. "He's afraid of the Elements that used to live at the Floating Islands."

"What, the Gravity Elements?" Irown asks. Mordan puffs out a breath. "Even the name sends a shiver down my spine." He lowers his head in shame. "I nearly died!" He walks away a few paces.

"It still haunts him to this day," Pree whispers to Eveara.

"I think we all have had many near-death experiences," Irown says.

"Please tell your story," Eveara asks Mordan, kindly. "It may help."

Mordan thinks for a moment and then slowly sits close to Pree.

"Way before the Great War, even before I evolved into a Solution, I was a young man, probably the same age as you Jaykin. It was a normal day helping my parents with chores, picking crops, as you do. I didn't hear or see anything when it arrived; it just appeared out of nowhere. 'Bow to me' it said. I turned to see this huge thing standing there. I had never seen one before. I didn't move, of course, as I'd thought it was joking. Then suddenly, I felt like someone dropped thousands of boulders on top of me. I fell to the ground and I couldn't move, not even a finger. Breathing was unbearable and I could feel my whole body shaking and being crushed. It stood there laughing at me. I was just a youngster."

Elra swoops down from Eragraph's shoulder and perches next to Mordan, rubbing her head on his hand.

"Since then, Mordan has never been anywhere near a Gravity Element," Pree says.

"What happened after that?" Seek asks.

"The best part of course," he says. "A Mind Element rescued me from that monster. She was amazing. Since that moment, I knew I wanted to be exactly like her; I wanted to be a Mind Element."

"Why didn't the Element erase your memory? Or why haven't you done it yourself?" Blint asks. Mordan smiles. "Because after she stunned the Element, she told me that she wasn't going to get rid of that memory, as it would remind me to be wise, strong and to never give up, even if I am being crushed by gravity."

"Wise and strong?" Pree says. "You aren't either of them, are you, Mordan?" she says sarcastically.

"And you know how to ruin my story don't you Pree." Everyone laughs.

"They sound terrifying," Dezil says.

"The Gravity Element is one of the most powerful Elements," Irown says. "You are lucky to be alive Mordan. But they are very helpful when on your side against other Elements during a Great War."

Q-Tech jumps out of the crater.

"Master Jaykin."

"How did you get on Q-Tech?"

"Not good."

"Why, what's wrong?" Irown asks.

"It is confirmed, this 'skyship' is not from Izara or Raziz."

"That's what I'm worried about," Jaykin

replies. "That means there are more invaders here."

"They might be close by," Eragraph observes.

"I have not seen any tracks yet," Seek replies.

"I can't sense anyone except for us," Mordan mentions.

"They may still be inside?" Irown suggests.

"No," Q-Tech replies. "Scan confirms, there is no one inside."

"Do you think we can use it ourselves then?" Jaykin asks.

"No," Q-Tech replies. "You'll need several passcodes just to get it to fly; and even more, to take it to space."

"Then what shall we do with it?" Pree asks.

"We'll just have to leave it here," Jaykin says.

"You can cover the door with crystal," Eragraph suggests.

"Yes, a good idea," Irown butts in. "They won't be able to get through it. You'll be able to sense it and come back here another time."

"Good thinking," Jaykin says and slides down the crater and stands close to the ship. He places his hand on the door and crystal forms over it. "No one can use it now," he says to himself.

***

Deep within the forest, Aren slowly wakes up with an awful headache. He tries to look around, but everything is pitch black. He can feel something wrapped around his head, which covers his eyes; and his hands are tied together.

"Where am I?" he shouts. But no one replies. He then hears loud thuds of what seem to be footsteps heading his way. "Who are you?" he asks but they don't answer, so he asks again but forcefully. "Who—" They hit him.

"We're the ones asking the questions, Aren," a woman's voice replies, interrupting him.

"How do you know my name?"

"I have my ways," she replies. "I can find out all your little secrets."

"No, I won't allow it."

"*You won't need to,*" she says telepathically, and places her hand on his head.

"No!" Aren screams.

***

On their way again, Jaykin sees that Irown is still trying to decipher the writings from the Western Light cave. He decides to take out his letter and have a look at it, maybe for the last time. He thinks about throwing it after finding nothing at the Western Light. It's been over a year now and it still hasn't made any sense. "*What you know places you in mortal danger. You must leave immediately. Look towards the Western Light, you will know where to go.*"

Blint notices him looking at the letter.

"Do you need some light Jaykin?" He sends an orb over his head.

"Thanks, Blint but—" As he is about to reply, he notices something on the paper that he hasn't seen before, but the orbs soar past him and it vanishes. "Blint, can you keep the orb still?" he says impatiently.

"Jaykin, that was very rude," Pree says.

"No, Pree, I've found something. I just need to see it again." He looks carefully at the paper. Some of the letters are shining in the light. "Look towards the Western Light," he says, then looks up at the orb floating in front of him. He holds the paper up towards the light and the letters flash in red. "T, R, A, V, E, L, T, O, W, O, N, O, G," he spells out in order.

"Travel to Wonog?" Irown asks. "What does that mean?"

"Wonog is a place, I think," Jaykin says. "Q-Tech have you heard of it?"

"Yes, it is on the planet, Raziz, but it is a vast ocean. There is nothing there."

"There must be something if the letter says so," Irown says.

"We will go there," Jaykin replies with determination and looks up at Raziz, trying to work out where Wonog may be. "I'm sure I will find answers there." He turns to Blint. "How did that work? I have looked at this letter in all sorts of light, but I got nothing."

"Let's have a look," he says, and Jaykin passes it over. Blint examines the front and the back then rubs it between his fingers. "Yes, we used this sort of paper during the Great War, to send secret messages."

"How did none of you know that?" Jaykin asks all the Elements and everyone shrugs.

"No one would have known that," Blint answers for them. "Because only the Light Elements

have the power for it."
Jaykin gasps.

"Then where did the Emperor of Lementes get this paper from?"

***

They continue on, until they come across a huge structure blocking their path. Partially buried deep in the ground, it is the first link in a chain, extending at an angle of forty-five degrees, high above them into the sky, where it connects to the edge of the Floating Island. Three other great chains, similarly connected, can be seen some distance away. They all jump off their goorit to inspect it. Irown is the first to touch the chain.

"It's metal," he says.

"It's one of four chain links that keep the island steady and secure," Q-Tech informs them.

"No kidding? I heard they're huge, but this is ridiculous," Jaykin says, also touching it.

"We're close then," Seek says.

"Great," Mordan says sarcastically. "I did wonder what that light is, over there."

They all notice a slight orange tint coming from the other side.

"Looks like firelight," Blint says.

"We better find out," Eragraph replies and clears the foliage around this first gigantic chain link. Their eyes follow the many links up to the Island, a landmass floating hundreds of metres above Izara, secured to the planet by its four great chains. Each of the links is huge and covered in a variety of different plants. The island itself is covered in lush vegetation and large rocks.

Back on land, underneath the Island, is a village.

"Jaykin did you know there is a village here?" Irown asks.

"No. I had no idea. I doubt anyone knew." he replies.

"Then we may have a situation," Irown warns.

"Something is wrong," Seek says. "It looks as if the people are in trouble."

"Come on, they may need our help," Eragraph says, leading the way.

On closer inspection, all is clearly not well with the village people. They wander listlessly around miserably run-down homes, mostly modest huts. Some appear to have been damaged by fire. One of the villagers, a woman, appears from behind such a hut. She holds onto a few possessions and stops in her tracks when she spots the Elements.

"Who are you?" she asks fearfully. "What brings you here?"

"Greetings," Eragraph replies. "Don't be alarmed, we're here to help in any way possible."

"We would like to meet your leader," Irown says.

"That's what he asked," the woman says angrily. Everyone looks at each other.

"Who?" Irown asks.

"The last outsider that came here," she replies. "The one from the north. Are you with him? Better not be."

"No, we are not with him," Irown replies.
The woman stares at each Element carefully then at Dezil, Jaykin and Q-Tech.

"You are from the cities, aren't you?" She shakes her head. "She will not be happy with your arrival, but I will take you to our chief." She puts down her belongings, then she looks at them all again. "You aren't allowed to take any of your weapons."

"We understand," Irown replies.
Eveara sees someone hiding behind one of the buildings and goes to investigate, discreetly leaving the others.

They head to a very tall hut that is undamaged. There is plenty of room inside for everyone to congregate. The Elements have no problem fitting in.

"Chief," the woman says.

"Yes, what is it?" she says, sounding agitated.

"More outsiders have arrived," the woman replies.
The Chief turns and faces them all.

"What is it you want?" she asks.

"I'll do the talking," Irown whispers to the others. "Greetings. My name is Irown. I am an Element. My friends and I are here on a quest."

"Elements? A quest? I don't really care for your quest or who you are right now," she says, sarcastically. "If you haven't noticed, we're in a crisis."

"What happened here?" Jaykin asks.

"One man did this," she replies. "He arrived here about four days ago. He also asked for me; claiming he didn't know much of our worlds. He asked many questions about the cities and their leaders. Then for some reason, he wanted to fight the strongest of my people." She lowers her head. "And they were all defeated," she finishes, bitterly.

"Where is this man now?" Jaykin asks.

"He left, three days ago when the Western Light vanished. I'm guessing he's there or the nearest city."

"He didn't go to the Western Light," Seek says. Everyone looks over at Dezil.

"It wasn't me," he says. "If he went to the city, he must have passed me. The only ones I came across were you lot."

"Or he travelled on the Air Element?" Irown mentions.

"Possibly, but I didn't sense anyone else on the Element," Mordan says.

"Could have been wearing the same armour?" Irown says.

"We are sorry about the latest attack," Eragraph says. "We will help as much as we can. If you would allow us."

The chief sighs and considers; trying to decide whether to trust in these new strangers. "Talking about helping, where is Eveara?" Irown asks, looking around.

"Oh, she's outside healing the villagers," Seek replies.

"Healing my people?" the chief asks, overhearing the conversation.

"We aim to assist you if we can," Eragraph says.

The chief ignores him and storms outside to take a

look. Numerous people are crowding around something: Eveara, kneeling and busily healing everyone with burns, cuts, bruises and even some severely damaged limbs. People walk away happily, some crying with happiness and emotion.
Jaykin and the others join the chief.

"We're on a quest to find Elements," Jaykin says. "They will help in the invasion. There is a ship outside of the village. I'm guessing that man you speak of isn't from this planet, and if one person can do this much damage, then imagine what hundreds or thousands can do. It is just the beginning."

"What do you need from us?" the chief asks.

Chapter 39

Farewell Izara

"I can't," the chief says. "I can't give you the island. It's been here for thousands of years."

"But you must understand, there is an Element there," Irown explains.

***

A couple of hours pass and with a great deal of persuasion, even begging, Irown finally manages to convince the chief to give them the island. But the chief imposes conditions, which they all agree to. First, they must give up all the goorit. Eragraph will make them all weapons and create large trees so the people can rebuild their homes. The village can also keep all the metal from the chains that hold the island in place. Jaykin will create a crystal for the village too, just like the one in Dreamora, but much smaller.

Their priority is a workable and effective plan of action. They need to detach the chains from the Floating Island, so it will rise to the planet Raziz, because they believe if Jaykin absorbs the crystal, then the island will crash land onto the village, causing even more chaos. To do this, they will be using fire to heat the chains halfway along their length. Too low or too high, the possibility of the chains hitting the village and the people is a huge risk. Eragraph creates a vast amount of wood, to keep the fires burning extremely hot and for a long time. Fortunately, the links are tightly connected, making it relatively easy to progress along the chain. Jaykin covers the fires with crystal, like a furnace, controlling the amount of air. His powers are limited as he only has one large crystal left, absorbed from Blint. He used the rest for the ship's door and the village's crystal. Many of the villagers help, carrying everything up for the fires on their back, as they are used to walking across the chains. The fires burn all through the day and most of the night.

Day 17

Pree helps everyone stay awake to complete their tasks. Three of the chains have now been severed with a huge crash and the Floating Island is beginning to tilt. Thankfully the ground beneath the chains had been cleared. The Elements all use their powers for this task and now there is only one chain left.

They say goodbye to the chief and to her people.

"I warn you," the Chief says. "No one has ever got to the middle of the island before. It may be impossible. The journey will not be an easy one. The closer you get to the centre the harder it becomes."

"We understand," Eragraph replies. "But it must be done."

"Then I wish you luck. You are all very brave to take up such a challenge." She bows to them.

"Thank you, Chief," Irown replies. "Good luck with the recovery." They all bow in return.

They head to where the remaining chain links attach to

Izara and start to walk across them.

"Who has actually been to Raziz?" Jaykin asks. All the Elements shake their heads.

"I have been there," Dezil replies. "It was many years ago though. Have you been?"

"No, never," Jaykin replies. "What about you Q-Tech?"

"Many times," it replies.

"Good, then you can help with directions if we get there."

"If?" Irown asks.

"The possibility of this working is…" Q-Tech pauses. "Very slim."

Everyone stops in their tracks.

"Well, that's encouraging," Irown replies.

"Do we have to take this talking, lifeless, walking thing with us?" Mordan asks.

"We do," Jaykin replies. "It's important and it's the only thing of Kanaren's that I have left."

As they reach the fire, the metal is nearly broken. The villagers who are guarding it make their way down when they see the group approaching.

Eragraph stops. "I will wait here," he says. "I will clear the area of the foliage and recover the crystal, which you will need Jaykin. Mordan, I will communicate with you when the chain breaks apart. Good luck everyone."

"You too Eragraph," Irown replies. Everyone continues walking, except for Jaykin, who seems reluctant to leave.

"Keep going Jaykin." He smiles and waves him away. "I'll be fine."

"I know. I just wanted to say thank you, and be careful."

"I'm always careful. You're the one that needs to watch out, or else we won't be able to find the crystal. Now go, unlock the Gravity Element." Elra squawks from his shoulder, as if in agreement.

"I will." Then he heads off up the chain. Eragraph watches him thoughtfully. Jaykin looks over his shoulder to see him sit down on the chain to wait, then he turns to catch up with the others.

They reach the gigantic island, covered in thick, green foliage and trees, all facing outwards as if they're all lying down. They can already feel the force of the Element's power. They decide that the best time to absorb the crystal is when the island is between the two planets, then the Element can have control and bring the island to a soft landing. They must wait for Eragraph's signal first.

"Something is moving underneath us," Seek says.

"Guardians," Irown replies. "We should have seen this coming. Prepare yourselves. Jaykin, go find the crystal."

"I'm on it," he replies and turns to Q-Tech. "Let's go."

The ground suddenly explodes around them all and an army of Guardians comes into view.

"*Mordan, I've untangled all the vines that were attached to the chains; we're ready to go.*" Eragraph doesn't hear a reply. "*Mordan?*" he tries again, but gets nothing for a couple of seconds.

"Eragraph, we're being attacked by Guardians," Mordan replies.

Eragraph curses and turns to the island. He can see at least a dozen Guardians making their way across the chain. He unravels his bow and loosens a few arrows which have no effect. Their bodies are made from stone. He looks around to see what he can use to help. Luckily there is still foliage that has been growing over the chains for thousands of years. This is the only defence he has now.

"Elra, fly to the island!" he shouts and she takes off.

With both hands, he wraps the vines around a few of the Guardian's legs, pulling them off the chain. They fall and smash into the ground below. Suddenly the chain buckles from the heat and breaks. Eragraph turns and tries to save Jaykin's crystal, but the island lifts too quickly and he misses it. It falls to the ground, with the lower half of the chains crashing down. He grabs onto the foliage nearby and so do the Guardians, as the chains that are still attached to the island swing around dangerously.

Everyone staggers as they feel the last chain break and the island rises. Jaykin is on the search for the crystal, making his way to the centre, where he can already sense it. He finds an entrance to a cave, large enough for a very big Element to crawl through.

"I've found it!" he shouts to the others.

Suddenly, two large Guardians burst from the earth in

front of him. Jaykin gasps and stands back. He can't use his powers here; he barely has
enough crystal, certainly not for two. He looks over at Q-Tech, then remembers Dr Rotnevin's words: "*There is a lot of gadgetry on there; one in particular, for when you're really in trouble. It's the voice command F-Q.*"
Jaykin stares back at both the Guardians, who are preparing their weapons, and at the top of his voice, he shouts. "F-Q!"

Q-Tech clicks and unfolds as if transforming into a flattened version of itself. It flings towards Jaykin and wraps around him, enveloping him
completely. He admires his new armoured body.

"Cool!" he says. Both the Guardians swing for him but Q-Tech's boosters propel Jaykin forward, between the Guardian's legs. He quickly turns and covers their feet in crystal so they cannot move.

"Q-Tech, can we destroy these things? Completely out of existence?" he asks.

"Of course, Jaykin," Q-Tech replies. And from two extremely fast swings to the Guardian's backs, they both crumble into pieces. Jaykin relaxes and sighs in relief. Q-Tech then unwraps itself from Jaykin's body and transforms back to its usual self.

"Thanks. We should definitely use that again," Jaykin says, as he absorbs the crystal holding the Guardian's feet. He turns and faces the cave again. He can feel some sort of force pushing him back.

He gazes at the crystal, levitating in the centre of the gigantic spherical stone cave. The walls are smooth where the gravity has pushed out over thousands of years. Irown explained to him earlier that day that the Gravity Element can use its power to pull and push gravity, changing it at will, and this one is undoubtedly hugely powerful. He can feel his whole body being pushed back and it gets difficult to get closer with every step he takes. He feels nervous, troubled, powerless. How is he going to get near it?

"I don't know if I'm going to be able to do this," he says. Even Q-Tech is struggling to move. "Stay here, in case any other Guardians appear."

"Understood," Q-Tech replies.

Sliding his feet forward, he pulls himself closer to the cave entrance, using all the rocks nearby for leverage. He grabs onto the edge of the entrance; it feels as if he is hanging off a cliff. He just manages to lift himself in and leans against the smooth cave wall, so he doesn't get pushed further away. He tries to reach out but can barely lift his finger let alone an arm.

"I can't get anywhere near it," he shouts out.

"Keep trying!" Blint yells. Close by, he is using his powers to try to blind as many Guardians as possible, but failing miserably. Instead, he draws his two swords and begins to fight them.

Jaykin tries sliding his body across the wall but cannot find any way of getting to the crystal.

"I can't; it's too powerful!" His breathing starts to get heavy with his chest being squashed by the gravity. "Someone, think of something!"

"Is there no other way to get near it?" Irown shouts, using his battle axe to take out a couple of the Guardians. Jaykin looks all over the cave.

"No!" he replies, despairing. "It's not going to work!"

"Don't give up!" Blint shouts. "Remember your training!"

Jaykin leans his head back onto the wall and thinks. He remembers the orbs of light, floating around him and that Blint controlled them with his mind. He tries his best to lift his hands, but it is still no good. Instead, he just tries to move the crystal closer to him. He holds his breath, feeling as if he is trying to lift the whole island, but still no good. He gasps, as the pressure builds up. If he can't think of something soon this island will crash into Izara or Raziz, possibly killing a lot of people. It will be over. He needs to open this crystal for a soft landing. Then he thinks, instead of trying to get the crystal to him, why not make a crystal behind him, to push him towards it?

"That should work," he says.

Everyone is fighting with at least two Guardians each, using all their weapons to fend them off, but more keep coming, as if the whole island is made from them. The Elements, Dezil and Q-Tech decide the best thing to do is to clamber into the cave with Jaykin, and they make it but, with the gravity force so strong, they are pinned to the cave walls.

Jaykin manages to place his hands behind his back and creates the crystal. It's as tall as him and it slowly moves him up towards the floating crystal in the middle of the cave. The pressure is very strong now. Jaykin holds his breath as it hurts to breathe. He stops all of a sudden.

"What is it, Jaykin?" Pree asks. But Jaykin hasn't the strength to reply. He's run out of crystal, again. He is only about a metre away.

The island quickly lifts higher into the sky above Izara. It gets colder and the air thins. Elra struggles to catch up with it. As Eragraph slowly climbs the chain, the rest of the Guardians climb down and block his way. He continues using his powers to try and clear the path.

"Elra!" he shouts. "Go back to the village. I'll come back for you!" but she continues flapping, ignoring Eragraph's call as if she doesn't want to leave him again. But it's too much for her. She stops and stares at him, letting out a loud squawk as the island continues rising.

Everyone holds their breath as the island passes from Izara's to Raziz's orbit.

"Now is the best time to absorb it, Jaykin!" Irown shouts.

Jaykin spreads his hands out wide and with all his strength he pulls the crystal closer towards him, millimetre by millimetre. Tears stream down his face; his whole body is in agony. He screams out loud and the Elements struggle to listen. Finally, it reaches him and surprisingly, his hands attached to it like magnets, absorbing the crystal. The gravity weakens and everyone detaches from the wall. The Guardians clamber into the cave and the Elements fight, once again. The crystal cracks, lowering to what is now the floor of the cave, with Jaykin still attached. Eveara clambers onto him and heals him as quickly as possible.

She realises he has broken ribs from the sheer effort of his task.

While she heals him, the Gravity Element falls. Loud clunking noises are heard from it. It wears extremely large thick dark purple and gold-plated armour. They can hear it struggling at first to lift it, then with ease, as it uses its powers to stand up straight. Ten feet tall, it surveys the scene. Seeing the Guardians, it flicks its wrist, smashing them into the wall and out of the cave.

"Wow," Jaykin says, admiring the new Element, but it doesn't react to him. It slowly moves its head from side to side, looking around at the others, who are all staring back.

"Something isn't right," Irown says.

"Oh no," Mordan says.

"What's wrong?" Jaykin asks.

"The Element is from Raziz," Irown replies.

Then, with a deep voicc, it speaks.

"You are all Izarian. You are not from here. You are all my enemies." He flicks his wrist again. Dezil and all the Elements are immediately pinned up against the cave wall.

"Jaykin, get out of here!" Eveara shouts.

"Stop, please!" Jaykin pleads, but the Element just looks down at him. "We're on a floating island heading towards Raziz. You need to stop this!" But he is ignored, and Jaykin feels himself getting heavier, forced flat onto the ground.

"You will all feel the full force of a true Razilian warrior!" the Element says with supreme confidence.

"Mordan, stop him!" Irown shouts.

There is a pause. "I can't. He has reflective armour on," he replies.

"Q-Tech, do something!" Jaykin shouts. It moves slightly but the Element pins it up against the wall too.

"Is this it?" the Element laughs. "Is this all you have?"

Eragraph reaches the island and looks around, searching for the others. He hears screams and clambers towards them. He tries warily to find an entrance to the cave, but suddenly feels himself jolt forward. He looks down. A sword; a Guardian's weapon, has pierced through his armour and into his chest. He drops to his knees and the Guardian touches his back and absorbs his powers.

"Jaykin," Eragraph whispers. "I'm sorry."

He falls to the ground.

***

In the city of Q-Ara, Meara stands on the roof of Emperor Mor's Palace with Co, the passengers, and the Knights. She looks up at the morning sky and watches as, all around the building, a fire breaks out. She is crying, worried out of her wits. She looks up and spots something in the sky; a massive shape, soaring slowly, up and away from the planet.

"Jaykin…"

***

Hundreds of miles away, deep within Izara's forests, hangs Aren; tied to a tree, battered, bruised, and slowly losing consciousness. All is quiet there. Behind him is where Mordan and Pree had met the invaders. Standing near the large ship are Q-Roids and Hunters who tried and failed to find the passengers, and never returned. Beside them are the other invading Elements.

Aren, too, sees the Island slowly flying through the sky. Blood trickles down his face.

"Jaykin," he whispers clenching his jaw.

The Elements around him all look up towards the island.

***

Jaykin tries pulling his arms away from the ground but the Element's power is too strong. He sees everyone else struggling too. He notices Mordan turning to Pree and overhears an exchange of tender words between them.

"Pree," he says, tears in his eyes; "I love you."

She turns to him in surprise and smiles, responding instantly.

"I love you too, Mordan." They reach out to one another and lock hands.

"*If they can't get out, I won't be able to either,*" Jaykin thinks. The Island starts to shake as if in an earthquake.

"This is the end for you!" the Gravity Element shouts out.

Panic, horror and sorrow show on their faces.

"Father, I'm sorry," Jaykin whispers to himself, and closes his eyes. "Where are you?"

Chapter 40

Before

1 year and 17 days ago

"Good morning, Q-Four," a man says, as he walks into a pristine white room and looks up at a screen.

"Good morning, Master. How are you this morning?"

"Doing well thank you. How is 'Project Assembling' coming along?" He walks up to a table in the middle of the room and starts to take off his long Hunter jacket.

"Nearly finished."

"Good, please send it to the Hunter, Kanaren. He should be in Lementes now. He'll know what to do with it." He places a few blank pieces of paper on the table.

"Of course, Master. It will be sent straight away. Do you think they still believe in this invasion?"

"They will Q-Four. It's taken us years to try and persuade the leaders of both worlds to even acknowledge its existence." He reaches over his back and takes out a Hunter's sword and a couple of Q-Azars and places them neatly next to the paper.

"What about the others that have supposedly gone missing?"
He stretches his neck and body as if all those things weighed heavy on him.

"They're fine too; don't worry about them." He turns back to the screen. "Q-Four, I will be…away for a while. I want you to look out for Jaykin for me."

"Understood. Do you think Master Jaykin will be okay without you?"

"He'll be fine, Q-Four. He's a clever kid; he'll work out the message eventually, and he should be able to find them all."

"Find what Master Jaylin?"

"The Elements."

Epilogue

The Mysterious Man

3 days ago

On the outskirts of the city of Dreamora, it is midnight and a huge storm is raging overhead. The rain lashes the ground. Guards patrol slowly up and down along the high wall. Suddenly, one of them catches sight of something in the corner of his eye, through the flashes of lightning. He looks harder, squinting and focusing intently on the long grass. Then his eyes open wide.

"Commander…commander!" he shouts. "Someone is out there." Sirens go off. A man struggling to stand drops to the ground, soaking wet and wheezing as if on his last breath. His face trickles with blood; he even struggles to crawl. His head falls, and he loses consciousness.

To Be Continued

Acknowledgements

I would like to say a massive thank you to everyone who has been extremely supportive all through this book's progression.

To my wife, Amy, who originally wanted to read this when it was completely finished but, in the end, helped beta read it; and for helping hand draw the world map.

To my parents, Kath and Kevin, who suffered a shock when I mentioned that I was writing something all those years ago, and never stopped.

To my mother-in-law, Jan; I cannot say thank you enough for your help with editing.

To my Beta readers, Diane, Laura, Lauren and Rose. Thank you for putting up with my writing and giving some amazing advice and suggestions.

To all my friends, who have been asking how the book is going, I can finally say: it's done!

To Arran, who designed the absolutely stunning cover, I cannot wait to see what you have for the next volume.

And lastly, to my not-so-little cousin and my number one fan, Harry, who, since he found out I was writing a book, has been very excited to read it. Now you finally can. I hope you enjoy it!

Printed in Great Britain
by Amazon

44433401R00300